Pure
as the
Lily

PURE
AS THE
LILY

by CATHERINE COOKSON

THE BOBBS-MERRILL COMPANY, INC.

Indianapolis / New York

AUTHOR'S NOTE

Street names and the actual times of air raids on Jarrow have not been strictly adhered to.

The Bobbs-Merrill Company, Inc.
Indianapolis • New York

I view you not, Jarrow, through
the misty, nostalgic glow of love;
around whose skirts I trailed my youth
and rattled into the gray, drab bosom
of your streets on the tram;
nor does the memory
of flamed skies,
last breath of dying slag,
touch my heart,
except to know
its glow
told me that men still sweated
to earn dignity, and bread,

And dreamed not yet
of hands turned white,
like lilies,
on the graves of their idleness,
nor saw themselves
shadows of lost youth
clumping through bone-chilling dawns
from Simonside tip,
spent cinders spilling
from their barrows,
on their way back
to Jarrow, dead Jarrow.

Yet, tho' I view you not
through love,
you draw me, in the wide-eyed night,
up the river that washes your feet,
the river on which I played
fifty years ago,
but as I walk
your new broad, shining streets,
I see them with no joy,
only as a facade,
covering the men and women
of my time;

for they are in my marrow.
They, whom the new generation
would forget,
they are my Jarrow.

CONTENTS

BOOK 1

Mary

JARROW 1933

1

"Da! Da! Wait a minute. Hie-on! Da."

Mary Walton came flying out of Biddle Street, turned up the narrow ash path between the low hedges and raced toward the man who had now stopped and was waiting for her.

"Eeh! you must be gettin' deaf; I've been shoutin' at you halfway down the street."

"Have you, lass? I never heard you. I must have been wool-gatherin'. But what are you doing round here at this time? I thought you would be home."

"Oh, I had to stay on; she's had one of her committee do's. Ten there were there. And the clearing up!"

"But why have you come round this way?" Her father raised his brows at her.

"Well"—she walked by his side now—"I was going to the allot-ment; I thought you'd be there. You're late, aren't you, I mean going over?"

"Aye." He nodded while looking straight ahead. "I've been across at Wallsend all the mornin'."

"Nothin' doing?" Her bright smile faded as she asked the question.

"No, no, lass. As if there would be. I must have been barmy to go; a waste of good coppers on the ferry." He turned to her and grinned. "I almost had to swim back."

When she pushed him with her elbow he laughed and went on, "It's a fact. You know, they were like a pack of mad dogs." The bounce went out of his manner now and he shook his head from side to side, saying, "Eeh! How people change. 'Where you from?' they asked us. There was about nine of us went over. It was said they'd be settin' on a good few, so we thought we might stand a chance. Chance! Not a chance in hell. We were loopy. By! You wouldn't believe it, lass." Again he shook his head. "When we said we were from Jarrow, you'd have thought we'd said we'd come over from Russia and were going to start another revolution. I'm not funnin', lass." His head moved in small jerks now. "They were for bashin' us. And Billy Teale was for havin' a go at them; we had a job to get him away. An' I can tell you we scampered for that ferry quicker than I've moved in weeks."

Mary looked at her father's profile. The face was sharp and thin, and gray-looking; his cap was pulled sideways over his brow and the peak was bent, giving his face a comic look. But her da wasn't a comic; he didn't take after her granda. Now her granda was a comic.

She was worried about her da. He was troubled in so many ways. It wasn't only that he had been out of work for eight years; it wasn't only that her ma kept on at him, although this she knew had a lot to do with how he felt, for there was that something indefinable that existed between him and her ma that she couldn't put her finger on. Everything had its share in making him look as he did now, a man without pride, and it was this loss of pride that seemed to hurt him most.

She was only eight years old when he was last in work, but she could remember how he looked then. He seemed taller. And yet he had never been really tall, being only five feet six and a half and thin with it, but he had carried himself straight in those days and held his head up and his chin out, and his cap had always been square on his head.

The little bit of happiness she had literally hugged to herself all the way from Mrs. Turner's and which she was going to present him with now seemed small, futile, inadequate against the diminishing man that the figure of her da presented to her, but nevertheless she was still excited about it.

They left the cinder path and walked into the open country that bordered the town. In the far distance to the right of them was what looked like a miniature mountain but which was only the dead slag heap of Palmer's shipyard. They walked over rough land, skirting puddles filled with January sleet and rain; then they rounded a hill that was but another camouflaged dump covered now with tufts of gray grass, and so they came upon the allotments.

Some wit had dubbed the allotments the escape route from Sedgefield, and the simile was a good one, for many a man had been saved from going to the asylum by being able to dig a patch of rough earth, and a little of his pride was salvaged when he was able to supplement with fresh vegetables the meager menu provided by the dole or the means test.

Before they entered the allotments proper Mary pulled her father to a halt, and, bending toward him and smiling into his face, she said, "You'll never guess what I've got for you."

"For me? No; what is it, hinny?"

She opened the bass bag that she was carrying and from between a pair of shoes and a soiled apron she drew out a little cone-shaped bag made of newspaper and, handing it to him, said, "Look an' see."

Alec Walton smiled at this beloved daughter of his before he unscrewed the twisted paper and gazed down at the heap of cigarette ends. Then, his eyes shining, he looked at her again, saying one word, "Tabs."

She nodded at him, her round face alight. "There's twenty-six of them, and they're not just butts, are they? Look!" She moved one aside with her fingernail. "That's three-quarters. And they're gold flake, not woodbines."

"My!" He shook his head in awe. "They must have had a beano."

"Aye. Yes, they did; they were smokin' like chimneys. And that's not all—look." She opened the bag again and held it toward him. "That's a bundle of sandwiches—tongue." And then, dipping her hand into the bag, she pulled up another twist of newspaper and, swinging it back and forward, added, "Tea."

"She didn't give you that?"

"Well"—Mary tossed her head—"would she? She gave me the usual two teaspoons, but she left me in the dining room for five minutes. And you know something, Da?" He shook his head. "I was drawn toward that caddy—just like a magnet it pulled me." She now leaned on his arm, her brow against his shoulder, and they both shook with their laughter. When she straightened up she said with slight indignation, "Well, she's so bloomin' mean at times, doling out two teaspoonsful! And I'm positive she measures what's left in that caddy every day. And you know she gets more than her money's worth out of me."

"Oh, aye. Well, I've told you, lass, she tricks you out of two and a half hours every week. I've told you. Half-day! She's got a nerve if you ask me. Nine till two, half-day!"

Mary sighed now, and they walked on as she said, "But still I get half an hour for me dinner and, give her her due, it's always a good meal. But sometimes I feel a bit peeved with her because, you know, I started on fourpence an hour, Da, and I'm still on it."

"Aye, and likely to be until you're twenty. But God forbid you're still there when you're twenty. Eight shillings a week for all you do, washing and ironing, the lot. By! Some of 'em would take the eye out of your head and come back for the socket. It makes me wild to think you're in place; you're worth something better than Mrs. Turner's, lass. It's you that should have gone to the secondary school, an' our Jimmy sent out."

"Aw now, no, Da, no. Be fair, that isn't right; our Jimmy's got brains."

"Brains!" He stopped and half-turned his head toward her. "You've got more brains in your little finger, real brains, than Jimmy's got in his whole body. He's mine, an' he's a canny lad, but the truth's the truth, he's been pushed into that school through fear an' no favor. And I'll say this again, if your mother hadn't kept at him all these years . . ."

"Aw, Da, be quiet, man. What she's done she's done for the best."

But had she? This thought had come to her more often of late: had her mother done everything for the best? She was afraid of the thoughts she had about her mother. There had been times, not so far back, when she wished she would die, and one of those times was when she had taken her from school and got her the job at Mrs. Turner's. Another time was when Jimmy got into the secondary school, for then she had cut down on everything to get him clothes. It was around this time that there had been constant rows in the house, and she remembered her da yelling, "You'd go whoring to get him what he wants." She thought her da was a bit jealous of Jimmy.

It was about this time, too, that her ma had got the job working for Mr. Tollett in his shop at the corner of the street after his wife died, and since then things had been better; at least in one way they had, for there was more food in the house because Mr. Tollett always gave her ma a basket of groceries on a Friday night besides her pay. But she had the idea that her da didn't like her ma working for Mr. Tollett. Her da called Mr. Tollett by his Christian name of Ben because they had been friendly when they were very young lads—that was before Mr. Tollett's father had got on and got the three grocery shops.

Alec now said, "Look there." He pointed over the drab squares of vegetable-stump-marked land, each dotted with a hut made of a conglomeration of old timber, boxes and corrugated iron, to a particular one at the far side. "The door's open; your granda's in."

"Oh, aye." Mary nodded. Then, turning to him, she said quickly, "Now, don't go and give him half those tabs, because he'll stick them in his pipe and they'll be gone up in smoke in a minute." She laughed. "You know what he is. I've got threepence; I'll give it to him to get some 'baccy."

"You'll do nowt of the sort; it's your night for the pictures. And anyway, if you were to give him the threepence, you know what would happen—he'd toss up whether it was 'baccy or beer."

Again she fell against his arm and laughed as she said, "And it would come down plonk into a gill of burton."

"Aye, it would that."

"Eeh! me granda."

She was still shaking her head and laughing as they entered the door of the hut, and there, on his hunkers and blowing heavily on a perforated tin of cinders, was Alec's father.

Peter Walton was sixty, but he looked seventy, until he spoke, and then his voice was so light and cheerful, had you not seen his face, you would have imagined it had issued from the mouth of a young man, a comic young man, for he laughed with practically every sentence he uttered, and if he didn't manage to convey his humor in the substance of his words, he did it with his inflection, a mixture of Irish and Geordie.

"Aw, there you are, the pair of yous!" His small round eyes glinted from their wrinkled settings. "Hello, me bairn."

"Hello, Granda. Can't you get it to go?"

"Damn an' set fire to it! That's what I say. . . . Oh be-god! look." He hooted like a young boy as a flame spiraled up from amid the damp cinders. "It did the trick. Damn an' set fire to it, I said. What d'you think of that?"

"Granda, you're making a smoke; you'll choke us." Mary coughed and flapped her hands, and Alec said, "It's a waste of cinders—we won't be stopping. By the way, did you go to the tip this mornin' and get me mother any? She was nearly out."

"No, I didn't go this mornin', I went last night. I got a bag of slack—she's bakin'. That satisfy you?"

Alec sniffed; then, looking at the fire, he asked with evident irritation, "What made you get it going anyway? Did you expect a tea party?"

"Aye, just that. Look." Peter screwed round on the dirt floor and pointed to a shelf behind him on which was reposing a two-ounce packet of tea and a small tin of condensed milk.

"Come into money?" Alec looked down at his father through narrowed eyes.

"Not that you could say, lad."

"Well, where did you get that pair? I bet me mother never gave you them."

"You're right there, your mother never did. She's a mean old scrub, your mother, the meanest old scrub I've known in me life."

"Oh, Granda!" Mary was laughing, her mouth wide. Eeh! her granda was a turn. To hear him talking you'd think he hated her grannie, whereas he thought the sun shone out of her.

"Aye, a mean woman, your grannie." He nodded at her. "Why, I've known her to put a piece of 'lastic on a penny an' stretch it to a shilling. Eeh aye! that's your grannie."

"It's as well for you she's been able to do that." Alec's nod toward his father was sober, sullen, and Mary wanted to turn to him and say, "Granda's only funnin', Da"; but her da was low that day, very low; that business over at Wallsend had hurt him. Oh, if only he could get work, work of any kind. All their problems would be solved, if only he could get work. Even her mother would be nice to him then. Oh, she was sure her mother would be nice to him if only he could get a job.

"Did you lift these?" Alec was weighing the tea and milk in his hand, and his father, turning on him with stretched face, said, "What! me lift anything? Now, would I? Ask yourself, would I?"

"No need to ask meself—did you?"

"God's holy honor!" Peter crossed himself, which symbolic action in his case was merely a relic from the days of his Catholic grandparents.

"Aw." Alec tossed his head to one side and repeated, "God's

holy honor!" Then, nodding at his father, he said, "One of these days you'll end up along the line, mark my words."

"Aye well, you might be right, lad. The only thing I hope is that they put me on a fast train." He now turned to Mary, and putting his head on one side and his arms akimbo, he took up the stance of a gossiping woman, and imitating a blatherer he bent toward her, saying, "You know, hinny, I cannot bear slow trains. Fast women an' slow trains, I cannot abear them."

As Mary again doubled up, Alec said sternly, "That's enough of your slaver, that's enough. Stop actin' the goat, man."

"I've got some sandwiches, Granda," said Mary quietly now; "it'll be like a picnic."

"Sandwiches, eh? Let's see." He looked down at the open parcel, at the curling edges of the dry bread, and, lifting a slice, he said, "By! tongue. My! has there been a banquet at the baronial hall?"

"She had a meetin'."

"What for this time?"

"Boots for bairns."

"Oh aye, boots for bairns. When are they doing anythin' for old men?"

"I'll ask her the morrow."

"You do that, an' tell her I'm in need of some linings. And your grannie wants bloomers."

"Da! give over, will you?"

Chuckling, Peter gave over and busied himself with blowing the fire until the water bubbled in the tin can; then he mashed the tea in a brown teapot with a broken spout, and when they were sitting on upturned boxes and a bucket drinking the hot, sweet liquid and eating the sandwiches, he broke the silence by looking at his son and saying, "You know where I've been the day?"

"No."

They stared at each other for a moment before Peter said, "*Shields Gazette* office."

"*Shields Gazette* office! All the way down there! You walked all the way to the *Shields Gazette* office? You must be mad, man."

"Oh, I didn't go to High Shields, not to the main office; I went to the one on the Dock Bank."

"Did they throw you out?"

"Aye"—he nodded, twinkling at his son—"just about."

"Small wonder." Alec turned his head completely away from his father and looked out of the open door into the twilight that was already beginning; and then he said, "You must be right barmy. Nobody's goin' to buy rhymes; they don't buy good stuff the day, never mind rhymes, man. . . . God, you really must be up the pole."

"They're not rhymes, I tell you once again, they're not rhymes, they're poetry. An' somebody'll buy them someday, you mark my words."

"Aw, Da." Alec was facing his father again, his head bobbing now, his face red. "You know what? You make me embarrassed, you an' poetry! You don't know the difference atween a full stop an' a bus stop."

"Maybe not; but neither did Robbie Burns."

"That's not it. Robbie Burns lived in a different age, and he had something to say."

"Well, so have I, lad, I've got something to say an' all. Listen to this." He thrust his hand into an inner pocket of his shapeless topcoat and pulled out a bundle of papers, but Alec flapped his hand backward at him, saying, "I don't want to hear."

"Oh, Da! Da." Mary was tugging gently at his sleeve, her voice placating. Then she turned to her granda. "Go on, Granda," she said, "go on," and Peter, holding a piece of dog-eared paper before him, said, "I'm goin' on, lass; it'll take more than me thick-headed son to stop me. Listen to this—it's called 'Value for Money.'" He tilted his chin upwards, slanted his eyes downwards and began:

> "We played ma's and da's
> Those years ago;
> Ma's apron and skirt,
> Da's shirt and old bowler.

Round the top corner
In the chimney breast
We played at houses,
In which the test
Was Birth.
Our Jimmy,
Three years old,
The bairn,
New delivered into the house
In the chimney breast,
Yelled like any new flesh
Feeling air upon its skin.
But him,
He yelled for taffie
Which was his pay
For playing the bairn
That day.

Now the day, he stands
Shiverin'
Outside the bedroom
From where he hopes
His firstborn
Will yell.
No taffie the day,
No pay,
Just sweating hell
And dim surprise
That from the dole queue,
The gap,
The Guardian's food ticket,
The corner end,
The tip,
The man somewhere in him not quite spent
Has the vitality
To earn the two bob
Allowed for a bairn
By the Government.

"There!" Peter nodded at his son's back and at his granddaughter's soft, tear-bright eyes.

"I think it's lovely, Granda." There was a break in her voice.

She bent in front of Peter and, her tone loud, she said, "Da, I do, I do; I think it's lovely—sad, but lovely."

Her father turned slowly toward her and said heavily, "All right, all right, it's lovely."

Since he was a small boy Alec had listened to his father's rhymes, and if his father had kept them within the perimeter of the family he would not have minded, but his father was convinced that he was a poet, a poet of the people, and when given the opportunity, and when not given the opportunity, he would create one and read his effort aloud. True, he would be able to put more into them than was in the written word because he was a bit of an actor when he got going, but as the years went on Alec found that he was more than a bit of an embarrassment: people laughed at him. And he didn't want his father to be laughed at; he was angered by it, for at bottom he knew that his father had something, something rare. Yet he felt that this something was a handicap, for even in the old days when there was work he didn't seem to hold down a job. Alec considered that if his father had put as much effort into earning his bread as he did into his rhymes, his mother would have weathered the slump for a number of years. But anyway his mother had had one advantage over other people—she had learned a long time ago, as his father had just said, to stretch a penny to a shilling. There were times when he admitted to a deep feeling for his father. He did not give it the name of love, but that's what it was; for who could help loving him, a man such as he was, a man who retained, in spite of everything, the joy of living.

Alec looked at Mary. Her eyes were pleading with him to be kind to his father. In a way she took after his father; she had the same kindness in her, and, like him, she was given to spurts of joy; only her joy didn't run to poetry, thank God. He smiled inwardly and his eyes lingered on her. What would he do with his life if he hadn't her? She was his one solace, his one joy. Some day she would marry and what then? Sufficient unto that day; let him enjoy her when he had her, for long or short. But from the way she was turning out he doubted that their time together would be long, for she was real bonny, and blossoming further every day. Her skin was pure milk and roses; and those eyes of hers, not usual; nobody on his side or on Alice's had green eyes. She had likely inherited them from far back. They were a deep, clear green, like looking down through water, and when they were soft and moist, as they were now, and shaded by her long lashes they did something to him, brought a constriction under his ribs. His love for her was like a pain; it gnawed at him at times, times when he dreaded anything bad would happen to her. She was as tall as he now and still growing. Some day, and not far off, she'd be a spanker, a breathtaking spanker, and she was worth somebody better than the fellows around the doors, for who were around the doors? There were fifty houses on their side of the street and only three men out of that lot in full-time work. The few lads who were at work were apprenticed and as soon as they finished their time they'd be out on their backsides. Of course, that didn't stop them from getting married. Some of them married while they were still serving their time and had a couple of bairns afore they were twenty. But that wouldn't happen to Mary; no, by God, not if he knew it. He didn't know how he was going to do it, but he was going to get her away from the street and from Mrs. Turner's and her fourpence an hour, if it was only into a shop, a good class shop. It would be a bit of prestige anyway.

He had been going down to the reading room at the Institute every morning lately looking up the jobs, not for himself, because that was hopeless—they didn't advertise for fitters in the newspapers—but something for her, for if he didn't do something for her, nobody else would. Her mother wouldn't. The situation, as it was, just suited her, Mary coming home in the afternoon to get the tea and see everything was ready for Master Jimmy coming in, and then do the ironing and all the odd jobs that she left her while she went out earning. . . . Earning! It used to be two hours in the morning at the shop and two hours in the afternoon, but now she was scarcely away from it.

"Da! Will you have another sup tea?"

"No, hinny, thanks. Look, it's getting on." He nodded toward the deepening light. "I think we'd better be making a move." He turned round on the upturned bucket, then pushed his father in the shoulder with his fist, saying jocularly now, "Come on, you, Poet Laureate!" And at this they all laughed.

As they dampened down the fire and gathered up their things, Peter said, "Aye, you never know. There's many a true word spoke in joke. Just you wait; there's time enough yet. I'll have the laugh on this town when I appear in *T. P. an' Cassell's Weekly*. Aye, an' *John o' London's*."

"Evenin' dress or mornin' suit, Granda?"

"Listen to her! Listen to her!" cried Peter, and father and son now looked at Mary, joined in this moment in their admiration for her, and Peter said, "There, you're so bloomin' sharp you'll be cutting yourself! Punch for you, me girl!" Then suddenly holding her face tightly between his two hands, he repeated, "Evenin' dress or mornin' suit? and out with it as quick as a knife. I tell you it's good enough for *Punch*. Aw, me love." He bent forward swiftly and kissed her on the side of her mouth, and she hugged him for a moment before he turned from her, blinking rapidly and crying, "Where the devil's it is it was I put it?"

"What, Granda?"

"Me pipe, me pipe."

"Asking the road, you know." Alec's voice was a mumble as he walked out of the door and along the narrow, winding path between the partly stripped stumps of sprouts and cabbages.

Back in the hut Mary pressed threepence into her granda's hand, and he held on to it as he said, "Ta, me bairn. Ta. I'll pay you back, I will. Somehow, some day I'll pay you back."

His head was bobbing all the while and she whispered to him, "I know you will, Granda. And mind"—she now poked her nose close to his—"I want interest."

They came out of the hut laughing loudly; and Peter put his

arm around her waist, and in a deep, musical voice he began
to sing:

"I love a lassie,
A bonny, bonny lassie;
She's as pure as the lily in the dell;
She's as sweet as the heather,
The bonny, purple heather,
Mary, me Scotch bluebell."

A man's voice came across the allotment, shouting, "You're
in good voice the day, Peter," and Peter called back, "Never
better, Sam. Never better. It's this warm weather."

They laughed while their breaths formed clouds in the biting
air.

When they came up to Alec, Mary walked between them, and,
thrusting the bass bag at her father, she said, "Will you carry
that, Da?" Then she linked her arms in theirs, and, laughing
and stumbling over the rough land, they went from the allotment.

They stopped when they reached Biddle Street, and Peter,
still in high fettle, cried, "We've come to the parting of the
ways, my love," and Mary, taking up his tone and mimicking his
voice, said, "Good-bye. Good-bye; we may never meet again!
Ronald Colman, big picture, last Tuesday night."

And as Peter and Mary laughed together again Alec said,
"You two should have your heads looked at. Come on, you"—he
grabbed Mary's arm—"else the town crier will be out lookin'
for us."

"Just a minute." Mary thrust her hand into her pocket. "Here,
Granda." She held out two candy mints toward the old man,
and when he took them he said, "Oh, mints! Good lass, I love
mints. But, you know"—he thrust his finger at her—"if I go in
suckin' one of these, your grannie'll be on me like a prairie dog,
she will, she'll swear that I'm just coverin' up me breath. An'
where did I get the money for drink! An', she knows me! An'
not another word will she hear. An' she's stood enough of me

coming in as full as a gun, an' she's going off with Charlie
Riddle."

"Aw, come on." Alec tossed his head impatiently as he pulled
Mary away from his father.

"Tar-rah!" called out Peter.

"Tar-rah, Granda." Mary called back. "Tar-rah!"

"Aw, tar-rah, good-bye, and so long!" said Alec. Then a few
steps farther on he looked at Mary, and Mary at him, and she
slipped her hand once again through his arm when they both
laughed softly, and Mary said quietly, "I love him," and Alec
replied, "Well, I hope you love him enough for both of us at
this moment, 'cos he got that threepence out of you, didn't he?"

"Oh, Da! what does it matter? Threepence!" And then she
remembered, he very likely hadn't threepence; the few coppers
her ma allowed him out of the depleted dole—depleted because
there were two people now working in the family—he would
likely have spent on his trip across the water this morning. She
knew he had felt a bit better when neither her mother nor she
was working and for six weeks at a time he could tip up twenty-
six shillings onto the kitchen table as if it were his wages. She
thought now she had been foolish; she should have given the
threepence to him and not to her granda.

2

Ninety-five Cornice Street was comprised of four rooms, a scullery and two staircases. It had a lavatory in the backyard, separate
from the one belonging to 93, but it shared the washhouse and
the only supply of water, a yard tap, with the tenants downstairs.

Alice Walton had been known to brag that her house was the
best-furnished in the street, and on this she was right. When in
1916 and at the age of seventeen she had married Alec, he was

just out of his time in the shipyard and, owing to the war, earn-ing good money. By 1918 he was earning treble what his father had been earning in 1914. From the first Alice had known what she wanted out of life and had been determined to get it. The determination had brought her from one furnished room at the top of the church bank to two rooms in Hope Street, then on to four rooms in Cornice Street. They had arrived in Cornice Street in 1921, when Mary was four and Jimmy two years old, and she had planned that their stay there would be no longer than three years at the most, by which time Mary would want a room of her own. She did not intend to have any more chil-dren, not if she knew it; and at this stage she had made it plain to Alec and told him he must do something about it. She didn't know what exactly she expected him to do nor did he know exactly what he was expected to do, except use something, and he wasn't going to all that palaver; so whether it was by chance or management they never knew, but they had no more children. This enabled Alice to set about furnishing her house properly.

By 1923 she had a real front room, containing a three-piece suite, a china cabinet, a glass-fronted bookcase and two oc-casional tables. The floor was not covered with lino but with a gray cord carpet right to the walls, a great innovation in those days; and in the living room she was the proud possessor of a drop-leaf table, a sideboard, four Georgian-type chairs, which she had bought secondhand and did not know the value of, only that their shape appealed to her, and two armchairs that had once graced a club room. In her own bedroom she had an austere satinwood bedroom suite and a double wooden bed; no brass knobs for her. She had, however, to be content with two iron beds in the children's bedroom. Her curtains were all heavy Nottingham lace, and there was deep imitation lace on the bot-tom of the yellow paper blinds.

It was in 1924 when she was looking further afield that her eye alighted on "Moat Cottage." Why a six-room cottage stand-ing in half an acre of land on the outskirts of the town should

have been given this name wasn't evident, because the ground
all about was level and there was no sign of a moat, wet or dry.
She had passed the cottage often in her walks into the country
with the children, but it wasn't until she saw it empty that she
coveted it. When, all agog, she put the proposed move to Alec
his first question was, "What's the rent?"

"Eleven and sixpence."

Almost double what they were paying for their present house;
was she mad?

Mad or no mad, she had said to him, she was going to have
that cottage; she wasn't going to stay all her life in a grubby
street like Cornice Street looking into somebody else's back
kitchen and somebody else looking into hers. Moreover, she was
tired of living next to a lot of numskulls.

At this he had answered quietly, "I have news for you: we're
on half-time next week."

And that had been the beginning of the end of her dream of
"Moat Cottage." It had also been the beginning of a change in
her character. Previously the objectionable facets of her nature
had found vent in the ambitious drive to get on, to have a better
house than the next, better-dressed children than the next, and
cleverer children than the next. Alec's place in the sphere of
her ambitions was the provider of the wherewithal to achieve at
least two of her ambitions.

On short time Alec became an irritant, but when he became
an unemployed man Alice's irritation leaped to bitterness bordering on hatred for him, and what little love she'd had for him
became centered, not on her firstborn, her daughter, but on
her son, James. James was going to accomplish for her all that
his father had failed to do.

She now looked at her son, where he sat on the corner of the
high fender, his knees almost up to his chin, engrossed in a dog-
eared comic, and said, "Put that away and get on with your homework!"

"What, Ma?"

"You heard me. Put that rubbish away and get on with your homework."

"But, Ma, I never start me homework until after I've had me tea." He peered up at her, and she said, "We're not havin' tea until those two come in; I'm not mashing twice. And where does she think she's got to? Almost five o'clock here and she finished at two. The more you do in this house the more you might—you get no help. . . . Do you hear me?" Her voice was shrill now. "Put that away and get on with your homework!"

Jimmy rose from the fender, folded the comic and was about to push it into his pocket when it was grabbed from his hand and Alice bawled at him, "How many times have I to tell you you're not to stuff your pockets with things! It puts them out of shape. God knows your clothes are hard enough to come by. Take your coat off and hang it up. I'm tired of tellin' you."

She sighed deeply, and, her voice dropping, she said, "Aw, boy, it's for your own good. Don't you realize that?" She bent toward him, and he answered sullenly, "Aye, Ma."

At this she closed her eyes, gripped her hands together and pressed them to her breast as she said, "Aye, Ma. Aye, Ma. What good is the secondary school to you when you cannot get away from the common jargon of the street? Aye, Ma. You can't even learn to say yes."

The boy stood with his head bent staring at his feet, and as she went to push him toward the little table in the corner of the room there came the sound of the bottom staircase door opening, and her chin jerked, then her head moved in a half-circle, nodding in its passage from one shoulder to another. "They've arrived," she said and marched across the room, pulled open the kitchen door that led into the scullery from where the back stairs dropped, and glared at Mary, who was ahead of Alec, and demanded, "Where do you think you've been, Miss?"

"With me da." Mary was taking off her hat and coat as she spoke. "I . . . I met him and went to the allotments with him."

"Went to the allotments!" Alice retreated back into the room, her hand thrust out toward the table that was set for tea. "This, Madam, is what you are supposed to get ready. You're supposed to be home here at three. There's a pile of ironing. It's been lying there three days, and"—she now turned her face in the direction of her husband but did not look at him as she ended —"not a drop of water up. And no coals either. Am I supposed to do it all?"

Alec never spoke. In the scullery he took off his coat and cap, hung them on the back of the stairhead door, went to the table under the little window on which stood a tin dish and an enamel jug of water, and, pouring some water into the dish, he washed his hands, rubbed the back of his clean hand over his mouth, then rubbed his damp palm over the surface of his hair, after which he went into the kitchen and silently took his place at the table.

The table was well equipped for a midweek tea in these times. There was a large loaf of new bread, a big square of marge on a glass dish, another glass dish holding plum jam, and a plate on which there were some thin slices of pale brown paste, their edges rimmed with yellow fat.

The tea poured out, the meal continued in silence for some minutes; then Alice, as if there had been no interval in her haranguing, exclaimed, "Three times a day, every day in the week, I have to go out, and do I get any hel—"

The crash of Alec's cup into the saucer startled them all. The tea spilled over onto the clean cloth, and it was this that Alice looked at as he jumped to his feet, crying, "There's nobody makin' you go out three times a day! It's your own bloody choosin'. You break your neck to go out. Aw!"

The sound of his teeth grinding caused Mary to hunch her shoulders and she did not look up as he stalked from the room; she did not look up until she heard the staircase door bang. At the sound, Alice, who for the moment had seemed taken aback by his sudden attack, got to her feet and yelled in the direction of the scullery, "No need to go out, you say? No need to go out?

Bad lookout for everybody in this house if I didn't go out. Bare legs and empty bellies it would be for the lot of you! . . . And you"—she turned on Mary, who was rising from the table— "where do you think you're going?"

"Just into the room." Mary's voice was flat.

"You'll sit down and finish your tea."

"I don't want any tea."

"You'll do what I say." Alice's hand on her shoulder thrust her down onto the chair, and the impact of her spine with the wooden seat made her gasp.

"And when you're finished you can get that ironin' done, me lady."

Mary turned an indignant face up to her mother. "It's Tuesday; I go to the pictures on a Tuesday, you know I do."

"Well, you're not goin' the night then."

"I am so!"

Alice drew herself up while she glared at her daughter, and, her voice low, she said, "You'll defy me then?"

Mary turned and looked down at her plate; she bit on her lip, and then she said, "It's the only night out in the week I have. It's only threepence, you know it is."

"Well, this is one night, threepence or sixpence or nothing, you're not going." And on this she marched out of the room and into the bedroom, where she grabbed up her coat and came back into the kitchen, buttoning it. Looking from one to the other of the solemn figures sitting at the table, she said, "Now I'm tellin' you; you both know what to do, you the ironing, and you your homework," and went out.

There was quiet in the kitchen, and the brother and sister did not look at each other but sat staring at their plates for some minutes, before slowly, as if activated by one mind, they started to eat.

When the rain began to pelt against the window, Mary went hurriedly into the scullery, and as quickly came back, saying, "He's gone out without his coat; he'll get soppen."

"Will I go out and look for him and tell him she's gone?"

"Yes, go on, do that. Go up Ellison Street first. He might be standing in one of the shop doorways, the dead shops, or down Ormond Street."

"Aye. Aye."

"And here, put your old mac on else you'll get soppen an' all. An' it's icy cold."

The boy felt grateful when Mary helped him on with his coat. He didn't know why this should be, for he never felt grateful for the kindnesses received from his mother. He had the same nice feeling when his da said a kind word to him. He knew that his da liked Mary better than he did him, but he didn't mind that, well, not really, for he liked Mary an' all. Yet he knew he would feel better if his da would take more notice of him, because he thought a lot of his da, no matter what his ma said. It wasn't his da's fault that he was out of work, but his ma talked as if it were. There were only four boys in his class with das in full-time work. Another two had das on part-time; for the rest, they were all in the same boat, so why should his ma go on like she did?

He found Alec standing in the doorway of a barricaded shop, a shop that had died when the shipyard died. He went in out of the rain and stood beside him, and, blinking up at him, said, "She's gone, Da."

"Who's she? The cat's mother?"

This was an attitude of his das he couldn't quite make out. He said softly, "Me ma's gone, Da."

"That's better. Don't they teach you manners at that school?"

Jimmy didn't answer this but said, "Mary said will you come back? She's keeping the pot hot." This last was a bit of his own invention, but he felt nice inside because he had thought of it.

Alec looked down on the boy, then he put his hand on his shoulder, and as he felt the porous mac he said, "You shouldn't have come out. You're wet through."

"We're both in the same boat then." The boy smiled up at

him, and now Alec smiled back and cuffed his ear, then they stepped out into the driving rain.

It was seven o'clock when Grandma McAlister came. Mabel McAlister was just an older replica of her daughter. She had the same thin face, sharp-pointed nose, and the same small overfull mouth, a feature that was at variance with her type of face; her hair was pale brown, fine of texture and sparse, and stuck out in wisps from under her blue felt hat; but the face still held the shadow of a one-time attractiveness. She was sixty-three years old, and when she was thirty-four, as Alice was now, she had likely looked the same and, like Alice, been entirely unaware that her claim to good looks was marred by her expression of peevishness.

Grandma McAlister looked at her son-in-law sitting in the armchair to the side of the high, slack-coal-banked fire, and her tone itself was an accusation as she said, "She not back yet?"

"No." Alec rose slowly to his feet. "She's a bit late but she should be in any minute. Sit down. Sit down, won't you? Will I make you a drop tea?"

"No; no, thanks. 'Tisn't long since I had mine." She sat down in the chair opposite and Alec resumed his seat. She had not spoken to Mary, who was ironing on the scullery table, which had been brought into the kitchen, nor had she spoken to Jimmy, who was sitting doing his homework. But after a few moments of stretching one leg out, and then the other, as if to ease a cramp, she brought her feet together, folded her hands in her lap, looked at Alec and said, "Nothing doing?"

"No, nothing doing."

"Ted Bainbridge, you know next to me, he got set on in Wallsend last week."

"Lucky for him. We were over that way this mornin'; we nearly got set upon, not set on."

"Well, you shouldn't go over there and cause a disturbance."

"Who said we went to cause a disturbance?" Alec's voice was rising. "We went lookin' for work. We'd been told there was

some going. Disturbance! What do you mean, causing a disturbance?"

"Well, look at what happened over at North Shields last year.
They say it was the Shields lot an' fellows going over from here
and incitin' them."

"Oh, my God!" Alec moved his head slowly. "They don't
need any incitement; their dole queues are as long as ours. What
you're on about was the demonstration. They were demonstrat-
ing against . . ."

"Demonstration! Better if they used their energy to look for
work."

"Oh, dear God!" Alec uttered the words to himself as if in
prayer. Could you blame Alice for going on like she did, being
brought up by that one sitting there? If ever there was a numskull in this world, it was her.

"She's a long time," Mabel McAlister looked round the room,
and her eyes came to rest on Mary and she said, "Your ma's a
long time. Go and see what's keepin' her."

Mary did not answer her grandma but glanced toward her
father, and when he gave her an almost imperceptible nod she
laid the flatiron on the fender, saying to him, "Will you take the
heater out of the fire for me, Da?" Then she went from the room
and into her bedroom, and there, taking her working coat, she
buttoned it up to her neck, tied a scarf tightly round her head
and went down the front stairs and out of the front door so that
she wouldn't have to pass through the kitchen and look at her
grannie again. She couldn't stand Grannie McAlister.

Their house was the last but one at the top of the street, and
at the bottom end was Mr. Tollett's shop, where her ma worked.

Mr. Tollett was a nice man, Mary considered, different. He
had only been in the shop about four years; he had come and
taken it over when his father died. His father and mother had
died within a month of each other; it had been very sad. Some
people said that they had died through worry because they'd
had to close up their other two shops owing to bad debts.

Mr. Tollett hadn't been married when he first came home,

but shortly after, he married a girl from Newcastle, from Jesmond, the posh end. They said she hardly spoke to anyone around the doors. Mary only remembered seeing her once or twice, because she never showed herself in the shop. She hadn't been bad-looking, but sort of uppish. Then last year she had gone and died, leaving a baby only a year old. It was from then that her mother had gone to work for Mr. Tollett. It was just the baby, the house and the meals she saw to at first; but then she helped in the shop. She went three times a day, even on Sundays.

Halfway down the street there was an alleyway leading to Crowdon Road. There was a lamppost on the edge of the pavement opposite the alleyway, around which there was always a crowd of children playing, but tonight, raining heavily as it was, there were no children. But as she approached the lamppost she made out two dim figures standing opposite in the shelter of the draughty passage, and when she recognized them her heart began to beat a little faster. They were Hughie Amesden and Paul Connelly.

It was Paul Connelly as always who spoke to her. "Hello, Mary," he said.

She stopped tentatively, standing in the middle of the pavement within the halo of the lamp. "Hello," she said.

"Going some place?"

"Just to the shop." She looked at Paul as she answered him but all the while she was seeing Hughie. She had no need to look at Hughie to see him; she saw him so clearly in the night that she almost imagined that he was sitting on the side of her bed talking to her, and the fact that he should talk to her would, she knew, be as great an impossibility as to find him sitting on the side of her bed, for he never spoke to her. He had once said "Hello," but that was the only exchange that had been between them, and she had known him since she was ten. He was so good-looking that even the texture of his skin made her ache to look at it; his face was long and pale, his eyes deep-set and dark, but his hair was fair and wavy.

Added to all these charms was Hughie's height. He was the
tallest boy in all the streets around—he must be all of six feet
now and still only seventeen. She'd never forget the first day
she knew she loved him. It was one Sunday night last summer.
Mrs. Turner had given her a frock. She had altered it and she
felt she looked bonny in it, so she had gone to church in the
evening, because more people could see you in church. If you
came out late they were standing about and they looked at you.
And she wanted people to see her new frock, because she had
never had one like it; what was more, she'd had to fight to keep
it, because her mother had wanted it—her mother took most
of the things that Mrs. Turner gave her; her mother liked dressing
up. The dress was of a dull yellow color, not gaudy. She didn't
know what the material was but it was like a fine wool. It had
a square neck and a full skirt. She hadn't the dress any more;
her mother had burned it. She had thrown it into the fire when
they were having a row. But on that Sunday night Paul Connelly and Hughie Amesden had been standing at the end of the
road. She had seen them immediately she left the church steps
because Hughie Amesden always stood out above everybody
else, and she remembered walking toward them, and then the
oddest thing happened. It was lovely but frightening. She saw
Hughie Amesden slowly disappear into a white light; there was
nothing left of him but white light—it even blotted out Paul
Connelly. And the other funny thing was she never remembered passing them. She was a full street away when she came
to herself and she thought, Where's he gone? and she had turned
round, and there they were right at the far end of the street and
she hadn't been aware of passing them. She had stood with her
hand to her throat and had gulped and then coughed, and a
woman passing by had stopped and said, "Are you all right,
hinny?" She had taken hold of her arm and added, "Why, you're
shivering, lass; you've got a summer cold."

She had nodded at the woman, then walked on; and she had
known she had fallen in love with Hughie Amesden, that she'd
always been in love with him since he had first come into the

neighborhood when she was ten. Yet he had never, never spoken to her, only that once when they were standing in the picture queue. He had come and stood by her side and said, "Hello," and she had said "Hello" back; and then he had gone into the six-pennies and she into the threepennies.

On the other hand, Paul Connelly was always wanting to talk to her. But she couldn't stand Paul Connelly. She didn't know why Hughie Amesden and he were friends, because Paul was only about half his size; they looked like Mutt and Jeff.

She now raised her rain-wet lashes and looked at the Adonis, and he looked back at her, and at this she dropped her head and muttered, "I'll have to be going. I'm going for me ma."

Neither of them made any comment on this explanation and the three of them stared at each other for a moment longer, then she turned awkwardly and ran down the street. She was trembling again; she always trembled when she saw Hughie Amesden.

When she came to the shop there were no children jumping up and down on the low sill or playing ball on the pavement. She put her face close to the window and saw that the shop was empty, which was a rare occurrence, because Mr. Tollett sold practically everything and there was always somebody wanting something from half-past seven in the morning until eight at night, ten on a Saturday.

The shop was situated on a corner, with one window in Cornice Street and another in Benbow Street, the short street that was linked with Crowdon Road. The back door to the premises was in Benbow Street, and it led into a backyard nearly always filled with boxes of all shapes and sizes. There were two rooms behind the shop that were used as storerooms. In the main one Mr. Tollett kept his tubs of butter and rounds of cheese and sacks of flour, and there were nails in the ceiling from which he hung the sides of bacon. The other room he kept for storing potatoes and greengroceries. The door from the backyard leading into the first room had a pane of glass in the upper half. Next to this door was another, which led into what had once been a separate house. The downstairs part had been turned into a garage, but the upstairs, consisting of four rooms, had been opened up to join those above the shop. Altogether, it was a grand place. She had been up there only once and had only glimpsed the sitting room, but had been amazed at the size of it. Mr. Tollett had had two rooms knocked into one; it was really lovely. Her mother had almost shooed her out. She had said she wasn't to come bothering. Mr. Tollett didn't want the street in. She had wanted to say to her mother that she wasn't the street, she was her daughter who had come with a message from her da.

She was going toward the door now that led into the house when she saw the outline of a figure moving behind the rain-smeared glass pane. That was her ma. Perhaps she was helping to put orders up. As her hand went toward the latch her face moved closer to the pane of glass and she could make out not only her mother but also Mr. Tollett, and saw that they were talking.

The room was brightly lit but the rain-patterned glass distorted her mother's features, and at first she thought that it was this that was making her look different. Then her hand dropped from the latch and she peered intently through the window. Her mother did look different, and it wasn't because of the wet glass. She had never seen her mother looking like this. She was looking into Mr. Tollett's face and her expression was soft and pleading; she looked young. She noticed that she kept wetting her lips. She saw Mr. Tollett bow his head while her mother kept on talking; she couldn't hear what she was saying because of the wind and the lashing rain. But now she saw Mr. Tollett pick up something from a chair. It was her mother's coat. She watched her mother put it on; her head was drooping now.

When Mr. Tollett suddenly came toward the door, she sprang back and nearly fell into the boxes stacked near the wall. If it hadn't been for the wind, they would have heard her scrambling to the side of them. She stood with her back pressed against a drainpipe that was blocked at the top, and the water splashed down onto her and almost blinded her, but she dared not lift her hand up in case it attracted their attention, because they were in the yard now.

She put her head to one side away from the water spout and she could see Mr. Tollett and her mother standing in the beam of light from the doorway. Mr. Tollett had his hand on the outside door and he was saying, "It isn't that I'm ungrateful, Alice, don't think that, but . . . but it wouldn't be right. Alec's a good man; I've known him for years, he's a good man."

Her mother's voice came to her now, thin and grim, saying, "Good man! You don't know. He doesn't need me, nor me him; there's been nothing, well, not for years. I tell you, Ben . . ." There followed a silence as if somebody had put a hand across her mouth.

Mr. Tollett was holding the back door open and she saw her mother step slowly through it and into the street. She saw Mr. Tollett thrust the bolt home, pause for a moment with his hands still on it, then turn toward the back door. She thought she heard him mutter, "God Almighty!" but she couldn't be sure. She remained where she was, frightened to move, until there came faintly through the wall the sound of the shop bell ringing. She let a few minutes elapse, then she groped her way to the wall door, undid the bolt and went out into the street, and strangely she wasn't thinking about her ma and Mr. Tollett, but about her da, and she kept repeating in her mind, "Oh, Da. Da."

It wasn't until she had almost reached the house that she thought, Me ma wants to go with Mr. Tollett; she was offering herself to Mr. Tollett. She recalled vaguely that her ma had known Mr. Tollett about the time when she first knew her da. Then Mr. Tollett had gone away to live in the South with an aunt and had worked in a car factory or had something to do with cars. It was all very vague, but she could just remember her da talking about it with her granda, and her da saying, "He won't take to the shop; he could never stand the shops—that's why he went away."

Her da had never been happy since he was out of work, but his unhappiness seemed to have deepened this last year, since her ma had gone to work for Mr. Tollett. And this was the reason. He knew about her ma wanting Mr. Tollett.

As her body's reaction was to tremble at the sight of her first love, Hughie, so it now ached with physical pain that was akin to anguish when it touched on the plight of her constant love, her da. Her da must be feeling awful, awful, because he must love her ma. He must have loved her, mustn't he, to have married her in the first place? And he must still love her, because if he didn't, he wouldn't be hurt as he was. So she reasoned.

Oh, her ma! She hated her ma. She was not sorry now that she wished at times she were dead. She would love to go in now and say, "I saw you all over Mr. Tollett. You're nasty, that's what you are, you're nasty." It would be difficult when her ma got at her not to turn on her and tell her that she knew all about her carry-on; but then she mustn't; her da had enough to put up with.

When she entered the house Alice started on her almost immediately. "Went to find me, did you? It's a straight road from here to the shop; did you make yourself invisible? Because I didn't see you!" When she advanced toward her and cried, "If you were up that alley, Miss, up to any carry-on, I'll skin you . . ."

But she did not finish, for her daughter spat at her, "Shut up, you!"

They stared at each other, eyes wide, while Alec, Jimmy and Grandma McAlister stared at them and the three marveled that Alice didn't take her hand and knock her daughter flying. All Alice did was to take in a long, deep, slow breath and turn away and attack the iron pan on the stove, grinding it into the embers as if in an effort to snap it in two.

Mary slowly took off her wet things, walked past her mother and went into her bedroom. Standing at the foot of the bed she gripped the iron rail and rocked herself over it backwards and forwards. Her mother knew that she knew. Well, now perhaps she'd be frightened and come to her senses. And another good thing could come out of it. She wouldn't lift a hand to her any more, for if she did, she would say to her, "You do, just you do," and that would be enough. Funny how things turned out.

3

It had snowed heavily on and off for a week, thawed, frozen, then snowed again; then in the night a fall of sleet followed by frost had turned the town into, as Alec put it, a skating rink.

He was waiting for Mary at the corner of Hurworth Place. Not that he was afraid she couldn't make her way home, because there was nothing better she liked than a good slide—she was still as bad as the bairns—but he was waiting for her because he had some news concerning what he considered might give her a better start in life.

When she came up to him she exclaimed, "Da! what you doing here? Man, you look frozen. Anything wrong?"

"No, no, nothin' wrong; I've just got a bit of news for you. Look, come on to your grannie's. I'm not tellin' you here; it's enough to cut the legs off you."

"Serves you right; you shouldn't have been standing about. Couldn't it have kept?" She caught hold of his arm and as she clutched the thread-worn overcoat she pressed nearer to him and said, "You might be getting a new coat, at least a new secondhand one, Mr. Turner's; she's been sorting his wardrobe out; she says he's ready for a new one. He's got two already and they're both good, but if he gets another, she'll likely give me number three. She's not bad, although she's stingy with the tea." She jerked his arm toward her, and he turned his head and laughed at her, "Aye, well, tell her to get a move on, else I'll be stiff."

"Where have you been the day?" she asked.

"Shields."

"All the way down there in this?" She paused. "Anything doing?"

"Huh!" He laughed softly. "You kiddin'?"

"Well, why did you go? Did you take the tram?"

"No, I felt like a walk."

"A walk into Shields in this? How far did you go?"

"The Market Place, Crofton's. Now, look." He dug his elbow into her side. "I'm not goin' to tell you any more till we get inside. Me breath's cuttin' me throat."

When they pushed open the back door of 7 Bingley Street, Grandma Mary Walton turned from the table where she had her hands in an earthenware bowl of flour and exclaimed in a high, excited voice, "Well! Look what the wind's blown in. Come in. Come in and close the door, else I won't have a hair left on me legs."

Banging the door behind them, they went in laughing, and, as Mary had noticed before, age seemed to drop away from her da when he was in his own home, at least the home of his youth, with his own ma and da. Her da was thirty-six and that wasn't really old, yet he appeared old to her, except like now when, blowing on his hands, he stood near his mother and said, "What you up to? Tea cakes?"

"No, nothin' so fancy, bread; but if you're staying long enough, I'll knock you up a bit stottie cake."

"I'll stay long enough, won't we, Mary?"

"Yes, Gran. . . . Where's Granda?"

"Listen." Grandma Walton looked toward the wall. "There's your answer."

They both looked and listened, and there came to them a snort, followed by a deep, rattling snore. "Go and wake him up." She nodded in Mary's direction, and Mary said, "Aw, let him lie for a minute." Then turning to her father, she demanded, "Well, come on, out with it! What have you got to surprise me with?"

Alec now took his overcoat off, pulled a paper from his inside pocket and, spreading it on the table, pointed to an advertisement that was ringed with pencil and said, "Read that." Mary read: "Young lady assistant wanted for dress department. Good prospects. Apply Crofton's, King Street, South Shields."

Without straightening her back, she turned her face to him and screwed up her eyes as she said, "But, Da! I won't stand a chance. There'll be a million after it. Crofton's. It's a big shop, not a huckster's."

"I know, I know, I've seen Crofton's afore." He nodded at her, his face half-smiling. "An' what's more, I've been in there this mornin'. Look what I've bought." He now pulled from his jacket pocket a startlingly white knot of tape.

"Tape?" Both Grandma Walton and Mary spoke together, and he nodded at first one and then the other and said, "Aye, tape."

"What did you have to go and buy tape for?" His mother asked him now, her small bright round face expressing a look of amazement.

"Not to slot through me knickers, Ma."

"Oh, go on with you, and stop it. You're as bad as your da with your vulgarities."

"God! Vulgarities." Alec was shaking his head while he laughed, and then he said, "Well, if you want to know, I'll put you both out of your misery. It's like this. Do any of you remember Jenny Broadbent?"

"Of course I remember Jenny Broadbent." It was his mother speaking. "She used to work . . ."

"Aye, she used to work in Crofton's. Then she left to get married; and he died, and she went back again. Well, she's on the haberdashery counter." He now inclined his head deeply toward Mary and, as if instructing her, said, "That's where they sell tapes, you know."

When she pushed him he laughed, then went on, "Well, anyway, when I saw this advert I thought of Jenny Broadbent, and

I thought me ma was good to her at one time, now see if she remembers that."

"Oh, you! our Alec."

"Yes, me, your Alec. Well, your Alec went down and said 'Hello, Jenny, can I have a knot of tape?' And she didn't answer for a bit, she just looked a bit stuck; and then she was half-laughing when she said, 'Yes, sir,' and as she passed over the tape I put the paper in front of her and pointed to that." He now stabbed the newspaper with his finger. "And I said, *sotto voce*" —again he turned to Mary—"that's under your breath, you know." Then after another push he finished, "I asked her if she could give you a helpin' hand, and she said aye, she could. You've got to be down there at half-past nine the morrow mornin'."

"Eeh! Da. Me in Crofton's! But . . . but it's a long way, and I'll have to pay me tram. What's the wage?"

"I didn't ask the wage, but it can't be less than what you're gettin' now, for God's sake, and anyway whatever it is, you'll have to meet your tram fare out of it. But it's a start for you— something better."

"Yes, yes." Her face was broadening into a wide beam. She looked at her grannie. "It would be nice, wouldn't it, to work at Crofton's, a big shop? Eeh!" Her head swung from side to side, and her chin went down toward her breast as if a deep shy-ness had overcome her as she said, "Eeh! fancy me getting a job in Crofton's."

"You haven't got it yet, lass."

"Now, be quiet, Ma; Jenny Broadbent's almost as good as her word, if I remember rightly."

"What do you remember rightly?" Peter Walton came into the room rubbing the sleep out of his eyes.

"I might get a job, Granda, in Shields, in Crofton's."

"Aye, aye!" Peter sat down. "What's it all about? Come on, tell us."

And they told him, and when they had finished he agreed with his son. "Aye, it would be grand, hinny, if you could get a real start in life, something refined like, not service. Although, mind, it hasn't done that one much harm." He thumbed toward his wife. "They learned her to bake and use her hands, although, mind, she still hasn't got much up top."

"For two pins!" Mary Walton lifted the lump of dough that she was kneading, threatening to throw it. "You may thank your stars, me bold boy, that things are as they are and I can't waste it, else you would get it."

"Well, hurry up and get it into the oven and less lip. Have you any currants to make me canny lass here a yuledo?" He nudged Mary. "And I could do with a sup tea. What you thinking about? No tea goin'!"

"Oh, Granda!"

As Mary went to push him he put his arms around her, saying, "Come on an' sit on me knee and give us a bit cuddle. Don't take any notice of them."

And they were sitting like this, Peter, his stubbly face pressed against Mary's shoulder, Mary, her chin resting on his sparse, untidy gray hair, both rocking each other, when the back door burst open and Jimmy entered.

The boy stood gasping for a moment, and they all stared at him, but just as his grannie was going to put a question to him he looked at his father and gasped, "I . . . I've been lookin' all over the show for you. Been to the allotments an' all. Me ma, me ma's hurt her leg."

"Hurt her leg! . . . Badly?"

Jimmy nodded at his father. "It seems so. They had to carry her up out of the street; she was yellin' blue murder."

"When did this happen?"

"Just . . . just a while ago. They sent me for you. I didn't know where to look." He drew in a gasping breath.

Alec was getting into his coat and Mary had already donned hers and was tying a scarf around her head when Peter said, "I'll come with you."

"No, no, Da," said Alec. "You'll be on your back afore you reach the end of the street; it took us all our time to get here.

I'll . . . I'll let you know. Come on." Scurrying now, the three of them went out, and Mary wondered why it was that nice things never seemed to last.

The house appeared full of neighbors, although there were only four of them: Mr. and Mrs. Ryder from the end house, and Mrs. Weir and her daughter-in-law from number 90.

"What's happened?" Alec stood looking down on Alice where she lay on the top of the bed with the quilt over her, but the only reply he got from her was a moan.

It was Jack Ryder who said, "I don't know if I've done right, Alec, but I've sent for the doctor; it's my opinion she's broken her leg. She passed clean out when we carried her up, an' screamed when we moved her. The road's like ice now, an' the bairns have made it a thousand times worse with their slides. It was on one of them she stepped, so they tell me."

Alec nodded back at the man. "Aye, you did the right thing, Jack. And thanks, thanks." He nodded from one to the other in the room; and they nodded back to him and filed out. He followed them on to the landing, saying again, "Thanks, thanks."

In the room Mary stood at the foot of the bed looking at her mother, and she watched her open her eyes and bite tightly on her lip before she said, "Here!"

Mary went up to her and bent over her, and Alice, looking straight up into her eyes, said, "Go on down to the shop. Tell Ben . . . Mr. Tollett what's happened to me. Tell him you'll . . . you'll help him out."

Mary stared at her mother for a time before saying quietly, "Yes, Ma."

Alice tried to move, then winced with pain. The beads of sweat were standing on her brow, and when Alec came back to the bed he said, "Lie still; don't move."

Alice didn't look at him but at Mary, where she was still standing gazing at her, and she said, "Go on."

"Where you going?" Alec turned from the bed as Mary made

to go out of the room, and she said to him, "Me ma says I've got to go and tell Mr. Tollett and . . . and help him out."

Alec kept his gaze on her, then looked at Alice again. But Alice had her eyes closed, and so he made no protest, and Mary went out.

She wasn't aware of picking her way down the street amidst the many slides; she only knew she felt guilty because of her feelings. She should be terribly concerned about her mother and her leg, but the only thing she could say to herself was, "You'd think she had done it on purpose, you would, you would." She had known what was going to happen before her mother laid down her demands; oh yes, she knew what was going to happen. She didn't want to go to Mr. Tollett's. Not that she had anything against him—in fact she thought he was a nice man, a kind man—but she just didn't want to work at Mr. Tollett's; she wanted to get that job at Crofton's. And her da would stand by her, yes, he would.

There were four customers in the shop and Mr. Tollett was very busy. She stood at the side watching him. She could see why her mother liked him; he was nice-looking. She knew he was thirty-five, only a year younger than her da, but he looked so much younger. He had a tanned skin and dark brown eyes and black hair—his grandfather was Italian. They said his grandfather had gone round with a hokey-pokey cart selling ice cream. He had a nice smile. He was making Mrs. Foggerty laugh. "Salty?" he was saying. "I've never sold a bit of salty bacon in me life. Briny, but not salty."

"Go on with you!" Mrs. Foggerty was pushing her thick arm toward him across the counter in a playfully menacing fashion. "Don't tell me I don't know when bacon's salty. It stuck to the pan."

"You don't know how to fry it."

"Eeh, did you ever!" Mrs. Foggerty turned for support to the other three women, and they all laughed, and when one of them said, "There might be something in that," Mrs. Foggerty's face lost its grin. But her tart reply was checked by the sound of a child calling: "Dada! Dada!"

"Oh dear, dear, here we go. Just a minute, ladies." As he moved along the counter he caught sight of Mary, and he said brightly, "Oh, hello. Hello there, Mary!" Then he opened the door of the storeroom and, looking down at the small boy, exclaimed, "How on earth did you get down here? Now, go on, be a good lad and get back upstairs. Alice'll be here in a minute."

". . . Mr. Tollett, me ma's hurt her leg—broken it, I think. She sent me to . . . to see to him in the meantime. Will I take him up?"

He stared at her across the counter. "Alice hurt her leg? Oh, dear me. Where?"

"When she was going back home she slipped on a slide."

"They want brainin', that lot," one of the women put in. "I nearly had me bloody feet whipped from under me meself. Something should be done about these bairns, or the lazy bitches up street should clear their fronts."

"Why should they when there's enough men to do it?" said another woman primly. "God knows they've got little enough to do, but clear the fronts, will they? Not them. Beneath the dignity of some of them to take a brush in their hands. The young'uns are the worst. Boxin' matches or their pitch-'n'-toss, they can find coppers for that. Oh, aye."

Mary passed Benjamin Tollett and stooped down to the child and picked him up in her arms, then went through the storeroom, out into the yard and up the other staircase, and entered a new world.

As angry as she was against her mother, she couldn't help but be impressed with what she saw. Everything was shining. She stood in the long room bouncing the child up and down in her arms and looked about her. There was a window at one end looking on to Cornice Street. It had a fine net curtain close to the panes, and at the sides hung green chenille curtains. At the other end of the room, along the side wall, was another window, and it had the same kind of drapery. There was a three-piece

suite covered in chintz; and the fireplace was even better than
the one in Mrs. Turner's; it was modern, very modern, all tiled
with a raised hearth. She had never seen anything like it. And
on each side of the fireplace, in the alcoves, were bookcases with
glass fronts. One held books, the other pieces of pretty china.
Set in the far corner of the room was a cabinet. The lid was up,
and when she walked toward it she saw it was a gramophone, a
fancy one called a radiogram. She had seen them advertised.

When the child said, "Tea. I want tea," she put him on the
floor, saying, "Oh, yes, dear; I'll get your tea. Come on."

She went out into the hallway again and opened the first door
going off it, and was amazed to see that this was a dining room,
not so posh as Mrs. Turner's, because there were only two pieces
of silver on the sideboard, but it was very nice. She hadn't
imagined Mr. Tollett going in for a separate dining room; she
thought they only ate like this round Bloom Crescent and Croft
Terrace and places like that.

The child struggled from her arms and impatiently ran across
the hallway and pushed open another door, which revealed the
kitchen. Here, too, net curtains were close to the window so that
people couldn't see in from across the road. She stood gazing
about her, and she told herself she wouldn't have believed it:
the kitchen was far superior to Mrs. Turner's. There was a
modern gas stove, and besides a larder going off, there was a
separate china cupboard. But most amazing of all, next to the
gas stove was a lift-up table and underneath was a copper, a
washing copper which, she saw, was connected to a gas pipe.
He had a gas copper; there was no need to use the washhouse.
Still, she didn't suppose they could get into the washhouse; it
would be full of boxes. But all this luxury amazed her.

The child tugging at her skirt and whining brought her out
of her dream, and she went about finding where things were
kept. When she asked him if he had milk with his tea he replied
bluntly, "No, tea . . . tea."

She gave him his tea on a little table set under the window.
It consisted of weak tea, bread and butter and jam, a piece of

Swiss roll and a plate of jelly and custard she found in the cupboard, and when he was finished he trotted away from her out of the kitchen, across the hallway and into another room, and she followed him into what was his own room. There was a cot in the corner, a playpen in the middle of the floor, and more toys scattered about than she had seen in the whole of her life.

"Gona play?" When he looked up at her solemnly she replied, "Yes, yes, I'll play. What do you want to play?"

"Engines." He proceeded to drag from a box an engine, coaches and wagons and pieces of rail, which he arranged with surprising dexterity in a circle on the oilcloth. She found that all she was required to do was to sit and watch him.

They were like this when Ben Tollett first saw them. He stood in the doorway and they weren't aware of his presence for some seconds.

When Mary became aware of him she jumped to her feet, saying, "He wanted to play."

"Yes, yes." He nodded at her. "He always wants to play. But tell me, what happened to your mother?"

"I don't really know." She was standing picking one nail with another as she spoke, conscious all the while of the thing that was between him and her mother, and yet wasn't, because he would have none of it. "They've sent for the doctor. They think her leg's broken. We . . . we were at me grannie's, me da and me, and Jimmy came for us. That's . . . that's all I know."

"Dear, dear!" He shook his head. "Well now, we're in a fix, aren't we?" He smiled, then asked her, "Do you think you can put him to bed later? I'll close early. They'll have to put up with it. And then I'll have to think of what I'm going to do, won't I?"

"Oh, I can see to him." She nodded her head, then looked down at the child, who now took his hand and swiped the whole arrangement of engine and trucks to the far corner of the room.

Ben put his hand to his brow and, smiling grimly, said, "He needs putting up with."

"He'll be all right. What time does he go to bed?"

"Seven, if he will."

"Can . . . can you tell me what you have for your supper?"

"Oh, anything. It doesn't matter about that. I can have something cold from down below." He jerked his head backwards. "Don't you bother, just make yourself comfortable and look after him. I'll be grateful for that." He nodded, then ended, "All right?"

"All right, Mr. Tollett," she answered.

Again he nodded while he kept his eyes on her for a moment; then, smiling, he turned and left the room, and on this the child made a dash from the corner of the room, crying, "Dada! Dada!" But Mary caught him by the hand, saying, "Come on, now. Let's clear this lot up, eh? And put them all away, and then we'll look at your picture books."

The two-year-old looked at her. He had never been told before to clear anything up—Alice cleared up after him—and to show he was having none of it he took his foot and kicked her on the shin. Her instant reaction was the same as if Jimmy had kicked her; her hand went out and she slapped him. There was a short silence in the room, because they both had received a shock; the child couldn't remember ever being slapped, and Mary felt she had done something terrible; not five minutes with the bairn and she had slapped him. But when he began to howl loudly she didn't pick him up; she just said, "Come on, now, be a good lad. We'll clear up together." And to her surprise he did as she bade him. But the clearing-up done, he sat on the floor, looked up at her and stated very firmly, "I don't like you," and as if she were a child again, fighting with a playmate, she poked her face down to him and said, "It's mutual. I don't like you either!" Again there was a short silence; but now it was broken by her laughter. She sat down in a low chair and began to laugh, and she became concerned when she found she couldn't stop. She put her hand over her mouth, and when the child came and stood by her side and put his hands on her knees and laughed with her, she found to her great consternation that she was laughing no longer but crying and gasping inside herself with each sob, "Eeh! me me. Me me. You'd think she'd done it on purpose."

It was ten o'clock that night and they were still arguing, at least Alice was keeping on. She might be in pain, but it wasn't stopping her tongue, and for the countless time she repeated the same phrase, "If any of them in this street get into that house, I'll never get them out. Don't think they'll give up the job when I'm better. I might be here a month, six weeks. You heard what the doctor said; me ankle's completely broken. I've got to stay put, an' who's going to keep us, I ask you? By the time they get round to gettin' you off the gap and on to the dole again we could starve to death. And that boy, he's got to be kept on at the high school. That's the main thing. And he's got to be decently dressed—he's not going to end up the same way as you have." She glared at Alec. "He's going to have a start in life, and to have a start he needs his school certificate, and if it's the last thing I do, he's going to get it.

"Crofton's! What do you think you'll get there?" This was to Mary, who was sitting sullenly with her back to the wall facing the bed. "Ten shillings a week at most, and then your bus fare to Tyne Dock, and another from there to the Market Place; you won't be able to do it under eightpence a day. Girl, you're mad. But you're not half as mad as him. He's put you up to this; I knew there was somethin' afoot." She nodded grimly at Alec. "Well now, you can both forget about it until I'm on me feet again, when you can continue with your high ideas. But in the meantime, you, me lady, will get yourself out of bed in the morning for a change and get down to the shop by seven, and get them their breakfast, and see to the bairn. You can tell Mrs. Turner you've got to finish at twelve; that'll give you time to get back and get them something to eat for one o'clock. You can arrange the meal the day afore; you'll have all afternoon and evening. I'll tell you what to do."

Alec hadn't interrupted Alice's flow, but now he turned from the darkened window, walked to the foot of the bed, and, look-

ing over the mound they had made out of a fire guard to keep
the clothes off her injured ankle, he said thickly, "She's not a
bloody dray horse."

"I'm not expecting her to be a dray horse. But she's had it too
easy up till now, and this isn't forever. I'm only asking her to
do it until I get on me feet again."

"Mrs. Weir would do it; she proffered." His voice was quiet,
dead-sounding.

"Mrs. Weir! Huh! She's just another of the bitches around
here who are waiting to jump into me shoes. They're as jealous
as hell of me working down there, because they know that we
eat better than any of them, have more than any of them. . . .
Aw, you! you can't see beyond your nose." She flung her arm in
a wide sweep, and its gesture threw him away from her. He
turned and went into the kitchen, and after a moment Mary
followed him silently, keeping her eyes away from her mother
as she passed the bed.

In the kitchen, where Jimmy was standing, a look of appre-
hension on his face because he was frightened of rows, Alec
looked from one to the other, and from deep in his throat he
ejected his misery and bitterness: "It should have been her
bloody neck," he said; "that's what it should have been, her
bloody neck."

4

The routine worked. After a few days the sullen look left
Mary's face, and at the end of a seven-day week she brought
home the pound Mr. Tollett had given her and also her reduced
wage of six shillings from Mrs. Turner, which she placed on the
bedcover and said to her mother, "There! twenty-six shillings."

As Alice's hand went out to take the money Mary quickly

picked up the six shillings and, looking straight into her mother's eyes, said, "I want more than a shilling pocket money."

"WHAT!"

"You heard what I said, Ma, I want more than a shilling pocket money. I . . . I want to buy some clothes; I want five shillings a week. As long as I'm doing two jobs I want fi—"

"You'll get my hand across . . . !"

"Ma!" Mary backed a step from the bed. "You're in no position to bargain, Ma. I've told you, I want five shillings every week, an' if I don't get it, I'm not going back there. You can't make me, you know." She poked her face toward her mother, who she thought for a moment was going to collapse.

"You're not gettin' five shillings, an' that's that!"

"No, I'm takin' it, Ma. There you are." She threw a shilling onto the bedcover. "I'm going to take it every week, say what you like. I haven't any stockings, and me shoes are nearly through. You see to Jimmy's things but you never do mine. I've never had a new thing that I can ever remember; it's been Mrs. Turner's, or afore that the market stall on a Saturday mornin'. I'm going to get something new, Ma."

"GET OUT!"

Mary went out and into the kitchen, and there she looked mischievously at her da and whispered, "I did it."

"And you got off with it?"

"I got off with it."

They both smiled at each other. Then, taking a half-crown from her pocket, she pressed it into his hand. But he pushed it back at her, whispering, "No, no!"

"Aye, yes; fifty-fifty."

"Aw, lass!"

He put his hand out and touched her hair. Then he turned and looked at Jimmy where he was sitting by the table staring at them, and Mary, too, looked at Jimmy, and she thrust her hand into her pocket again and handed him a sixpence. But he didn't take it, not right away; he looked from her hand up to her face, then said, "For me?"

"Aye, who else? It's not for coffee-Johnny, or Tommy-on-the-bridge, 'cos they haven't done nowt for me." Whereupon Jimmy put his head down and his hand tight across his mouth to smother his laughter. But he was unable to restrain it, and as she pushed the sixpence into his hand there came a querulous shout from the bedroom. "You, Jimmy! Do you hear me there? You, Jimmy!"

When they were left alone Alec whispered, "You'll have nowt left, lass."

"Don't you worry, Da." She slanted her eyes up to him. "I'm on to a good thing here; it's a gold mine, or a silver one. Look." She pulled from her pocket another half-crown. "Mr. Tollett gave it to me for meself. He emphasized that. He said, 'Now that's for yourself.'"

Alec smiled at her as he said, "Well, that was kind of him."

As she looked back into his face the mischievous smile left her own and she said, "He is kind, Da. He's a nice man."

They stared at each other and then he nodded slowly. "Aye, Ben's all right"; then he asked, "Do you like it there?"

"Yes, Da. Aw, yes. It's lovely; it isn't like work at all. The way the place's set out it's grand. Have you seen it?"

"No, no, I haven't seen it, lass. What's it like? Tell us."

So she proceeded to tell him, and he gazed at her, not taking in all she was saying but thinking, It'll be God's pity if she takes up with housework for good; she's worth something better, oh aye, something better than that.

It became the regular procedure that Alice would instruct Mary what she was to cook for Ben and how she was to cook it, and Mary would listen dutifully and say, "Yes, Ma. Yes, Ma," knowing that at half-past twelve she would hurry panting through the backyard and up the stairs, to warm up, or finish, the dinner she had prepared yesterday, a dinner of her own concocting.

She would talk to the child, joke with him, make him laugh. She had given new names to all his toys. His cloth doll she called

Ching Lang Lou. What did it matter that it was a Negro with black wool curls? They had great fun with Ching Lang Lou. Then, the meal ready and set in the dining room, not the kitchen, she would call Ben up, while she herself would take his place in the shop.

One day he had said to her, "It's a pity we can't sit down together, Mary," and she had answered, "Oh, that's all right, Mr. Tollett." She had added, "I eat more when I'm on me own," and at this they had laughed loudly as if at a great joke, and shaking his head while he gazed at her, Ben had said, "Aw, Mary, Mary."

She got on well with Mr. Tollett. But it was odd how little they saw of each other; they were just like that saying, ships that pass in the night. He was already in the shop when she arrived in the morning, and they spoke to each other for only a few moments when she took his place twice so that he could have his meals. Very often when she took down his three-o'clock cup of tea she just left it in the storeroom and tapped on the door, and he would call to her, "Thanks. Thanks, Mary." The only time she ate with him was on a Wednesday when he had his half-day.

One night, as she was leaving, she did say to him, "You're busy enough to have an assistant," to which he replied, "I did have one, but he assisted himself, Mary, a little too much."

"Aw, like that, was it?"

"Yes, it was like that."

"You can never trust people."

"Yes, that's a fact, you can never trust people, Mary."

She had every opportunity of helping herself from the well-stocked cupboard upstairs, and a half a dozen spoonfuls of tea wouldn't have been missed from the caddy each day, but she wouldn't do that, not to Mr. Tollett. Why, the basket of groceries he had given her ma every Friday night and which he still continued to give her couldn't be bought for fifteen shillings! No, she wouldn't take a grain of salt belonging to Mr. Tollett.

She was happy as she had never been happy before, because she had now things to give, money to give to her da and their Jimmy, the price of an ounce of 'baccy to her granda, and a quarter of hard candies for her grandma. But she didn't pay for the hard candies, because when she offered Mr. Tollett the money for them, he wouldn't take it, even though she said to him, "They're not for me, so if you don't take it then I'll have to go some place else next week to buy them."

"Who are they for then?" he had asked. "Your mother?"

"No." Her no had been flat-sounding; but her voice had risen on, "Me grannie! She loves them."

"Well, give them to your grannie with my compliments."

"Oh, thanks, I will. But mind, next week you'll have to take the money."

Oh, Mr. Tollett was nice. She hoped her ma's leg stayed as it was for months. Not that she wished her any harm, only, as things were, life was wonderful.

And then she got the St. Valentine's card.

"You've got a letter," Alice said, staring at her very hard as she went into the bedroom to make her daily report, which was anything but accurate.

"A letter! Me? Who from?"

"That's what I'd like to know. You carrying on with a lad?"

"Me? A lad!" Mary's face stretched; her tone held deep indignation as if she had never thought about having a lad in her life. "No. You know I haven't got a lad. What time have I got for a lad, from early morning till late at night? What time, I ask you? Where's the letter?"

Alice picked up the letter from the bedside table and handed it to her. It felt stiff. She examined it back and front, noting that the postmark was Jarrow, before she opened it, then she drew out a card. The card had a large rose on the front, deep red and of a cabbage variety. She stared at it, turned it over, then read: "From a silent admirer."

The face that now looked at Alice was as red as the rose on the card.

"Give it here!" Alice's hand grabbed, but Mary withdrew her arm quickly and said, "It's mine."

"Who's it from?"

"A friend."

"You said you hadn't any lads—you've been havin' truck with somebody, haven't you?"

"No, I haven't. Anyway"—she thrust the card back into the envelope—"what if I was havin' truck with a lad? I'm past sixteen. Janie Anderson from across the road was married last week, remember, and she's not seventeen yet."

"Don't you talk to me about Janie Anderson, that trollop. Do you want to land up in the same way as she did, going to the altar with her belly full?"

"Oh, Ma! Ma, what do you think I am?" Mary's tone was indignant.

"I know what you are." Alice nodded her head viciously at her. "And let me see you havin' any carry-on with any of them round these doors and I'll whip you till you can't sit."

Bitterly they stared at each other, and the knowledge that was between them rose to the surface, and Mary was just prevented from hissing it out by Alec's entering through the open door.

"Come out of it." He pulled at her arm and thrust her out of the bedroom. Then, looking at his wife, he said slowly, "What a pity you didn't take your own advice, isn't it?"

Alice made no answer to this, but her lips parted to show her teeth tight-clenched. The muscles on her neck went into cords as Alec went on, still quietly but authoritatively, "If she wants to have a lad, she's havin' a lad; as she said, she's turned sixteen. And should she get one soon, she could take after her mother, couldn't she, and have to run for it? Janie Anderson isn't the first trollop." And on this he turned slowly and went out of the room.

In the kitchen Mary was sitting at the table. She had taken the card from the envelope and was staring at it, and she turned to Alec and, handing it to him, said, "I haven't got a lad, Da, and I don't know who it's from."

And she didn't know who it was from, not really, but she hoped it was from Hughie Amesden, because he was silent. Although he had only spoken to her that once, somehow she felt he was as much aware of her as she was of him.

Alec read the message on the back, looked at the rose again, then said, "It's bonny. . . . No idea who it's from?"

"No, no, Da. Well, there's just one lad I know who doesn't talk much; but then"—she shrugged her shoulders—"I really don't think he would send me a card."

"Well, anyway"—he flicked his fingers at her—"it's a start. You'll see, they'll be comin' every post from now on."

"Oh, Da, don't be daft."

"The lads in my class think you're bonny."

They both turned and looked at Jimmy where he had been bending over his books in the corner of the room, seeming uninterested in what was going on, and her da laughed aloud as he said, "There you are; that's fame for you."

"Oh, Da!" She pushed him, then said, "Oh you, our Jimmy! Talk about spinning them."

"I'm not, I'm not, Mary. Honest. They were talkin' about lasses one day and one of the lads said you were a cracker."

"How old was he?" Mary was standing very straight now, her head up, her chin to one side.

"Same as me, fourteen."

"Fourteen!" She slumped with her mirth and laid her head against Alec's shoulder, saying, "Fourteen, Da, fourteen!" and Alec, laughing too, said, "Well, he'll grow; there's plenty of time."

"You, Jimmy!"

The voice came from the bedroom, and Jimmy got up wearily from his seat and looked at them for a moment, and they at him; then he bowed his head and went from the room.

Wearily Alec turned toward the fire, saying below his breath, "You know, of the three of us I'm beginning to think he's got the worst deal."

Suddenly Mary felt sad, not because of what her da had said about Jimmy, but because he was no longer pretending that everything was all right between her ma and him. It was three against one now, but she knew that the one was stronger than the three put together.

5

Mary had been working at the shop for six weeks when Alice said, "I'm havin' no more of this. I'm gettin' on me feet."

"Don't be silly, Ma. The doctor said it would be eight weeks, and you had to be careful."

Alice stared at her for a moment before she said grimly, "Mr. Weir says you can get crutches if you go down to the Infirmary; your da 'll go the morrow and get me them, and once I'm on me legs I'm comin' down there to see what you're up to, me girl."

"What do you mean, Ma, what I'm up to?"

"Just what I say, 'cos I know you're not takin' two penn'orth of notice of what I tell you. I don't know what's going on, but you're too happy by half. There was me having to practically beg you to take it on, and now I'll likely have to hammer you to give it up. But you'll give it up, me girl. Oh aye, you'll give it up, I'll see to that."

Mary bit on her lip, shook her head and walked out.

The day being Wednesday, she sat down to the table to dinner with Ben, and they were almost finished with the meal when he said, "Is there anything wrong, Mary?"

She gazed at her plate before she looked up at him, saying, "I'll soon be finished; me ma's on her feet again—at least she will be the day; she's gettin' crutches."

"Oh!" He went on eating for a moment, and then he said,

"But she'll be a few more weeks on crutches. She won't be able to put her foot down to the ground for some time yet."

Again she looked up at him. "Me ma will," she said flatly.

When she had cleared the pudding plates and was carrying them into the kitchen, Ben followed her and, standing in the doorway, asked simply, "Would you like to stay on, Mary?"

She looked at him over her shoulder. "It's me ma's job."

"It's anybody's job I choose to give it to, Mary."

"Me ma would never stand for it." She turned her head away from him.

"I'm very satisfied with the way things are, Mary. And . . . and the child's taken to you; he's been happier and more obedient these last few weeks than ever I've known him. He . . . he wanted a playmate, sort of." He smiled gently.

Although she didn't turn to him but went on scraping the bits from the plates, she knew he was smiling; she could tell by his voice. She had learned a lot about Mr. Tollett during the last few weeks; she could in a way understand why her ma liked him—liked him too much, because he was different from her da. But there was nobody like her da, nobody; her ma should be satisfied having a man like her da.

"She wouldn't stand for it," she said.

"Oh!" His tone had a touch of authority to it. "It isn't what she'd stand or not stand. If you want to stay on you can, and welcome. The only thing is, I think it's too much for you doing the two jobs; the hours are too long. If . . . if you decide to take it on full time, I'll pay you accordingly. You won't lose by it."

She turned and looked at him now. His brown eyes were kind and had a great depth to them; sometimes she felt uneasy when they were on her.

"Will you think it over?"

"I . . . I don't need to think it over. I'd stay and be pleased to, very pleased, but it's . . . it's me ma."

He nodded at her now, a slow smile covering his face. "If that's how you feel, Mary, we'll meet trouble when it comes.

Just carry on as you are doing." He went to turn away, then
stopped and looked at her again and said, "Would you do me a
favor?"

"Oh aye, yes, Mr. Tollett."

"Well, on Friday night I'd like to go out. There's a dinner in
Shields, a businessman's do; it only comes once a year, and if
you'd stay with David until I get back, I'd be very grateful."

"Oh yes, yes, of course, I'll stay. It'll be a pleasure." She
nodded at him.

"Thanks, Mary."

When she had the kitchen to herself she stopped what she was
doing and stood looking through the meshed curtains. There
were white tufts of cloud scudding over the chimney pots and
she watched the sun come out and turn them to pink, fluffy
banks. The day was suddenly bright; her life, her future were
suddenly bright; she could have this job for good, full time, and
what could her ma do about it if Mr. Tollett told her straight?
And if she stayed on, she would, in a way, be killing two birds
with one stone, for she would be making not only her own future secure but also her da's; her ma couldn't get up to anything
if she wasn't coming back to the shop, could she? Of course, her
ma would be mad—she knew she would—but if she went on too
much she knew what she would do. She'd go and live at her
grannie's. There was a spare room there, and her grannie would
be only too glad to have her. It would be lovely living with her
grannie and granda; fancy being able to work here all day in this
lovely house, and then at night not to have to go up the street
and face her ma, but go to her grannie's. Oh—she sighed deeply
—the prospect was too good to be true.

On Friday night she ran up the street with the basket of groceries and her pay and hurriedly handed her mother the twenty-
one shillings.

"Wait a minute! Wait a minute!" said Alice, as she went to
hurry out of the room. "You're like a devil in a gale of wind."

"Well"—Mary turned to her—"you know I've got to get back

as Mr. Tollett's going out. I'm taking over the shop. I've got to get back."

"Taking over the shop! . . . YOU! by yourself, and it Friday night, the busiest of the week? You, taking over the shop!"

"Yes me, Ma." Mary took a step back into the room and poked her chin out toward Alice. "And if he didn't think I was capable, well, he wouldn't let me, would he?"

"Get out of me sight. When I'm properly on me feet, girl, you won't cheek me like this. By God! I'll take it out of you when I'm on me feet an' can manage those crutches."

Mary stared at her mother and was on the point of saying, "You've got a surprise coming to you, Ma," but she left it; there wasn't time, and as Mr. Tollett said, "Meet trouble when it comes."

In the kitchen she hurriedly gave her father the half-crown and Jimmy the sixpence, and Alec, walking with her to the top of the stairs, asked, "What is it, lass?"

Turning to him, her face straight, she said under her breath, "She's got a surprise coming to her, me ma. Mr. Tollett wants me to stay on; he doesn't want her back."

"He doesn't!"

She was about to run down the stairs but was checked by the look of consternation on her father's face.

Slowly Alec said, more to himself than to her, "That'll put the kibosh on it—it'll break her up."

She had thought her da would have been pleased at the news, but apparently he wasn't.

"But you wouldn't want to stay on in service, lass, if you could get something better, would you?" he said.

"It isn't like service, Da, it's like a holiday there. I like it."

With an absentminded movement he pushed her gently toward the stairs, saying, "Go on; we'll talk about it later."

In the shop she went straight behind the counter. Ben had just finished serving a customer, and as the woman left the shop he looked at Mary and said, "Now, you're sure you can manage?"

"Yes, of course. I've done it afore, I mean serve."

"Yes, but Friday night's different. Toward nine you'll be getting some of those scroungers in at the last minute. But remember what I told you, no tick, not a penn'orth to the Mulhattans, the Fawcetts, the MacMullens and the Romneys. If they see me going out, you'll bet your life they'll be in here like a swarm of ants. But particularly keep a lookout for Hannah, Hannah Mulhattan. Don't let her talk you round, because she's got a voice like best butter. She still owes me four pounds ten. It was six pounds, and I wouldn't really have minded it being eight if she had continued to bring her bill, but when she owed me three weeks' bills and she walked down to Shields with her pay packet on a Friday night and never showed her face, and had the nerve to come in the following week"—he laughed now and, thumbing the counter, went on—"She put thirty shillings down there and in her smooth Irish way said, 'Will you take that thirty shillings, Ben?' Of course I said, 'Yes, and pleased to, Mrs. Mulhattan.' And I took the thirty shillings, and I got her bill out and I said, 'Now that'll leave four pounds ten between us.' I said it just the way she says it, you know?"

"I know." Mary laughed at him.

"Well, then she said to me, 'Can I have a few things in me basket?' and I bent over, just like this"—he now demonstrated—"and I said, 'Mrs. Mulhattan, you can have your basket full to the brim and running over as soon as you pay me the four pounds ten.' Well, I can't go on and tell you, Mary, what she said to me after that because you'd be so shocked you'd pick up your skirts and fly up the street."

"Oh, Mr. Tollett!" She laughed and tapped her hand against his arm, then said, "Don't worry, I'll be up to her, and the rest. That's Mrs. Mulhattan, Mrs. Fawcett, Mrs. MacMullen and Mrs. Romney?"

"Yes, that's them. Anyway, I'll go out the back way; the van's in the lane, and I might escape their notice."

Half an hour later she was in the middle of serving a customer when she heard him call from the storeroom: "Mary, just a minute." And she called back: "Be there in a tick, Mr. Tollett."

In the storeroom she stopped and stared at him and her mouth fell into a slight gape. He looked different. She hadn't seen him dressed like this. He had gone out on a Wednesday dressed up, but then he had just had an ordinary suit on. Now he was wearing a dark gray suit that fitted him perfectly, a white shirt with a stiff collar and a gray tie. His shoes were black and shiny, and hanging loosely around his neck was a white silk scarf. And he tucked this in as he put on a black overcoat.

She wanted to say, "Eeh! you look grand." She had always thought he was nice-looking, but now she saw he was good-looking, handsome. Again she could see why her ma compared him with her da and felt for him as she did.

"I'll be back about eleven; perhaps before—I might get bored. Anyway, if I'm not back by half-past eleven, you'll know I've got blind drunk and somebody'll be carting me back." He smiled a wide smile and his teeth looked whiter than ever against his tanned skin.

All she said to this was, "Oh, Mr. Tollett."

"You never know, I'm let out so little that I just might get paralytic. Anyway"—his voice dropped—"as soon as you close make yourself comfortable. I've left you some eats on the table, and I've picked out some records that you might like to hear. Put them on and enjoy yourself."

"Oh." Her voice rose. "Oh, that's nice. Oh, I'd love that. Oh thanks, Mr. Tollett."

"David's sound, sleeping like a top . . . and there's the bell." He pointed toward the shop. "Bye-bye."

"Bye-bye, Mr. Tollett. Enjoy yourself."

"I shall."

"And"—she put her hand to her mouth as if she were calling him over a long distance and whispered—"get tight if you like."

"Thanks, Mary. Thanks."

Both laughing, he went out one way and she the other.

She was supposed to close the shop at nine but it was nearly twenty past when she got rid of the last customer. As Mr. Tollett had said they had come swarming in at the last minute; but she hadn't had to deal with any of the bad-debt lot.

She was tired when she got upstairs, and she flopped down immediately into an easy chair in the sitting room. The curtains were drawn, the fire was blazing merrily, and the light was on. It had been nice of him, she thought, to leave the light on and nobody in the room. She looked toward the radiogram. Yes, there were the records on the side, and next to them a big dish of sweets.

She pulled herself up and walked over to the table and picked up the dish and exclaimed aloud, "Oh! a walnut cream whirl." How did he know? She had never told him that these were her favorites. Only twice in her life had she had a walnut cream whirl. She took the walnut off the top, then put it back as she thought, No, I'll keep it for after; I'll have a cup of cocoa and something to eat first. I'll keep that for when I put the records on.

Her tiredness forgotten, she almost skipped into the kitchen, made herself some cocoa, put a slice of boiled ham between two pieces of bread, then sat down at the little table near the window to eat it. She wouldn't take it into the sitting room; no, she didn't want to make any crumbs there. When she was finished eating she washed her face and hands because she felt sweaty, and as she dried herself on the roller towel behind the door she turned her face to the side and looked in the little mirror hanging on the wall, Ben's shaving mirror. She stared at her face. Was she bonny? Men often said she was bonny; not only her granda and her da but Mr. Weir and Mr. Tyler and Mr. Knowles. If she passed them at the corner, they would laugh at her and say, "By! you're getting a bonny lass, Mary." She liked it when they said that, although she would shake her head at them and say, "Eeh! Mr. so-and-so."

She went into the sitting room again and looked at the records. Ketelby's "In a Monastery Garden." Tchaikovsky's "The Sleeping Beauty." The "Blue Danube" waltz. Victor Silvester's Dance Band. Oh, she'd put that on first; she liked him.

"Oh lovely! lovely!" The exclamation she made aloud covered both the whipped cream whirl and the music, and as she bit through the hard chocolate and into the cream she waltzed: one-two-three, one-two-three, one-two-three, and she laughed to herself as she went round the room, weaving in and out of the furniture. She loved dancing; she would love to be able to dance properly. She had once gone to a dance in the Catholic school-rooms with Teresa Hewitt. It had been wonderful, but her mother had found out, and that was that. She had told her she was going to the half-pound night in the Methodist recreation room behind the Chapel. Her mother couldn't stand the Hewitts because they were Catholics; but then her mother could stand hardly anyone in the street, because she considered they were all common.

She had never been able to keep a real girlfriend, because she couldn't invite her into the house; everybody in Cornice and Benbow Streets was below her ma's notice—they were all common. She wondered if her ma knew what the neighbors said about her, because when she was having one of her yelling matches she sounded as common as muck herself.

Da-da-d'dah, d'dah, d'dah! Oh, this was lovely: a big warm room lit by a pink-shaded light, and wonderful music, and a chocolate cream whirl. She licked her fingers, then ran swiftly into the kitchen and wiped them on a flannel, and ran back into the room just as the record was finishing.

She played four records and danced to them all, even to "In a Monastery Garden." Then, her legs feeling tired, she decided to read a little. The bookcase presented an assortment of litera-ture. The top shelf showed her books by Ethel M. Dell, Elinor Glyn, Ruby M. Ayres and many others. The next two shelves, the books were thicker and heavier-looking. There were some by Dickens. She knew about Dickens; she had learned about him at school. She didn't care much for Dickens; it was the pic-tures in the book that put her off. The other names were new to her: Thackeray, Conrad, Conan Doyle, Edgar Wallace. Oh, she had heard of him. But she didn't think she'd like to read any of these. She reached up to the top shelf and picked out *The Way of an Eagle* by Ethel M. Dell. Then she settled herself in the armchair with the dish of sweets to her side, and she was just getting interested in the story when suddenly, feeling very tired, she let the book drop from her hand, put her head back in the corner of the chair and dozed.

It was a noise from the street that woke her, boys running and yelling as they kicked a tin. She sat up with a start and looked at the clock. Half-past ten. Eeh! she must have fallen asleep. She felt very tired. She stretched and yawned, then got up and replenished the fire, after which she made herself a strong cup of tea. She didn't want to be asleep when Mr. Tollett came back; he would think it had all been too much for her. She dabbed her face with some cold water, nipped her cheeks to bring more color into them, which was unnecessary, put a comb through her hair, then went back into the room and put on another record. She had picked the "Blue Danube" waltz again.

Slowly she began to dance, but just backwards and forwards in front of the gramophone. When the arms came about her and she was swung round and into the waltz, she stifled her scream. Then, to the beat of the music, she gulped, "Oh! Mis-ter Toll-ett. Oh! Mis-ter Toll-ett."

"Da-da-d'dah, d'dah, d'dah!" Ben sang as he waltzed her round the couch, in between the chairs, around the occasional table and back toward the couch, and when the record ground to a halt she gasped again as his arms tightened round her in a vise-like grip, and for a second she was pressed close to him, her cheek to his cheek, his lips near her ear. Then she was standing an arm's length from him, where he had thrust her, and, her breath almost choking her, she gaped at him. He . . . he was tight, she told herself, he was tight.

"Oh, Mary! I'm . . . I'm sorry, b-but, you see you're to blame. I did what you told me, I got tight. I'm . . . I'm not drunk, not real drunk. I . . . I didn't stay long enough. I thought I'd better get back while . . . while I could."

"Did . . . did you enjoy it, Mr. Tollett?"

"Yes and no, Mary. Yes and no. And Mary." He lurched toward her now and caught hold of her hands again and stared into her face. "Don't call me 'Mr. Tollett.' I've wanted to tell you for . . . for weeks not to call me 'Mr. Tollett.' 'Ben,' call me 'Ben.' Go on, say 'Ben.'"

"Oh, Mister . . ." She shook her head and laughed with a nervous, high laugh, then said, "Ben."

"That's better."

As she looked at his face she felt her legs begin to tremble and go weak at the knees as if she had been running for a long time. His eyes were bright and dark. The look in them was deep; it was a look she had seen before but it was much deeper now. She tried to stop the trembling creeping up through her body. She said, "Thank you. Thank you for the sweets, an' . . . an' I loved the walnut cream whirl."

"Aw! For God's sake, Mary, be quiet! . . . Thank you for the walnut cream whirl!" He gave a quick, impatient toss to his head; then bringing his face close to hers he murmured, "Don't you know I want to give you things, haven't you seen it? Oh my God, Mary!"

She couldn't stop him. She didn't know whether she would have if she could, but he was on his knees before her, his arms were around her thighs, his head was pressed into her waist, and his voice sounded as if he were actually crying when he muttered, "Aw, Mary. Aw, Mary, don't you know, I love you, girl? I love you . . . I love you." Each time he said "love" he pressed his head hard into her waist. "I've been driven nearly crazy these past weeks—haven't you seen? Aw, love!" He now raised his face and looked up as he said softly, "Don't be afraid. Don't be afraid of me. Please don't be afraid of me, Mary."

Her bottom lip trembled as she said, "I'm . . . I'm not."

And she wasn't afraid, even while she was. She couldn't un-

derstand herself. Mr. Tollett was telling her he loved her and
. . . and he was right in what he said, he had been telling her
that for weeks and she hadn't let herself catch on. That had been
the look in his eyes. Her breath was pushed out of her body
when he again pressed his head into her, and his words were
muffled now as he groaned, "I love you, Mary. Oh God! how I
love you. I've never loved like this in me life. NEVER!
NEVER."

She could say nothing. She knew of no way to answer talk
like this. All she wanted to say was, "Get off your knees, Mr.
Tollett," for it didn't seem right that he should be on his knees
to her.

As if he had heard her, Ben pulled himself to his feet but
still kept close hold of her. Leading her to the couch he pulled
her down beside him. And now she was in the circle of his arms
again and he was asking softly, "Do you like me a little bit,
Mary?"

She paused before nodding her head; and then she said, "Yes."
And this was true, she did like him.

"Do . . . do you think you could love me?"

She looked at his face. He was good-looking but in a different
way from Hughie Amesden. She had been in love with Hughie
Amesden for years. Did she still love him? She didn't know; she
only knew she was excited now, even while she was frightened.
Perhaps this was love; it must be something more than liking,
but it wasn't the same feeling that she had for Hughie Amesden.
She had never seen a white light around Mr. Tollett—around
Ben. She would never be able to call him "Ben"—it sounded
cheeky. "Presumptuous" was the word. She knew all about pre-
sumptuousness, because Mrs. Turner was always thinking about
this one being presumptuous and that one being presumptuous,
and getting above themselves. Yet he was saying he loved her.
But what about her ma? "What about me ma?" she said.

Now he was shaking his head impatiently, and, his voice low
and stiff, he said, "Listen, Mary. If you don't come back the

morrow, your mother's never comin' in here again, not to work or anything else. I . . . I might as well tell you she's been a great trial to me, your mother."

"I know."

"You know?"

"I . . . I saw her once through the back shop window. It . . . it was the night you put her out the backyard door."

"Oh, dear God!" He bowed his head. Then lifting it sharply, he said, "But there was never anything between us, never. Years ago when we were bairns together she used to trail me. I never could stand her, honest. I shouldn't say this, but I never could stand her. When Jane died I was at my wit's end and I was glad of her help, but I never imagined that she would start again, else I wouldn't have let her in the door. . . . And you know something, Mary? From the minute you came in the house I've been amazed that there isn't a bit of her in you. You take after Alec; he's a good man, your da."

"Yes, yes, me da's a good man." She could love him for that alone, for saying her da was a good man.

"He should never have married her, but she was determined to be married. Do . . . do you know something else? She was one of the main reasons why I went down to me aunt's in Dorset an' was apprenticed in the car trade. I was really scared of her in those days; she was dominant, even then. You see we all lived near each other in the early years. Your da and me lived in the same street and . . . and she lived opposite. It was impossible to get out of the back door, you know, or the front without running into her. And then when Dad died and I came back and found her living in this very street, Lord above! But anyway, she was married, so . . . so I thought that was all right. . . . Then I married Jane and Jane was the kind of person who could keep people in their place. . . . Oh y-es, yes indeed."

He took his hands from about her now and, cupping her face, said gently, "Don't tremble so. . . . Look, I'm . . . I'm going to tell you something that I've never told a living soul, an' likely I wouldn't even tell you this if I wasn't . . . well, slightly tight.

But, but I feel you should know. . . . Well, what I'm goin' to tell you is this, just this. I never was in love with Jane. I never felt anything for her, not like I feel for you, not like the feeling that's in me now. And I'm speaking the truth, Mary, I'm . . . I'm not just pushing a line, but . . . aw God, I should have met you when I was seventeen, eighteen, nineteen. Aw, Mary, aye, I should, I should have met you then and felt then like I do now. Do you know something?" He moved her head gently between his hands. "I was nearing thirty and I'd never met a lass that I liked. I . . . I thought there must be something wrong with me, I did. I did. You know?" He now shook his own head and closed his eyes for a moment as he went on, "You wouldn't understand, you wouldn't understand, but I wanted a wife, and I wanted children, and a home of me own; I was tired of living with me aunt, but I didn't want to come back to Jarrow and me people. Oh no"—he pulled a face at himself—"Jarrow wasn't for me. Then Mom and Dad died, an' I was alone here, stark alone. An' then I met Jane and . . . and I can say this, it isn't conceit, but Jane married me, I didn't marry her. Yet I was glad to be taken over. Can . . . can you understand? No. No. What am I talking about? You cannot understand any of it—you're not old enough. . . . But a funny thing happened with Jane, very funny. She voted to stay here"—he jerked his thumb downwards—"and not in Gosforth. It was, Mary, it was really funny, for, with all her high-faluting ways, she had the same ideas as my own dad—and my mam, because she could see us in no time at all having a chain of shops. It was no use me telling her that me dad had just closed two. No; she said the slump would come to an end sometime, and this was the time to buy property, when it was going cheap, and to keep on buying shares, the ones that were right down. My Aunt Bridget had started me on that game, shares. That's how she was so comfortably off.

"Aw, Mary"—he smiled wryly—"you look amazed, an' no wonder, no wonder. Aw, what am I keeping on about? Shares, shops, there's only one thing I really want you to know—I love you." The words came out on a thin whisper. "I love you, Mary, an' I need you. You're so beautiful, fresh, soft . . . kindly . . . aw an' kindly."

When he drew her to him and put his mouth on hers the shivering spiraled up through her body; it whirled round her head and sent her floating away. She had dreamed about being kissed, she had dreamed of Hughie Amesden kissing her, but even when she had imagined his lips on hers it had never been like this. She was weak and faint; there was no air in her body; she couldn't breathe. When his mouth left hers she drew in a shuddering breath and gasped, and his lips began moving over her eyes now, onto her ear, down to her chin, onto her neck, right down to her breast bone. "I love you, Mary, I love you, Mary, I love you, Mary." His voice was like a chant going round and round in her head.

"You love me? Say you love me, just a little bit. Say it, Mary. Say you love me just a little bit." His brown eyes were looking into hers. They were wide. She had never seen eyes so wide and dark and deep.

"Say it, Mary." It was like a whisper coming along a tunnel. "Say it, Mary. Say it, Mary."

"Yes, yes, I do." She sent the whisper back along the tunnel. And then her breath was cut off again; she was smothered with kisses and she didn't know what was happening to her, but she was kissing him back. And now he seemed to be kissing her with every part of his body. She was hot, sweating; she had the funny feeling that she was swelling all over fit to burst.

They were lying along the couch now side by side, and then all of a sudden she felt herself falling, and they rolled onto the floor. They remained quiet for a moment and looked into each other's face, and she heard herself laughing. And then she was in his arms again and they were rolling over like two bairns down a bank after their paste eggs on Easter Sunday. His hands were warm and soft and he kept saying, "I'll never hurt you, Mary. Don't worry, I'll never hurt you." But he did, for she was suddenly shot through with pain; and the world stood still.

6

"What is it, hinny? What's the matter with you?" Grandma Walton bent over Mary. "You're all out of sorts these days. It's far too much, these two jobs; it'll be a good thing when your ma gets back. She'll soon be on her feet again; she had her foot to the ground when I was in yesterday."

"What is it, lass?" Now Peter Walton bent over her, his merry face holding a troubled look. "What is it? Has your ma been making trouble for you? Aw"—he did not wait for an answer—"don't take no notice, that's her. You should be used to it now. Aren't you going to eat this bit cake? Look, your grannie just baked it this mornin'; it's as light as a feather."

"No, thanks, Granda. I don't feel like eating; I've . . . I've got a headache."

"But you seem to have had a headache on and off the last few weeks, hinny. Now, if it doesn't let up, you'll have to go and see the doctor. Have you told your ma?"

Mary was looking downwards as she said, "No."

"Then you should."

Her grandfather now put his arm around her and hugged her to him as he muttered gently, "Your da's worried, he's worried sick; he can't make you out."

Oh, if she could only make herself out, if she could only tell somebody. She had come round to tell her grannie 'cos her grannie was good at breaking news. She had promised Ben she wouldn't leave without telling her grannie. They had been over it time and again; he had wanted to go up the street and tell her da. He had said, "I'm glad it's happened, love, I'm glad. Do you hear me? Because now it'll have to come into the open and you'll marry me."

He had asked her to marry him the very next morning after what had happened. When she had gone upstairs, she hadn't been able to look at him, but he had taken her in his arms and laughed and said, "Aw love, I'm the happiest man on earth. I'm going along to see your da right now." And at this she had seemed to go mad for a minute, because she had cried at him, almost screamed at him, "No, no! you mustn't. No, I tell you, I don't want you to go and see me da."

She had realized fully, after a wakeful night, that there was nothing that her da didn't know about Ben and her ma, and that somehow, no matter if Ben was in the right, her da still thought that he had taken her ma away from him. And now if Ben were to go up and say that he wanted to marry her, her da would go mad. Instinctively deep down inside her she knew he would do something, because, besides everything else, Ben was old enough to be her father, and if her ma had got him as she wanted to, he could have been at that.

Ben had pacified her. "All right, all right," he had said, "we'll leave it and do it in your time. But you're not vexed at me, are you? You don't think I'm a frightful man?" And she had looked at him, and then she had surprised herself by falling against him.

No, she hadn't been vexed at him, for she liked him. She hadn't liked what had happened that night, but nevertheless she liked him. He was kind and nice . . . and lovable, and he looked different from any of the men around the doors, better-class like.

But it wasn't only her father she was afraid of knowing—it was her ma.

Now she had missed her period and she knew what that meant: when you stopped having your period you were going to have a bairn. And she didn't feel very well inside herself.

She looked from one face to the other bending over her, their expressions full of concern, and she said, "I want to talk to me grannie, Granda."

Peter straightened his back and said, "Oh aye, lass." Then, with an effort at his old jocularity, he added, "Well, I'd better away. Did I tell you I had business to attend to in the Town

Hall? There's a meeting of councilors the day, a real covey of them. They've asked to see me; I think they're going to put me up for Mayor."

When this evoked no answering smile from her he went out, and Grandma Walton, pulling up a wooden chair to the table, sat down and caught hold of her hands and looked into her face for a long moment, and with the knowledge of years she said quietly, "No, lass, not that?" and Mary, knowing that there was no need for detailed explanations to her grannie, just dipped her head once.

"Aw, my God! bairn."

"Oh, Grandma!" She flung herself into her grannie's arms, and Grandma Walton rocked her as she patted her back, asking quietly, "Who is it? I didn't know you had a lad."

She was sobbing so bitterly she couldn't answer for a while. Then, raising her head and sniffing and wiping the tears from the end of her nose with the back of her hand, she said, "It isn't a lad, Grandma, it's Ben."

"Ben?"

She looked at her grandmother's screwed-up face.

"Mr. Tollett."

"Oh, my God!" Her grandma dropped her hand as if it were a hot cake she had just taken out of the oven. "You're jokin', lass?"

"No, no, Gran."

"Aw, what a swine! to take advantage of a bit bairn. . . ."

"He didn't, he didn't. Listen, Gran, listen." It was she who had hold of her grandmother now, shaking her by the arms. "He didn't. It wasn't like that at all. He wanted to marry me straightaway, an' I wouldn't, 'cos I was frightened to tell me da, or me ma. The other, it . . . it just happened. And . . . and I want to marry him, Gran."

"You do, lass?"

"Yes, yes, Gran."

"Then why were you frightened to tell them at home?"

"I couldn't, Gran. You see . . . well, there's a reason."

"Yes, go on."

"Well, Gran, I don't know how to say it, an' I shouldn't say it."

"You've said enough, and you'd better tell me the rest, lass. If you don't want it to go any further, you know me."

Yes, she knew her grannie; it wouldn't go any further. She said quietly, "Me ma's been after Ben all the time she's been working in the shop. He . . . he pushed her off. I saw him, actually saw him one night and heard him tell her that he . . . he wanted none of her because me da was a good man."

"Your ma . . . after him? No! . . . and," she said vehemently now, "your da is a good man? But he didn't think that when he took you down. . . ."

"He didn't take me down, Gran, not like that. I've got to say it, I . . . I was willin'. If I hadn't been, he wouldn't have. But you see I couldn't let him tell me da, because me da's known about me ma wanting him, I mean Ben, and he would look upon it, well, like a double insult."

"Well, things haven't changed; how do you think he's going to look upon it now? And you're right when you think he's not going to like it. He's going to play it up, and that's putting it mildly. You know, your da thinks the sun shines out of you, lass; he thinks you couldn't do wrong, not if you were tempted by ten devils. He thinks of you like your granda's song 'Pure as the Lily in the Dell.' Aw! Mary, Mary, why had you to do this?"

"Gran, I didn't, I didn't, not on purpose." She was crying again. "It just happened."

"Well"—Grandma Walton sighed deeply—"he's got to be told, and you want me to tell him, is that it?"

"Yes, Gran."

"In that case I don't think I'll wait for him comin' round; it'll be better to kill two birds with one stone and tell them together. I'll get me hat and coat."

Fifteen minutes later they walked out of Bingley Street, into Grant Street, went past the station, hardly exchanging a word until they stopped outside the shop. Then Grandma Walton said, "You'd better go and prepare him. Your da will come storming down, you know, and you'll need some soft soap and sugar to smooth him, I'll tell you that."

Mary stood for a moment watching her grannie walking up the street, her black coat shining with use, her black hat perched straight on her head. Her figure was thin and small and she looked for all the world like a girl playing at grannies.

She did not go in the shop way but entered by the side door and went up the stairs, and she hadn't been in a moment before Ben joined her.

"Well?" He stood in front of her.

"Me grannie's gone up now to . . . to tell them."

He wiped his hand back and forth across his mouth; then with a short laugh he said, "Well, I must say I'm not looking forward to the next hour or so, but I'm glad it's come. I've got the same feeling in me stomach as I had in the war after I had been called up and thought of the day I would have to go over the top, and what it would be like." He smiled wryly. "Now I know." He stared down into her face; then swiftly he pulled her into his arms and kissed her long and hard. After a moment, with gentle fingers he traced the outline of her mouth, saying, "It's a small price to pay for you, Mary." And with that he turned from her.

This was the last time she was ever to see his face clear-cut and handsome.

Alice stood near the table. She was holding on to the edge of it with clenched fists, her knuckles, like bleached bones, sticking up white through the skin. But her face, in contrast, was red, purply red, as if she were about to go into convulsions. The red was reflected in her eyes; there was a madness about her.

In contrast, Alec stood to the side of the fireplace, one hand stretched outwards holding the brass rod, his mouth open and his face gray. He appeared relaxed, as if he were going to sink down onto the fender. And he could have done just that; he felt in a state of shock, sapped of strength, unable to move. His mother was standing there telling him that Mary was pregnant by Ben Tollett. He had taken the words in—he knew he had, for he was repeating them in his mind—but he couldn't do anything about them. His face even refused to express surprise. It wasn't that he disbelieved his mother, he did believe her; this is what had been wrong with Mary for weeks now. He remembered the day she had suddenly changed. It was after the night she had had to stay, waiting for Ben coming back from the dinner in Shields. She had come in sort of exhausted, and he had said to her, "You can't go on like this. It's these jobs; two jobs are one too many." She had never been right since then.

He recalled vividly now the look on her face. That was when it had happened, that night. Ben Tollett, not satisfied with having Alice on the side, had to take Mary, Mary . . . HIS MARY!

Of a sudden his mind came alive. Ben Tollett had taken Mary. He would kill him. That's what he would do, he would kill him. Nobody was going to take his Mary down, least of all Ben Tollett after the carry-on he'd had with Alice, 'cos you couldn't tell him that there had been nothing between them, her breaking her neck to get down there every minute, and she had not let him near her since she had started at the shop. She hadn't been much for it before, but this last year or so, nothing, so you couldn't tell him. . . . And he had taken his Mary.

His body refused to move as quickly as his mind, and his slow pace as he walked from the fire brought Alice's attention from her own blind rage for a second. She watched him go toward the stairhead door, and when Grandma Walton shouted, "Alec lad! Alec lad, don't go. Not like that!" and made to go after her son, Alice suddenly grabbed her fiercely by the arms, steadying herself by her hold on the older woman, and she screamed, "Let him go! Let him be! Let him bash his face in! Do you hear? Let him bash his face in!"

"Steady, lass, steady." Grandma Walton shook off Alice's grip and, in turn, took her by the arms and pushed her into a chair.

But Alice was no sooner in it than she was out of it. Hobbling to the top of the stairhead, she screamed down it, "Smash him! Smash him up! And his shop an' all. Do you hear? Do something worthwhile in your life, smash him up!"

As Alec went down the street his step quickened. "Smash him up," she had said. "Smash his shop an' all." She had no need to tell him what to do; he knew what he was going to do.

He thrust the shop door open so fiercely that it bounced against a bag of potatoes and sprang back at him, and for the second time he thrust it open. Then he was standing in the middle of the shop looking past the two women at the counter to Ben, whose skin seemed to have bleached.

After a moment of staring, of silent waiting, even on the part of the women, Alec said, "You bloody swine, you!" The words came quietly from his throat, but deep. Then on a higher note: "You dirty, whorin' swine, you!" On a higher note still: "A bairn. Little more than a bairn! A young lass, pure. She was pure!"

"What is it, Alec?" One of the women had come to his side, and he thrust her away so quickly and hard that she stumbled back against the counter that held the stationery and birthday cards and comics and women's weeklies.

"Alec!" There was a tremor in Ben's voice. "Look, come in the back. This is a private affair—come in the back."

"Come in the back, he says." He was now looking from one woman to the other. "Come in the back. Do you hear him? Come and hide it up. He's taken my lass down and he's askin' me to come in the back! Do you know that, Mrs. Wilson, and you, Mrs. Cooper? He's taken our Mary down; this dirty swine has taken our Mary down."

With a spring, he was leaning across the counter, his two hands full of Ben's gray linen shop coat and his shirt and vest.

"Leave go, man! Leave . . . leave go!" Almost choking, Ben wrenched himself free, and as he staggered back against the partition on which the tin stuff was stacked Alec flung up the counter flap and was on him again. As they struggled together and the tins rolled from the shelves and the counter shuddered and a half round of cheese went tumbling to the floor, the women screamed, and one of them ran into the street shouting, "Help! Help!"

By this time the two men were wedged in the opening left by the flap and already blood was pouring from Ben's face. Then, like froth pouring out of a bottle, they spurted into the middle of the shop and crashed against an ornamental biscuit stand, wherein the tins were set at angles, fronted by a long glass door. The stand rocked backwards and forwards twice, then fell inward toward the window with a resounding crash.

The women, who had been trapped in the corner, now slipped through the counter lid and caught at Mary as she came dashing from the storeroom yelling, "Oh, Da! Da!"

"You can't do nowt, lass, you can't do nowt. Let them have it out." The women held on to her, and it was at this point that Ben managed to throw Alec from him. But as he did so he slipped on the spilled fruit on the floor and went sprawling backwards. In a flash Alec reached to the left of him and picked up a glass jar of sweets standing on a shelf at the back of the shop window facing Cornice Street. For a moment, just for one moment, it was poised in his hand; the next it crashed down onto Ben's face, and the jar split in two as if it had been cut by a knife, the two pieces falling one to each side of his head while the jube-jubes spilled over him and instantly became bathed in his blood.

Ben didn't move. Nobody moved. Not Alec, now leaning back against the counter; nor the woman holding Mary; nor Mary, straining forward; nor all the children in the shop doorway; not until the men rushed in and exclaimed one after the other, "My God! God Almighty! Christ alive! what's happened?" did the tension break. Then Alec, pulling himself slowly away from the counter, went from the shop. He did not look toward Mary; he looked at no one. His clothes were torn, his face was splattered with blood; but it wasn't his own blood. Blindly he went through the crowd at the door and the larger crowd on the pavement and the road. The whole street was out, and they made way for him. And when he saw the policeman come hurrying down toward him, with a woman at his side, he half-stopped. But when they just hesitated as they looked at him, then went on, he, too, went on.

When he entered the house again his mother said, "Oh, my God! Oh, my God! what have you done? You're all blood. What have you done?"

And Alice cried, "Did you do it? Speak, man! Did you do it?"

He looked at her long and hard as he said, "Aye, I did it, I did what you said. Aye, I did it. You satisfied now?"

Then he went and sat down by the fire and held out his hands to the blaze, and when his mother took a towel and began to wipe his face he did not push her away.

Mary cradled Ben's head until they brought a doctor, and when he came and the shop cleared, except for two men, a woman and the policeman, she still knelt on the floor by his side until they brought the ambulance. Then she rode with him to Harton Hospital in Shields.

"Are you his daughter?" the nurse asked.

"No. No."

"His wife?"

She shook her head.

"Who are his next of kin?"

She didn't know, except that he had a cousin who lived in Wallsend, but she didn't know the address, and anyway she was crippled.

Half an hour later, when the nurse came to her and said, "He's ready for the theater," she asked in a whisper, "Is it bad?" and the nurse shook her head and looked down as she answered, "They'll try to save his eye."

Oh, God! his brown eyes, his beautiful brown eyes. Her da had done this to Ben. She couldn't believe it. She had known he would be mad, but not this kind of mad. She thought he would have gone mad with his tongue going for her, then not speaking to her for a while, but after which he would come round. Her da was a gentle man; he wouldn't hurt a fly. And it was all through her. She wished she were dead. Oh! oh! how she wished she were dead.

Half an hour later still they took her into a side ward and gave her a cup of tea, and the nurse said, "What are you to him, a relation?"

She shook her head and turned it away, and the nurse raised her eyebrows and asked no more questions.

An hour and a half later they brought him out of the theater, and the sister herself came to her now. "You'd better go home," she said; "you won't be able to see him until tomorrow."

"What did they do to him?" Her voice cracked on the words, and she had to repeat, "What did they do to him?"

"Well, they had a lot of stitching to do. His face was badly cut; there were pieces of glass in it."

"His . . . his eye?"

"Oh, I think the eye will be all right; the cut just missed it, fortunately. He was very lucky really, much more so in his neck, for the slash was near an artery." She nodded sympathetically and said, "You can see him tomorrow. Go home now, dear."

She turned dumbly away and walked out of the hospital, down the long drive, through the iron gates; and only then did she realize that she hadn't any money for her bus journey back to Jarrow. Blindly she began to walk, down Talbot Road, along Stanhope Road and into Tyne Dock. She passed through the Dock arches, went up the long, quiet road toward East Jarrow. But before she came to the New Buildings she crossed the road to sit on a seat because her legs were aching. Her whole body was aching; her head and her heart were aching. She was weighed down with a great ache, and pain, and anguish. She loved Ben, she knew now she loved Ben, but she also loved her da. What would happen to her da?

She had no answer to this. She looked across the road to the marshes, the open timber pond that filled up twice a day with the tide from the river and the North Sea. Children were playing on the timbers, running back and forward yelling gleefully. It wasn't long ago that she had played and laughed and been happy; that was when she wasn't in the house. She had been happy, too, with her da and her granda in the hut on the allotment; and she had laughed when she was at school, especially at playtime. She would never laugh again.

She started to walk on, up past the disused Barium Chemical Works, the tramsheds, round by the Don Bridge and St. Paul's Church, and when she entered Jarrow she did not go up the church bank but cut across the salt grass, and so wended her way through the maze of streets until she came home . . . to the shop, because, although she hadn't thought about it, she knew now that this would be her home; if Ben lived, this would be her home. She'd never go into number 95 again.

Mrs. McArthur had been looking after the child. Mrs. McArthur was a nice woman, not gossipy; she minded her own business and she was one of Ben's best customers. The shop door was locked; she went round to the side door and up the stairs.

The child was crying and Mrs. McArthur said, "I've tried to pacify him, but I couldn't."

Mary lifted up the boy in her arms and began to rock him, and he said, "Da-da. I want me da-da," and she answered, "He'll be back soon. It's all right, David, he'll be back soon."

"Is he bad, lass?"

"It's his face."

"Did they do anything?"

"They operated. I don't know what they did, they only . . . they said"—she gulped in her dry throat—"they saved his eye."

"My God! My God!" Mrs. McArthur shook her head. "And your da. He's the quietest man in the street; I wouldn't have believed it. Is it about you, lass?"

"Yes, Mrs. McArthur. I'm going to have a baby, Ben's baby."

"Aw, lass! lass! Well"—Mrs. McArthur raised her eyebrows, then shook her head—"these things happen. I was going to say, it's God's will, but I won't. What are you going to do about the shop, lass?"

"The shop? I hadn't thought, Mrs. McArthur."

"Well, it's Friday the morrow, lass, and people will want their things. You've got to keep the business going until Ben comes back."

"Yes, Mrs. McArthur."

"Look, I'll tell you what I'll do. I'll go round and see to my lot and then I'll come back to give you a hand, because, my God, there's a shambles down there."

"Thanks, Mrs. McArthur."

"Sit down, lass, you're almost dropping. Look, I'll make you some tea afore I go."

"Thanks, Mrs. McArthur." She felt she was going to faint; the child slipped from her arms to the floor but stood close to her knees whimpering.

Mrs. McArthur was bending over her now, saying, "Now look, don't you pass out, lass. Is there anything in the house? A drop of whisky?"

"There's some spirit in the cupboard over there." She pointed.

When Mrs. McArthur put the whisky to her lips she sipped at it and shuddered, but after she had drunk it she felt less faint.

"I'll be going now, lass. Will you be all right?"

"Yes, thank you, Mrs. McArthur."

"I'd better tell you, lass." Mrs. McArthur stood with the door in her hand. "They're looking for your da, the police. They went up home, but he was out. Then they went along to your grannie's, and he wasn't there. And I think they've been to the allotments. I don't know whether they've got him yet. He'll get into trouble for this; you know that, don't you, lass?"

She looked at the kindly woman. She couldn't say, "Yes, Mrs. McArthur," she just nodded.

7

She opened the shop on the Friday morning at nine o'clock; the first person to enter was a policeman. "Can you tell me where your da is, lass?"

"No."

"I'll have to look upstairs."

"You can; he's not there."

"I'm sorry, lass, but I'll have to."

"You heard what I said, you can." She lifted the flap of the counter and he passed through. A few minutes later he came down.

"If you know where he is, lass, you'd better tell us, 'cos he'll be found in the end."

"If I knew where he was, I'd tell you." And she meant it, because if she knew where he was, and he was alive, a little of the terror might seep out of her.

"It's a bad business," he said. "I'm sorry for you; I'm sorry for you all."

"Thanks," she said.

"Mr. Tollett's in a bad way, they tell me."

She didn't answer. She knew he was in a bad way; she had phoned early this morning.

"Let's hope for all concerned he doesn't snuff it."

She stared at him, but still made no comment.

The shop had never had so many customers all at once since it had been a shop. People who had never spent a penny in it before came in just to look at her, and by the end of the morning she was answering their looks straight in their eyes and defying them to say anything.

She couldn't understand the feelings that were in her. Part of her was terrified for her da and the consequences of his act, part of her was sick with anguish for Ben, Ben who was so kind and good, and part of her was full of defiance, and this was supplying her with a strength, strength to keep the shop going, strength to let them all see she could keep the shop going, and the house going, and look after the child. And when the customers' eyes, especially those of the women, rested on her stomach, she made herself stare back at them . . . hard.

And in the afternoon when Mrs. Mulhattan came into the shop and greeted her affably, saying, "Oh, me dear, it's heart sorry I am for you. Aye, trouble, trouble, and him a quiet man who never said a wrong word to a body in his life. It's good of you to keep things goin', it is, it is that. Now, I've brought a bit off me bill. There's ten shillings; fair's fair. I'm not the one to withhold what I owe an' a man out of action." Mary took the ten shillings, flipped back the pages of the ledger, marked it off Mrs. Mulhattan's account, then wrote on a piece of paper: "Received from Mrs. Mulhattan ten shillings, balance owing four pounds," and handed it across the counter to the beaming, flabby-breasted Hannah, who said, "Well now, me dear, just a few things to be gettin' on with. I'll have . . ."

She got no further before Mary said quietly, "I'm sorry, Mrs. Mulhattan. I've got me orders from Mr. Tollett; you can't have anything on tick until the bill's cleared."

The big woman stared at Mary for a moment, then looked to the right of her where stood a boy with a holey jersey and an empty pop bottle in his hand, then to the left of him where Mrs. Brown stood looking at her. Mrs. Brown was a Nonconformist, a ranter, a woman to be spoken to every day of the week except Sunday, when Mrs. Brown attended chapel with the other Holy Joes, while she herself went to claim contact with the true God at Mass. Then looking back at Mary, she said, "You brazen young bitch, you! Who the hell do you think you are! Give me back that ten bob this minute."

"I'll . . . I'll do nothing of the sort, Mrs. Mulhattan. And if you cause any disturbance, I'll send for the police, I will. Georgie!" She looked at the boy with the bottle.

"Aye, Mary?"

Then she looked back at Mrs. Mulhattan, and now the infuriated woman backed toward the door, and there, with deep eloquence, she exclaimed, "Bugger me eyes! but I'll see me day with you, miss, and the bastard you're brewing."

After the door had banged Mary stood silent for a moment and a shiver passed over her body. Then she looked at the boy, who said, "I wan'-a quarter o' custard creams an' a bottle o' lemonade, two ounces o' paste, an' a quarter o' boiled ham."

She served him and put it on the bill, and did not wonder at such an order from a boy with a jersey hanging in threads, because, although his father had been out of work for ten years, he had a brother still working in the mercantile, and his married sister, who lived with them, had turned their front room into a secondhand clothes shop.

The business of the shop on this, her first full day in it, the way of living that for years had been all about her, yet had come into vivid actuality for the first time when seen from across the counter, helped her to stem the panic that threatened to make her dash out of the place and to run helter-skelter—but to where? To the hospital? or to search for her da?

At seven o'clock she closed the shop and ignored the bangings and rattlings on the door as she put the child to bed. Then she washed herself hurriedly, got into her coat and hat, and was ready to go when Mrs. McArthur came up the back stairs.

"Let them knock—don't go down," she said to her, and Mrs. McArthur answered, "Not me, lass. How long are you likely to be?"

"It'll take me a good forty minutes to get there, I may have to wait, and the same back. They likely won't let me stay. I . . . I should be back just after nine. . . . I'll . . . I'll pay you, Mrs. McArthur, I'll pay you."

"Oh, that's all right, lass; we'll talk about that later."

Mary now nodded toward the child's bedroom, saying, "He's settled down; you needn't go in unless he cries."

"Good enough, lass."

"Make yourself some tea or something."

"Go on about your business. I'll see to meself, never fear."

When she came to a panting stop outside the ward door and caused the sister to look up from a table in the middle of the ward at which she was writing and say, "You're too late for visiting," she walked slowly toward her.

". . . I couldn't get any sooner. I just wanted to know how Mr. Tollett was. I've . . . I've been looking after his shop and . . . and the child; I couldn't get any sooner."

"Oh, yes." The sister now stood up. "Mr. Tollett? Oh well, you can only stay a few minutes, mind. Come along." She led the way up to the top of the ward, to the last bed, which was ominously curtained, and, pulling the curtain aside, she allowed Mary to pass her, and she said again, very softly, "Only a few minutes, mind."

She was standing above him, looking down onto one eye and a bit of his cheek. The rest of his face and his head were swathed in bandages. One hand and arm were bandaged to the elbow, but the other lifted toward her, and she gripped it and brought it to her breast as she bent over him and murmured, "Aw, Ben. Ben."

"Mary."

"How . . . how you feeling?"

"Better."

"Oh! Ben, what can I say?"

He was blotted from her sight by the tears spurting from her eyes, and he muttered low, "Don't, Mary, don't. I'm all right . . . better tomorrow."

She hastily wiped her eyes. "The shop, it's all right; I'm keeping it goin'. And David, he's all right an' all."

"Good. Good."

They stared at each other. She wanted to say something to comfort him, like "Ben, I love you. I'll . . . I'll always love you," but she couldn't, not here.

His hand brought hers slowly up to his cheek, which now no longer looked brown but deathly white, and there was a faint movement of the muscles below his eye as if he were trying to smile. She was torn inside by the sight of him. As she bent over him the smell of ether that still hung around him made her feel sick and faint.

A voice behind her said, "You'll have to go now."

She turned and looked at the nurse, then back to Ben. "I'll come in the morrow night, but I'll phone in the morning to see how you are." She wasn't saying anything she wanted to say.

He stared at her while she backed from him; and then she was walking blindly down the ward. When she came to the sister at the desk she stopped, and, aiming to make her voice steady, she asked, "Will . . . will he be all right?" and the sister said, "It's too soon to tell, but we hope so."

The following day she had a visit from Ben's cousin, Annie Tollett, who lived in Wallsend. She was a little woman with a club foot. She had a thin face and thin body, and when she spoke her voice was deep, laughingly deep, almost like that of a man. She came into the shop, saying, "I'm Annie Tollett. I hear Ben's had a mishap; bad news flies fast. You'll be Mary. Get out of me way and let me through."

At this, she pushed up the flap of the counter and walked into the storeroom, and there they surveyed each other. After a moment the little woman said, "You needn't be scared of me. I'm not going to interfere. Ben's business is his business and mine's mine, but I hear you're going to have his bairn."

Mary stared at the woman. She lived in Wallsend across the river. It was as she said, bad news flew fast. She did not know who had told her and she did not ask; she just said, "If you wait a minute, I'll put the lock on the door and make you a cup of tea."

"You needn't bother. I'm quite capable of making meself a cup
of tea. You don't want to lose any customers. . . . How's the
bairn?"

"He's . . . he's all right; he's in his playpen."

"Well, I'll go on up. Come up when you have a minute."

Mary watched the little figure hobble out of the storeroom
and into the yard and disappear through the door that led to
the staircase. She was a funny little woman but not nasty; sharp-
tongued but not nasty. She didn't look a little bit like Ben,
though; there was nothing about her to connect her with Ben
or his family.

She had just got back into the shop when the door opened
and her granda came in. Her hand went instinctively to her
mouth, and as if she were expecting him to attack her, she
stepped back and leaned against the framework of shelves and
waited for him as he came slowly forward. When he stood opposite her she saw that he was indeed an old man; he seemed to
have put on years since she had seen him on Thursday. His
voice, too, sounded broken as he said, "Don't look so frightened,
hinny, I'm not going to reproach you."

"Oh, Granda!" It was like a soft whimper. She moved toward
the counter and put her hand across it, and he took it.

"I'm sorry, Granda."

"I know you are, hinny, I know you are."

"Me da? Have you seen him?"

"That's what I've come to tell you. They picked him up. I
say they picked him up, but he wasn't trying to run away—he
was just bemused. He had been lying under the slag heap all
night."

"Oh, Granda! Granda!"

"Now, don't cry, hinny, don't cry."

"Where've they taken him?"

"To Shields."

"The police station?"

"Aye."

"What'll they do to him?"

"I don't know, lass. But you've got to prepare yourself; he'll likely have to go to jail, 'cos he nearly killed Ben. You know that, don't you?"

She nodded slowly, and, her head deep on her chest, she murmured, "Oh, Granda! I feel terrible, terrible. I want to die."

"It's no use lettin' go like that, so don't talk daft."

She said now, "Me ma? Does she know?"

"Yes, she knows."

"Is she going down to him?"

"No, lass. Don't expect your ma to go down. Your grannie and me, we're going down; and if you get a minute, and you're down that way, you could go in and ask to see him. They mightn't let you, but on the other hand they might. I . . . I think you should."

She stared at her grandfather. She wanted to see her da. She wanted to tell him that she didn't blame him for what he had done. But how could she tell him that when he had nearly killed Ben, and who knew—as the sister said the next few days would tell—but that it might turn out that he had killed him. She loved her da, she still loved her da; what he had done he had done for her. She was in torment, torn all ways.

"You should, lass."

"Yes, Granda, I will, I will."

"Ta-rah, lass."

"Ta-rah, Granda."

She put the bolt in the door and went upstairs. The little woman had made tea and was bouncing David on her knee, and she asked abruptly, "Have you seen him?"

"Yes."

"How is he?"

"He's in a bad way, a very bad way."

"It was your da that did it, wasn't it?"

"Yes."

"I know about your da. Ben's always spoken well of him. But not about your mother; your mother's a Tartar by all I can make out, and no better than she should be, and not as good as she could be. And I know about you an' all; he often spoke about you."

Mary stared at the woman. Ben had never mentioned his cousin Annie. He had gone off in the van sometimes on a Wednesday afternoon and taken a box of groceries with him, without saying where he was going. But then, when she came to think about it, they'd never had much time to talk, not until that night, the night he had waltzed her round the room. It had all started that night with the "Blue Danube."

"I'm not going to interfere and don't think I'm pushin'"— the thin finger was wagging up into her face now—"but I'll come across now and again and look after this one"—she bounced the child on her knee—"to give you a break. Have you anybody else comes in?"

"Mrs. McArthur. She's very good. But I'd be grateful if you would."

"I'm not interfering, mind."

"I know. Oh, I know."

"But the shop'll have to be kept going. At a time like this he could lose customers. Not that we need worry about that so much, but it's always well to have more than one iron in the fire. Well, there's the bell going, get yourself down."

"Yes, yes." She turned from the little woman. She should feel annoyed, vexed at the abruptness of her, but she didn't; strangely, she felt she was going to be a comfort. She wasn't to realize for many years that some comforts could be mixed blessings, and that all, everything, must be paid for.

8

It was nine o'clock on Sunday morning when there was a knock on the back door. When Mary opened it Jimmy slunk into the yard and, closing the door quickly behind him, stood with his back to it and looked up at her. "I'm on me way to me Grandma McAlister's," he said, "but . . . but I wanted to see you for a minute."

They stared at each other.

"How are you?"

"Awful, Jimmy."

"Have you seen me da?"

"No, I'm goin' this afternoon, after I've been to the hospital."

"Is Mr. Tollett . . . is he going to die? They're saying he's going to die."

"When I phoned last night he was a little better, quite comfortable they said."

"Aw"—he drew in a sharp, short breath—"I miss you."

"And me you."

He looked down at his boots. "I'm goin' to help Grandma McAlister bring her things; she's . . . she's coming to stay for a while."

Mary said nothing to this but looked at Jimmy gulping on his spittle as if to get over an obstruction in his throat; then, his eyes cast down, he said, "Me ma's awful, going on all the time, like mad. Mary." He was looking up at her now. "I'd watch out."

"What d'you mean?"

"She keeps sayin' what she's going to do to you."

"She can't do anything to me."

"You never know. You know something?" He gulped again. "I heard me grannie telling me granda that she egged me da on, she told him he had to go and smash Mr. Tollett up, and smash up his shop an' all. She egged him on, screamed at him."

"She did?"

"Aye."

"Oh, me ma! She's wicked, Jimmy."

"Aye, I know. I wish I could come and live with you, Mary."

"Aw, Jimmy, Jimmy, be quiet. I . . . I don't know how long I'll be livin' here meself. If anything happens to Ben, I'll have to go to me grannie's."

"I wish I could come with you to me grannie's."

"Well, you know you can't; you've got to be educated. That's her mania, educating you."

"I know, and I don't want it. I don't, really I don't, Mary."

She shook her head and looked down at the square paving stones in the yard, then at the boxes lining the walls, as if searching for an answer to her thoughts, and she almost said, "It was to get you clothes for school that she came here in the first place, so you've got to stay there." But she knew that wasn't right; she knew why her mother came here. It wasn't for money, for she already had a good job doing for Mrs. Bainbridge, three doors down from Mrs. Turner.

"I'll have to be going."

"Wait a minute!" She went back into the shop and took a shilling from the till, and when she pushed it into Jimmy's hand, she cautioned him, "Hide it, and don't let on."

"Oh ta, Mary, ta. I . . . I will."

"The best thing to do is to leave your coppers at Grandma Walton's and pick them up when you need them."

"Aye, Mary, I will. And . . . and you'll look out for me ma?"

"Yes. Don't worry, I'll look out."

She hadn't really needed Jimmy to warn her; it had been at the back of her mind, like another peril to be faced.

"Ta-rah then."

"Ta-rah, Jimmy."

At twelve o'clock Annie Tollett came and took over. At one, Mary left the house for the hospital, and not until she was standing with the other visitors did she realize how empty-handed she was; everybody was holding either bunches of flowers or bags of fruit. But what did it matter? Ben wouldn't mind.

When the doors were opened and she entered the ward she saw with relief that the curtains were no longer around his bed. She approached him slowly and stood over him and said softly, "Hello, Ben."

"Hello, Mary." He had difficulty in moving his lips.

"Are you feeling better?"

"Yes . . . oh, yes."

Self-consciously she pulled a chair nearer the bed, and then she sat down and took his hand. "You're going to be all right?"

"Yes."

They stared at each other for a long while until he said, haltingly, "The time . . . is long. I've been . . . waiting for you."

She nodded, and then whispered, "And me, I've been wishing the hours away."

He pressed her fingers. The grip held some strength and brought a small smile to her face. They sat in silence, just looking at each other, and then he said, "I'm sorry, Mary, I've . . . brought this trouble on . . . on you."

"No, no, it's me."

He closed his eye as if in protest. "No. No, you were innocent, too innocent." When he opened his eye it looked deeply sad, and there was silence between them again until he murmured, "Mary, you'd better know I'll . . . I'll be disfigured. There'll be a scar . . . from top to bottom." He touched his bandaged face.

She gazed down at him, and she saw that he was greatly troubled about this, and he would be, because he was a good-looking man. She said quickly under her breath, "It'll make no matter to me. I don't care what you look like."

Again there was a pressure on her hand and again silence. It was difficult to talk; people who were in both their minds must not be mentioned, her da, her ma.

After a while she told him about the shop and about Mrs. Mulhattan coming in and how she had received her, and his hand kept pressing hers in appreciation of her efforts. And then she told him what she had meant to tell him the moment she came into the ward, about his cousin Annie coming over.

"That's good. . . . Annie's good at heart; bluff, but good at heart." Then after a moment, during which he seemed to gather strength, he said on a surprised note, "And she came over the day?"

"Yes."

"That's something; you can't get her out of her house on a Sunday as a rule."

When the bell rang she stood up immediately; then, bending, she shyly placed her lips to the side of his mouth and held them there for a moment.

She was standing then, holding his lopsided gaze. "I won't see you till Wednesday, visiting day, but I'll phone."

"Bye-bye, Mary."

"Bye-bye, Ben."

She walked backwards for a short distance and his eye lingered on her.

There was a drizzly rain falling when she got outside. She was glad of it, because it hid the fact that she was crying, and she chided herself sternly for this. If she was crying now, what would she be doing in a little while when she met her da—if she met him.

She took a tram from the corner, down Fowler Street to the center of the town, from where she made her way to the police station.

Sunday seemed to have settled on the police station as well as on the town, and she pushed the door open into the dusty room that looked like an office. There was nobody to be seen, but when she reached the counter a door opened at the far end of the room and a policeman came in. He stood behind the counter, his hands flat on it, and smiled at her. "Aye?" he said. "And what can I do for you, Miss?"

"I'm . . . I'm Mary Walton."

"Yes."

"Me da."

"Aw, you're his daughter, Alec Walton?"

"Yes."

"Well"—he put his head a little on one side—"he's all right, lass."

"Can . . . can I see him?"

He looked down toward the floor at one side of the counter, then to the other side, then back to her again before he said, "Just a tick."

When he returned to the room there was another policeman with him, and they both stood looking at her over the counter. Then the second policeman looked at the first one and said, "Well, I don't see why not," and, turning to her, he added abruptly but not unkindly, "Come along."

She followed him through the passage and down steps to a corridor where there was a line of doors, all with gratings in them at the top. He inserted a key in the second door and pushed it open, saying, "I'll come back for you in a few minutes."

She was inside the room, the awful little room, the cell, and her da was sitting staring at her from a plank bed attached to the wall.

Alec rose slowly to his feet and they stood, their eyes linked in an agonizing trance.

She was the first to move. She took a step toward him, saying, "Da! Oh, Da!" and at this he seemed to come awake. Actually, for the first time in days, he came fully to himself. His head swung slowly from shoulder to shoulder; he took his hand and rubbed it across the stubble on his mouth and chin, back and forward his hand went; then in a characteristic fashion he pushed it up over his brow and through his hair. When his body began to rock from side to side she flung herself forward and took him in her arms, and they hung together, swaying, crying, moaning, but saying no word.

After a time, when the paroxysm of their joint grief had subsided a little, they sat on the edge of the bed and from her tormented being she dragged up the mundane question, "How are you?"

He couldn't speak but he nodded his head as he took a dirty handkerchief from his pocket and wiped his tear-washed face.

"Are . . . are they all right to you?" She moved her head back in the direction of the door, and at this he blew his nose violently, then nodded his head again, blinked his eyelids rapidly and spoke for the first time. "Aye," he said, "they're very good, considerate." He looked at her, and he too made the mundane inquiry, "How are you?"

"Oh, all right, Da."

They stared at each other, still in pain, and then, his teeth digging into his lower lip and his head swaying again, he said, "I . . . I must have been mad." His head stopped swinging and he looked into her eyes. "I . . . I think I am going mad, lass."

"No, Da. No!" She was holding him and looking into his face. "No. No, it's just been too much, everything and then me. I'm . . . I'm to blame."

"You're not! No!" The emphasis was deep.

"Yes, yes, I am." Her emphasis was equally deep. "I'll carry it to me grave; I know I am."

He shook his head twice in denial, then said, "There's only one person to blame an' we both know who that is." His eyes still on her, his mouth working against asking the question, the seconds passed before he could make himself say, "What happened to him?"

Seconds passed again before she answered, "He's . . . he's in hospital, Da."

"I know that, I know, they told me. But what I mean is, what did I do to him?"

She looked to the side, to the painted brick wall. She noticed there was writing on it; she couldn't read it. She looked back at him. "His face is cut."

"Much?"

"Down one side."

"Will he get better?"

"Yes." She was quick to answer now, to reassure him. "Oh yes, he's on the mend, don't worry." She lifted his hand and held it between her own.

He said very quietly, "They'll send me to jail, lass, you know that? But . . . but don't worry, I don't mind, honest to God I don't mind. I'll be out of it for a time. And when I eat me food it won't stick in me gullet; I'll have nobody to thank for it but"—

he gave a painfully mirthless laugh—"the country." He asked then, "What's happenin' to you, lass?"

"Oh, don't worry about me, Da, I'm all right." She did not say, "I'm looking after the shop, I'm staying in Ben's house, I'm sleeping in Ben's bed." What she said was, "I can always go to me grannie's."

"Aye, you go to your grannie's."

At this moment the key was turned in the lock and they both started and looked toward the door where the policeman stood. She turned round again and said suddenly as if he, too, were in hospital, "I should have brought you something, Da. I never thought."

"Ah, lass, you brought yourself. Thanks, lass, thanks for comin'." He held her tightly and as he did so he whispered against her ear, "Try to forgive me, lass. Try to forgive me."

She couldn't answer. She tried; she tried to say, "Oh, Da! me forgive you?" but the words were blocked, and she turned from him and went out, and the policeman had to lead her up the steps because she couldn't see them.

In the office once more, the two policemen looked at her, and the first one she had seen said, "Don't take on, lass, he'll be all right." He came round the counter and put his hand on her shoulder. "These things happen." And now he tried to make her laugh as he bent down to her and said, "We'd be out of our jobs if they didn't, don't you realize that?"

She was going out but stopped at the door, and, turning toward them where they were both standing looking at her, she said, "Ta . . . thanks," and simultaneously they nodded their heads toward her.

In the street a man and a woman paused and looked at her. She supposed it was a disgrace to be seen coming out of a police station; you were in trouble when you were seen coming out of a police station. But it was funny, she hadn't thought about the disgrace of it, not once. It would be her ma who would think about that, the one person who was to blame for it, her da had said, and he was right there.

She dried her face and boarded a tram, and as she was driven through the dead and deserted Sunday town she realized she felt a little better. Now she had seen her da and made her peace with him, she would cope; she would cope with anything now, even her ma.

It was nearly a week later when she had to cope with Alice, but she had been forewarned. Just as she had been about to close on the Thursday night Jimmy had slipped into the shop. "Me . . . me ma's coming down to you," he had gabbled. "Could be the morrow, anytime; I heard them talkin'. She wants your wages."

She gave him a loud "Huh!" and said, "Can you see me givin' her them?" and he replied, "She says she'll knock hell out of you, Mary."

"Let her try, just let her try."

He had hung his head as he muttered, "She's threatened to thrash me an' all if I speak to you."

She had put her hand gently on his shoulder. "Come the back way anytime. I keep the back door locked, but you knock on it like this. Rat-ta-tat-tat. Rat-ta-tat-tat. You know?"

"Aye, Mary."

All day on Friday she waited. With every tinkle of the bell she looked up, expecting to see Alice in the doorway. And when she hadn't put in an appearance by four o'clock she thought of a way to fortify herself for a late attack. She called Andy Robson from the roadway where he was playing football. He was a lad of twelve, sharp-witted and wily, and would do anything to earn a penny. She took him into the storeroom and said, "I want you to play outside the window, Andy, and if you should see me ma come in, I want you to follow her into the shop, understand? And when I say to you, 'Go and get the police, Andy,' you say, 'All right, Mary,' and dash out. But don't go and get him, just go round the block, understand? And if you do that, I'll give you threepence."

"Oh, I'll dee that, Mary," he said. "I'll dee that all right."

By half-past seven she was still waiting. She had supplied Andy with bread and jam so that he had no need to go home for any tea, and he was still waiting to earn his threepence.

Her nerves were taut, she was very tired physically. She had been on her feet from early morning either in the shop or upstairs. She'd had to have the child downstairs with her behind the counter for an hour or so, and he got in her way. She was afraid to ask any of the children in the street to mind him, for Ben had never done this, and if anything should happen to him . . . well. She wished she were in bed. Oh, how she wished she were in bed and asleep with all her thinking cut off.

It was just on closing time and the shop was empty for the first time that evening when Andy came sidling in and up to the counter and whispered conspiratorially, "Your ma, she's been standing up near the alley for the last ten minutes or so. And your Jimmy has just passed the shop and looked in and gone up to her."

"Thanks, Andy," she said. "Go on outside and do what I told you."

She knew why Jimmy had passed the shop—her ma had told him to tell her when it was empty.

She waited, busying herself cleaning the counter with a damp muslin cloth. She was covering up the cheese and the bacon when the door opened and Alice entered. She was walking with the aid of a stick and her face looked all white bone, except her eyes, which were sunk in her head and were blazing. She hobbled over the step into the shop and went to thrust the door shut behind her, but Andy jerked it open and sidled in. For a moment she turned her ferocious glare on him, saying, "Get out!" But he didn't get out, he merely backed toward the side counter.

Slowly Alice hovered toward Mary, and when she came face to face with her, she was standing almost in the same place in which Alec had stood some days earlier. She looked at her daughter, and, her lips moving square from her teeth, she said, "You dirty bitch, you!"

Mary made no comment, but she gripped tightly on the muslin rag and waited.

Alice seemed nonplused by her silence and now she burst out, "Me money! I want me money."

"What money?"

"Don't come that with me, Miss. Hand it over afore I take it out of your skin."

"You're gettin' no money from me, now or ever again." The words were slow, deep, flat, and they seemed to have the effect of stretching Alice's body upwards. Her face took on color again; her anger and indignation came out in sweat.

"YOU GIVE ME ME PAY!"

"It isn't your pay, Ma, it's my pay. I've worked for it, and I'm not livin' with you any more. You're gettin' nothing from me again ever, not a penny, so get that into your head now."

"You brazen, dirty bitch! You filthy, stinking . . . !"

"Shut up, Ma! Shut up afore I tell you something."

"You tell me something? I'll tell you something! Who's looked after you all these years? Who's brought you up? Done without meself to see that you were fed; worked for you for years; slaved down here in this shop."

"You slaved, Ma! You slaved, as you call it, in this shop to suit yourself, not for me, nor me da, and not even for Jimmy; no, I know why you worked here, an' you know that I know." She watched her mother choke and gulp again, then lift up her stick.

"You do!" she cried. "Just you do, Ma, and you'll be sorry."

Alice was trembling visibly from head to foot. She now looked round the shop as if for some support and cried loudly, "Your da's in prison because of you."

"Not because of me," Mary cried back at her. "It was you who egged him on. 'Smash him up,' you said; 'smash his shop up,' because you were jealous. That's your trouble. You wanted Ben for yourself. You threw yourself at him an' he wouldn't have you."

She sprang to the side as the stick came down with a sickening thud on the counter and across the spot where she had been standing.

With lightning speed she lifted the hatch and was in the shop confronting Alice, with only a yard between them.

Shaking from head to foot, she cried, "Get out of here this minute! or I'll send Andy there for the police."

Andy couldn't have got out of the shop door at this stage because Alice was standing in his path. Nor did she seem to hear the threat, for she shouted back, "You think you're on to a good thing, don't you? You think you're going to marry him and be set fair for life an' all this!" She waved her stick widely. "But, by God! I'll see you don't; if it's the last thing I do, I'll put a spoke in your wheel. You're under age, you know that; you can't do it without my consent. I can get you put away in a home. That's something you didn't know, isn't it? I can get you put away in a home."

"Get out! Get out this minute!"

"Tell me to get out, would you?" She threw her stick aside and her hands came out like talons and clawed at her daughter's hair.

Mary screamed and struck back, and now Andy didn't need to be told to run for the police. But whether he would have gone searching or not he was never able to answer, for there, not ten yards from the shop, was Constable Power on his round, and so he yelled at him, "She's at Mary! Her mother's at Mary."

"What? What is it?" Without waiting for an answer the constable followed the boy's pointing hand and hurried into the shop, and he had to use almost brute force before he could disentangle Alice's hands from Mary's hair. Holding the screaming woman by the shoulders, he shook her, shouting, "Be quiet, woman! Be quiet, do you hear me?"

When Alice, gasping and spent, stopped her screaming he said to her, "Now, look. Now, look you here, Missus. Take my advice and get back home."

"She's me daughter and . . . and she's not stayin' here and . . ."

"Listen to me, Missus. I'm giving you a bit of advice. It's up to you to take it or leave it, but if you don't go quietly home this minute you might find yourself alongside your husband. Now, it's up to you."

Alice drew in a deep, shuddering breath.

The policeman stooped down and picked up her stick, which he handed to her, and like someone drunk she stumbled to the door. But there she turned, and looking back at Mary where she was standing leaning on the corner, her pinafore hanging from her shoulder where it had been ripped and her hair tousled into a busby round her face, she cried, "You'll never know a day's luck in your life. That's me prayer, and I'll say it every night for you. You dirty bitch, you!"

The policeman did not follow her into the street and through the small crowd, mostly children, that had gathered outside, but he closed the door after her and turned to Mary and asked, "Are you all right, lass?"

She pulled herself up from the support of the counter and moved her head wearily.

"She hurt you?"

She put her hand through her hair. Her scalp felt as if it had been torn apart in several places, and as she drew her fingers over it the loose hair came away in her hand. She looked at it, and the policeman said consolingly, "Don't worry, it'll grow again. But are you all right otherwise?"

"Yes, yes, thank you." As she looked up at him, slow tears welled into her eyes, and he said, "There now, there now. Lock up and get yourself to bed." Again she nodded at him. He was the same policeman who had locked up her da, the one who had come into the shop and found Ben on the floor; he knew all about her; he knew all about everyone on his beat. And nobody liked him; she wondered why.

He said to the boy, "Get what you want and come on."

Andy looked at Mary. His eyes were wide. He had seen some

fights in his time between women in the back lanes but he had never seen anyone look as mad as Mary's mother.

"Wait a minute." She went to the till and took out threepence and handed it to Andy, who said, "Ta, Mary," and went with the policeman.

She locked the door, then put the lights out and went slowly upstairs, and just as she was she threw herself on the bed and sobbed her heart out. What was happening to her? What was happening to all of them? Life had gone mad.

The following morning she put her hair up for the first time. She combed out her plaits, twisted the hair into coils and pinned it up on the back of her head with hairpins from the shop, and immediately she felt different.

She didn't realize how different until eleven o'clock in the morning, when Hughie Amesden came into the shop. He had never been in the shop before, at least whilst she had been serving, and somehow she guessed that he didn't usually come at all, for he lived streets away, near Staple Road.

She had been stooping down, stacking some blue wrapped-pound bags of sugar that she had just weighed, and when she stood up there he was, as tall and as handsome as ever, more so, beautiful . . . and young.

"A packet of cigarettes, please," he said.

She was a second or two before she turned round to the box and picked up a packet of woodbines. As she placed the packet before him he pushed the tuppence toward her, and with their hands on the counter they looked at each other.

He stood gazing at her through narrow lids as if he had never seen her before. He had likely come in, she thought, to see if she had changed and was finding that she had. Yet the putting up of her hair that morning hadn't made her into a woman—she had been a woman for days, inside; the putting up of the hair was only the outward sign. She knew in this moment that she would never feel young again.

"Ta," he said.

"Ta," she said.

He turned and walked slowly out of the shop. He was her youth gone. Had she ever loved him? Had she ever seen him enveloped in a white light? Yes, yes, she had; once a long, long time ago. Did she still love him? He had spoken to her. She had heard his voice say something, more than that one word "Hello," and she was surprised that it wasn't beautiful like him. It was an ordinary voice, like that of any of the lads about. She had heard he was no longer at school and had gone into the mercantile docks to serve his time as a draftsman.

But did she still love him?

It was almost as if she had taken her own hand and impatiently pushed herself back from the counter; for, leaning against the rack, she was confronted by the question, what was she really doing? She was thinking like a lass, a girl, and she was no longer either. She was carrying a bairn inside her. In an odd way, she realized that from now on her life would be weighed down with responsibilities.

Her surroundings seemed to fade away, and as if she were looking at a film, she saw the responsibilities stretching down the years: starting with Ben, a disfigured Ben, and his child, and her child; her father, and her Grandma Walton, and her Granda Walton, and their Jimmy; and strangely there was tacked on to the end of her responsibilities the little crippled figure of Annie Tollett.

And then to ask herself that fool question, Did she still love Hughie Amesden?

9

Alec was tried at Durham. It was the end of the day and his was the last of a long line of cases. The court was practically empty but for a few sightseers, mostly unemployed men, and a young woman dressed in a brown coat and a brown felt hat which merged with the color of her hair.

Mr. Justice Broadside glanced at the prisoner as he listened to the prosecuting counsel. He looked an inoffensive enough creature, slight, thin; yet he had nearly murdered a man, so the prosecutor had just informed him. But it would appear he had had provocation. He looked over the court to the girl sitting in brown. Was she whom it was all about? A pretty piece, and likely more to blame than the man concerned. Girls of her age played havoc with older men, and this particular man had nearly paid with his life. He looked around. He wasn't in court. He motioned the two men below him to the bench, and to his question the clerk to the court said, "From medical report, Your Worship, he will be badly scarred, facial scars."

"And that, you say"—Mr. Justice Broadside now lowered his head and looked over his glasses in the direction of the brown-clad figure—"is the person in question?"

"Yes, Your Honor."

"The man is still in hospital?"

"Yes, Your Honor."

"Hmm!"

Mr. Justice Broadside slowly straightened his back and the two figures solemnly receded from the bench.

Well, let him get this over. He was hungry; it had been a long day. "Alec James Walton, you have admitted causing grievous bodily harm to one Benjamin Arthur Tollett."

Mr. Justice Broadside now paused as if he were waiting for some comment from the prisoner, which would have surprised him had it been forthcoming. Then he went on to tell the man in the box that he couldn't do this kind of thing and hope to escape the consequences, not in this country, and not in this particular county. People like him, if they couldn't restrain themselves, would have to be put under restraint by those in responsible positions. True, he had been provoked, and he was taking into consideration the understandable feelings of a father and, therefore, would not make the sentence actually fit the crime but would show leniency toward him. He ordered him to prison for a term of eighteen months.

The prisoner made no response, neither of surprise nor of dismay. When he was turned about and taken from the box his actions were those of a puppet.

Eighteen months! Oh, Da! Oh, Da!

Mary stood waiting in a bare room. They said she could see him for a few minutes. How could she look at him? How could she bear to look at him? Eighteen months in prison. But then she supposed he had got off light, because they had been making bets in the street on the length of time he would get. Jimmy said some of them were betting it would be five years because it had been close to murder, and he was lucky he wasn't swinging.

She didn't remember his coming through the door; she wasn't aware of anything until his arms were about her and he was saying, "There, lass. There, lass. It's all right, it's all right. Look. Look at me." She looked at him. "I'm not worried, I'm not, only for one thing." He paused, then said with a break in his voice, "Do something for me, will you, Mary?"

"Yes, Da, any . . . anything, anything."

"Tell Ben I'm . . . I'm sorry."

She nodded, then clung to him; and after a minute he gently pushed her from him and said, "You'll come an' see me?"

She was unable to answer; she could only nod her head, and then he was gone. . . . But it was queer, she thought, his wanting Ben to know that he was sorry, for the fact still remained that Ben had given her the bairn. Her da had never mentioned her condition; it was as if it had escaped his memory. Yet that's what it was all about, wasn't it?

All the way down in the train from Durham to Newcastle she cried, and people looked at her. One woman sat beside her and patted her arm and said to those sitting opposite, "She's likely had someone sent to prison," and they all nodded.

At Newcastle she was so confused she got on to the wrong platform for the Shields train and missed it, and had to wait for the next. When she alighted at Jarrow the twilight was deepening and she walked slowly back to the shop.

Mrs. McArthur was waiting for her. "What did he get, hinny?" she asked.

"Eighteen months!"

"Oh, that's not bad. I thought it'd be twice that. If he behaves himself, he'll get out afore his time, too."

Oh, she wanted to die, she did, she did; she wanted to fall on Mrs. McArthur's neck and sob out her misery. But she must wait until she got to her grannie's later on. Neither of the old people had been able to come to Durham with her because her granda was in bed, bad with his chest. They were afraid of angina or something and her grannie couldn't leave him. She felt responsible for this, too, for whatever her granda had, had been brought on by worry.

When Mrs. McArthur put her arm about her shoulders, she didn't wait any longer before giving way completely.

A week later she took Ben's clothes down to the hospital and for the first time saw him without the bandages on his face, and she hardly stopped herself from exclaiming aloud.

The red scar started near his scalp, came down over his eyebrow, taking the corner of the top eyelid with it, then went on down the cheek to the chin. He had another scar that ran in a diagonal line across his neck. But it was the scar that pulled his eyelid down that gave his face the strange, sinister effect. It made him look, she thought, like one of the men in the squeally vampire pictures.

When she put the case down by the bed their faces were on a level, and he stared at her and said quietly, "Well, Mary?"

She made herself look at the good side of his face as she said, "It's all right, Ben; it'll get better."

"That's what they tell me. They say the redness'll go; they say it'll tighten. But the more it tightens, the more me eye will be

pulled down. That's how I see it. How do you see it, Mary?"
His voice was as tight as the skin of his face.

"Aw, Ben, Ben."

"It's all right." He closed his eyes. "Don't distress yourself;
we'll talk about it when we get home. . . . Did you order a
taxi?"

"Yes."

"Well then, I'll get into me things." He got up and pulled a
dressing gown around him and, having picked up the case, went
through a door, while she sat by the bed waiting.

When he came out dressed, he had his face turned to the side
as he spoke to someone, and he was Ben again, and she told herself she must keep looking at this side until she got used to the
other side. She mustn't let him see how it affected her, because
he was still the same; no matter how he looked, he was still the
same.

She noticed that the sister and the nurses were nice to him.
They were all shaking hands with him; he seemed very popular.
Then he would be: Ben was attractive; at least he had been. Oh,
what was she thinking? She was acting small, mean, ordinary,
letting herself be affected by the look of him. She should be
ashamed of herself, she should that. She would never forgive
herself, never, if she made him feel worse than he already did.

She smiled at the sister and added her thanks, and then they
were walking out of the hospital, and the taxi was waiting for
them.

She did not know whether or not it was on purpose, but he
placed himself in the cab with his bad side next to her, and although he held her hand all the way home, he didn't speak.

When they entered the house Mrs. McArthur set the pattern
for future reactions. The sight of the scarred face brought her
mouth open and she exclaimed, "Oh, my God! lad; he did make
a mess of you."

After swallowing deeply Ben made an attempt at lightness,
although his tone was grim as he retaliated, "I was no oil paint-
ing to begin with." But Mrs. McArthur imagined she was help-

ing matters when she stated flatly, "Oh! now, that's a lie, if ever there was one."

Mary had the desire to take the kindly woman by the shoulders and run her down the stairs. "Where's David?" she put in quickly.

"Oh. Katie Smith and young Bella took him to the park. I thought it'd do him good; he hasn't been out much lately."

Five minutes later, when Mrs. McArthur had gone, Ben took Mary by the hand and led her into the sitting room. There, sitting her down on the couch, he brought his face squarely to hers, saying, "Now take a good look. She's right, Alec did make a mess of me. Let's face up to it, let's try to face up to the whole bad business. Your da's in jail, I'm marked, and"—he lifted her hand now and placed it over his eye—"what you've got to realize is that I'm going to be like this for the rest of me life. You won't always be able to look at this side." He patted his cheek. "The only hope they've given me of improvement is that later when the skin heals they might be able to cut the lid and lift it. But that's in the future; now, as you know, I want to marry you, Mary. I've wanted you"—his voice dropped low now—"I've wanted you since the day you first set foot in the shop. You know all that, and if I hadn't gone mad that night, none of this would have happened. But I did go mad; you can't undo what's done. But the point is now I'm not going to hold you to it; you can have the bairn and I'll bring him up as me own, but I'm not going to hold you to marrying me."

The bigness of him, the kindness of him, and even the wonder of a love such as his for somebody, as she put it to herself, with nothing much about them and no education, brought her falling against him, and she cried, "Oh, Ben! Ben, I would marry you if it was on both sides." Now she made herself put her lips to the corner of his drooping lid, and the act completed her transition into a woman.

BOOK 2

Jimmy

JARROW 1943

"Burrows!"

"Yes, sir." The tall boy unwound himself from his desk and stood up. The book held before him, he blinked a number of times before saying, "The twentieth sonnet, sir."

Jimmy smiled inwardly. "Carry on," he said.

"A woman's face, with nature's own hand painted.
Hast thou, the master-mistress of my passion;
A woman's gentle heart, but not acquainted
With shifting change, as is false women's fashion;
An eye more bright than theirs less false in rolling . . . !"

"There's a comma in that line; you must use it. It reads: 'An eye more bright than theirs . . . less false in rolling.'"

The tall boy nodded, then went on:

"G . . . gilding the object whereupon it g . . . gazeth."

There was a smothered titter and when Jimmy cast a withering glance over the class the sound died away, but an echo of it remained in himself. Why did Burrows pick a piece with two g's in one line? He could never manage his g's; they had been waiting for those g's.

When the boy finished he looked at the master, and Jimmy said, "That was quite good, Burrows," and the boy, his face pink, eased himself down into his seat like a snake uncoiling.

Poor Burrows! Five feet eleven and not sixteen. He knew what it felt like; he had experienced it. On his sixteenth birthday he had been five feet ten and his hands and forearms had been hanging out of his coat's sleeves like tortured limbs from a rack. To add to his humiliation she had sewn cuffs on the sleeves. (He always thought of his mother as she.) The cuffs had been fuller than the sleeves and of a softer material and looked like frills, and the lads had ribbed him. Poor Burrows; he was of the same breed. But he had the excuse that he couldn't get clothes because of the lack of clothing coupons.

"You, Felton! What have you chosen?"

"The sixty-sixth, sir."

As he nodded to the boy to begin he congratulated himself. He knew little Felton would pick that one. He was a romantic, was Felton—at the opposite pole from Burrows, for he was small, even undersized, but his heart was big. He would suffer, would little Felton, even more than Burrows.

When the boy finished with the lines:

> "Tir'd with all these, from thee would I be gone,
> Save that, to die, I leave my love alone,"

he thought, Poor Felton. He liked little Felton; he hoped that one day he would find a love that he would hate to leave alone. God, what was he thinking about, finding love? Get on with it! What was the matter with him?

"Quite good." He nodded at Felton. "But you use a little too much emphasis. Let the words speak for themselves. Our author knew where to lay on emphasis, don't you think, Felton?"

"Yes, sir, yes." The small boy smiled and sat down.

"You, Weir!"

The thick-set, bull-headed boy began in a Northern accent that could be cut with a knife:

> "Let me not to the marriage of true minds
> Admit impediments. Luv is not luv
> Which alters when it alteration finds. . . ."

Luv is not luv which alters when it alteration finds! How would a numskull like Weir tackle love? Like a dog let off a chain.

"Cook!"

"Riley!"

"Fawcett!"

"Youlden!"

One after the other they recited the sonnets of their choice as part of the Friday afternoon English lesson. Then after Youlden's oration there was a sound of scuffling feet and something being kicked along the floor, and as if another man had suddenly entered the skin of the benign, gangling English master he now burst forth in a voice like a sergeant major's, "MILLI-GAN! Leave that . . . gas mask case alone! How many times have I to tell you? Stand up!"

Milligan stood up. He was red-haired, square-faced, and he was grinning.

"If you want to practice football, there's a schoolyard in which to do it. Why must you keep dribbling that . . . that gas mask case? Give it here."

The boy stooped down, retrieved his gas mask case and came down the aisle, his body rocking from side to side with a half-sheepish, half-defying swagger.

"Put it on my desk." He stared at Milligan, and Milligan looked up at him, an innocent expression on his face now.

"Don't you stand looking at me like that, Milligan, guileless. I know you; you're the biggest irritant in this class. Well, what have you to say?"

As soon as he uttered the last words he knew he had asked for it. He had given Milligan an opening.

"You were going to say 'bloody,' sir; you were going to say, leave that 'bloody gas mask case alone.' And then you were going to say, 'That damned . . . !' "

"Quiet! GET!" He thrust his long arm out, and Milligan got. He walked back up the aisle with the whole class roaring.

"Silence!" He banged the long ruler on the desk, and after the tittering had died away they all looked at him bright-eyed, while he stared at Milligan, seated now, innocently looking back at him.

He liked Milligan; you couldn't help but like Milligan. You could murder him, but you couldn't help but like him. Funny how some of them irritated you and you could still feel for them. But there were others, like Crockford, for instance, whom, no matter what they did, good, bad or indifferent, you loathed.

In the past month he hadn't once asked Crockford to stand up and speak his piece; even last week when they were doing *Henry VIII* and he knew Crockford was willing him to say, "And now you, Crockford"; because, as Crockford had once boasted, he had done Wolsey so often he felt he was Wolsey. What was it about the lad he couldn't stand? His self-assurance? His sharp nose? Those round, dark, all-seeing eyes? Or was it because Crockford saw through him and, like one or two of the old brigade in the common room, thought he was out of place here, and if it hadn't been for the war he would never have got his nose inside the school, he with only his Teachers' Training College behind him? He had heard old Dixon, the Latin master, say, "War or no war, it would never have happened in my day."

It was a sore point with some of them that the products of the Teachers' Training College were getting a foot in. He would like to bet he could teach better than half of them on the staff; he had proved it with these fifth-formers.

He had been given the fifth form because Watson had been called up, and they were hard put to get someone to fill his place, but he knew that the head was pleased with the progress that the lads were making. He himself knew his own worth as a teacher. He knew he had the knack of drawing them out; he never used sarcasm and didn't hold with the theory that thirty-five silent and solemn boys formed a disciplined class. Yet he stood no nonsense. Oh, no! They knew how far they could go. That is, all except Crockford. But there was always a Crockford in a form; there was always one whom you detested.

The class was silent now, still bright-eyed and waiting. He looked at his watch. There was ten minutes to go. Should he? Crockford was holding him with that hypnotic stare of his; he could not go on ignoring him forever; the others would notice. He moved his book slightly to the left on the broad, flat table, wet his lips, reached out for a pencil as if about to write something further on a sheet of paper already half-filled with notes, then lifted his head and, looking at the boy sitting in the third desk from the front, said, "Ah yes, Crockford. What did you select?"

There elapsed ten whole seconds before Crockford rose to his feet. "Forty-three, sir." The voice was thick and deep, like that of a man.

"Well, carry on."

There was a silence now such as an actor might create before delivering some profound oratory. Then in modulated tones the boy quoted:

> "When most I wink, then do mine eyes best see,
> For all the day they view things unrespected;
> But when I sleep, in dreams they look on thee,
> And, darkly bright, are bright in dark directed;
> Then thou whose shadow shadows doth make bright,
> How would thy shadow's form form happy show
> To the clear day with thy much clearer light,
> When to unseeing eyes thy shade shines so!
> How would, I say, mine eyes be blessed made
> By looking on thee in the living day,
> When in dead night thy fair imperfect shade
> Through heavy sleep on sightless eyes doth stay?
> All days are nights to see, till I see thee,
> And night, bright days, when dreams do show thee me."

The complicated rhythm, the sense, and only sense to those acquainted with Shakespeare, had been mastered by the speaker. The eyes of all the form turned in admiration on Crockford, but Crockford's eyes were looking into the master's, laughing into the master's.

Since he had taken over the form he had suffered—and the word was "suffered"—Crockford's own and particular way of hitting back, which took the form of laughter—clever, vicious, secret laughter . . . and insolence.

> For all the day they view things unrespected.

They were waiting for him to make a comment on the performance. He tapped his pencil on the table, put his head back as if thinking, then said, "Well now, what about my own contribution? I am sure you would want to hear something from me."

The giggle that went round the class was almost girlish. They knew Willowy Walton (Jimmy's nickname) wrote poems. It was said that he had done a book of them and that they would have been published if it hadn't been for the war. There were cries from the boys now of: "Yes, sir!" "Oh yes! sir."

Jimmy held up his right hand for silence, and placing his left hand in the vent of his coat in Nelson fashion and taking an exaggerated stance, he began in the voice of an indignant child:

> "He said it was a   BLUEBOTTLE,
> I said it was a   FLY.
> He said it was a   BLUEBOTTLE,
> And then I asked him   WHY?
> 'Just 'cos,' he said, 'just 'cos.'
>   That's all.
>   Wasn't any answer,
>   WAS IT?
>   At all."

The class was convulsed. He let them have their way for a moment or so, then brought it to a teetering stop by saying, "That's all, joke's over! Clear up."

He kept his eyes away from Crockford. He supposed it had been a mean trick, ignoring such a performance, then stealing the boy's thunder, even ridiculing it with a few lines of childish gibberish.

Aw, he was glad it was Saturday tomorrow. Yet was he? Didn't he always long to get back on Monday morning?

A boy now called, "Please, sir, please, sir. What will we have to get ready for next week?"

He was gathering up some books from his desk when he stopped and looked at the boy. He would like to give them "The Rape of Lucrece" or "Venus and Adonis," and he would and could if it weren't for Crockford. He lifted up the books and walked toward the door, then stopped, and covering the whole class with the sweep of his eyes he said, "Walter de la Mare next Friday."

"Three jolly gentlemen
In coats of red
Rode their horses
Up to bed."

"Study, but do not try to emulate, this writer." He then walked briskly out.

A rippling murmur followed him into the corridor, which pleased him. Modestly, he prided himself on the quality of his exits—and entries, and he felt flattered by the knowledge that this fifth form in particular waited expectantly for them.

He decided not to go into the common room; there was no need. Anyway, he hadn't much time; he was on Home Guard duty tonight. But first he wanted to look in on Mary. If he was quick he would likely have half an hour there; that would get him home about quarter past five and he'd be in time to get something ready for Betty coming in at six.

He hurried out of the gate, thrusting his way between groups of boys, hurried to the end of the road and jumped on a bus. Fifteen minutes later he was going up the back staircase to the rooms above the shop and breathing a sigh that again he had managed to get in without his mother's detecting him.

"Oh, hello there." Mary had heard his step on the stairs and met him in the hall. "What a day! You look frozen."

"I am." He took off his coat and was about to go toward the sitting room when she said, "Come in here," and pushed the dining room door open. "Ben's just popped up for a cup."

"Hello there, Jimmy." Ben looked up from the table.

"Hello, Ben. By! it's a snifter." He stood before the fire, his knees bent so that his buttocks should be nearer the heat.

Ben asked, "Well, what kind of a week has this been? Murdered anybody?" He laughed.

"No, not quite, but I had the strong inclination to this afternoon. I've got a kid in my class called Crockford. I just can't stand him; he gets under my skin."

"Dim?"

"No, no." Jimmy tossed his head, "Dim, no. Just the opposite, a very bright boy. Perhaps that's the reason I don't like him, competition." They laughed together.

"Here, sit down. Have this cup of tea." Mary motioned him to the table, then said, "I've got a bit of beefsteak pudding left from dinner time—not corned beef"—she pulled a face—"the real stuff. Would you like it?"

"Would I like it!"

"Well, drink your tea. It won't take ten minutes to heat; I'll put it in the oven."

"Ta, Mary." They exchanged a warm and intimate smile before she went into the kitchen.

Mary was not, naturally, the girl of ten years before; she was a fully developed woman, a beautiful woman. If her mirror didn't tell her so, Ben told her, at least once a week, and that, she considered, after ten years of marriage was something.

When she looked back it didn't seem that she had been married to Ben and living in this house for ten years. Strangely, compared with those early months in 1933, nothing much seemed to have happened in the past ten years, except that the war had started and was still going madly on. Inside herself, too, she seemed to have remained stagnant; her resolute outside appearance was only a facade, for underneath she still carried the burden of fear and doubt, and remorse.

Although she had become used to looking at Ben's disfigured face, there were times when she was bowed down with the responsibility of his changed appearance and the effects it had had on him. Ben was still kind, still thoughtful, still loving, oh yes, still loving, but there was a bitterness in him that hadn't been there before her father had crashed the bottle of sweets down on his face. But the bitterness was a subtle thing; it wasn't evident to anyone but herself. She doubted if Ben himself realized it, perhaps because he had given it the outlet through an ambition to make money.

Before they had married she had learned about his hobby, the thing called "stocks and shares." His father, he said, had started him on it. His father and his cousin Annie had been at it for years. Even the shock of Clarence Hatry, the millionaire financicr, going broke in 1929 about the same time as the New York Stock Market crash hadn't deterred them. Hang on, his father had said; the end of the seesaw that was down was sure, by the very length of the plank, to come up top on the next swing. And he had been right, for most of their shares at least.

After the child was born he had spent more and more of his time reading papers that dealt with these shares, and then he had taken the small profits from the shop and spent them on buying more shares, and in 1938, when the slump was seen to be visibly easing itself out of the North, he had opened another shop, which he managed himself, while she, with the assistance of young Teresa Bennett, had kept this one going and seen to the house. Then, just a week before the war broke out, he had taken a third shop, mostly greengrocery this one, and put a young fellow in as manager.

She had felt sad about his putting a manager in, thinking that if things had been different it would have been a wonderful opportunity for her da, for since Alec came out of prison at the end of 1934 he hadn't done a stroke of work, and since the very night he was let out he had lived with her grannie and granda. That night, when he went home, her ma had told him that he'd have to sleep on a shakedown in the front room because Grandma McAlister and she were sleeping together, and she had got rid of . . . that one's bed. On this, he had turned on his heel without saying one word and walked out and gone to the home of his childhood. And there, like someone sucked dry of dignity, he had remained, living quite unconcernedly on the old couple, who could not, in the ordinary way of things, have supported him if it hadn't been for the pound note Mary slipped into her grannie's hand once a week.

Her da remained as a living recrimination that tainted even her happiest days. There was plenty of work for him to do now, if he could have done it; but the term of imprisonment, coming on the years of idleness which had sapped his manhood, together with his conscience, which had lashed at him all during his prison confinement, added to which the final degradation of being relegated to the floor in his own house, all combined to turn him into a sick man, both mentally and physically. He had never been big, but now he seemed to have shrunk to half his size, and he looked as old as his father.

When people talked about him they blamed him. He had no gumption, they said. These things happened to other people and they got over them. Life had to be lived. Only Mary herself understood, because these things had happened to a gentle man, a gentle man who loved and trusted one person, and it was this same person who had betrayed him. Now she knew she'd have to carry him for the rest of his days. Yet, strangely, she did not feel the burden of him as she did that of Jimmy. Why this was so she couldn't fully understand, for Jimmy had a good position— he was a schoolteacher. Her mother had done something here. Her mother was answerable for so many things; she was even answerable for warping Jimmy's life. Yet she had this to her credit; she had equipped him, or been the means of his being equipped, to earn his living at the one thing he wanted to do, teach.

He was clever was Jimmy; he would go far. So she thought. So why was she always worried about him? Was it because of his drinking? Not really; everybody drank these days. If you could manage to get it, you bought it even if you didn't really want it. It was like everything else: anything that could be eaten or drunk that was offered you, you bought. But the trouble with Jimmy was he couldn't carry his drink, not like Ben. After a few whiskies Jimmy acted like a daft lad. But he had drunk hardly at all until he had married Betty.

Betty! Why, in the name of God, had he to take someone like Betty! Hadn't he had enough of their ma? Couldn't he see that Betty was a replica of their ma? She mightn't be half the size of their ma, being tiny, "petite" they called it; but the first time she met Betty she had seen beneath that petite surface, beneath that smiling face and childish manner, to a cast-iron character that was every bit as hard as their ma's.

She remembered the first time she had met Betty. It was on a Tuesday in September of '41. She remembered it because it had been given out on the radio that the Shah of Persia had abdicated that morning and was to be succeeded by the Crown Prince, and that the Duke of Kent had returned from Canada on Sunday and that since he left London he had traveled fifteen thousand miles by air. Little things like this always stuck in her mind when they were attached to events, and it had been an event meeting Betty, for she had acted baby-like and gushed and swarmed all over her. But her baby ways didn't alter the fact that she was a lot older than Jimmy, as it turned out seven years, in fact. She had longed to say to him, "You're mad, lad, you're mad." It wasn't so much about Betty's being older than he, as his not seeing that the front she put on was just an act.

She had clear gray eyes and a sharp little face, and both the eyes and the face had a cutting effect on Mary. In a way she could have been her ma's daughter. Yet because of her skittish ways, Jimmy imagined she was the antithesis of their ma. He saw her as someone he could rule and at the same time love and pet. How wrong he had been, and how he was paying for it now.

Jimmy, in a way, was her da over again. He was soft inside, kindly and sensitive, and in taking Betty he hadn't got away from their ma, he had only saddled himself with a younger ma. But the strange thing about it was that her ma and Betty got on like a house on fire.

When Jimmy had first broached the subject of marriage she understood that their ma nearly went up the wall, and he ran the whole gamut of her recrimination: Look what she had done for him; how she had slaved for him; how her life had been ruined; how she had been left alone to work for him; and this is what he was doing; as soon as he was earning, going off and getting married!

But he had stood his ground and said he was going to marry Betty whether she liked it or not.

This was one time when Mary wished her mother had got her own way. It would have saved a lot of trouble in the end.

When she went into the room with a plate of meat pudding Jimmy was saying on a high note of surprise, "The Moat Cottage! Oh! I heard it was empty."

"And has been for the past six months," said Ben; "that's why it was going cheap."

"By!" Jimmy said after a moment, jerking his chin upwards; "you've got a business head on you. How many is that you've bought now?"

"Oh, let me see." Ben was smiling quietly, as the left side of his face showed, even though on the right side the corner of his mouth remained straight, held in stiffness by the jagged line running up to his eyelid, which now, although not drooping so noticeably, was still pulled slightly downwards, and he said, "Six. Yes, six," he added. "And Mary there, she spotted the last two; she's getting good at it."

"But isn't it a risk?"

"No, we don't pay any rates as long as they're empty, and the war can't last forever. When it's over there'll be a rush, not enough houses, and everybody coming swarming back. Of course, the property deals in places like Jarrow won't be anything like those in the seaside towns. There'll be quite a few fortunes made out of properties along the coast. . . . But still, I'm not grumbling, and if you had any sense"—he nodded now toward Jimmy, where he was eating the meat pudding appreciatively—"you'll give up that schoolteaching and come in with us."

It was nice, Mary noticed, that Ben always referred to the business as theirs and not simply his. When he turned to her and ended, "What do you say?" she answered, "The same as you. But then"—she shook her head and made a face—"we'd likely have to sack him, because he'd spend half his time sitting behind the counter scribbling that poetry of his."

"I . . . I don't write poetry." Jimmy wiped each side of his mouth with his fingers, swallowed, then said, "I wouldn't dare give it that name; verse, that's what I do, verse. By the way, where are the bairns?"

"Oh"—Mary glanced at the clock—"Annie should be in any minute; she's gone round to a pal of hers. You'll hear her long before you see her. And David is along at the Flake Street shop, can't keep him away from there. He asked his dad yesterday"— she laughed toward Ben—"if he could wangle and get him off school, a sort of war-work wangle, so that he could work in the shop. I'd like to bet that by the time he's twenty he'll have a chain of them stretching from here to Whitly Bay."

"Newcastle."

She laughed outright at Ben and said, "All right, Newcastle." Then, turning to Jimmy, the laughter still on her face, she asked, "How's Doo-lally getting on?"

"Oh, Doo-lally!" Jimmy, about to take a drink from a steaming cup of tea, put the cup back onto the saucer, and wagging his head over it he said, "Poor Doo-lally. But you know, it's a shame, Mary, she's no more doo-lally than I am; it's just the look of her. And yet why call anyone who looks like her 'Doo-lally'? Sophie Tucker would be a better title, because she's all bust and buttocks. Note"—he looked from one to the other, laughing—"how politely I described her anatomy."

They were all laughing when he said, "But seriously, she's a good eyeful. How she came to marry that big lout of an individual I'll never know. And Lord! When I hear him going at her I could go in there and land him one—if I dared." His head flopped backwards in self-derision. "But he'd just need to breathe on me and that would be me horizontal." He demonstrated by leaning back and throwing his arms wide. Then after the laughter had subsided again he said, "But still, it makes me mad. Saturday night after Saturday night, I don't know where he finds the booze. I feel like asking him; I wish I could get as smashed as that."

"Oh," put in Mary, "it's the booze you're worried about, not her!"

"Yes, perhaps you're right. It could be."

"Why doesn't she leave him?" asked Ben now.

"Aw, I don't know. The usual; she's just had another miscarriage. They tell me this is the third. You know, you can't imagine her putting up with it, not the way she looks. You want to hear the lads when she passes the corner: it's like a wolf pack. But she just turns round and laughs at them. She's so good-natured. And they call to her, 'Hello, Doo-lally!' I mean, fancy calling her Doo-lally to her face. But as Barney Skelton on the top floor says, 'Half the men for streets around would be only too glad to swap her for their wives.' Mind, I don't think she's got any money sense. I think that's what the trouble's about between him and her, because they say even when it was possible to buy things, when they were first married at the beginning of '39 and he gave her his pay, she'd go straight out and spend the lot on the daftest things. They say she'd bring home huge pieces of steak that would do a family for a week, and cream cakes, and things like that, or she'd go and rig herself out in something fancy—and how fancy! But that's the only daft thing I can see about her; for the rest, I find her, well, nice, kindly." He laughed again before adding, "We've been in that flat about four months and, you know, I don't think I've gone through the front door once but she's poked her head out of her door as if in great surprise and said, 'Oh, it's you, Mr. Walton. How are you?' And you know, I've nearly always got to check myself from saying, 'Oh, all right, Lally.' It's funny, but you want to call her Lally."

"What's her real name?" Mary asked now, her face straight.

"Jessie, I understand, so Skelton tells me. Jessie Briggs. It used to be MacAnulty before she married. Her father was Irish; her mother, of all things, was Spanish. And she's as blonde . . . well, as blonde as peroxide. Anyway"—he grinned as he rose from the table—"she . . . she affords me a little amusement in my darker hours. . . . That was lovely, Mary, thanks. Now I'll go home and have me tea."

"I bet you will an' all. I wouldn't care if you showed anything for it." Mary pushed him toward the door.

"I'm the thoroughbred type, long, lean and laconic. Ah well, here I go. Nice seeing you, Ben. Ta-rah."

"And you, Jimmy. Ta-rah."

Mary followed him out of the room, across the hall and down the stairs, and when they stood in the yard she said to him, "How's things?" It was as if they had just met, and, his face straight, his shoulders hunched, he replied, "Same as usual. No, no, that's not strictly true, getting worse would be more correct. You know what the latest is?"

"No, but I could give three guesses."

"She wants to come and live with us."

"Oh, I've been expecting that for a long time, ever since Grannie McAlister died."

"And Betty's all for it. We went at it tooth and nail last night. Apparently both she and me ma agreed that the bit of money she's earning would help the finances of our establishment, therefore enabling me to save and buy a house. This is the latest, buy a house. No reason, they say, why I can't get a job in a school, say, in Newcastle, or Whitly Bay, somewhere round the coast, in a respectable—refined—quarter." He emphasized the last two words with a deep nod of his head. "Neither of them has ever known such a common place as Jarrow. Not only is it dull, dirty, and more depressed than before the war, but its people are dull and vastly ignorant and, for the most part, depraved. And this, mind you"—now he had his face down and close to hers—"as you and I know, from two people who have never been more than a mile or two out of the town in their lives—Newcastle's the farthest."

He straightened up and looked at the top of the backyard wall as he said, "Oh, Mary, I wish I weren't teaching. I wish I hadn't this smattering of education, because instead of its broadening my mind and enabling me to make allowances, it does the opposite and makes me look down my nose at the pair of them. You know, their combined ignorance and bigotry is almost too much to bear at times."

As he brought his troubled gaze to her she saw the small boy who had, over the years, come rat-a-tat-tatting with his special signal on the backyard door here, telling her his tale of woe, pouring out of himself the burden of his mother. At more than one stage in his young days he had begged her to let him come and live with her, until she was forced to say to him, "If you ever did that, Jimmy, she would do murder, and I'm not just saying that. I know she would, for she lost our da, she lost me, and"— she had stopped herself from saying, "She lost Ben," and ended, "but me da and me would be nothing, because she never cared for either of us, but you, she always thought the sun shone out of you. No, Jimmy; get that out of your head. You can never come here, not to live. Pop in as often as you can, but be wary, for, you know, once she gets wind of your coming she'll put a stop to it. Oh aye, and slap you silly in the bargain."

It seemed strange that over the years her ma had never got wind of Jimmy's visits to her. Whether she thought that he wouldn't dare go against her wishes and therefore had not bothered to watch him she didn't know. And there was one thing she thanked the neighbors for: if anyone had seen him coming in, they hadn't split on him. It didn't sadden her to know that her mother was heartily disliked, even hated; rather it reassured her with regard to her own feelings, which at times she thought could be taken as unnatural, for after all, as the old women said, blood was thicker than water.

Jimmy said, "I didn't say anything upstairs—I couldn't—but it's funny about your buying Moat Cottage, because they were both on about it the other night, not talking to me, but at me. They conceded that to live there would mean still living in Jarrow, but on the outskirts of the better part, and me ma said she had always admired the cottage. By! I wouldn't like to hear what she says when she knows you've got it."

"It doesn't matter to me," Mary said, "what she thinks or what she says. I'm past her and all she can do to me." She asked now, "Have you been along to me grannie's this week?"

"Yes," he said. "I called in the night afore last. It was rather late. I'd been on fire watch. And me da came in. He was three sheets in the wind."

"Really!"

"Yes. I don't know where he got the money from. You been giving him any?"

She glanced away. "I give him a little now and again."

"Well"—he walked toward the back gate—"I don't blame him. If I knew where he got it, I would have gone with him and we could have got blotto together." He grinned down at her, and she said sadly, "Oh, Jimmy"; then added, "I wish you wouldn't."

"Wouldn't what?"

"Well, drink."

"Ben drinks."

"Yes, I know."

"You mean, I can't carry it?"

"It's not that. . . ."

"It is that, and I know it's that; but you've got to have a bolt hole, at least I have. I've got to scoot out between those two somehow to some place. God!" He put his hands to his scarf and pulled it tight. "You know what, Mary? At times I wish I were dead."

"Oh! our Jimmy. Our Jimmy. Stop talking like that!"

"All right, all right." He grinned down at her, then punched her gently in the cheek. "I'm only kidding. Well, I must be off. I'll have the bellmen out else. Be seeing you."

He went out into the street, and as he heard her lock the door the sound was like a gate clanging shut on his main bolt hole or, rather, private heaven, because in comparison with his own home that house to him had always appeared like heaven.

Fifteen minutes later he entered the tall house in Haven Terrace that had been turned into four flats. As he entered the hall a door on the right opened quickly and he looked at Mrs. Jessie Briggs. She was as he had described her, big, blonde, with prominent bust and buttocks. She was no more than twenty-five; her skin was pale, and her eyes were big and blue and arched with dark brows that contrasted strongly with her very fair hair.

"Oh, it's you, Mr. Walton. I thought it was Albert. How are you?"

"All right, Mrs. Briggs, thank you."

"Cold, isn't it?"

"Yes, yes, it's very cold."

She came from the doorway and took a step into the hall. "I heard something about you today, Mr. Walton."

"Did you, Mrs. Briggs?"

"Aye."

He waited while she smiled broadly at him, and he noticed that there came from her an odor. It wasn't scent and it wasn't body sweat; it was something about her, and whatever it was it was an attractive smell.

"I was talking to Mrs. Wright in the fish shop, and she got on about her boy—he's in your class at school—and mind, this is true"—she pushed her head toward him—"she said the boys think the world of you, and she said you had written a book. Yes, she did; a book of poetry."

He felt himself turning scarlet, like a second-former being brought up before the head for some misdemeanor, a personal, sexual misdemeanor. "Oh, that's not right, Mrs. B-Briggs." He was even stammering.

"Oh, but she said it was. A book of poetry, that's what she said."

Oh, my God! He closed his eyes and shook his head. "Oh, oh, that was a long time ago before the war, Mrs. Briggs. I . . . I used to dabble in it. Everybody does, you know, before they're twenty; it's something that comes with spots."

They were both laughing now and she said, "Oh, Mr. Walton, something that comes with spots! Poetry! Oh, Mr. Walton! You know something, Mr. Walton? I like poetry; I read poetry. There's bits by Ella Wheeler Wilcox in the paper and I read them. Oh, I do like a bit of poetry."

"I'm glad to hear that, Mrs. Briggs, I . . . I . . ."

At this point he was thrust forward by the door being opened, and there entered Betty. She stopped and stared from one to the other.

As if addressing a friend, Mrs. Briggs said on a high note, "Oh hello, Mrs. Walton," but Betty, turning on the big blonde woman a look that was meant to floor her, passed by her husband, took out her key from her bag and opened the door—and left it open. And now Jimmy, as if he had as many legs as an octopus, found difficulty in turning round and away from Mrs. Briggs; but as he did so he gave her a weak smile and a nod, and she returned his salutation with a broad smile and a nod.

"WELL!"

"Yes, well! Now, what can you make of it?" He forced himself to smile. "Caught red-handed in the hall with a blonde!"

"Don't be facetious. Why do you speak to her? Common, low slut of a woman!"

"How do you know she's a common, low slut?"

"Anyone who can use their eyes can see that. But of course you couldn't."

Jimmy stared at his wife as she tore off her outdoor things. He had known her three years and he had been married to her for two, but at times he felt he had known her from the beginning of his first memory, and that memory took him back to a day when he was three years old and was struggling to get out of his mother's arms and down onto the floor, and she wouldn't let him but held on to him and kept kissing him. Why hadn't he seen his mother in her? There was a psychological thing here. It was explained in Freud; put in a nutshell, it was that. Although he had resented his mother and had always wanted to get away from her, she had emphasized the tie between them so much that he couldn't unloosen it. In choosing Betty—or in Betty choosing him—he realized now, although with her skittish ways he had imagined her as being the antithesis of his mother, that somewhere in the mysterious depths of him he had been willingly marrying his mother. It was like an act of self-abnegation, a voluntary giving up of liberty.

"Standing gossiping to her and not a cup of tea ready and on six and you being finished since four! Where've you been?"

"Trying to get drunk."

"Stop being so childish. Do you know"—she turned her small tight, slim body toward him and gazed up at him with open disdain as she said—"you're utterly childish, immature? God only knows how you teach."

He had the desire to take his hand and with one swipe knock her flying. That would settle it; once he hit her that would settle it. But he couldn't do that, no. No, he wasn't going to start being another Briggs.

He watched her prance into the kitchen. He heard the kettle being banged on the stove, and her voice came at him, saying, "If it's not too much trouble, set the table. . . . Coming home after a day on me feet and not a bite ready!"

As he set the table he thought that cordite actually poisoned some people; they just couldn't stomach it. She packed cordite all day, and it never seemed to do her any harm. Oh—he jerked his head at himself—the quicker he got drunk, the better. Friday night he was generally lucky at the Ellison for a drop of liquor; it would soften his attitude to the whole world.

As she came into the living room with the teapot she said, "I saw Mam as I was getting off the tram. She'll be around about half-past six."

"I'll be gone by then. I'm on fire watch at seven."

"You know something?" She stared at him. "You're the most ungrateful sod I've ever met in me life."

It was funny about her and swearing. She was so small, so refined-looking, until she opened her mouth. Her swearing grated on him. He could stand men using language that would raise the roots of his hair, and he had heard some women that were good second-bests, but their swearing, even their obscenities, didn't affect him as when he heard her swear. She had a way of saying "sod" that caused his stomach muscles to tighten.

"Your mother's worked for you all your life and you haven't really got a good word for her. Where would you be without her, I ask you? You and your sister are tarred with the same brush. The things your mother's had to put up with from you two! An' then your da. . . ."

He looked down at her, his face stretching slightly, his eyes widening. It was odd, oh, more than odd, really strange, mystifying, but she liked his mother. She was about the only person he knew who liked his mother. And his mother liked her. After threatening what she was going to do to him if he married, as soon as she saw Betty they were like that—in his mind he entwined his fingers. It was said that people who were really alike didn't get on, but under the skin there wasn't a pin to choose between his mother and Betty, and they got on so well they had almost become one; when he saw and heard one, he saw and heard the other. It was uncanny. Why had this happened to him?

Now, if he had only married someone like Mary, or—he gave a hic of a laugh inside himself—Mrs. Briggs! Now, Mrs. Briggs wouldn't have nagged from morning till night; she might have spent all his money. But didn't Betty? What did he get out of his pay? She grabbed his check as soon as he got it, and from the first she had seen to the finances. She allowed him three pounds a month, and that was for bus fares, cigarettes and— beer. She arranged their financial life like any first-class account- ant. There was a box for everything in the house from coal to candles. Yes, candles; they had to have a store of them in for when the lights failed. He had been daft to put up with it; he had been daft from the start. Was it too late to change? Aw, what was the use? He'd go and have a drink, do his fire-watching stint and, if there was time, have another. That would see him over tonight; tomorrow he'd be in a better frame of mind. And he had enough money left over from the sweepstakes to keep him going. Good job he had the sense to keep that to himself. He was lucky at sweeps. Three this year he had won, forty-five quid in all.

"Mam's coming here to live."

"WHAT!"

"You heard."

"Oh, my God! She's not."

"I say she is."

"Well, let me tell you: if she comes here, there'll still only be two, for when she comes in permanent I go out. Now, have it your own way."

"Where you going?"

"To get drunk. To get bloody well drunk. I needed a drink before, but now I'm gasping for one."

"Sit down and get your tea, and don't act so stupid, like a kid!" Her voice was full of disdain.

"Don't call me STUPID . . . or a kid, Betty." He took a step toward her, and although she didn't back from him she pressed herself against the table, and again he said, "Don't you call me stupid! There was only one time when I was ever stupid and I'll give you a guess as to when that was." And on this he turned round, grabbed up his coat and hat and went out.

Before he went on fire duty he managed to get a pint and a double whisky; and after, just on closing time, another two

pints and two doubles. He was on his way home, warm inside
and happy, when, just after leaving Ellison Street, he met Mrs.
Briggs coming out of the fish shop.

"Aw, Mr. Walton, is that you?" She peered at him. The moon
had come out from behind a group of scudding clouds and for
a moment the street was illuminated and everything was softened and mellow. Doffing his hat, he said, "It is, Mrs. Briggs, it
is." And at this they both laughed and turned and walked up the
street together.

"I've been lucky. I got some fish and chips, Mr. Walton."

"And I've been lucky. I've got slightly tight, Mrs. Briggs." He
bent right over her, and again they laughed, even leaned against
each other for the fraction of a second.

"Oh, you are funny, Mr. Walton."

"Do you think so, Mrs. Briggs?"

"Aye, but nicely funny. You know what I mean? No offense?"

"You couldn't offend me, Mrs. Briggs. You know something,
Mrs. Briggs?" He stopped and swayed gently like a tree above
her as he said solemnly, "I like you. I think you are a very nice
person, Mrs. Briggs."

"Eeh! Mr. Walton, thanks. An' I like you an' all. An' do you
know what I think you are?"

"No. Tell me, Mrs. Briggs."

The clouds were still scudding across the moon, sending dark
patterns over their faces. She seemed to be floating before him,
just a little off the ground, and her voice came to him softly,
saying, "Well, I think you are a gentleman, Mr. Walton."

The clouds obliterated the moon and he couldn't see her face.
He put out his hand and found her arm, and felt the warmth
coming through the paper of the fish and chips.

When the moon showed her face again it was no longer smiling, nor was his when he answered, "You are a very nice woman,
Mrs. Briggs. You're very kind, and . . . and you are the very
first person who has called me a gentleman. I shall not forget it,
tight as I am." He dropped his chin onto his chest. "And I know

I'm tight, but I shall not forget it, Mrs. Briggs. You know what I'll do? I'll write a poem about you. Yes, I will."

"Oh! Mr. Walton."

"Yes, I will. The very next time I'm on fire duty I'll write a poem to you. I . . . I wrote one tonight. I . . . I wrote it 'cos I'm inadequate. Yes, yes, I'm inadequate. An' not only in one way, for I cannot write real poetry. Poetry, you know, Mrs. Briggs, is not just rhymes. Oh, no. That's where people, ignorant people, make the mistake; they call rhymes poetry." He was flapping his finger at her face now, which he could just see faintly, and he went on, "Real poetry is made up of metrical com . . . composition, you know, and so many, many more things. Oh, yes."

"Really, Mr. Walton?"

"Oh, yes, Mrs. Briggs. Real poetry, real poetry is composed of prosody an' stanza, an' feet. Now, a foot, let me explain, Mrs. Briggs, is what they c-call . . . a metrical unit. Aw, Mrs. Briggs, there's a lot more in p-poetry than da-de-da, you know; for example, Mrs. Briggs, you know that little piece that goes:

"Tiger, tiger burning bright
In the forests of the night.

Well, did you know that this is a very, very good piece of poetry? It's composed of tetrameters. You know what a tetrameter is, Mrs. Briggs? Of course you don't, Mrs. Briggs, so don't be ashamed, Mrs. Briggs, 'cos so few people know about tetrameters. . . . Well now, pay heed." He laid one hand on her shoulder. "It's the lifting and falling of the voice like, you know, the inflection—short and long, or long and short: Ti-ger. Get it? Long-short. Ti-ger, ti-ger bur-ning, long-short, bright, . . . Oh, Mrs. Briggs, I'm boring you to death." His face was now close to hers; the smell of his whisky-laden breath was mixing with the fumes of the fish and chips, and she laughed gently and said, "No, Mr. Walton, I love listenin' to you. Mind you, I . . . I've got to confess I don't understand about it, but I like listenin' to it."

He straightened up and began to walk along the street again, and after a moment he said solemnly, "You are very, very kind, Mrs. Briggs," and to this she answered, "Not at all, Mr. Walton."

They were in darkness again when she said, "Eeh! you can't see a speck."

He stopped and stood swaying and looked up toward the sky, crying, "Come out! come out, you mad orb!" and when the moon came from behind the clouds she burst out laughing and held on to his arm, saying, "Oh! Mr. Walton. Oh! Mr. Walton, that was funny."

"Ah, Mrs. Briggs, when I'm in me cups I can command the heavens. I'm a god when I'm in me cups." He stopped again, and, gazing at her in the bright moonlight, he said solemnly, "When I'm in me cups I forget about everything: people, war, children, everything; except one thing, Mrs. Briggs; one thing I never forget, an' that is I want to write poetry, real poetry, you know. Not that I want to use great . . . long, bewildering stanzas, no Rubaiyat of Omar with its decasyllabic rhyming. No, I don't want to do anything in a big way. I just want to write poetry that the ordinary man or woman c-can understand. Would—would you like to hear what I wrote tonight, Mrs. Briggs?"

"Yes, Mr. Walton. Oh, yes, I would."

"Well then, you shall."

He drew from his pocket a piece of paper; then, looking up at the sky again, he cried, "Keep shining," before he unfolded the paper, and in deep and sonorous tones read:

> "From areas of longing
> That fill my life with strife
> To stretch my intellect
> To those I read,
> And express my thought
> In high flowing screed
> That would bewilder all,
> In turn, as I am
> By minds

That burn
To impress,
Thus transgressing
The art to convey,
I pray you,
God of words,
Keep me simple
For this day.

"There! Mrs. Briggs."

"Oh, Mr. Walton, that was luvly."

"But it wasn't po-poetry, Mrs. Briggs."

"No, be-buggered! you're right there, mate, it wasn't." The
two men passing, one an air-raid warden, laughed uproariously
and Jimmy, looking after them, shouted, "I abhor the unhal-
lowed mob and hold it aloof!"

"Good for you, chum," they called back.

"Never mind, Mr. Walton. It sounded poetry to me." Her
voice was consoling. "They're ignorant."

"No, no, Mrs. Briggs." He was shaking his head widely from
side to side now. "They're right; it's not even rhyme. Blank
verse is the only name you could give it, but that's what the
books say there isn't any of. And you know what there isn't any
of? Poetic prose; they say there isn't such a thing as poetic
prose. . . . Your fish and chips will be getting cold, Mrs. Briggs."

"I can always warm them up, Mr. Walton. But you know
something? I was lucky to get them. It's the first time Pearson's
been open this week. Mr. Fielding tipped me off. I didn't know
they were open and there was only ten afore me. I was lucky."

It was as if they both had decided they'd had enough culture
for one night.

"Yes, you were lucky, Mrs. Briggs. You know, I think you're
very lucky in all ways, Mrs. Briggs."

"What makes you say that, Mr. Walton?"

"Oh"—he was swaying and when he tripped off the curb she
put out her hand quickly and drew him on to the pavement
again, and he said, "Because the gods that be made you kind."

His voice faded away into a whisper as he finished; his head drooped onto his chest again, and as they turned into Haven Terrace the moon was obliterated by the clouds and they were shoulder to shoulder as they groped their way up the street. And when they opened the door and stepped into the dim, blue-painted-bulb-lit lobby he made a dramatic gesture in placing his fingers on his lips and whispered, "Good night, Mrs. Briggs, it's been a ple-pleasure"; and she whispered back at him, "And for me an' all, Mr. Walton." Then he was tiptoeing to the door.

The door opened straight into the passageway, and there at the far end stood his mother and Betty, and they were both staring at him as if with one pair of eyes.

"What did I tell you?" Betty was looking at Alice, and Alice, coming slowly up to him, glared at him as she said, "You're in a nice pickle, a picture you are. A schoolteacher, and look at you! To think I'd see the day."

"To think you'd see the day, Ma." He shook his head sadly at her.

"Aw! what have I done to be made to suffer this an' all?" She turned her head and looked at Betty. "One after the other of them, and now this, a sot!" She glared back at her son. "'Cos that's all you are; that's all you are a sot, a drunken sot. . . . An' where'd you get the money from?"

"Yes, Ma; that's all I am, a drunken sot. . . . An' where do I get the money from? Why, Betty, Betty. Betty's kind, Betty is."

As he turned to go into the sitting room Betty cried after him, "We've been waiting for you to take your mother home"; then, "Come on, Mam," she said. "By! I'll have something to say to him in the morning."

When the door banged he sat down and stared through the open sitting-room door into the passage. They had gone, the two women that were one; funny, he'd never be able to get over that mystery. Of all the people in the world that he could have chosen, or could have chosen him, he had to pick on Betty, Betty who was his mother, and his mother who was Betty. As he stared toward the far door he seemed to see through it and across the hall, into the house opposite, where Mrs. Briggs lived, and he had the greatest desire to get up and go to her. But then there was Mr. Briggs, and Mr. Briggs was big, very big.

He stood up now and said aloud, "Mr. Briggs is very big. Remember that, Jimmy; Mr. Briggs is very big."

2

It was Saturday, a week before Christmas. The queues outside the outdoor beer shops were as long as those outside the butcher's—longer. Everybody was trying to stock up for Christmas and, of course, for what was much more important, the New Year.

It was half-past one and Jimmy had managed a couple of whiskies and two pints, and he was feeling very mellow as he went upstairs to Mary's.

"Hello there."

"Oh, hello, Jimmy. Fancy seeing you at this time! We've just finished dinner but there's plenty left. Like some?"

"Like some? Fancy asking me such a silly question. Why do you think I came? Where are the nippers? I'm going to take them down to the market; who knows what we might pick up?"

"I'm afraid you're out of luck, Jimmy." Mary had left the sink, where she had been washing up, and was piling a plate with cold meat, cheese and pickled onions. "David's down in the Flake shop—as usual"—she dipped her chin—"and across there" —she pointed out of the kitchen and toward a far door—"the other one's in bed; she's got a cold on her, and I'm afraid she'll be stuck with it over the holidays."

"Aw, that's too bad." He went out of the kitchen, pushed the bedroom door open and, thrusting his head around it, said, "Who's got sniffles and sneezes, coughs and wheezes?"

"Oh! Uncle Jimmy."

He stood over the bed with his hands on his knees and looked down on the flushed face of Annie. "You feeling bad, love?"

"Awful, Uncle."

"Aw, rotten luck. I was going to take you to the market."

"Were you, Uncle Jimmy?" She smiled wanly, sniffed, then said slyly, "I'm all stuffed up but I can still smell you've been drinkin'."

"What!" In mock indignation he stretched his six feet three high above her. "That's libel, that is. Me drinking! I've never touched a drop in me life." He turned to Mary, who was standing in the doorway. "Do you hear what your daughter is accusing me of? She says she can smell I've been drinking. What are you going to do with her?"

"Give her a prize for telling the truth."

"Tell us a story, Uncle Jimmy." Annie moved restlessly in the bed, and Mary put in quickly, "He's going to have a bite of dinner, and you get to sleep, Miss."

"Aw, Uncle Jimmy, give us a rhyme then. Go on."

A rhyme. Jimmy walked round the foot of the bed clapping his hands gently together, saying, "A rhyme, a rhyme, give her a rhyme. Ah, yes." He stood with one arm outstretched. "I know one about your favorite subject—and mine. Drink. It goes like this:

> "Annie stood outside the Ellison Arms
> And watched the men go in.
> They all walked straight and spoke to her
> And they asked her where she'd bin.
>
> "She waited behind Haggerty's wall
> And she watched them all come out.
> They all wanted to talk at once
> And began to lark about;
> And their legs began to wobble
> And some went in-and-out.

"Then Annie began to wave her arms,
Kick up her legs and shout:
I take after me Uncle Jimmy
And I've had a bottle of stout."

Annie was lying now, her hands covering her mouth, shaking with laughter while Mary, smiling primly, pushed Jimmy from the room saying, "Go on with you!"

When he was seated at the table she looked at him and said, "She was right—you stink of it."

"I don't." He flapped his hands at her. "I've only had one. No"—his head went back on his shoulders—"I'm not going to be like most drunks and lie about it. I've had a couple of straights and two pints."

Mary's eyebrows moved up just the slightest. "Is that all?"

"That's all."

"Well, it doesn't take much to knock you over, that's all I can say. And I've said it before."

"I know that, Mary, dear, but just let me get this down and it'll soak up the liquor and I'll be ready for more." He only just prevented himself from pointing to his coat lying over the chair, and in the inside pocket of which was a quarter bottle of whisky that he was going to keep for Christmas—if he could.

Mary poured herself out a cup of tea and sat down opposite him and said quietly, "I'm worried, Jimmy."

"Ah, now! Now!" He wagged the fork at her. "Don't, don't. I don't want you on me conscience an' all. Well, what I mean is, I don't want to have it on my mind I'm adding to your lot. Your . . . your plate's full enough as it is."

"Well then, keep that in mind and go steady. By the way, we've got Cousin Annie coming across to stay; she's been bombed out."

"No!"

"Yes, it happened yesterday in that early-morning raid."

"I heard they got it across the water but that there wasn't much."

"No, only one bomb. It didn't, of course, hit her place, but it's taken the roof off."

"Do you mind her coming?"

"No, not really; she's a fusspot but she's good at heart."

"Where are you going to put her?"

"Oh, we'll find some place. A shakedown in the front room until Ben gets that cubbyhole of his cleared out. He's going to take all the stuff down to the Rington Road shop, and then I'll fix it up for her—that's if she's still here. They'll likely get round to doing her place afore long."

"You're going to have your work cut out."

"Oh, no. No, she shouldn't be any trouble; in fact, she'll be a help." She smiled wryly but more to herself than at him. She could do without Cousin Annie's help because a little of her went a long way.

After a silence between them he said, "What's the news, did you hear it?"

"Oh, yes, nothing much. Talking about the Pacific; it seems to be full of aircraft carriers."

"Well, I wish they'd do something soon and get those Japs out of the way."

"They took Tarawa."

"That all? Nothing else?"

"I didn't hear, but then I was going back and forward."

Jimmy got up and walked to the window and stood looking through the border of blackout paper that surrounded it and started to sing quietly "I'm dreaming of a white Christmas."

"And that's what we don't want, thank you very much."

He turned to her abruptly. "It would have been different if they had taken me."

"Well, they didn't. And don't start and go through all that again."

"Well, I still can't understand it. Flat feet!"

"Well, you are flat-footed, and that's that. Anyway, somebody has to stay behind and see to the children; your job is just as important as if you were over there."

"Aw." He turned his head slowly to one side and his voice held utter scorn. "Who you kiddin', Mary? You're talking to me, Jimmy. I'll tell you something"—he was pointing at her—"I feel like crawling when I'm standing at the bar next to any of them in uniform. Half my size and years younger, and in uniform, and they look at you and say, 'Deferred, mate?' And how they say it!"

"Don't be so bloomin' soft." Her voice held real anger now. "And use your head. If it weren't for you and the men in the docks and the women in the factories, they wouldn't be in uniform. What your trouble is, you're too thin-skinned. Go on, get yourself out. Take a walk into Shields, to the market as you intended. The air will do you good, get rid of the fumes and clear that stupid mind of yours. And, by the way, if you see anything fresh going—in the market I mean—get it for me, no matter what it is."

He turned to her, saying, "You're kiddin', aren't you, with your own private black market running here?"

"Oh, our Jimmy! it isn't a black market." She was indignant but she was smiling. "If we exchange a little butter and sugar for a little meat, or some such, what harm's in that? We have our coupons like everybody else."

"Aw, Mary!" He pushed her in the shoulder, and she pushed him back the same way and they both laughed. Then she said, "Well, you be thankful anyway, you get your share of it."

"I am, and thank you very much, Mrs. Tollett."

"Go on." She pushed him toward the door, then, pulling him to a stop, said, "Go steady, Jimmy, please."

"I will, Mrs. Tollett, God bless you, Mrs. Tollett. God bless you." He kept touching his hat, and she lifted her foot but missed in her aim and nearly fell over. He ran down the stairs and, at the bottom, stopped and looked back up at her. They were both laughing.

In the street he hummed again the Bing Crosby song "I'm Dreaming of a White Christmas." There was snow in the air; the air itself was like a knife on the throat. The sky was low and the atmosphere a pale gray haze, and all the way into Shields, in one way or another, everyone seemed to be endorsing the title of the song.

"By! it's enough to cut you in two."

"It won't be long now, you can smell it."

"Bet the place is thick by the morrow . . . as if we hadn't enough to put up with."

"One blessing: it'll stop the bloody raids."

He got off the bus at Laygate and made his way down the mill dam bank toward the market; at St. Hilda's Church a bedraggled figure was shaking a box in front of the passersby while he cried, "Help to get bits for the poor bairns." He thrust the box in front of Jimmy. "It's for the bairns, sir." As Jimmy, a wry smile on his face, went to put his hand in his pocket a passerby laughed and said, "You must be barmy, man; it's more like beer for his belly." Whereupon the benevolent old man came out with a mouthful of abuse that both startled and amused Jimmy. He put his hand back in his pocket and walked on.

Would you believe it! They got up to all kinds of tricks, and a war on. What a pity, what a pity that people cheated, especially at Christmas. It was a time of goodwill, Christmas, even with a war on. That's what they said they were fighting for, wasn't it, goodwill to all men? Mind your eye, not that he believed in the religious reason for all the Christmas waffle; the whole thing was a colossal fable, but nevertheless it was a nice fable. It was the kind of fable that you could do with more of, and if people weren't nice to each other at Christmas, then they'd never be nice to each other. . . . Would Betty be nice to him? Would his ma be nice to him? Would he be nice to her and say, "Come on, Ma, it's Christmas, come and live with us"? He should practice what he preached, shouldn't he?

There were very few stalls in the market, but the place seemed thronged with people coming from King Street and from the direction of the ferry, or making their way back and forth across the square. And there was a deal of traffic about, military stuff, most of it. Yet it added to that feeling of excitement that was about. Yes, it was a good fable, Christmas.

He stopped. The Salvation Army had started to play. Good old Salvation Army. You couldn't beat the Salvation Army. No going to church for them in their best clothes; and no hiding their talents in the ground either. They did good, did the Salvation Army. "Away in a manger." He started to hum to himself:

"Away in a manger,
No place for his head. . . ."

Suddenly he felt cold and shivery, and very much alone. He wished the bairns could have come with him; they would have kept him laughing.

He went down East Street, looked about him to see if the coast was clear, whipped the bottle out of his pocket and, putting it to his mouth, drank half of it.

He shuddered as he felt it burning down his long length. That was better. Oh yes, that was better. He'd walk round the market and over toward the Salvation Army; then he'd make his way home. He'd walk back to Jarrow. As Mary said, it would clear his head. He laughed to himself; it would need more clearing now than ever.

When he drew near the Salvation Army he found a crowd gathered in front of them. It was a mixture, two or three soldiers, a few airmen, some sailors tight as drums—they were lucky, they got a navy ration as well—some young lads and lasses, a few A.T.S., and families with children.

He came to a stop near two girls in khaki uniforms. They were singing and they glanced at him as much as to say, "Well, it's Christmas." He smiled back at them, and as he inclined his head down to them he picked up the words: "The Little Lord Jesus laid down his poor head." His voice caused the girls to stop singing for a moment and laugh, and their laughter turned into giggles when, high above the rest, his voice soared, "The stars in the bright sky looked down where he lay." They were still laughing when they joined their voices to his, and when he put his arm through that of the girl nearer to him and interrupted his singing to nod toward the other, at the same time putting in quickly, "Link up," the girl, choking with her laughter, did as he bade her and linked her arm with that of her companion.

The band hardly paused before going into "The First Noel." The crowd had now grown to almost twice its size by people stopping in their walk across the market, and most of them had joined in the singing.

From the advantage of his height Jimmy looked over the crowd and for a moment he felt a power running through him. It was as if he had created this scene; he felt that he had brought all these people together—goodwill to men. In this moment he experienced a feeling of joy. He was so warm and happy inside, he wanted to express it in some gesture, such as waving his arms about.

The winter twilight was deepening. Although it was a heavy gray twilight, the faces all about him seemed to him to be illuminated from within. . . . And then there came the first flakes of snow.

To the cries of "Oh!" and "Aw!" and "Here it comes!" the faces were upturned toward the falling flakes.

The band played louder; they knew that they had the crowd with them. Two of their members were smilingly pushing themselves through the throng, shaking tambourines while waiting for hands to be withdrawn from bags and pockets. The response was better than they'd had all day; they put it down to the love of God.

Now the band was playing "I wish you a Merry Christmas, I wish you a Merry Christmas, I wish you a Merry Christmas and a Happy New Year." The girl in khaki turned her face up to Jimmy and sang it to him, and Jimmy, bending his head down to her, still with his arm in hers, sang it back to her; and then everyone around seemed to be singing it to his neighbor. It was one of those moments which can happen in wartime and at no other.

Whether it was the girl who started it or he, he never remembered, but he did remember that when they pushed him forward as their leader, he was gratified that this was so. The girl grabbed his waist from behind, then her friend did the same with her, and from then on a chain formed as fast as a piece of gasoline-soaked rope burns.

Everyone was singing. What matter if, at the head of the crocodile, it was "I Wish You a Happy Christmas," while further along it was "Away in a Manger," and further still, "Knees up Mother Brown" with the tail end, "We'll Meet Again"?

When Jimmy led the way behind the band in a sort of rumba step dictated by the pressure of the girl's hands on his hips, one of the Salvation Army men laughed at him and cried, "Are you happy, brother?" And he shouted back, "Yes, indeed; I'm happy, brother." And the girls behind took it up and yelled, "Are you happy, brother? We've got them on the run. Are you happy, brother? We've got them on the run. Germany, here we come! Are you happy, brother?"

He came to the road leading down to the ferry, and his reaction was to stop at the curb, but the girls behind pushed him on, yelling now, "Stop for nothing, brother! Stop for nothing, brother! Look out, Adolf, we're on the way!"

As he went to cross the road there was a shrieking of brakes when a lorry pulled up sharply, and two soldiers sitting in the cab grinned down on them and shook their heads.

When he led them across the end of the road leading down from the mill dam bank into the market there was another shrieking of brakes, this time from a line of vehicles making their way out of the market and toward the bank and toward home, but the chain behind him suddenly disintegrated into a crowd which surrounded him and the policemen, and the two A.T.S. girls shouted, for no reason that he could see, "Leave him alone! Leave him alone! What harm is he doing? We were only having a bit of fun. Little enough we get. It's Christmas Eve. Perhaps you've forgotten, it's Christmas Eve."

"Break it up! Break it up! Get going!" The policemen began pushing. One of them pushed at Jimmy with the flat of his hand so hard that he staggered and would have fallen but for the support from behind, and this angered him.

He was brave with the warmth of the whisky inside him. There was no need for this kind of thing. "Now look," he said. "What d'you mean?"

The policeman had no time to tell him what he meant, for he was trying to prevent his helmet from being knocked off; but he was just a fraction too late and when he bent to retrieve it someone placed a boot on his buttocks and sent him sprawling.

It was amazing how quickly the crowd divided to let the policeman fall. Now the other policeman was laying about him, and as if they had been conjured up out of the snow-filled air, there appeared more policemen, six of them.

When two of them gripped Jimmy by the arms and pushed him through the crowd, which parted almost docilely, he struggled as he cried, "Look! you've made a mistake. Let go of me, man, do you hear? I've done nothing, an' you don't know who I am."

"There's plenty of time to tell us, mate."

As they dragged him along Barrington Street toward the police station the two girls followed, shouting, "He was just singing carols, that's all, he was just singing carols. You must be short of a job." And one policeman turned and called back, "If you don't get away this minute, I'll have another JOB of taking you in an' all."

When they bundled him into the police station the joy and gladness that had so lately filled him was replaced by a deep fear: he was being locked up like his da. God in heaven! He was being locked up. He tried to explain to the policeman, using his most persuasive manner, "Look, sir, I was only singing carols."

"All in good time," said the policeman from behind the counter. "You'll have plenty of time to explain."

That was all they could say: he would have plenty of time to explain. What were they going to do with him? No, no, surely not; they couldn't be going to put him in a cell. Why, he had only been singing carols and leading a crocodile. After all, it was Christmas Eve.

When he was taken to another room he said as much to an officer who sat behind a desk writing things down, and when the policeman who was standing to his side began speaking he gaped at him, for he was saying, "Drunk and disorderly. Holding up traffic and obstructing the police in the course of their duty."

He cried at him, "I did no such thing! I never obstructed you; you pushed me and I never raised my hand to you. As for be-being drunk, you'll have to prove that; that's libel."

The policeman by his side was now looking toward Jimmy's coat pocket, and the one at the desk, following the look, said, "Would you mind removing your overcoat, sir?"

"I don't see why. What's that got to . . ."

"Would you mind, sir?"

His head bowed, he took off his overcoat, and the policeman, taking it from him, folded it inside out as if careful not to crease it, and in doing so exposed the upper half of the flat bottle of whisky reposing there.

Of a sudden Jimmy knew he was going to be sick. He put his hand over his mouth and immediately he was led along a corridor and into a washroom.

It was dark when the shop door opened and the blackout curtain was pushed aside and the blonde woman came hurrying in and said to the girl behind the counter, "Mrs. Tollett, can I see Mrs. Tollett?"

"I suppose so." Teresa went through the storeroom, picked up a broom and, directing the handle ceilingwards, knocked three times, then yelled, "Mrs. Tollett! Somebody to see you."

When Mary came into the shop and saw the woman she instinctively recognized her; she was Jimmy's Doo-lally-tap, and her mouth fell into a small gape as she looked across the counter and said, "Yes?"

Lally, her expression greatly troubled, as if she were about to burst into tears, said, "Can . . . can I have a word with you?" Then she glanced at the curious eyes of the customers directed toward her, and Mary said, "Yes, yes, come through."

She did not stop in the storeroom but led the way out into the backyard and up the stairs. In the sitting room, she said, "Sit down, Mrs. . . ."

"Briggs. Mrs. Briggs."

"Oh, yes, Mrs. Briggs."

They stared at each other until Mary said, "Are you in trouble?"

Lally gulped, hitched her bust up with her forearm, and muttered, "No, no, not me; it's . . . it's Mr. Walton."

"Jimmy?"

"Aha. You see. . . . I . . . I'll sit down if you don't mind."

"Yes, yes, of course." Mary pushed a chair forward toward the fire. "Would you like a cup of tea?"

"I wouldn't mind. Ta. But I think . . . I think you'd better listen first. You see, I've been down to Shields. Albert's auntie lives there. She's old an' on her own an' I drop in when I'm down there, you know. I was coming back 'cos I wanted to get back afore it was blackout, you know?"

She nodded her head toward Mary, and Mary said, "Yes, yes, I see." She was becoming conscious of saying, "Yes. Yes."

"Well, it started to snow just as I got on the bus at the bottom of King Street. And then, when we got into the market place we got stuck, like. I'd never seen such a crowd in me life, never, honest." She shook her head. "Eeh! it was. Well, as a man said to me, it was like as if the war was over, you know?" She laughed here, and then, as if apologizing, she looked at Mary for a moment with a straight face and went on, "Well, as I was sayin', the noise was terrible. There were people hootin' motor horns, singing an' yelling an' dancing, everybody was going round in a chain holding on to each other. I'd never seen anything like it, honest."

When she stopped and smiled Mary wanted to say, "For God's sake, get on with it, woman."

"Well, there I was sittin' and I looked out of the window and I saw Mr. Walton." Her voice dropped, and her face fell into straightness again. "He . . . he was talkin' to the police. And then there was a scuffle and he nearly fell and . . . and then I saw them takin' him away."

"JIMMY! Our Jimmy?"

Mary now had one hand covering her cheek and Lally said, "I got off the bus, but I couldn't get through the crowd. When I did he was gone; they'd taken him to the station. And there were two lasses there—they seemed to know all about it. They were A.T.S. and they said they had just been singin' carols with the Salvation Army band, that's all. Everybody had been happy and singin' carols, and he had started a sort of crocodile dance round the market. It was like one big happy party, they said. And then the police had come and they'd got nasty."

"Oh, my God!" Mary's head was bowed deeply on her chest, and then Lally said, "I thought I'd better come and tell you. You see, his wife—well, she don't talk to me much. An' I heard he comes to you a lot 'cos he's fond of you, like . . . an' it was on me way. I hope you don't mind. . . ."

"No, no, I'm glad you did, and thank you very much. It's very good of you."

"It's a shame, he's so nice, is Mr. Walton. He would do nobody no harm, nobody. I've never known a man like him, not so polite in his manner and such."

"No, he would do nobody no harm," Mary repeated, and then added, "Only to himself."

They looked at each other; and then Lally said very thoughtfully, "Aye, well, that's life, isn't it?"

As Mary looked back at the big, rather blowsy blonde figure, she thought, What makes them think she's daft? But Jimmy, their Jimmy. Oh, my God! The police station. She never wanted to see the inside of a police station again as long as she lived, but she'd have to go down. Ben would get him out on bail. But

Betty, and her ma, my God! This would give them a handle on him. Quickly she said to Lally, "I wonder if you would do something for me, Mrs. Briggs?"

"Anything, anything I can, Mrs. Tollett, an' pleased, yes."

"Well, would you not tell his wife, or anybody, until I get him home and then he can do the telling himself?"

"Oh, I won't say a word, Mrs. Tollett. No, not a word. Anyway, as I said, I didn't want to go to his wife 'cos she's no room for me. Not that I've done anything to her. No, I won't say a word."

"Thank you. I'll get you a cup of tea."

"No, no"—Lally had stood up—"you'll want to get on. It's only five minutes' walk home. Thanks all the same."

"I'm grateful to you, very grateful." Mary gave her a small unmirthful smile as they faced each other and added, "I've heard about you from Jimmy."

"You have!" The big pale face lighted up, and as the blue eyes sparkled with warmth Mary could see what attracted their Jimmy—the girl, or woman that she was, looked so kindly.

"He always speaks very well of you."

"Does he? Well, fancy! But then, I couldn't imagine him speaking bad of anybody. I'm not just saying it 'cos he's your brother, Mrs. Tollett, but I think he's a gentleman, I do, an' I don't care who hears me say it."

Mary stared into the big placid face for a moment, then said, "It's very kind of you to say so. Well, thanks again. I'll get ready now. I'll . . . I'll have to get me husband to go down with me. I'll see you out."

She saw Lally to the back door, where she shook her hand and again thanked her; then she flew back into the house and into the dining room to Cousin Annie, who was enjoying her tea, as she did all her meals, and she said quickly, "I've got to go and see Ben; give an eye to her, will you?" She nodded toward the wall.

"What's your rush? Who was that came in—Mrs. McArthur?

What you going off like the devil in a gale of wind to see Ben for? He'll be along shortly."

She was going out of the door as she said, "I'll tell you all about it when I get back." She went into her room, grabbed up her coat and hat and put them on as she ran down the stairs; then she was stumbling through the dark streets toward Flake Street and Ben.

Jimmy in prison. He'd be thinking of their da all the time. Oh, the fool! the fool! But in a way it wasn't unexpected, for she had been waiting for something like this. And this was only the beginning. Yes, the way he was going, this was only the beginning. But singing carols in Shields Market to the Salvation Army band!

3

"What's he been up to?" Alice looked at Betty. "Everybody's been sniggering around the doors for days. And then just this morning, her across the road, the Cooper piece, shouts to me, 'Goodwill to men. By! your Jimmy's a lad.' What's he been up to?"

"How should I know? Goodwill to men? What was she meaning?"

"That's what I'm askin' you, lass."

Betty looked around the living room at the three-piece suite, at the shining modern sideboard, at her glass-fronted china cabinet; then she brought her eyes to rest on her hands where they were making steam marks on the lacquer polish of her extending table, and she looked at Alice and said, "You know, when you come to think of it, he's been funny, quiet"—she nodded—"more quiet than usual, because you can't get a word out of him."

They studied each other; then Alice said bitterly, "Well, whatever he's been at, I bet our Mary's put him up to it. He'd never have the gumption to do anything on his own. He's me own son and God forgive me for saying it, and I never thought I would, but he's gutless. He takes after him, he's gutless."

"Goodwill to men." Betty was nodding to herself now. "Yes, he has been funny since afore Christmas. He looked pasty-like as if he was in for the flu or something."

"Where's he gone?"

"I don't know. He went out first thing this morning dressed up."

"Dressed up?"

"Ssh! Here he comes."

They listened to the door being opened; they listened to him pausing in the hall as he took off his coat; then he was in the room facing them. Alice spoke first. "What's all this about?" she asked quietly.

"All what about?"

"That's what I'm askin' you. Why should somebody shout across the street to me, 'Goodwill to men. By! your Jimmy, he's a lad'? What've you been up to?"

"Oh, that!" He looked from one to the other with raised brows now, then said quietly, "Oh, you'll know soon enough."

"Know what soon enough?" They were both on their feet, but it was Betty who asked the question.

"Get the evening paper. It'll be in there."

"What are you talking about?"

He looked at Betty. "About me being summonsed for causing a disturbance; it'll all be in the paper."

"WH-AT!" they both breathed the word out together.

"Yes; I thought I'd let it come as a surprise. Anyway, if I'd told you when it happened, you might have worried, being concerned for me."

"Jimmy Walton, what have you done?" Alice moved a threatening step toward him, and he said, "It's no use me telling you, Ma. I'd only spoil it. Reporters do it better. Why don't you slip along to our Mary's, Ma? The papers'll be in the shop. It'll save you a long trail into Ellison Street, and Mary will give the whole details; she bailed me out last week. Or, I tell you what." He turned to Betty. "Slip over the passage and ask Mrs. Briggs. She's a kind woman, is Mrs. Briggs. She was in court this morning."

He was getting pleasure out of this bit of tormenting. He hadn't often the chance to get any pleasure out of either of them, but when Betty's hand reached out suddenly and grabbed the knife from a tray of cutlery and crockery that she had just washed up, he said, a grimness in his tone now, "I wouldn't if I were you, Betty, because once you've been in court, it's funny, you lose your fear of it. You don't mind going back."

On this he turned from them both, walked into the passage, put on his coat and went out of the house again, leaving them gaping at each other. But only for a minute.

Alice sat down as if her legs were weak; but there was no weakness in her voice as she said quickly, "Go on. Go on, get the paper."

Betty did not need to be told twice. Within minutes she was out in the dark, groping her way toward the newspaper shop. In the dim light of the shop, she scanned the headlines; then she doubled the paper up and scurried as quickly as the black-out allowed back to the house.

She went straight into the room, slapped the paper on the table and started flicking the pages, with Alice standing by her side now. They went right through it but couldn't find what they were looking for.

More slowly they started at the beginning again, and there it was, in the corner, at the bottom of a page,

SCHOOLTEACHER FINED FOR CAUSING
A DISTURBANCE IN THE MARKETPLACE

In the Shields Magistrates Court today James Arthur Walton, of 25 Haydon Terrace, Jarrow, was fined five pounds and bound over for twelve months to keep the peace. James Walton had pleaded not guilty to knocking a policeman's helmet off and tripping him up, but guilty to

creating a disturbance by leading a number of people in singing and dancing around the marketplace, thus causing the traffic to be brought to a
halt. Private Rene Willsden and Corporal Millicent Bailey spoke in his
defense, saying it had started innocently with them all singing carols together.

Police Constable Tatting, in giving evidence, said that the accused had
been drinking heavily and a quarter bottle of whisky was found on his
person when he was taken into custody.

They sat down weakly. They were stunned, utterly stunned.
Then Betty began to cry, and her voice and manner took on the
girlish role that had once been habitual with her. "The disgrace! the disgrace! I'll never be able to show my face at work
again. I would have known about it if I had been in this week;
if I hadn't had this cold, I would have known about it. And he
said that her, that overflowing bleached, blowsy . . . she was
there in the court. Oh, Mam!"

Alice wasn't crying; her eyes were as dry as her voice when
she said, "Something's got to be done, and something drastic.
You can't manage him. I've got to say it, Betty: you can't manage him. He needs a firm hand; he's his father all over again. I
can see it in him every day. Oh"—she closed her eyes as she
dropped her head back on her shoulders—"why was I cursed
with him! With a man like him, and then an ungrateful pair—
what have I done to be served so!" Then bringing her head
forward with a snap she leaned toward Betty. "Well, there's one
thing you can do for a start: you can put your foot down with
that one across the passage."

Betty dried her eyes and nodded emphatically back at Alice,
saying, "An' I will. By God, I will."

The headmaster said to Jimmy: "This is not quite the thing
we expect from our masters, Mr. Walton," and Jimmy replied,
"No, sir, I'm aware of that."

"There'll be questions from the board, you know that, don't
you?"

"Yes, sir."

"Apart from your own reputation, it gives the school a bad name and leaves a bad impression on the boys."

As for the common room—well, the common room was divided, some for and some against him. But not so the school. For a couple of days Lanky Walton's prestige almost equaled that of the honored dead of the Battle of Britain and those men of the Tyne who had died a hero's death in convoys.

But, like all such episodes, the one in the marketplace would have died a natural death, remembered only as the day Lanky Walton led the Salvation Army. And if it hadn't been for Albert Briggs throwing a party, it would have. But before the second incident recalled the first vividly to mind again something happened that left an indelible mark on Jimmy and almost broke Mary's heart.

It was early in the New Year and things had been quiet for a number of nights. Although the air-raid siren had gone twice within the past week, each time it had proved to be a false alarm. On this particular night the siren moaned out its warning at quarter-past seven. Jimmy had just come on duty in the back room of the Nonconformist Chapel. Ned Pritchard turned from the table, on which there were two telephones and a rough switchboard, and said, "Here we go, Jimmy!" and Jimmy, who had been about to take off his overcoat, replied, "Well, it's about time; I've been wondering where they've been."

Ned Pritchard turned from the table and called to the man who was going out of the door, saying, "Bill! Tell Arthur Pilby to stick around Bolton Street end, will you? That bloody lot around there won't go in the shelters. But then, some of them would be hard put to get in, with the stuff they've got stuck inside. But tell him to keep his weather eye open."

"Will do."

"And you, Jimmy, you'd better stick around here until we know where they're leaving their visiting cards."

It wasn't long before they heard where the visiting cards were being left, and as the dull thud reverberated through the hall Ned Pritchard said, "By! they've been quick. They must have slipped through. Where are the bloody antiaircraft lot? Asleep?"

As they listened it was evident that the bloody antiaircraft lot weren't asleep. The pop-pop-popping was continuous. There was another dull thud, nearer this time. Ned Pritchard got up from his seat and, putting on his steel helmet, said, "They're getting cheeky." Jimmy answered, "Yes, they want their faces slapped," and they both looked at each other and grinned.

The next thud wasn't so dull, and they threw themselves flat on the floor and rolled underneath the steel table as the building shook and the plaster came splattering down from the ceiling. When they raised their heads Ned Pritchard peered at Jimmy and remarked, "The bugger does want his face slappin'."

"I'd better get out," said Jimmy quickly, "and see what's happening."

"Aye," said Ned; "somebody will have been unlucky with that one."

Outside Jimmy called to dim figures who were running up the street: "Where was it?"

"Felton Street, I think," someone called back to him.

And it was Felton Street, or what had been Felton Street. The flames were illuminating the sky. Three children were pressed against a wall that was still standing; they were crying, but their crying was muted as if they were dreaming; men were putting their shoulders to jammed doors while flames burst from the windows above them; there were voices shouting, giving orders; there was the rattle of fire engines coming down from the other end of the road.

Jimmy shooed the children from the wall, then began tearing at a tangled mass of splintered timbers and bricks out of which a hand was sticking upwards as if in salutation. Two other men came and worked alongside him, and when they got the woman out she was quite dead. She was wearing a pink pinafore, and gripped in one hand was a women's weekly magazine. The man next to Jimmy, who was dry-eyed but had tears in his voice, said, "They won't go into the bloody shelters; they think it's over."

Jimmy said hoarsely, "The shelters!" When they scrambled over the smoking ruins there were already men unearthing the blocked entrance to the shelters, and as he feverishly began to help, one of them said, "They've got Wearside Row. They say it's flat."

Jimmy stopped in the act of lifting the frame of a door from the rubble and, grabbing the man by the arm, said, "Wearside Row? You're sure?"

"Aye. Well, the warden's just said."

His grannie and granda were in Wearside Row; they had moved there not two months ago when their house in Bingley Street was shattered. Wearside Row! Oh, my God, no!

He turned from the men and scrambled across the rubble and ran in and out of the fire hoses and the ordered chaos now filling the roadway, round corners, down back lanes and through alleyways until he came to Wearside Row, or where Wearside Row had been.

The eight little houses were now as flat as a toppled pack of cards, except for the end one. That still had some walls remaining, and inside it a fire was blazing; it looked like a magic lantern. He stood with one hand on top of his tin hat and the other across his mouth until a man passing him said harshly, "Don't stand gaping there, lad; get a move on."

Gulping, he clutched at the man. "Everybody out?"

"What do you mean, everybody out? If you mean dead out, aye, it hit the center. The bloody bastards! God! I wish one would come down on a parachute, just one. Christ! Oh aye, just one. You know somebody here?" His voice had dropped.

Jimmy shook off the faintness that was overwhelming him. "Num-number s-seven. Me grannie and granda."

The man looked toward the smoking rubble and the men tearing at it. Number 7 had been one from this end. He now turned and said, "Come on, lad, we'll see."

It took them two hours before they saw, and then the sight made him vomit. He turned his back and staggered across the road and leaned against the standing wall and retched his heart out.

It was near ten o'clock when, with dragging steps, he made his way to Cornice Street. He didn't know whether or not Mary had been informed, but he'd have to go to her.

He heard her before he saw her. The deep, heart-wringing moans came to him as he lifted one weary step after the other up the stairs. When he opened the door he saw her sitting on the couch with Annie by her side. She was rocking the child backwards and forwards as she cried, with that dreadful moaning sound. Opposite her, Cousin Annie was sitting with her arms folded tight about herself; tears were running down her cheeks. Teresa was standing at the table pouring out cups of tea; tears were streaming down her face, too; and Mrs. Mc-Arthur, her face awash, was standing at the head of the couch, saying, "You must get hold of yourself, lass, you must get hold of yourself."

When he entered the room they all turned and looked at him. He went slowly up to Mary and lowered himself beside her and said, "You know?"

She made one deep nod with her head, then moaned, "Oh! Jimmy, Jimmy. He was such a good man. There'll never be another like him, never. . . . And David. David and he loved the shop. . . . Both of them. Oh, my God! Why? Why? Why, Jimmy?"

When his mouth fell into a deep gape and he put his hand across it and slowly turned his head away from her, she came to herself for a moment. "What is it? Where've you been? What is it, I ask you? You're all muck."

He was going to be sick again. As he rushed from the room she followed him, pushing Annie's clinging hands away from her.

In the kitchen she grabbed his arm as he bent over the sink, "What is it? Who? Who else?"

He didn't answer—he couldn't; he kept vomiting. He didn't know where it was all coming from. When at last he straightened up and wiped his mouth, he looked at her and his head wagged several times before he could bring the words out: "Gran and Granda."

"No!" She backed from him. "NO!" Her voice was high, bordering on a scream, thrusting off the knowledge. "No! Four of them! The . . . the only good ones, four of them. NO, JIMMY! NO!" She was tearing at her hair when she rushed past him, and he ran after her and caught her in his arms and held her tightly to him, and they rocked back and forward as if they were grappling in battle.

4

They could bury Ben and David whole, for, strangely, there'd been hardly a scratch on them. It had been the blast that had done it; it had blown through the shop taking the young manager, three customers, Ben and David with it. Two of the customers had survived and were in hospital.

There were a lot of burials going on in the cemetery; a great number of people were about, black-clothed, stooped people, all with heads down, looking toward the earth.

They buried Mary and Peter Walton in a mass grave with the remnants of fourteen other people. They buried Ben and his son together, the smaller coffin on top, and as Mary watched them go she thought she would go mad; she couldn't bear this. "Ben, Ben, come back." The words kept whirling in her mind: "Ben, Ben, come back." She knew it was silly, stupid, childish to keep on, for Ben would never come back, nor David. She had loved David as if he were her own. He had looked upon her as a mother; he had called her "Mam"; he had never, not once, asked after his own mother; and he had looked like Ben. David had promised to be good-looking, handsome.

Ben had been handsome; even with the scar disfiguring one side of him he had been handsome. In the darkness of the night when he would hold her close and whisper, "I love you, Mary. There's not a cell in me body that doesn't love you, adore you. To me you're the most beautiful thing in the world. Do you know that?" she had thought, "And you are beautiful an' all, Ben. Right through you are beautiful." But she didn't tell him, not in words she didn't. Ben liked to talk in the dark. During the day his affection might have taken the form of a slap on the buttocks, the sudden holding of her face in his hands and looking deep into her eyes, but in the night his loving had been something that a woman dreams of. She knew she was lucky. If only she hadn't felt responsible for his face, and responsible for her da going to jail, she would have been happier than any woman in the land.

And now he was gone. She had said to him, "What do you want to go out in this for? It's enough to cut you in two. David can make his own way home. He's out often enough in the blackout." And he had replied, "I want to see how things are going." She had laughed at him and said, "Aw, you!"

"And the same to you, Mrs. Tollett," he had said, then had gone out smiling, and she had never seen him smile again.

It was over. They were walking up the path, Jimmy supporting her, young Annie and Cousin Annie behind them, and Cousin Annie's crying was audible. It sounded as if she were drunk.

She didn't know what she would have done without Jimmy

these past few days; he had turned up trumps, acted and talked strong. He had always looked older than his years but never sounded it.

At the intersection of the paths a man walked across them, and they had to step out of his way, for he was walking with his head down, as were they. When she looked up she recognized him: Hughie Amesden. He was changed. He was taller and broader, and still good-looking, but in a different way to what he had been as a young lad. He was crying. They stared at each other through their tears and she said gently, brokenly, "You an' all?" and he bowed his head again and said, "Me daughter; she was seven." He turned and looked a little way back along the path from which he had come to an elderly man and woman walking one on each side of a younger woman, supporting her. "Me wife," he said; and then he gulped before ending, "Our only one."

He walked straight across her path and she and Jimmy walked ahead.

Life was funny. NO, NOT FUNNY! The denial screamed in her head. She'd never use that word again when thinking of life. Life was not funny in any way. And she had it to live and she did not know how she was going to manage it. There was Annie to see to and . . . and her da. Yes, her da.

As if her thoughts had conjured Alec, she saw him standing half-hiding behind the corner of the church wall. As she caught sight of him he drew back, and she looked at Jimmy and said brokenly, "Me da, round the corner. Go and bring him."

And Jimmy brought him.

Alec, at forty-six, appeared like a man of sixty. He had a bewildered look in the back of his eyes. He sat in the motor opposite Mary and Jimmy and he didn't raise his head or speak. When the car put them down outside the shop he made to walk away, but blindly Mary groped for his hand and led him round the corner, through the yard and up the stairs and so into her house for the first time.

What she wanted to do more than anything was to go into the bedroom, throw herself on to the bed and moan out her pain; but there would be time enough for that during the long nights ahead. She tried to make herself remember that she wasn't the only one who had suffered loss; her da had lost an' all; at one go he had lost his mother and father, and through their going he had lost his support.

From the couch where he sat looking about him in a kind of amazement his eyes came to rest on her and he said quietly, "I hadn't . . . I hadn't left the house ten minutes, Mary. If only I'd stayed behind, if only I had, that's all I'm sorry for. If only I'd stayed behind."

"Don't be silly! Don't talk so." Her voice was sharp.

Mrs. McArthur came into the room and said, "The tea's ready, lass," and they all went into the dining room and sat round the table, Cousin Annie, her own Annie, Jimmy, and her da. And as she looked at them, one after the other, even at her own daughter, who was gulping on her tea whilst she cried, she wished them all far away. She had lost the only one who mattered, really mattered; she had lost the only one who held her to this place. There came into her mind a very odd thought for a moment such as this, for she was saying to herself: If the war were over now, I would sell everything and travel, yes, I would. I've always wanted to travel. Ben's made sure that I've got enough to keep me in comfort for the rest of me life. I would travel, that's what I'd do, and damn everybody.

Her thought was snapped off as Jimmy said, "Drink your tea." She drank her tea, and they all came into focus again, and she knew that they all needed her as she had needed Ben. But this didn't stop her from wanting to throw them off, for the weight of them was piling the years on her, and she knew the reason. Ben had always treated her as a young girl; even now she was twenty-seven, he had still maintained the vision of her as she had been at sixteen; and Ben was gone, her support was gone; she had to shoulder them alone.

5

"Do you hear that?"

"Wh-what!"

"That racket next door, or are you deaf?"

"No, I'm not deaf, but, but I was asleep, and if you went to sleep you wouldn't hear it either."

"How can anyone sleep in that! Where's the police, I'd like to know?"

"Police?"

Jimmy turned over, raised himself, then, leaning his elbows on his knees, supported his head in his hands while he said slowly, "They're having a party. You can't have a quiet party—you're allowed to make a bit of noise at a party."

"Put your knees down! Might as well not have any bedclothes on at all. Haven't you any consideration for anybody but yourself? . . . Party, you say! It's been going on for hours. Do you know what time it is? It's twenty-five minutes to four. Party! I've never closed me eyes. Do something."

"What"—he turned on her—"what can I do?"

"You can get up and tell them to stop it."

"Me go over there and tell them to stop it?"

"That's what I said. If you were any kind of a man, you would have been over hours since when they first started."

It was a fortnight since the mass burials at the cemetery and she'd been quiet since then, even civil to him, so much so that he had come to think that if it weren't for his mother, they might have a chance.

He had never liked his mother, but after she had stood in his kitchen the day after the bombs had dropped and had looked at him and said, "God's slow, but He's sure; when He pays back

He doesn't use small coin; she's got her deserts at last," there had risen in him a hate of her. He had almost sprung on her; something in him had leaped at her and taken her by the throat and choked her; he had felt the blood draining from his face as he stared at her, and then he had said, "I hope God forgives you, but He'll have His work cut out." Then he had left her and he hadn't spoken to her since. He passed her in the house here as if she didn't exist; when she talked at him, tried to rouse him, he ignored her. He felt it was better to ignore her, for he mightn't be responsible for what he might do or say if he once opened his mouth.

He had drunk very little since Christmas, a few pints, that was all; he had determined to try to give it up, especially the hard stuff, for he knew he couldn't carry it and still be himself. No man could really, but he could carry less than most.

"What you sitting there for like that, as if you were miles away? Get up, go to the door and shout. . . . Listen to them. They're going mad. It's a wonder Barney Skelton hasn't been down. Oh, I forgot, he'll be one of them. And the Pinchers from next door on that side, and the Wilsons on this side. Go on!" She gave him a dig in the back that almost pushed him out of the bed, and he turned on her, his temper flaring up as it was apt to do at times, and shouted, "Don't you do that! You'll do it once too often."

Slowly he got out of the bed, pulled on a thin dressing gown and his slippers and went out into the hallway. The noise of the singing and yelling echoed through the house; then with startling suddenness the door opposite him was pulled open and the sound came at him like a wave.

In the doorway stood Albert Briggs, his arms round a woman; they were both singing at the top of their voices. Behind him came two other men and another woman, and there were more people behind them again.

"Ho! who've we here, eh?" Albert Briggs loosened his hold on the woman and waved his hands above his head, crying now,

"Look! It's Mis-ter Walton. Mis-ter Walton's come to join the party. Have you come to join the party, Mis-ter Walton?"

Albert Briggs lifted his seventeen stone toward Jimmy. He had no coat on and his shirt sleeves were rolled up showing arms knotted with corded muscle. Albert was a docker and proud of it, and proud of his strength, and with one big hand he now gripped Jimmy's shoulder.

Although they were of similar height, Jimmy was like a reed compared with Albert Briggs, and Briggs could also give Jimmy ten years. Briggs actually shook him when, stressing the appellation "mis-ter," "Mis-ter Walton," he said, "Mis-ter Walton 'as come to honor us with his presence. You know somethin', folks?" He turned to the rest of the company who were now crowding into the hall, their faces silly with laughter. "Mis-ter Walton is a gen-el-man, he is. Lally says he's a gen-el-man 'cos Mis-ter Walton can write poetry. What do you think of that?" He ended this by giving Jimmy a half-playful punch in the stomach.

Gasping for his breath, Jimmy stepped out of Briggs's way and forced himself to say, "Now, look here, enough's enough. It's nearly four in the morning; I think it's about time you gave up, don't you?"

"Listen! Mis-ter Walton is speakin'. Bill, ya bugger, come here a minute." He motioned to a man at the back of him, and when the man came forward Briggs said to him, "This is MIS-TER Walton, the gen-el-man."

"Albert, Albert, stop it!" It was Lally's voice shouting now. "Do you hear me, our Albert? Stop it! and come on in." But Albert took no notice of his wife but went on addressing his companion. "What'll we do with Mis-ter Walton, what, Bill, eh? What'll we do with him, eh? Look. Look." He grabbed at Jimmy's pajama legs. "He wears ja-mas! Mis-ter Walton, the gen-el-man, wears ja-mas! Aw, Bill, fancy a man havin' to wear ja-mas, eh? Ja-mas only get in the way, don't they, lad?" There was uproarious laughter before Briggs ended, "Wonder would they fit me?"

Jimmy looked apprehensively around the laughing, beer-

blotched faces, then toward his own door. But Briggs was between him and the door.

When Briggs's hands came out and clutched him around the
waist he fought back with both feet and hands, but Briggs had
the grip of a gorilla, and he was being assisted by three of the
other men. Laughing like maniacs, they got him on to the floor,
where he was helpless against their hands, and they pulled off
his pajama trousers while Lally screamed above the din, "Stop
it! the lot of you. You dirty, rotten lot of swine, stop it!"

"Shut her up, somebody! Shut her up!" It was Briggs shouting, and one of the men got hold of Lally and pushed her,
struggling, back into her room, and none too gently; then, banging the door, he held on to the knob.

"Wha' about the trashcan, eh, wha' about the trashcan?"

There was a chorus: "Aye, aye! that's an idea. Come on,
heave-oh!" And with this, four of the men hoisted Jimmy up,
covered now only in his pajama top, while he bawled at them,
"Stop it, you mad lot! Let me down! Do y'hear? Do y'hear?
Briggs! Briggs! You'll pay for this, Briggs!"

"Yell ya bloody head off, chum. Come on, out the back way.
Mind the bloody blackout. Can's in the backyard."

Briggs was yelling instructions, and it was Barney Skelton
who emptied the trashcan. Then while Jimmy still fought them
they doubled him up like a wire clothes peg and rammed him,
buttocks first, into the bin, and of a sudden he was quiet.

"Open the yard door. Go on, open the yard door, you silly
bugger. We can't roll him in here—not enough room. An' shush
your hush. We don't wanna bring the bloody wardens on us."

Reeling now and with suppressed, almost insane laughter,
they carried the can into the back lane, remarking as they went,
"His legs are like two matchsticks."

"He's got no flesh on his arse, just bones. Over you go!"

They tipped the trashcan across the narrow gutter that ran
down the middle of the lane and began to roll it. But it had
revolved only about three times when Lally came tumbling out
and stood square in its path. She had a flashlight in her hand

and she flashed it over them, crying, "Stop it, you dirty buggers! Stop it. I've got a poker here, and I'll brain the first one that comes near him. I'm tellin' you." Then opening her mouth wide, she yelled, "Polis! Polis!"

Showering oaths on her while they still laughed, they scrambled back through the yard door, Briggs among them, and when it had clashed shut she stooped down, and, putting the flashlight on the cobbles of the lane, she gently eased him from the bin, muttering all the time, "Oh my God! Mister Walton. Oh, I'm sorry! Oh I am, I am that."

Even out of the bin, Jimmy was unable to get to his feet; he was bruised from head to foot. It is true to say that if they had rolled him the length of the back lane he would have been dead before he reached the end of it, for his nose was scraped and bleeding, the skin was off one cheek bone, and, what was worse, at this moment he felt that his body would never straighten out again.

He had never been one to go in for sports, being too lanky, but he had often done a few exercises such as touching his toes and skipping. But to be bent like this! He thought they had broken his back.

Oh God, God! The humiliation of it. He was cold, both inside and out, icy cold. It seemed to have encased his heart. What was happening to him? Why were things happening to him like this?

"Come on, try to stand, and get inside; you'll die out here in this cold." She took his arm.

When he stood up he was embarrassingly aware of his nakedness but thankful to God that it was dark. She mustn't turn the flashlight on him.

Like a child walking over a pebbly beach, he stumbled over the cobbles toward the back door. She had one arm around him now to support him, and when her other hand tried to open the door and it didn't move she cried loudly, "Open the door, you dirty buggers! Open the door!" But there was no answer to her calling.

"Come on. Come on," she now said quickly. "We'll get in the front way. Your wife will let you in. Even if they've closed the door, she'll . . . she'll open it."

Hobbling still, and his teeth now rattling like castanets, he stumbled toward the end of the lane, and round the corner, and his feet had just touched the smooth ice-coldness of the pavement when the light flashed over them.

"Well! an' what do you think you're up to? What's THIS?"

The light showed the constable a man, naked except for a pajama jacket, and a woman in a skin-tight dress with a low neck, a blonde.

"What do you think you're up to?"

"It's all right, con . . . constable. The . . . the back door was locked—we couldn't get it." Lally was gabbling.

"How did you get out?" He was addressing Jimmy now. "You've forgotten something, haven't you? What's your name?"

"I tell you it's all right, constable." Lally's voice was high, and there was a note of fear in it.

"I'm speaking to him. What's your name?"

Jimmy couldn't answer for a moment because of his chattering teeth, and then he said, "Look, they were having a prac . . . practical joke."

"A practical joke! What kind of a practical joke? A naked man and a woman in the street at this time of the morning! Where's the practical jokers? I can't see any." He swept the light from one side of the road to the other. "What's your name?"

Oh! dear God. Oh! dear, dear God. There was a voice crying from the depths of him, as if in prayer, for help out of this situation. He stammered again: "It's . . . all a mis . . . mistake . . . con . . . constable, they. . . ."

"Stop waffling. What's your name?"

"Wal . . . Walton."

"Where do you live?"

"Sev . . . seventeen Haydon . . . this street."

"Well, we'll go to number seventeen."

The door into the hall was open but the doors on each side were closed. Jimmy went to turn the knob of his door and found it locked and he shook it vigorously, angrily. And now he yelled on a stammer: "Be-Betty! Betty! Op-open the door, Betty."

"I . . . I live across there." Lally was pointing now.

"Oh, yes!" said the policeman.

"Yes!" She barked back at him now, then went and tried the door. But this, too, was locked; and now she was yelling. "You, Albert! you, Albert! you rotten swine you! open the door." But still there was no sound, not even a drunken giggle. Then she turned and looked at the policeman in a sort of mute desperation.

Suddenly Jimmy's door was opened and there stood Betty in a dressing gown, and when she saw her husband trying vainly to hide his nakedness she gave a girlish gasp as if she had never seen him bare before, and she cried plaintively, "Oh! Oh!"

"You know this man, Missis?"

"Know this man!" She turned her head to the side as Jimmy pushed past her and went into the house.

"Can you account for his being in the street naked at this hour of the morning?"

"No, I can't." She glared across the dim hall toward Lally. "Nor can I account for her being with him."

So that's how it was. "May I come in a minute, Missis?"

Betty's head rolled from one side to the other, but before she could speak Jimmy was back at the door buttoning up a pair of trousers, and he barked, "No, you can't come in for a minute. Whatever details you want you can have here. My name's Jimmy Walton; you know my address; you know how you found me, so make what you like out of that. Get inside!" He turned and thrust Betty into the room; then, with the door in his hand, he pointed to his bleeding nose and cheek, and his scraped feet and said, "I've been having fun, look. I was stripped and put in a trashcan and rolled down the back lane. Put that down in your little book. You won't believe it, but put it down because that's my story." And at this he banged the door in the policeman's face, and the policeman turned to the blonde woman standing leaning against her door as if she were half-drunk, and said, "And what have you got to say to all this?" And her defiant answer was, "Just what he said, word for word."

6

It caused a great laugh; after the horror of the bombing such an incident was welcome. The poor fellow was unlucky; it said so in the papers. He wasn't accident prone, he was just dirty-trick prone. This was the same man, it was said, who had been brought up and bound over for leading half the populace of Shields in a dance round the market square to the strains of the Salvation Army band just before Christmas. Now the poor fellow, through no fault of his own, gets caught naked in the street. He had got up at half-past three in the morning to quieten a party that was going on in the flat opposite and the revelers had taken him out, stripped him, put him in a trashcan and rolled him down the back lane. Now that kind of trick could be done on a young lad, but when you do it on a six-foot-three man there's bits of him bound to protrude, and Mr. Walton's protrusions had become very sore points for days—the reporter had a great sense of humor.

Although the incident was very funny, the reporter went on to say it might have been less funny for Mr. Walton, who it must be remembered was bound over to keep the peace for twelve months, if it hadn't been for Mr. Barney Skelton, who had come forward and said that he had been at the party and had taken part in the practical joke. They were all a bit tight and it had just been done for a bit of fun; nobody had anything against Mr. Walton. Mr. Skelton had pressed that Mr. Walton was a decent chap; he was sorry for what had happened, and, yes, it was true they had locked the back door and locked Mrs. Briggs out of her front door as well.

The magistrate had commented that he considered the members of the party had a warped sense of humor, and he thought it was a pity that the old rule "an eye for an eye" did not still obtain. He wondered how Mr. Skelton and his friends would like to be put naked in trashcans and rolled down a cobbled back lane at four o'clock on a winter's morning. And did Mr. Skelton and his friends realize that there was still a war on, and did they, the magistrate had asked pointedly, stay away from work the following day because they had thick heads? It was a great pity, he considered, that the men concerned weren't in the armed forces; men were dying at the present moment for people like them.

When Barney Skelton had come out of the court room he had said to anyone who had a mind to listen, "That's what you get for doing the right thing; I was the only bloody fool who came forward."

The headmaster could do little about this. He did not send for Jimmy, but Jimmy was aware it was another black mark against him. The effect of the practical joke on him had been much worse than the business of the marketplace. He had come out of that affair with some dignity—at least he hadn't been aware of the entire loss of it—but now he felt stripped, a butt, a fool. He knew if he had any gumption he'd pack and leave. But where would he go? There wasn't a place in England where he could go these days and not be traced through either his identity card or ration book. Oh yes, if it was the last thing she did she would trace him and make him keep her. The only solace he had was Mary. No, that wasn't true; there was one other that could be of solace to him, great solace. But he couldn't go to her; as much as he wanted he couldn't go to her. Funny how you got to like people, and from liking to loving them; the most unusual people, people who weren't your type, so others would say.

When he went along to Mary's he said airily, "Well, seen

the papers?" and for answer she said, "Oh, Jimmy! Poor Jimmy!"

"Aye, poor Jimmy."

She stared at him lovingly and said quietly, "You know, when the war's over you want to get yourself away from here; you want to go far away."

"Not a bad idea," he said.

She looked out of the kitchen window onto the rooftops opposite, where the slates were of different shades, showing the patchwork after blast damage, and she muttered, "That's what I want to do, get miles and miles away." She turned her tear-washed eyes on him and said, "Your da's in the front room. Go and have a word with him."

"How is he?"

"Oh, just the same. He's like a child, you know, so grateful for what you do, it hurts. Remember when he used to take me to the allotment when I was small? It was like having little holidays to escape to the allotment, and it's odd, but in a way I feel I'm back in those days, except that . . . that now I'm him. You know what I mean? I'm taking him by the hand now."

"He'll likely pull himself together now he's with you."

"That remains to be seen."

"Are you keeping him for good?"

"What can I do? Where can he go?"

"Aye. Yes, that's the question, where can he go? It's going to be hard on you."

"I don't mind."

She said she didn't mind, and three parts of her didn't, but then there was that vital quarter that protested. She could see herself going right down the years burdened with one after the other of them. But she wouldn't mind the burden; she wouldn't mind anything if only she had Ben back. . . . Oh, if only she had Ben back. She was so lonely, lost, empty.

Jimmy said to her now, "I know how me da feels, as never before I know how he feels, because, like him, I've been stripped of dignity. I remember when I was about thirteen seeming to see him for the first time. He was standing at the corner with a bunch of other men and I thought, he's hump-backed, gray, skinny, and I felt ashamed of him. But just for a moment, for then I realized that all the others were stooped, gray and skinny, and they all had their hands in their pockets. I started to look at the men after that. There were groups at every corner and they all looked alike and they all lacked one thing. I couldn't put a name to it then, but it was dignity. That's what they lacked, dignity. Some of them have regained it, since the war gave them work, but not me da. And so I know how he feels."

"Don't talk so, Jimmy. Look, pull yourself together, face up to it. You were the victim of a joke; nobody's going to think the worse of you for that."

"No, no," he said; "they won't think the worse of me, they'll only see me with me pants off; particularly five hundred pairs of young eyes in the school hall looking at Lanky Walton with his pants off." He turned from her and went into the sitting room.

She looked out of the window again and startled herself when she whispered, "I will! I will! As soon as the war's over I'll get away, just Annie and me. I'll put me da in a nice little house, and Cousin Annie with him. They could look after each other for a time. And I'll travel, and perhaps I'll see some part of the country I'd like to settle in, some place softer, less harsh, where I wouldn't have to look out on rooftops."

The door opened and Cousin Annie came in. She was limping more than usual and she flopped onto a chair, saying, "Oh, me leg's playing me up. They said I'd have to have the hip joint seen to, and it'll likely come to that in the end. I would have had it done ages ago only I was afraid it would stop me walking altogether. But I've got to face up to that, I suppose. Are you making a cup of tea, lass?"

"Yes," said Mary. "Yes, I'm making a cup of tea."

"And I'll have a scone and butter," said Cousin Annie.

"We'll have marge today," said Mary.

If an unexploded bomb had dropped in the kitchen, Cousin

Annie couldn't have looked more startled. "Why?" she demanded, her small body bristling.

"Because, Annie, it's about time we did."

"Time we did?" queried Cousin Annie. "But you're not short of butter?"

"No, but we should be. We should just get our rations like everybody else."

"Oh!" Cousin Annie wagged her head. "It's going to be like that now, is it?"

"Yes, Annie, it's going to be like that."

Mary hadn't known when she would make the stand about the rations, but ever since her particular bomb had dropped, she had, as it were, become conscious that there was a war on. It was 1944 and she hadn't really felt that war up till now. It had laid waste various parts of the town but had caused them nothing but inconvenience, such as blackouts and working late at night with coupons. It had, on the other hand, made them quite a bit of money even with the restrictions on foodstuffs; as for their table, it had been no different from what it had been in 1939.

Her new moral outlook was going to make her very unpopular, she knew that. Mr. Gregson would cut down her meat. Well, let him. And then there were the clothing coupons. Well, she could do without those. They would say she was turning into a holy Joe. They'd just have to say that.

It wasn't only the day or yesterday that she had been vitally aware that there was too much fiddling going on, but she hadn't been able to do much about it because they were doing their share of it. Now, however, she felt forced to take a stand. She couldn't really explain why except that in a minute way it would help to get back at those who had killed the four people dearest to her.

Cousin Annie was hobbling from the room as she said, "It's going to be a poor lookout for the lot of us if you're going to turn sanctimonious. I would have thought you could have put your mind to better ends."

She mashed the tea and ignored the remark, then went down the stairs, across the yard and into the shop, and there, calling Teresa into the storeroom, she said, "I've made a cup of tea. Go up and get it; I'll see to things. And by the way, Teresa, in future just weigh up Mr. Gregson his rations. That also includes the Richardsons, the Browns and the Connellys; if they want any explanations, tell them that's your orders and to come to me."

Teresa screwed up her eyes and looked at Mrs. Tollett, but she didn't immediately say anything. She just thought her employer must be going a bit funny; the bombing business had turned her head. Then she muttered, "As you say, Mrs. Tollett, as you say."

Mary had been serving in the shop for about five minutes when the door opened and a tall man entered. She hadn't put the light on yet and the shop was dim with the blackout covering most of the windows, but she sensed he wasn't one of the regular customers. When he stopped further into the shop she saw it was Hughie Amesden.

It was ten years since she had last seen him in the shop. She had seen him once or twice during that time in the street with a girl, a pretty girl. She didn't know whether she was the one who had become his wife, because she had only caught a glimpse of her that day at the funeral.

He waited until the rest of the customers were served before he came to the counter. He did not ask for anything straightaway but looked at her and said, "How are you faring?"

"Oh, not too bad, Mr. Amesden. And how are you yourself?"

He jerked his head. "Putting up with it."

"How is your wife?"

"Oh, she's taken it pretty badly. She . . . we thought the world of her, Christine, you know."

As she put in, "Yes, yes, I know," she wanted to add, "But there's one solution for you and your wife, you can have others." But she didn't, because she knew that would be no solace at the moment.

They stared at each other over the counter, then she said, "It's getting dark," and moved from behind the counter to the window, where she pulled the middle blackout blinds down, drew the gray blanket curtain across the door, then switched on the light. All the while he watched her, until she lifted the hatch and went behind the counter again. Then, looking steadily at her, he said quietly, "I was very sorry to hear about your husband and son. I . . . I didn't know him, but I'd heard of him; he was highly respected."

"Yes, yes, he was."

"And . . . and I've popped in the day because . . . well, I've just heard you lost your grandmother and grandfather at the same time. That was a terrible blow."

"Thank you, it was kind of you. Yes, it was a terrible blow."

He smiled faintly at her. "I remember the old people. You used to go round there a lot. I used to see you when we walked round there, Paul Connelly and I. You may remember him?"

"Oh, yes; Paul Connelly."

"He went down with his ship last year."

"No!"

"Yes."

"Oh, I'm sorry."

"He was an only son an' all. It . . . it seems years since those days, doesn't it, the time when we used to meet on the streets?"

She stared at him, her eyes widening slightly. . . . The times they'd met on the streets, he said, yet he'd never opened his mouth to her; only once in all those years had he said, "Hello." She remembered the card from a silent admirer. She had it upstairs somewhere. Jimmy had brought it when he sneaked her few possessions out of the house. She wondered if it were he who had sent it. But no, no; it would have been Paul, Paul Connelly.

The shop bell rang and two children entered.

He said, "Well, I just wanted to say how sorry I was."

"Thank you, Mr. Amesden."

He continued to look at her and when she glanced back from

the children to him he said quietly, "I never thought I'd want to get back into the thick of it again. I was discharged last year." He tapped his chest. "A bit of shrapnel did its best to stop me breath." He smiled weakly. "But now, every hour of the day I crave to be back."

She nodded at him as she said, "I know how you feel. It's had the same effect on me, but . . . but in a different way."

"Well"—he moved a step from the counter—"I'll say good-bye."

"Bye-bye, Mr. Amesden."

When he had gone she stared at the door for a moment before saying to the children, "Yes, what can I get you, hinny?"

And as she served them she thought that he hadn't come to buy anything, he had come just to pay his respects. That was nice of him. And he had remembered ten years ago, ten years ago when they were young.

7

Life for Jimmy on the surface looked as if it had slipped back into the normal. The weeks passed and ran into months; spring came and went; the war would soon be over, victory was in sight; D-Day had taken place in June; everyone in the world who had access to the radio and the B.B.C. knew all about the beachhead at Arromanches. People still talked of Monte Casino, which had been taken in May, and it was prophesied that the war would be over by Christmas—that is, Hitler's war. There were, of course, still the Japs. Things were going marvelously— Jerry was on the run; men were still dying in their hundreds— but things were going marvelously.

Jimmy taught as well as ever; at least he thought he did. His temper was apt to flare up a little more often, but that was the only difference he noticed in himself, in his relationship with his pupils, that and the fact that he didn't joke with them now, except on rare occasions.

Then something happened that altered the view he had of his whole future and brought a glow to him; the glow was dim and distant, but it was there nevertheless.

Albert Briggs died; he was killed. He was working on the deck of a ship when the chain slipped from a loading crane. It wrapped round his body like a snake and he was dead when they picked him up.

Jimmy commiserated with Mrs. Briggs but did not go to the funeral, although he could have, since it took place on a Saturday morning. Mrs. Briggs became the talk of the street, and of his own home, because she had gone to her husband's funeral in her ordinary clothes, without even a black band around the arm of her gray coat.

Indecent! Betty said. It was thoroughly indecent. But then she was bats. She had certainly earned her name of Doo-lally-tap, if anybody had. Everybody knew clothes were hard to come by, but she could have worn a black band, couldn't she?

"Perhaps," Jimmy put in quietly, "she's not a hypocrite."

"Of course you would stick up for her." Betty came back at him, and he looked at her and replied quietly, "Of course."

He had seen Lally only three or four times since the night of the trashcan episode until Briggs's death. The first time he met her he had thanked her for coming to the court and she had said, "Well, it was as little as I could do, Mr. Walton." Twice he had walked home with her in the blackout. But on each occasion he had been sober and so had not read poetry, or tried to explain its mysteries, to her.

But following Briggs's death he made a point of going to a certain public house near High Street where he had seen her the last time they had met. On Tuesday and Friday nights, when he would stroll casually in, there, seated in the corner of the saloon, would be Mrs. Briggs, and he would say, "Oh, hello there, Mrs. Briggs," as if he were surprised to see her. And she would reply, "Oh, hello, Mr. Walton. How are you?" Then he would say, "Do you mind if I sit down?" and she would answer, "No, of course not, Mr. Walton. Not at all."

The polite addressing of each other became laughable; until last Tuesday night he had said to her, "You know it's daft, this 'Mr. Walton' and 'Mrs. Briggs.' I'm going to call you Lally."

"Oh!" She had laughed and blushed like a girl as she replied, "That's nice of you, Mister Wal—" And then they had laughed together.

"What's your real name?"

"Jessie. I used to be Jessie Falconer; it was Albert who gave me the nickname of Lally. I didn't like it at first because 'Doo-lally-tap' means . . . you know." She tapped her temple with her finger. "I'm not very bright, but on the other hand I'm bright enough to know that I'm not what it means, am I?"

He looked at her sadly for a moment, and he hated Briggs as he conjured him up in his mind. Yet the man might have said it in a joke when she had done something silly: "Aw! you're Doo-lally-tap." But he had kept it up, and others had picked it up, and it had stuck.

"Not that I mind really," she said.

"I'll call you Jessie," he said.

"No, no, call me Lally. I like Lally—it's soft-soundin'." She flapped her hand out to him. "The things I say. I condemn me-self, don't I? That's what they say: the prisoner condemned himself out of his own mouth."

He didn't answer but he gazed at her, into her blue eyes, her kind blue eyes. Her big blonde face looked washed out, pale. "How old are you, Lally?" he asked.

"Twenty-five, going on twenty-six, but . . . but I know I look older." She smiled pathetically. "I've just got to look in the glass an' I know I look older. . . . It's the misses you see, miscar-riages," she explained to him in a whisper, and he nodded at her as he thought: And Briggs's fist to help things along.

"Funny about names, you know. I bet you don't believe me"—
she was leaning toward him across the little table—"but I don't
know yours, honest, honest, I don't."

"You don't?"

"No. No, not your first name. Sometimes I've listened to try
and catch it, well, you know when . . . when your wife's"—she
lowered her head and shook it from side to side, then she raised
it and, looking at him, finished quietly, "We all go on at times,
but I could never catch it."

His own face was soft as he gazed back at her. She had listened
trying to catch his name while Betty was going for him.

"It's Jimmy."

"Jim-my! JIMMY! No."

"Yes. What's wrong with 'Jimmy'?" He drew himself up in
mock indignation.

"Well!" Her full bust wobbled as she tossed herself from side
to side. "Jimmy! Aw now"—she put out her hand, her face
serious—"no offense meant, but Jimmy! Anybody could be called
Jimmy. Jimmy . . . well, it's ordinary."

"I'm ordinary."

"No, no, Mr. . . . ." She laughed again, then went on softly,
"No, you're not ordinary."

They were gazing at each other silently when the barman
came in and asked for their order.

After a while he said, "What are you going to do now?"

"Oh, just carry on. I'm goin' back to me job. The doctor says
I shouldn't for a few weeks—I've got debility—but I get fed up
in the house. The days are long, and you can't keep cleanin' all
the time, can you?"

"Don't mind me asking," he said, "but how are you off?"

"Oh, I'm all right." She looked at him without speaking for
a moment. "It's nice of you to ask. But shortly I'll be better off
than ever I've been in me life. They're going to give me com-
pensation for Albert. And then"—her chin flopped onto her
chest and her body shook with silent laughter before she raised
her head slowly and looked at him from under her eyelids—"I

can go daft again. I go daft when I have money, you know. I just want to go out and buy and buy. Not that you can buy much now; but it's like a craze, I just want to spend. I don't want to buy things for meself so much, you know, but I like buyin' presents, givin' things."

She was one big present. Just being herself, she was one big present. He wanted to stretch out his arm and pull her into him, feel the bigness, the softness, the warmness of her.

As they walked home through the blackout he kept a distance from her, not letting his arm touch hers.

When they entered the lobby Betty was at the door and at the sight of him she turned her back and marched into the house, and as he followed her he told her, "I met her at the corner of the street."

"You're a damned liar!"

"All right, I'm a damned liar."

"Do you know what you are?"

"What am I?" He began taking his clothes off.

"You're a bloody fool. People are talking, they're laughing. Mam says they're laughing about the schoolteacher being seen with a woman like her, Doo-lally-tap! But if you want my opinion there's not much to choose between you. There's a couple of you, both doo-lally-taps. But let me tell you, you're not going to show me up. I'm warnin' you now, if you don't stop seeing her, I'll . . ."

"Yes, Betty?" His voice was quiet, ordinary.

"Oh!" She gripped the rolling pin that was lying to the side of the draining board, and he said, still quietly, "I've warned you, Betty, never to throw anything; the repercussions might be surprising."

That was Thursday over a week earlier, and every night since, she had been at him, and he had seen neither hide nor hair of Lally. She hadn't been in the pub this Thursday, so he guessed she couldn't be well. He had nobody of whom he could inquire and so had been tempted to knock on the door and find out what was wrong with her. But on six of the seven nights when he arrived home from school he had found his mother already in the house. The bone of her contention and her main topic now, as it had been for months, was the fact that Alec and Mary were together. "Shame to waste two houses on them!" she said in one breath, and in another, "That bitch has just taken him in to spite me further."

His mind became like a battlefield, his principal enemies being Betty and his mother, but their reinforcements were many and came in the shape of the headmaster, who sent for him at least once a week about some petty misdemeanor; some members of the common room; and on the fringe of them, arrayed in all their young armor, the boys, nerve-racking, irritating, bloody, although he told himself he shouldn't hold anything against the kids. Except one or two, like Crockford. . . . And Crockford—that young swine!—had better look out, he was getting under his skin.

It was Friday afternoon again. The exercise for the afternoon had been an essay, the subject to be chosen from past School Certificate papers, or alternatively, a poem.

As he said "Well, Youlden, let's hear it, your epic," he thought to himself, Five-past three; just another hour.

Today, more than ever, each individual nerve in his body had a frayed end; each seemed to be rubbing against the skin, causing him to twitch. Twice when his neck jerked upwards out of his collar he had drawn the eyes of some of the boys toward him. Little Felton had looked at him with some concern, and Burrows had stared at him so long that he had indicated with a pointing finger that he continue with his work.

His head was fuzzy; he felt tired. He had been fire-watching till late, and then, when he got to bed, he hadn't closed his eyes until five o'clock in the morning. When the alarm went he couldn't believe he had to get up. He hated getting up in the morning, for the torment would start again.

He wished he could unburden himself, really unburden himself to Mary, tell her about Lally and how he felt, but he knew that he was afraid of the look he would see on her face, because at one time he had laughed about Lally; like everybody else, he had made game of her. And anyway, Mary had her hands full at present. She seemed changed since Ben had gone. Naturally she would be; but she was making life harder for herself. Cousin Annie had made a fuss since Mary's rethinking on the ration business. And then there was his da, gliding like a lost soul about the house, wanting to be helpful, yet only succeeding in being ineffectual in whatever he did.

"That's very good, Youlden, but you've put the cart before the horse. You've described the air raid, then you go on to tell us of the people's feelings in the shelter before the air raid in a series of flashbacks. That technique would work very well in a novel, but it only complicates matters in this short essay. It is out of place with this commonplace—and I'm not using that word literally—subject. This subject requires for its strength straightforward treatment. You see what I mean?"

"Yes, sir."

"Nevertheless, it's very good. You have got feeling into it. . . . You, Riley."

Crockford's eyes were tight on him; he had a number of papers on his desk which spoke of some erudite exposition. He was willing him to say, "And you, Crockford."

Riley said, "I wasn't able to, sir."

"Why?"

The boy hung his head for a moment, then muttered, "We've had . . . to . . ."

"All right, all right." He didn't want to drag Riley's domestic life into the cold scrutiny of the classroom; Riley's father was in the Navy and his mother considered her war work the supplying of the needs of any man in uniform, and so her moving was not caused by enemy action but through the moral actions of her neighbors.

He swung his gaze from Crockford to Felton.

"Felton!"

"Yes, sir."

Felton stood up, moved from one foot to the other, then said rather sheepishly, "I've done a poem, sir."

"You have?"

"Yes, sir."

There was a slight titter from one or two desks, and Jimmy said coolly, "We won't laugh yet—it may not have any humor in it. Go on, Felton."

Felton, the paper in his hand, looked at Jimmy and began to explain, "It was when I was in the bus, sir, going from . . ."

"Read your poem, Felton; it should tell us what you were doing."

"Yes, sir." The boy began hesitantly:

> "From Birtley to Prudhoe,
> Walking singly
> In twos,
> Or grouped,
> Dark-clothed,
> Capped;
> This Sunday morning
> Standing in sockets
> Of doors,
> With hands in pockets. . . ."

The boy glanced up nervously and Jimmy nodded at him, and he went on:

> "Why do the men
> Walk so?
> Stiff from shoulder to hip,
> No easy stride
> When forearm is locked
> To the side."

Again the boy glanced up; then, after wetting his lips, he went on with more confidence:

> "Was it as bairns,
> Their noses running cold,
> Blue, numb,

Their eyes gummed with rime,
Feet like long-dead flesh,
That caused their hands
To seek burial?

"All along the way
On this summer's day
Like manacled slaves they go,
Hands in pockets
Faces shewing no glow,
The men of the North."

There was silence in the class. Some of the boys had turned and looked at little Felton; then their eyes came back to Jimmy, waiting for his comment. When it didn't come immediately, Felton gulped and stammered, "It . . . it . . . it was just an ob-observation, sir, not real poetry."

"You have no need to make excuses for that, Felton. If that isn't poetry, then I have never heard poetry. Some clever people who might call themselves authorities would quibble and bamboozle you by saying it has no decasyllabic line, that it's not pentameter or tetrameter. They would dissect it until it was gutless. You used the word 'observation.' Poetry is observation, Felton, observation put in a crucible; and the essence that is drained from it is a something we can only describe as poetry. I myself strive to put into words my observation, but the resulting essence is, unfortunately, not poetry; but you, boy, have been given some essence; nurture it."

Little Felton's face was red with pleasure, his head wagged self-consciously once or twice, and then he sat down.

Somehow Jimmy was reminded in this moment of his grandfather. His granda had written poetry and he hadn't one piece to remember him by; the essence, and the result, which he had kept in two boot boxes had been blown to bits. Why hadn't he talked to him years ago about poetry? Well, taking his cue from his da, he hadn't thought much of it. There had been an excuse for his da, because he'd had no foundation on which to stand and judge, but he himself should have recognized something, that special something in his granda. And he had just before the end. One night he and the old man had got talking and the decades between them had melted away. For a brief moment they had recognized in each other the meaning of truth, and he had known that what he possessed had come from this dauntless man. He remembered vividly one line he had said, a profound thing: "Waste is the essence," he had said; "what we use today is the waste of yesterday. A simple lump of coal is the essence of rotting trees." He had known all about the process, as every schoolboy did, whereby coal came into being, but he had never thought to put it into poetic language. "Waste is the essence."

Crockford's eyes, like a magnet, were drawing his now. Crockford was like a thorn in his flesh. He had mentioned Crockford yesterday to Melton, who taught history. There was a Crockford in every class, Melton had said; in fact he had two of them. He had said at times he hoped the war would go on long enough so that his two would be called up, then blown up. He had laughed as he said it, although there was in him, as in himself with regard to Crockford, the germ of a desire that this could come about.

The classroom door opened and a boy came in. When he came to the desk Jimmy said, "Well?" and the boy said, "Can I get the file, sir, the form file for Mr. Smith?"

Jimmy looked at him. It wasn't only that he had to have a target to take his mind off Crockford for the moment; it was this business of grammar. How often had he rammed it home and to this very boy. He turned a cold eye on him, "What did you say?"

"Can I get the file, sir, for Mr. . . ."

"What did you say? Your name is Beechwood, isn't it?"

"Yes, sir." The boy was looking surly now.

"Well, what did you say, Beechwood?"

Beechwood glanced at the class. Most of the faces were bright, expectant; they were in for a bit of fun. They knew what Lanky Walton was after; they'd all had it. Beechwood should have been prepared.

"Say it again."

"Can I . . . have . . . the . . . ledger?"

"Say it again . . . again."

Light dawned on the boy and his chin jerked to the side as if he had just woken up out of sleep and he said, in a muted tone, "MAY I have the ledger for Mr. . . . ?" His voice trailed away.

"Yes, you may, Beechwood. Remember you are not asking yourself the question. Can I get the ledger? Of course you can get the ledger; you are capable of getting it, aren't you? But you are asking my permission to get the ledger: May I have the ledger? You follow me, Beechwood?"

"Yes, sir."

"Then take the ledger." He pointed to the other side of the desk. The boy took the ledger and as he went out the class made a quiet tittering, and Jimmy felt slightly ashamed of himself. This was the kind of thing for which he blamed Bennett, sarcasm. There was an excuse when you were putting it over in a lesson. . . . Now for Crockford.

The door opened again. It was the headmaster's boy.

"Sir, the head would like to see you if you have a minute."

"Very well, Ramsay. Burrows, you take over, and if any of these—GENTLEMEN act up, make a note of it. That goes for you, Milligan, especially."

"Yes, sir." Milligan grinned from the back seat, then added cheekily, "But you needn't worry, sir, I haven't got me gas mask case."

Jimmy stopped near the door and stared at Milligan, then went out. And he was tempted for a moment to look through the small glass panel in the door to see what Milligan might be up to. It would be easier to intimidate a regimental sergeant major than Milligan. Why did Milligan always carry that empty gas mask case? It couldn't be his original one—that must have been kicked to bits very early on. He smiled wryly to himself, then wondered what the headmaster wanted with him now.

When a few minutes later the headmaster handed him his

monthly check he thought, I must be in a bad way—he had forgotten it was payday.

He had reached his classroom again; his hand was going to the doorknob when, looking through the panel, he saw a figure standing behind his desk and facing the blackboard. It was Crockford. He was writing something on the board and Burrows was apparently remonstrating with him, because he kept flinging his arm toward the door.

When Crockford's hand stopped moving on the board and he stroked the chalk with a great flourish across the bottom of it, Jimmy recognized the impersonation of himself. Then Crockford was standing where he usually stood; rising on his toes now, swaying gently, bending his long length forward, placing his hands on his hips, then pushing one hand after the other through his hair. This was himself to a T.

He felt a flame of anger sweep over him.

He thrust the door open, and his entry was made in total silence. The boys sat stiffly, wide-eyed, some with mouths agape, waiting. Burrows began to say something.

Jimmy lifted his hand, palm upwards, to quiet Burrows, then walked to the front of his desk and looked at Crockford, who was standing to the side of the board and for once appearing unsure of himself, even looking a little scared. Then he turned his eyes to the board, and what he read was:

"Wet Lanky Walton's whistle with whisky and he'll waffle about Warwick, Westmoreland, Wellington or Watt; not forgetting POETRY—Poetry, prosody, pentameter—the sot. Why doesn't the Salvation Army call him up to empty their trashcans?"

He couldn't read the last words for the flame of his anger.

What happened next was done so quickly that the boys didn't stir from their seats for some seconds. With a movement that was a spring, he gripped Crockford by the neck and, swinging him round as if he were a small child, dragged him sideways to the board, and there, pushing his face against it, he rubbed it unmercifully over the chalked words.

The harder Crockford struggled and fought to free himself, the harder Jimmy pushed his face back and forward. He was quite unaware now of the pandemonium behind him, of Felton and Burrows, and Cook and Riley and Fawcett and Youlden, all impeding each other as they pulled on his arms, shouting, "Sir! Sir! Leave go, sir! Leave go, man!" of boys running from the room and masters running in. He was only slightly aware of them trying to get his clutching hands from Crockford's collar and of the superior tone of Mr. Bennett, crying, "Walton! Walton! Have you gone mad? Take hold of yourself, man. Leave go! Do you hear me? Leave go!" Of the senior math master, saying, "Come on, Jimmy. Come on, Jimmy," in a coaxing voice.

But it was not because of either of them that he let go of Crockford; it was because the rage suddenly seeped from him as if someone had opened a trapdoor in the soles of his feet. He felt the strength running down from his arms and his ribs and his legs, leaving him limp and shaken. He didn't remember how he got from the classroom to the common room, but he did remember as he left the classroom hearing someone saying, "His nose is bleeding. It's only his nose." And he remembered putting his hand up to his face. But it wasn't his nose that was bleeding; it would be Crockford's.

When the headmaster came in he stood silent for a moment looking down at him, and then he said stiffly, very stiffly, "You had better go home, Mr. Walton, and see your doctor."

They had brought his coat and hat, and when he got into them the headmaster said, "You will see Mr. Walton home, Mr. Quilter?" and the master said, "Of course, sir."

It was then that Jimmy put his hand out toward them in a delaying movement. He didn't speak but he made a small movement with his head, and then he walked past his colleagues and the headmaster and went across the hall and out into the school yard, out into the sunshine, out of the school gates, and out of this kind of life forever.

He was finished, finally finished; at least this part of him was finished. But there was another about to begin. He knew what

he was going to do. It was as if he had been rehearsing for weeks
and had just given the first performance.

It was half-past four when he got into the house. He looked
about him; he was no longer dazed but he was still trembling.
He went to a cupboard under the stairs and pulled out a couple
of cases, then packed them with his belongings. He gathered up
all his books and put them in cardboard boxes. These he stood
in the hallway, in the shadow of the stairs, and his full cases he
put back in the cupboard. It was five o'clock.

He looked in the mirror. His face was pale and grim. He was
twenty-five years old, he was a man, and he was going to act like
a man; for the first time in his life he was going to act like a man.
He was Jimmy Walton, the man; gone was Jimmy Walton, the
lad, the young fellow who had to be thankful to his mother for
putting him on his feet; gone was Jimmy Walton, the young
husband, who had allowed himself to be browbeaten by a slip
of a Tartar, five feet of pure bitchery.

He straightened his tie, smoothed his hair back, and as he did
so he was reminded of Crockford. He wasn't sorry for what he
had done to Crockford; he'd had it coming to him. He should
have done it months ago. But no; he had done it at the right moment.

He went out and across the little hall and knocked on the door
opposite. When Lally opened it, he stared at her before saying,
"Hello. May I come in?"

She did not answer as she stared back at him, but she opened
the door wider, and he passed her and went into the room, then
turned and looked at her.

"I . . . I haven't seen you this week. Have you been sick?"

"Yes. I got a cold an' had to stay in bed."

"Oh."

"Come on in and sit down."

He looked about him. He had never been in this room before;
it was ordinary, cheap-looking. He turned to her and took her
hand and led her toward the fireplace, where a low fire was

smoldering. Then, pressing her down into a chair, he drew up
another to her side, and again taking her hand he looked into
her face and said simply, "I love you, Lally."

Her blue eyes softened with bewilderment as they widened
and she shook her head and pulled in her chin; then she said,
"Eeh! no, Jimmy. Eeh! no. Well, what I mean is . . ."

"Listen. I love you, I need you. God, how I need you. I've
wanted to put me arms around you like this." He now slipped
from the chair onto his knees and drew her to him, and when
he felt the nearness of her, of her soft, warm flesh, he became
still inside. How long had he wanted to do this, for how many
months, for how many years, for how many eternities? Since he
was born he had longed to do this, lie against Lally. There was
a need in him, there had always been a need in him, and since
the first time he saw her he had known that she could fill that
need. The need was well-deep; it went right down, past Betty,
past his mother, past those torturous days at the secondary school,
past the torment of his long arms dangling from his cuffs and
the bottom of his trousers straining away from the top of his
boots; past this life and into another only dimly comprehended.

She was saying, "But, Jimmy, your wife—I don't want to cause
trouble."

He brought his face up from her neck and looked into her
eyes. "What do you think about me, Lally?"

"Aw." She closed her eyes for a moment and her face dropped
into a great expanse of warm tenderness. "Oh! you should know
that. I think you're wonderful. I've always thought you were
wonderful, clever, so . . . so."

"I don't mean that way, Lally. What do you think about me
as . . . as a man, not the schoolteacher?"

She bit on her lip and her head drooped for a moment; then
she lifted it as she said quietly, "I . . . I love you, Jimmy. I've
. . . I've always loved you, ever since I first saw you in the passage. Albert knew, he sort of guessed, that's why . . ."

He drew in a long, deep breath as he pulled her sharply to
him. "That's all I want to know, that's all I'll ever want to know."

When he kissed her he felt like a god. And was he not kissing a goddess? For she was built like a goddess, like those of old. Oh, wonder of wonders! Her mouth was soft and warm and enveloping. He was swimming into her flesh. How in the name of God had he done without her all this time? But never no more, he'd never let her go now. From now on there wouldn't be a day or a night when they would be separated.

He drew his lips from hers and, looking into her great blue eyes, said, "Now this . . . this is what I want you to do. I want you to pack a case, just with what's necessary for the time being, and I want you to go along to our Mary's—you know, the shop—and wait for me there."

"But . . . but Jimmy, w-won't she . . . ?"

"No buts." He put his fingers on her lips.

"But, lad, just a minute." She pulled his hand down and held it tightly. "Do you really know what you're doin'? 'Cos you know what they'll say, they'll say you're up the pole. Some of them around here think I'm soft in the head, and I haven't done much to prove them wrong. As I told you, Jimmy, I'm daft with money. And then there's your sister. Won't she go off the deep end?"

"No, Mary won't go off the deep end." He wasn't sure of this, but he said it emphatically.

"But the other teachers at the school, Jimmy, they'll look down on you 'cos of me."

"I'm finished with school."

"You've left?"

"Yes, you could say I've left. This is going to be a new start. We'll find a house somewhere, we'll set up and I'll get a job. There's plenty going, don't you worry about that. Now do what I tell you." He got to his feet and pulled her up with him. "Pack up straightaway and get down to Mary's and wait there; when we find a place you can send for your stuff." He was going to add, "What you want of it," but realized they might be glad of it, because you couldn't buy new furniture for love nor money, and little of secondhand stuff either.

While they stood near the door, close again, she touched his face and said, "I can't believe it, Jimmy. I was sittin' here feeling lost, lonely. I haven't seen a soul to speak to in the last three days; everybody's out at work and about their own business . . . you know"—she nodded—"and I didn't feel up to going out and . . ."

"You feel up to it now?"

"Oh aye, yes." She leaned her head against his neck and said simply, "I'd walk on hot coals to get to you, Jimmy."

"Oh! Lally. Lally."

He had to force himself to let her go. Then he admonished her once again: "Now, hurry up and get out as quick as possible for there's likely to be a few high-jinks later on. And wait, I'll bring these boxes in." He opened the door and pointed to the cardboard boxes. "They're my books."

A minute or so later she caught hold of his arm and said, "But what'll I say to your sister?"

"Just say Jimmy sent you and may you stay there until I come. That's all, say nothing more. Mary won't ask any questions; she'll see and understand."

"Eeh! I can't believe it." She shook her head. "It's fantastic, you wantin' me . . . oh! Jimmy."

He looked at her lovingly, took her in his arms again; then he hurried across the hall and into his own house.

Betty came in at six o'clock. The first thing that caught her eye was the bare tea table. She went into the bedroom, where Jimmy was tearing up papers from a box he had placed on the bed, and she said, "Oh! you're in. Why isn't the tea set? What you doing with that old box on the clean cover?"

His reply was brief. "I'm not staying for tea."

"You're not on tonight."

"No, I'm not on tonight."

"One of those moods, is it?" She flung off her outer clothes and went into the kitchen. He heard the banging of the kettle on the stove and the rattle of crockery.

He gathered up the torn papers and returned them to the box; the others he tied together with some tape and put them in the pocket of his overcoat, which was lying across a chair; then he went into the room where Betty was setting the table in no quiet manner, and he said, "You needn't set it for me, but you can set it for two. I want you to go and fetch me ma."

"You what?"

"You heard what I said, I want you to go and fetch me ma."

"Now?"

"Yes, now."

"What's up with you? She'll be round about sevenish."

"I'm not waiting until seven. Stop doing that"—his voice was rising—"and go and get me ma."

"You gone mad altogether?" She shook her head. "You've been on the bottle." She peered at him in silence and seeing that he hadn't been on the bottle she asked, "What do you want Mam for all of a sudden?"

"You'll know when you bring her; I'm not going to waste breath on both of you."

"What?"

"Do I have to repeat everything? I said I am not going to waste breath on both of you. Go and bring me ma now if you want to hear what I've got to say."

He swung round, went into the bedroom, brought back her hat and coat and flung them into her arms, saying, "Go on!"

When he slowly advanced toward her she backed from him, staring at him, her mouth agape, and she pulled on her coat as she opened the door. Then she peered at him again and, repeating the headmaster's words, said, "You had better see a doctor, that's what you'd better do, an' soon." Then she was gone.

They returned quicker than he had expected. He had given them half an hour, but they were back in twenty minutes. When they came into the room they looked at him standing near the table dressed in his good suit, an overcoat hanging over the back of the chair and, by the side of the chair, two cases. The sight of him standing thus bereft them both of speech for a moment, but it was Alice, as usual, who got her word in first. "What's this?" she demanded. "What you up to now? And this, this!" She pointed from one case to the other.

"You've been plaguing to come and live here for the last couple of years, haven't you, Ma?"

Alice didn't answer this, but she pulled in her chin and screwed up her eyes and waited. And Jimmy went on, "Well, now I'm giving you the chance. You can have it all to yourselves, the both of you"—he nodded from one to the other—"because I'm leaving."

The two women exchanged glances; then they looked at him again and their reactions took different forms. Betty realized that this could really be the end and that she'd have to do something quickly, use the same tactics that had got him in the first place. She dropped her head onto her chest and began to whimper: "You can't, you can't mean it, Jimmy? We've had our differences, but you can't mean . . ."

Alice's voice cut her off, yelling, "Leave! is it? You'll leave here with that lot"—she kicked out toward the case—"over my dead body."

"Well, I just might do that, Ma, I just might, because I'm going to tell you now"—he moved one step toward her, which action impressed her more than his statement—"it's been as much as I could do to keep me hands off you for many a long day, even as far back as the night you locked me in the bedroom and offered me da the shakedown in the front room. I had the greatest desire to claw your face that night. So your words might just come true. I wouldn't put them to the test if I were you, because you know something? I'm at the end of me tether and, driven too far, God knows what I would do. I've been in court twice. What's one more time? And me da wouldn't be in it once I started. Quiet men are like that, tigers under the skin, you know. Or don't you? No, you'd never learn. You drove me da to bash Ben almost to death when with a few sensible words you could have altered the whole scene. You could have said: 'These things happen. Ben's still a young man, and he's a marvelous catch for our Mary.' But no, you didn't, because as I understand it you had your eye in that quarter yourself. And another thing, I don't have to thank you for what you did for me; what you did for me was to boost your own ego, if you know what that means. Put in simple words, in your case, get one up on everybody in the street."

"You thankless, God-forsaken, weak-kneed scum! for that's all you are. You're like her. Birds of a feather. You're going to her, aren't you? She's done this. She's been egging you on for years. . . . You long, weedy simpleton!" She couldn't go on. The saliva was running over her bottom lip.

Betty was sobbing aloud now, sitting by the table, her head in her hands, her shoulders shaking. Jimmy looked down on her and said, "It's too late for that, Betty. Don't come the soft, down-trodden little woman at this stage, because there's no softness in you; you're as hard as nails. I should have seen it from the beginning. But me ma's right about one thing—I am a simpleton . . . at least I was." He turned and, picking up the coat from the chair, threw it over his shoulder, then lifted the cases and, looking at his mother, dealt her the last but one final blow. Yet for her it was the final one. "You'd like to know," he said, "that I won't be teaching any more. I wiped the blackboard with a lad's face and the headmaster didn't like it. . . . And although our Mary's got nothing to do with this business, you're right, I am going to her, just for an hour or so. I've got somebody waiting there for me." He walked toward the door through a clear path, and there he turned. "I'll better tell you, because you'll know soon enough—it'll take the Home Guard to put the fire out when it gets around. I'm going off with Lally."

Betty was on her feet, her face looking fiendish now, and she screamed at him, "No! You won't! You won't disgrace me with her, that dippy . . . !"

"HER, that brazen, barmy blonde an' you! Why, you!" Alice rushed to the table, but he had the door open when a tin of condensed milk, already spilling its contents, hit the stanchion.

But when the cup caught him on the side of the face his teeth clenched and he felt the anger from earlier in the day returning. He was for putting the cases down but thought better of it; instead, he dragged the front door open and went into the street. He could hear the commotion behind him and their yelling in the hallway, but he knew that neither of them would follow him into the street. They both considered themselves above the types that took their battles into the street, which was odd, because when either of them got going you could hear them for doors down.

When he turned the corner his pace slowed. He was free. He was free. The words rose to a crescendo in his mind like a great, concerted shout, and he paused for a moment to let them escape, but when they came through his lips they were a deep whisper that released his body of its weight.

By the time he reached Mary's he had come down to earth somewhat. He was still married to Betty and she'd likely make him pay through the teeth with a maintenance order. But nothing on God's earth could make him go back to her. He had escaped; he was free, free to love and be loved by Lally.

It wasn't until he was going up Mary's stairs that he realized that he had his check on him. In shock, both of them had forgotten it was his payday. He chuckled and smiled, and he was still smiling when he entered the hallway and Mary came from the sitting room. But the smile slid from his face when he saw her.

Mary watched him drop the cases and throw his coat over them; she watched him straighten his back and stretch his neck upwards. They stood looking at each other, until she said under her breath, "What's all this about?"

"Come into the kitchen."

In the kitchen with the door shut he said, "I hope you don't mind, I told Lally to come here and wait for me."

"Lally. You mean . . . ?"

"Aye, yes, I mean what you think. I've left her, Betty, and I did it in one grand finale. I sent her for me ma, I made her go for me ma, and when she came I told her she was welcome to stay. You know how she's plagued me for years to come and live there. Well, now they've got each other." His voice dropped. "I couldn't stand any more, Mary. The climax came at school. I . . . I hammered a boy."

"You what!"

"Oh, he had it coming to him." He turned his head to the side. "He wrote something on the board about me and I rubbed it off with his face."

She put her hand to her cheek; then grimly she said, "You know what usually happens when you attack somebody in the face."

"Oh, it wasn't like that." His tone was sharp now. "I made his nose bleed, that's all, and gave him a fright."

"They'll likely sack you."

"Oh, that's a foregone conclusion. I'm not going back."

"And"—Mary moved her head slowly up and down—"you're going off with her?" She jerked her head toward the door.

"Yes."

"Oh, my God! Our Jimmy!" Her tone, her manner, her look were all derogatory.

"Now, don't you start, Mary, you're me only hope. And she's all right. She's . . . she's wonderful. She may not be very bright, but I've got enough brightness for both of us. Betty was bright, brittly bright, bitchy bright. I know inside that Lally is what I need. And she's nice, she's kind."

"I'm not disputing that." Mary had her head turned away now. "She might be all that. . . ."

"She is all that. When you get to know her you can't but like her."

"That may be true an' all, but have you thought what you're doing? Betty won't take this lying down. Even if she would, me ma 'll see to it that she'll get the last farthing out of you; you'll have to keep two houses."

"I'll manage somehow. That will be the least of my worries. Bread and scrap and a board bed wouldn't hurt me; it's people that hurt me, Mary. You should know that, the same one that's hurt you—her! Even Betty, as bad as she is, wouldn't have gone to the limit if me ma hadn't encouraged her. There's a devil in me ma, she's a bad woman. It's dreadful to say such a thing." He turned away and looked out of the kitchen window. "Aye, it's dreadful when you've got to say that the one who bore you is bad, rotten."

There was a silence between them now; then Mary asked quietly, "Where you heading for?"

He turned to her. "That's the point; I've no place as yet. I was going to ask a favor of you. The Flake Street shop, the rooms above, they're damaged, I know, but . . . but I could fix them up for the time being. There's nobody in there, is there?"

Mary blinked, bit on her lip, then said quietly, "No."

"Then . . . then will you let us have them just until I find a place?"

She looked at him. What could she say? The thought of the Flake Street shop spelt pain to her. What she did say was, "They're bare; there's no bedding there, nothing."

"If you could let us have a few blankets or something until tomorrow, we'll send the cart for Lally's things."

She heaved a sigh. "Yes, I could do that."

He walked toward her and took her hands and said gently, "Thanks, Mary. You know something? I've never been happier in me life than I am at this minute. I can't remember one real happy day, not even"—he gave a hic of a laugh—"not even the day I married Betty, because the previous night some little thing that she said clicked in my mind and linked her with me ma, and if I could have got out of it then, I would. . . . You want to see me happy, don't you, Mary?"

"You know I do."

"Well, I'll be happy with Lally. . . . Where is she?"

"In the dining room with me da. Funny"—she gave a small laugh—"they're talking together as if they'd known each other for years; I've never heard me da talk so much since he came into the house."

Jimmy smiled now as if she had paid him a compliment and said, "There, what did I tell you?"

She turned from him, saying, "Well, come on. Take your coat off and have a cup of tea."

Two hours later they were ready to go. Jimmy had made the journey with the van to Flake Street and deposited there some bedding, which included a single mattress, together with their cases, and now Mary was in the sitting room alone for a moment with Lally. They were both standing looking at each other. Mary thought, This woman is a year younger than me, only twenty-six, but she looks thirty if she's a day. And she looks blowsy, not Jimmy's type at all. Jimmy was the brainy type, clever, intellectual. He should be doing something with his brain. But what had he done? Lost his job as a teacher. With that record behind him he'd never get teaching again. And now he was going to start his life with this woman, her with the nickname of Doolally-tap, and you didn't get a nickname like that around here unless there was some reason for it. What was Jimmy thinking about?

She started as Lally put out her hand and touched her gently and, as if reading her thoughts, said, "I know I'm no catch. People'll say he's mad. An' perhaps he is, 'cos I'm not bright, but at the same time I know some things that other people don't. I don't think you need to be too bright to make a man happy, an' I'm going to make Jimmy happy. I'll spend me time, all me life, trying to make him happy. An' . . . an' I'll tell you something: if he wants to leave me after a bit, I won't try to stop him. I'll just be thankful for what I've had. It doesn't come everybody's way every day to get a man like Jimmy."

Her humility was embarrassing, it was throat-catching. She could see now what had got Jimmy, the simplicity, the truth, and the depth, yes, a depth welling up out of the big body. She swallowed hard before she said, "I think you will make him happy, Lally; he . . . he needs a little . . . a little love. He's had a rough passage."

They both nodded at each other, and when the door opened Mary said briskly, "Well now, I suppose you'd better be off. But"—she looked toward Jimmy—"come round for breakfast in the morning and we'll get down to things. When I've had time to think there may be some place more suitable than Flake Street."

Jimmy said nothing, he just smiled at her; then taking Lally by the arm he led her into the hallway, where Alec was standing. "We'll be off then, Da," he said.

"Aye, lad, aye." Alec nodded at him and then at Lally. "Be seeing you, lass," he said, and Lally answered, "Oh yes, be seeing you, Mr. Walton. Pleasure meetin' you."

"An' you, lass, an' you."

Mary did not go down the stairs with them, and when the sound of the door closing came to her she turned and looked at Alec, and she saw that he was smiling. She couldn't remember the last time she had seen him really smile. She looked toward the stairhead doorway. She had the strange feeling that her da, too, had gone off with Doo-lally-tap.

8

It was over. The world had stopped going mad. That is, all except the Japs. But they would soon be put in their place, and the best place for them was in graves. So said everybody that came into the shop.

Wasn't it marvelous! Soon they'd be able to come in and say, "Couple of pounds of best butter, lass; three pounds of cheese; two pounds of the best shortback, smoked, mind; half a dozen bars of chocolate; no, no, make it a dozen; two pounds of biscuits, mixed, custard creams, chocolate, lemon slices, the lot."

And Mary brought censure down on herself by answering one

customer who was prophesying this order by saying, "Yes, Mrs. Jacobson; but in the meantime you'll have your rations, for four, isn't it?"

There were victory teas in the streets, one street vying with another in laying a table for the bairns, and lavish enough to represent victory.

"Come on, Mary." Mrs. McArthur smiled at her. "You can scrape the bottom of the barrel. It's for the bairns, a bit extra fat and sugar. You'd be surprised what I could do with a couple of pounds of each. They say they're using liquid paraffin to make their cakes across the road"—she nodded in the direction of the houses over the back lane—"but our Lizzie's Monica—she's nursing in Harton, you know—well, she told our Lizzie to be careful in using too much of that, things can happen to your inside, she said. So as I said to Mrs. Wright and Mrs. Farthers, we're havin' none of that, we're not having that on our conscience." She laughed here. "We don't know what's in the bloomin' marge, and the sugar might be half sand, but still that's the government's fault. What about it, lass?"

Mary smiled wryly, "All right, I'll see what I can do."

"Good lass." As Mrs. McArthur went to leave the kitchen she turned and said, "And you'll come down and look in? It's no use broodin', lass, you cannot bring them back."

When she had gone Mary thought, She's right, you cannot bring them back. But she went into the bedroom and lifted up Ben's photo and that of David from where they stood on the chest of drawers, and she looked at them for a long while before replacing them. Then of a sudden she grabbed up Ben's photo again and held it to her chest, murmuring, "Oh, Ben! Ben!"

She was lonely. She seemed to be getting more lonely with every day that passed; time wasn't helping her. Here she was, surrounded by people all needing her, making demands on her and filling her with guilt because she wanted to push them off. Over the past months the feeling of wanting to get away from them had been strong on her, but since May 7th, the day on which Germany surrendered, she'd had the added urge actually to pack up and rush off somewhere. But where? The war over, she saw the world open to her; she could travel. She'd always wanted to travel, and she'd have enough money. Ben's hobby would pay off now. He had initiated her into his hobby. He had shares in about fifteen different companies. Not a lot; perhaps only two or three hundred, and some of them weren't worth more than a shilling or two each as they stood, but Ben had told her time and again, Let the war be over and within a year or two most of these would rocket. Once he had turned to her and said, "Don't ever sell these, Mary, I mean thinking that they're not worth anything because they're low," and she had replied, "What on earth are you talking about? How could I sell them?" And he had said, "Well, you never know what happens. I'm just warning you."

She would heed his warning; he had made her sensible where money was concerned. Then there were the shops. The property was theirs—hers now; besides the six houses and the cottage, Moat Cottage. But she knew what she was going to do with the cottage. The day Jimmy and Lally went in there she was going to hand him the deeds. It would be a surprise, a nice surprise, and it would give him a feeling of security and add a final touch to his happiness.

At times lately she had felt a bit green about Jimmy's happiness. He was going around like a tall beacon light, shining with it. He had been right: Lally had been what he needed. And Lally herself—nobody could help liking Lally. She was big, naïve and lovable, and she was someone who had to be cared for and directed, and Jimmy had never had anyone to direct, or prove himself master of. He had been bullied, dominated and mastered all his life.

During the last year she had watched her brother become a man. The dreaminess had gone, and since the bairn had been born . . . well, anybody would think that it was the first baby that had been delivered into the world. But then it was Lally's first baby.

It was odd how things had gone for him since he had taken the final step away from her ma and Betty. He had got a job as orderly in the infirmary, and he had not only endeared himself to most of the staff with whom he worked, but had managed to bring the interest of the doctors to bear on Lally, owing to her three previous miscarriages; in consequence, she'd had the best of care and had been admitted to hospital during the latter part of her pregnancy. She'd had to have a caesarean in the end and it was doubtful if she'd ever have another child. But that didn't matter; she'd given him a son, and he had called him Ben.

She had been very touched that Jimmy had called the child Ben, and so, in order that his son could be brought up in decent surroundings, away from the scum of the streets and the back lanes, she had suggested to him that if he put in some spare-time work on the cottage, with what old bomb-site timber he could get his hands on, and decorate it, even if only with battleship-gray paint, then they could move in there. His delight had been so great that you would have thought she was offering him Buckingham Palace.

Yes, she was glad, happy that things were going well for Jimmy, even if his doting attitude toward Lally was a little too much at times.

As she went quietly from the bedroom she saw her daughter hastily push a bag of sweets into her coat pocket and gulp at the one in her mouth, and she called, "Annie!"

"Yes, Ma." Annie's expression was surly.

"I thought you were going to give your rations in for the Victory tea?"

"Well, I am; I did."

"What's those you put in your pocket?" She went toward her and drew from her pocket a bag holding about six ounces of toffees, and she put her head on one side and surveyed her daughter, and Annie surveyed her in return and said, "Ma, you're niggardly."

Yes, she supposed she was niggardly. Who else in her position

would deprive her daughter of a few sweets? What was the matter with her anyway? She handed the bag back to Annie, but
asked, "Who gave them to you? Teresa or your granda?"

"Me granda."

"Go on." She pushed her, and she smiled wryly as she watched
the child flounce down the stairs. Her da would have done the
same for her years ago.

A few minutes later she entered the back shop. Alec was
weighing up sugar at a side table, while he hummed to himself
the song that had been his father's favorite, the song that got
on her nerves, the song that in a way she took as a reproach to
herself:

> "I love a lassie,
> A bonny, bonny lassie.
> She's as pure as the lily in the dell.
> She's as sweet as the heather,
> The bonny purple heather,
> Mary, me Scotch bluebell."

There were times when she wanted to scream at him, "Oh
da! for God's sake change that tune."

She recalled once when they were walking along the cinder
path, his arm about her shoulders, and he was singing—someone
had stood him a few pints that day—and he looked down into
her face as he sang the line

> "She's as pure as the lily in the dell."

Lately she had thought that perhaps even without her ma
agitating him he would still have beaten up Ben. Looking at
him now, small, stooped, quiet, inoffensive, a prematurely aged
man, who would think that he had ever been capable of acting
as he had done?

Since she had given him the job of weighing the dry goods
and packing up orders she had seen glimpses in him of his
former self, especially on the nights when Jimmy and Lally came
round. Then he would sit with Annie between his knees and
talk, and even chaff. And she knew that in these moments he

was happy; he had his family around him as he had never hoped to have, and never had in their young days.

What hurt her most with regard to him was his subservient manner toward herself; it was always "Yes, Mary. Aye, Mary. Yes, I'll do that, Mary." It made her the boss, and somehow she didn't want to be the boss. The boss of him, and Annie, and Cousin Annie, and Jimmy, and Lally. Yet they all looked to her as the boss. She didn't want to be their boss, anybody's boss— not even Arthur's in the Charter Street shop, or Teresa's in this one. She wanted to get away on her own.

Alec said, "How's that?" He pointed to the row of sugar bags, and she said, "Fine. Fine, Da. Go on up now. I've made your cocoa."

"Oh ta, Mary; I could do with that. Is there anything else you want specially doin' when I come back?"

"Well, you could start on the potatoes. Do them up in three-pound bags."

"Aye, aye, I will, Mary. I won't be a minute."

"Take your time." Her voice was impatient. Then she looked at him gently and smiled. "There's no hurry; take your time, Da."

"Aye, lass, aye. All right." As he went out she sighed and put her hand to her head; then she was walking toward the shop door when Teresa came through it, saying hurriedly, "There's a man in the shop wantin' to have a word with you."

Without speaking, Mary followed her back into the shop, and there at the other side of the counter, standing with a number of women customers, all from around the doors, was Hughie Amesden.

"Good morning, Mrs. Tollett."

"Good morning, Mr. Amesden."

He was standing near the counter and when he looked from one side to the other she said, "You would like a word with me, Mr. Amesden?"

"Yes, Mrs. Tollett."

"Will you come through then?"

She ignored the looks of the women and lifted the hatch and allowed him to pass in front of her and into the storeroom.

They stood looking at each other for a moment. He had his hat in his hand. It was a soft trilby. She had noticed that he never wore a cap, and this sort of made him stand out from the other men about the place. He pulled the rim of the trilby between his fingers and thumb as he said, "I . . . I just wanted to say good-bye to you."

"Good-bye? You're going away?"

"Yes." He nodded. "The first stage is Southampton. We're leaving the morrow, and . . . and then America."

"America?" She bowed her head toward him.

"Yes, you see me wife's got an aunt over there. Her son came over here during the war and he married an English lass. They live in Southampton. He's billeted there. Well, the long and the short of it is me wife can't settle here; she's crazy to get away since we lost our girl, you understand?"

She moved her head again.

"And her cousin's going to see about getting us a passage. We might have to wait a bit, but René—that's my wife—thinks that if we're on the spot we'll have a better chance."

"America, it's a long way."

"Yes, it's a long way."

"Are you looking forward to it?"

He looked into her face for a full minute before he said, "No. But you know how it is."

She nodded again, but she didn't know how it was. She wouldn't know until she, too, was able to say to someone, "I'm going away. I'm going to America."

He was twisting his hat around in his hands as he said with a half-smile, "It's funny. We haven't met often during the years, although we were brought up together . . . well, quite near each other. But I thought, well, I thought I would let you know I'm going, just to say ta-rah."

"It was very kind of you, Mr. Amesden, and I wish you all the luck in the world."

He didn't answer, and they continued to stare at each other until the silence became so great, so heavy that she felt herself going red in the face, and she searched frantically in her mind for something to say. And what she said was, "You'll be glad to get away. It's . . . it's depressing here."

"No. No"—he shook his head vigorously—"it isn't that I find it depressing. Well, not more so than any other place during the war. Blackouts and everything, you know; places don't have a lot of effect on me—it's people."

How true, how true. She said aloud, "Yes, you're right, Mr. Amesden. Places don't matter all that much; it's the people."

The back door opened and Alec entered and they both turned and looked at him with blank faces, and he said, "Oh."

"This is Mr. Amesden, Da. He's going to America."

"Oh aye." Alec put his head back and looked up at the tall man. "I wish you luck, lad." He put out his hand. Hughie took it, and they shook hands gravely.

He now turned to Mary with his hand extended, and she placed hers in it. It was the first time they had touched. His hands felt big, warm, firm.

"Well, I'll say good-bye then, Mrs. Tollett."

"Good-bye, Mr. Amesden. I hope you get on well."

"I hope so."

"If . . . if you ever come on a holiday, you must look us up."

"I will, Mrs. Tollett, I certainly will." He still had hold of her hand, and when he dropped it he stood for a second longer looking at her, then turned away and went toward the door that led into the shop. She did not follow him to show him out but turned toward the back door as Alec said, "He seems a nice chap. I seem to know his face. Is he from around these parts?"

"Yes," said Mary. "Yes, he's from around these parts."

When she got upstairs Cousin Annie put her head out of the kitchen and asked, "Do you want turnips done with the potatoes to mash like?" and she looked at her and said "What? Oh, yes. Yes, that'll be all right, Annie." Then she went into the bedroom and, sitting on the side of the bed, looked at the photo of Ben and bowed her head. What was wrong with her? What was up with her anyway? She had the feeling that she had just sustained another great loss.

9

"Come on, love, and sit down and get this toast." Jimmy pulled Lally down into a chair by the side of the table; then, pointing to the fire, he said, "That's a blaze for you, isn't it? And there's enough rotten bits outside there to keep us going for a month. By! I was lucky to get that load. Arthur Stanhope— he's in the boiler house, you know—he's going to put me on to another lot. His brother's on cleaning the bomb sites—that's how he gets the tipoff. A couple of bob on the side"—he nudged her with his elbow—"and we're set."

He looked around the room, his face bright. Then he said, "Isn't it marvelous! Ours. Fancy our Mary giving it to us! Just fancy. I still can't believe it, not even yet. By! she's good."

"She's wonderful, is Mary." Lally looked down into her cup, then stirred it slowly before she said thoughtfully, "You know, Jimmy, most women are bitches. Oh, they are." She looked at him and nodded as if he had denied this. "But when you get a nice one it makes up for all the rest."

He put his hand across the table and gripped hers, and he said quietly, "You're telling me that. To me there are only two good women in the world, you and our Mary."

"Aw, Jimmy." She looked at him with her big, limpid blue eyes for a moment; then pulling her hand away from him and sitting up straight she said, as if coming to a grave decision, "I'm not goin' to dress so flashy. I'm goin' to pick quiet things."

Jimmy let out a roar of laughter, leaned back in his chair and almost did a back somersault. Gripping on the table, the tears running down his face, he said, "Lally! you're priceless."

And she was priceless to him. He'd had a year of such happiness that it was impossible to imagine. He had never dreamed that any human being could hold so many beautiful emotions in his body at one and the same time. Why, why did he love her like he did? According to modern educational standards she was, as she said, dim, at least dim about some things, but on others so unconsciously profound that she astounded him. At such times he felt that there was a door in her mind that had something behind it stopping it opening, and that once that door could be forced back he would have, in his Lally, a sage. But did he want a sage? No, he just wanted her as she was, he never wanted her any different, because as she was she had made a man of him. And her need of him, her love of him, would go on keeping him a man.

During the past year he had done so many things he never thought he'd be capable of. He had used his hands. Just look what he had done to this place at odd times during the last six months! He had made cupboards; he had boarded in the old-fashioned sink; he had sanded all the grease and dirt off the great stone slabs of this kitchen; he had reinforced the stairs; he had even built Lally a kind of dressing table in the queer little niche in the bedroom up above, and now that the authorities were allowing a pound's worth of new wood a month for reconstruction, there was nothing he wouldn't be able to do during the next year or two. Among that great pile of charred and oiled wood outside the door there were two large beams he was going to preserve—he already had an idea what he was going to do with them. The front room was eighteen feet long and still held the old-fashioned iron fireplace. Well, as soon as he could get down to it he was going to have that out and put one of these beams across the top and make an open fireplace. He had seen the picture in a magazine, seventeenth-century style. Oh, the ideas he had in his head. And then the garden, back and front: he'd have that all dug before the winter and designed. He'd make a sandpit for Ben at the back, and when he could get his hands on some cement he'd make him a little pool. He'd bring South Shields sands into his own backyard. . . . The things he was going to do.

Lally, looking from the blazing fire to him, now said, "Oh, Jimmy, I don't want to leave. Now the fire's on I feel we're home . . . for good. It seems a long time till Monday when the things come."

Jimmy, who was sitting close to her holding her hand, looked at the fire, too, and said, "I was a fool; I should have got them to move us today or tomorrow. I don't know why I said Monday. Oh yes, I do." He nudged her. "I thought we'd all come in together, and as we're not picking up Ben from the hospital until Monday I thought, Wherever we go, whatever we do, we'll do it together, the three of us."

"Aw, that was a nice thought, Jimmy, doing everything together, you, and me, and Ben. Do you think his ear will be all right?"

"Yes, yes."

"I wouldn't like for him to be deaf, Jimmy."

"He won't be deaf." He shook her arm. "He's got a bit of an ear infection, that's all. And we're lucky, we're favored. Don't forget, it isn't every bairn they take in and look after. First-class care—we're favored."

"It's 'cos of you."

"Tripe!" He stood up, saying, "Well, it's getting dark; we'd better be making a move if we want to call at Mary's."

"Oh aye. Oh aye. Are you going to bank down the fire, Jimmy, afore we go?"

"You bet. Oh, you bet."

"It's a shame, it's such a lovely blaze."

He looked at her as she stood now gazing down into the fire, and then he pulled her round toward him, saying, "I'll tell you what I'll do. Billy Sollop won't be doing anything tomorrow. He'd given me the choice, Saturday or Monday. Look, I'll slip in to him as we're going home and ask him if he can do it tomorrow. Anyway, it would be more sensible to have the place all straight for Master Benjamin Walton returning home, wouldn't it?"

"Oh Jimmy, will you?"

He took her into his arms. "You'd like to come in tomorrow, wouldn't you?"

"I'd like to come in now." She pulled a face at him.

He smiled at her, then said airily, "Well, Mrs. Walton, you may, if you wish, sleep on the stone floor or, if you prefer the boards, upstairs, but for me, my old bones need a mattress."

"Oh, Jimmy! You're funny." She pushed, then pulled him toward the door, and they went out, he having to stoop to avoid the low lintel.

They were halfway down the path when he swung her around and they surveyed the cottage. It was deceptive-looking; it suggested it might have two rooms down and two or three up, whereas in fact it had, besides the large kitchen and equally large sitting room, another twelve-by-ten-foot room, a scullery, a large washhouse that gave access into a wooden outhouse, which Jimmy had already planned as a workshop, and upstairs it had three bedrooms. It was a place that had great potential, and the artist that was in the poet saw this. Moat Cottage was going to be a showplace. In his mind already he saw it completed.

Arm in arm, tight-linked, they made their way in the gathering dusk into the town, lit now with street lamps but still showing the scars of war. The nearest way to Mary's would have been along Croft Terrace, down the road and cut through Haydon Terrace, but he kept clear of Haydon Terrace and took the long way round. He had come across Betty twice during the last year. The first time, the day she had taken him to court for a maintenance order, and he had been committed to pay her fifteen shillings a week. The second time was when he had found himself sitting opposite her in the bus. He had only been seated a minute and there were her eyes boring into him as if they would stab him. He got to his feet and jumped off the bus with the conductor shouting after him, "What's up with you, mate! Want to break your neck?"

His mother he had seen only once and he never wanted to see her again. It was on the day everybody was going mad with victory. He had been pushing his way through a crowd blocking the roadway near Ellison Street. He had Lally by the hand pulling her after him, and there was the face to the side staring at him out of the crowd. The only face that wasn't laughing, the only mouth that wasn't open. He saw that she had her teeth gritted, her lips back from them in a snarl, like that of a dog, and it had crossed his mind that she looked like a madwoman.

But he could go in by Cornice Street from the top end now—he always did when coming back from the cottage—and it gave him a sort of kick as he walked down the street with Lally on his arm. From the beginning he knew what they would be saying: "Brazen bugger! Did you see the pair of them? Talk about being bare-faced! All right, all right, granted Betty was a bit of a Tartar, and his mother . . . well, they all knew what she was. But for him to walk out on them and to take up with that one, Doo-lally-tap, he must be as daft as her. And always arm in arm, a pair of brazen buggers, if ever there was. Oh, he's barmy all right. Well, remember what he got up to—the Salvation Army thing? And then the trashcan? And to wipe a blackboard with a lad's face! If you ask me, they're well matched." As if they were shouting in his ear he could hear them. But it didn't matter to him; they couldn't penetrate his private world, this island on which he was living, this beautiful island called Lally.

In Mary's he announced loudly, "We're going in tomorrow, Mary. I was daft; we have all the weekend to get straight."

"Now you're talking sense." She nodded from him to Lally. "I wondered to meself why you were leaving it till Monday."

"Aw, just a fad, a kink. I'm gone up here." He tapped his brow.

"You needn't stress that fact." She laughed at him. "Go on, have something to eat. Give me your coat, Lally."

"Mary."

"Yes, Lally?"

"I was just sayin' to Jimmy, the next things I buy with me coupons I'm goin' to get something quiet like, and I'd like you to come with me and . . ."

"Come on, you big fathead." Jimmy tugged her so hard by the arm that she fell against him, and Mary just smiled, but she was laughing inside. Lally in quiet clothes! If you put her in a nun's garb, she'd still look like Lally. How could she ever hope to hide that bust and that backside? But it said something for her that she wanted to dress quietly. She thought now, as she had thought before, that it was a pity she was stamped with the telling title of Doo-lally-tap. In one way she could understand how she had come by the name, but in another she thought it was quite unfair, because Lally, at bottom, was no more doo-lally-tap than she herself was.

When they went into the dining room she said to her da, "They're going to move tomorrow. You could give them a hand."

"Oh aye." Alec nodded at Jimmy. "Oh aye, lad, I'll give you a hand to get straight, and pleased to. An' I tell you what, I'll come and dig your garden. Oh"—he looked at Mary—"that's if it's all right with you, lass?"

"Yes, it's all right with me, Da," Mary said softly.

"Oh, I'd like to get me spade into the earth again. Oh, I'd like that." He jerked his head at Jimmy, and Jimmy said, "Well, I'll give you plenty of what you like, Da. You can rely on me, I'll give you plenty of what you like." And they were all laughing as they sat down at the table.

10

Alice sat to the side of the window looking through the thick Nottingham lace curtains into the street. Across the road Peggy

Hurst was washing her windowsill. Not before time, she thought, and even now she was only giving it a lick and a promise. Dirty cat, that Peggy Hurst. And there was that Mrs. Keely with her two bairns; likely off to Shields Market to spend her money on trash. She never could keep the bairns nice, and her man had been in good work for years. These women! Men slaving for them, working from Monday morning till Saturday night for them, and half the women no better than they should be, while here she was having to fend for herself, neither man, chick nor child to speak a word to her or give her a penny. Badness and sin paid off. They talked about God being good; had He ever been good to her? What was before her? Work, and more work, five days a week until she died. She was only forty-six, she was no age. But she felt old; and no wonder, she'd had enough in her life to make anybody old. Oh, God, if only she could get her own back on them—just once—just once. That's all she asked.

She rose from the chair and began to pace the room. They were all together now, her husband, her daughter and her son, not forgetting his fancy piece, all together like a pack of thieves. They said Jimmy and that daft piece were never away from her shop. Why hadn't a bomb fallen on her and the shop? Decent, hardworking, God-fearing people had to be taken while others, like her, were left. She was her own flesh and blood, but God! how she hated her. All the ills in her life, all that had happened to her stemmed from their Mary.

She stopped in her pacing. And where was Betty? She was hardly in these days, either. She had some fellow in the offing; she could smell a rat before it was stinking.

The door opened at this and Betty came in and dropped the basket of groceries on the table.

"Where've you been? You've taken your time, haven't you?"

"Oh, for God's sake! Mam, you haven't got a stopwatch on me, have you?"

"Well! well! There's no need for that."

"Oh, my God!"

Alice turned from Betty and, putting her hand to her head, held it as she said, "Don't you start. Now, don't you start, Betty, because that'll be the last straw."

"Well, you will keep on. You're getting on my nerves—you keep on and on."

Alice subsided slowly into a chair. Her face was grim, her lips tight and trembling.

Betty tossed her head from side to side, tore off her coat and hat, went into the bedroom, then coming out again, said, "You're not the only one who's going through the mill. What do you think I've just heard?"

Alice's head came round quickly, her lips slightly open now, the eyes wide in inquiry. "What?" she asked.

"Your Mary's given them a house, a cottage."

"She's what!"

"Just what I said, she's given them a cottage. On the outskirts of the town, Moat Cottage or some such name."

Alice was out of the chair, standing straight, rigid. "Moat Cottage. Our Mary's given them Moat Cottage!"

"That's what I said. I met Phyllis Bradley and she told me. Apparently your Mary's owned the cottage for a long time, or her man did. But Master Jimmy's been doing it up and . . . your daughter"—now Betty's small head was bouncing on her shoulders—"your daughter's given it to them, lock, stock and barrel, deeds. What do you think about that? Phyllis Bradley's girl plays with the McArthurs' child. She got it through her."

"Moat Cottage!" Alice's eyes were wide, her jaw was sagging. She was looking at Betty, yet through her, and beyond her, and she said again, "Moat Cottage!"

"Yes, that's what I said. Do you know the place?"

"Yes . . . yes, I know the place."

Did she know Moat Cottage? Moat Cottage had been her Shangri-La. She had come from the Church Bank, through Hope Street, into Cornice Street; they were just stops on the way toward Moat Cottage. She could hear herself saying to Alec, "It's to be let at twelve and six a week," and him replying, "Dou-

ble what we pay here. You barmy, woman?" And now their Mary
had given it to their Jimmy, and he was taking that woman
there, that big, fat, slobbery bitch of a woman. No! NO, not to
Moat Cottage!

"Our Mary . . ."

"What?"

"Our Mary, she's done this on purpose. She knew, she knew
I always wanted that place. Why, I nearly went to live there.
She's done it on purpose, you see." She was standing over Betty,
gripping her arms, and Betty, shrugging her off, cried, "Stop it,
Mam, you're hurtin' me." Then she said, "You were going to
live there?"

"Yes, years ago I was, but he was frightened of the rent. Alec,
he was frightened of the rent. But she knew, our Mary, she knew
what I thought about that place. I used to take them when they
were bairns, her and Jimmy, and show it to them. It had a long
garden back and front. Right out in the country it was then, with
open fields all about, and the sky." She lifted her hand and
waved it back and forward, and Betty said sharply, "Mam! Mam!"
and as if Alice had been recalled from a distant time, a distant
place, she stared at Betty and asked, "Are they in yet?"

"No, they're moving in on Monday, so I understand. The
McArthurs' girl said they are going in on Monday and are going
to have a sort of party. By the way"—Betty turned her back on
Alice and her voice shook as she said—"there's a further bit of
news: the bairn came over two weeks ago. You're a grandma
again, once removed. . . . It's a boy."

"My God!"

They both sat down now, and there was quiet on the room for
some minutes before it was broken by Alice's saying, "Moat Cottage! Moat Cottage!"

"Is that all you can say, Moat Cottage?" Betty was screaming
now, and she jumped to her feet and ran into the kitchen, but
Alice still sat, and she still repeated, "Moat Cottage! Moat Cottage!"

11

"Mam! Mam!"

"What? What is it?" Mary came out of layers of sleep. "What do you want, child?"

"Listen, Ma; there's somebody knocking at the shop door downstairs. Listen."

Mary pulled herself up and listened. Then, getting out of bed and pulling on her dressing gown, she ran into the sitting room, switched on the light, then went to the window and, opening it, looked down into the dark street.

"Who is it?"

A light flashed up into her face. "Mrs. Tollett?"

"Yes, that's me."

"Can you come down a minute? It's the police."

Police. Even the word could make her stomach turn over. "Just a minute." She shut the window and looked at Annie for a moment in amazement, saying "Police." Her eyes lifted to the clock on the mantelpiece. Quarter past three in the morning. In the hall she pulled a coat over her dressing gown and said to Annie, "You stay put, and don't wake your granda or Cousin Annie."

But Alec was already at his bedroom door, asking, "What is it? What's up? Is she sick?" He was looking at Annie.

Mary said, "No, no. There's somebody knocking at the shop door. Now stay where you are until I find out what it's about." Her ma, she thought; something had happened to her ma. She didn't add, at last. But her thoughts went on, they'd come for her da, naturally.

As she unbarred the shop door, the policeman said, "I'll come in a minute if you don't mind." There were two of them. They walked past her, then turned and faced where she stood with her back to the door. "It's . . . it's about your brother, Mrs. Tollett."

"Jim . . . Jimmy?"

"Yes, Jimmy, and . . . and his wife. There's been an accident . . . a fire."

"A what! A fire? The cottage?"

"Yes, yes, I'm afraid so."

"They're . . . they're not hurt?"

The policeman opened his mouth, then moved his head downwards.

"Aw, no. Oh, dear God, no!" She was rocking herself while she held her face now. "They're not . . . ?"

"Your brother's all right, that is, he's badly burned, but he's alive. But I'm afraid, Mrs. Tollett, his wife's dead."

"Lally? His wife? I mean Lally? Lally? . . . No!"

The policeman stared at her, and she pushed past him and walked to the counter and pressed her back to it, tight against the edge, and she flapped her hand at them, saying, "No, no, no! He'll go mad. Lally . . . Lally wouldn't hurt a fly. What is it? What happened?"

"As far as we can gather," said the policeman softly, "the fire had caught well alight by the time your brother awoke. They were overcome by the fumes. He . . . he opened the window and tried to get her out that way, but couldn't, and then . . . well, by what I can gather he dragged her down the stairs; the place was blazing. She must have been dead before he got her outside. And it's a cold night, extremes, you know. He tried to revive her. Some people in a car passing along the main road saw the flames and when they got to him they couldn't do anything; well, it was natural, he was like someone demented. By the time the fire brigade arrived there was nothing much left of the cottage."

She felt herself going down into the darkness, then her da was saying, "Lass! Lass! Drink this."

She opened her eyes. The policemen were still there. She

didn't remember their bringing her upstairs. She looked at her father. The tears were running down his face, and Annie was crying and whimpering, "Oh! Uncle Jimmy. Oh! Uncle Jimmy. And me Aunt Lally." It hadn't taken Annie long to adopt Lally as an aunt.

Cousin Annie came hobbling out of the kitchen with a tray. She had been making the inevitable cup that cheers. She, too, was crying.

"Where are they?" Mary's voice was level.

"In the Frederick Road Infirmary, Shields. We've got the car outside—we could run you down."

"Yes, yes."

They helped her to her feet.

"I'll get me things on," she said.

"Have this cup of tea, lass," said Cousin Annie.

"I don't want any tea." She walked past them into the room, and as she got into her clothes she thought, What's wrong with us? There's a blight on us. He'll go mad. I hope he dies an' all; he wouldn't want to live without her; she was like a stay to him, a great, warm, comforting stay.

For days Jimmy lay in a daze of pain, mental and physical. He prayed to die. If they had left any means near him he would have seen to it that he died. They stuck needles in his arms to quiet him, but it didn't obliterate the pain in his mind. He had killed Lally, burned her alive.

For the thousandth time he was back in the room. He had put the gramophone on and he had said to her, "It's lucky we have the gramophone. And we'll get a battery radio; I don't want electricity, nor gas. I like the lamplight, don't you?"

"It's lovely, Jimmy, lovely," she had said.

"And you're lovely." He had pulled her up out of the chair and waltzed her round the uneven floor, and she had cried, "You're tipsy."

"And so are you," he had answered; "we're both tipsy. Come on, let's get more tipsy, let's finish this. It's a celebration, it's a housewarming. We would have had it on Monday anyway." And as he poured the glasses of whisky out he said, "The last time I felt like this I led the Salvation Army around Shields Market, remember?"

They had fallen on each other's neck and laughed as she said, "Eeh! you're a lad, Jimmy."

"And you're a lass, Lally. You're a strapping, North Country lass, and I love you . . . love you . . . love you." With each "love" he had hugged her tightly to him, and she had gasped and laughed loudly and said, "Jimmy, it seems too good to be true. It's like heaven."

After that they had sat down on the mat in front of the roaring fire and, as she leaned against him and looked at the sparks flying up the chimney, she had said, "I never want to die."

That is what she had said, "I never want to die." And then they had gone upstairs, and she had died. And it was his fault, because he had banked up the fire with wood. She had warned him not to. "Eeh!" she had said. "Don't put any more on." But he had laughed at her, saying, "This old chimney will stand it. It's brick all the way up; there's no timber going across it. And it'll soon die down, and the room will be warm in the morning when we get up."

When he had next looked down into the room over the banister it was like looking into a blast furnace. He had dragged her heavy body from the bed and tried to push it out of the window, but the window was too small, and only one side of it opened anyway. Then he carried her to the stairs. But when he was only halfway down he had lifted his hands from the burning banister and had fallen, and then he had dragged her through the heap of burning furniture. Most of the bedroom pieces had been left downstairs because the men couldn't get them up the narrow stairs; they'd had a job to get the bed up. They'd had to take the box spring apart, and he had said he would manage the furniture himself; he could unscrew it and put it together again. And there it was like a mighty bonfire, and when he'd got the door open there was more of it. The pile of wood outside was ablaze and lying across the door. He hadn't wondered how it got there, he just knew he dragged her over it. And then he was holding her, rocking her, yelling. He could hear himself yelling, "Lally! Lally! Lally! God Almighty, Lally!" . . .

On the evening of the third day, when he came round, Mary was sitting by the bed. She said, "Hello, lad," and he just stared at her. He couldn't move his hands or arms because of the bandages, and they had bandaged his head. He remembered his hair catching afire and being wafted into a blaze when he went outside, and he had bashed at it with one hand while still hanging on to Lally.

"You feeling better?"

For answer he said, "My fault, Mary."

"No, no, Jimmy."

"Yes."

"No, no. What makes you think that?"

"The fire, I . . . I heaped it up. I . . . I got tight"—he closed his eyes, then said, "I got tight, Mary. Things always happen when I get tight."

"Ssh Ssh!" she said. "Don't talk, go to sleep. But it wasn't your fault, it was nobody's fault."

The next time he was aware of her sitting by the bed was two days later. His mind was clearer then.

She said, "Are you feeling easier?" and he answered, "Yes." Then he looked at her and said, "Couldn't last, Mary; it was too good to last, too wonderful."

She gulped in her throat but couldn't speak.

"I wasn't worthy of her and . . . and I should have known something like that would happen because . . . because I saw me mother; in the afternoon I saw me mother. She was coming out of Brooker's Lane, not far from the cottage. She didn't see me—I kept out of her way—but I remember wishing I hadn't seen her. I should have known, shouldn't I? She put a curse on me."

"Be quiet. Be quiet. Don't say such things." But even as she said this her mind was working rapidly. Her mother along Brooker's Lane? Brooker's Lane joined the rough road on which the cottage stood. What was her mother doing round Brooker's Lane?

It was three days later when she knew what her mother had been doing round Brooker's Lane. The insurance man called, together with the local insurance inspector, and another man who had come down from Newcastle and whose particular work was to deal with fire claims, and what he said to her was, "I'm sorry, Mrs. Tollett, but we have to go into the matter of your claim; there's more in it than meets the eye. Now, we're not exactly sure of this, but there will be more investigating to do. But as it stands now there is a theory that the fire did not start in the chimney inside but was started from the pile of wood outside with an application of paraffin."

She stared at the three men. Then she poked her head toward them and said, "With an application of paraffin?"

"Yes, Mrs. Tollett; that's what they suspect. Do you know anyone who would have reason to set the place on fire?"

She did not shake her head or answer; she just continued to stare at them.

Her insurance man said, "You did tell me, Mrs. Tollett, that their original plan was to go in on Monday. Whoever set the place afire, if someone did, that is"—he looked at his two superiors—"very likely they didn't know that anyone was inside."

Somebody set the place on fire with paraffin from the outside. And Jimmy had said, "I saw me mother coming out of Brooker's Lane. She didn't see me." "Do you know anyone who would have reason to set the place on fire?" the man had asked.

Oh, no. NO! She couldn't have done THAT. But she could, she was capable of anything, her ma; disfiguring or burning alive, her ma was capable of anything.

"Don't distress yourself, Mrs. Tollett"—the inspector was speaking—"your claim will be met. There's no doubt about that, but there'll be an investigation."

Courteously they left. They left her sitting staring in front of her, churning up such a rage that she knew that if she didn't take hold of herself she would give vent to it in screaming.

Annie came into the room, saying, "Mam, can I go and play with Bella?" and she said to her, "Yes."

"Mam, are you all right?"

She looked at her daughter. "Yes, I'm all right, hinny. Go and play with Bella. I'm going out for a short while. I'll go out the back way. If your granda wants me, tell him I won't be long. Tell Teresa also that I've gone out for a short while."

"Where you going, Mam?"

"Just on a bit of business, dear."

"Not down to the hospital?"

"No, not now, not down to the hospital. I won't be long." She put on her hat and coat and went out.

The time that it took her to get from Cornice Street to Haydon Terrace was filled with the admonition, "Don't touch her. Don't touch her. Don't lay a hand on her." Yet from all areas of her brain, it seemed, the question came at her, How could she resist laying a hand on her?

She had never been in the house in Haydon Terrace, but from Jimmy's description she knew the layout.

She went in the hallway and stopped at the door on the left-hand side. She knocked once, a hard, sharp knock, and when it opened Betty was standing there. When she saw who her visitor was she put her hand over her mouth and muttered, "No, no."

"Get out of me way."

As she went into the room Betty grabbed at her arm, saying, "It's no good. Leave her be."

"Where is she?"

Betty jerked her head back toward the door. "You can't do anything, it's no good."

With a sharp push she threw Betty off and went to the door and thrust it open, and there, opposite her, in a double bed lay her mother. Her two arms were lying limp on top of the patchwork quilt, her head was tight against her shoulder and the corner of her mouth was drawn upwards into her cheek.

"You see. You see." Betty was by her side now almost jabbering. "She can't speak, do nothing; she's had a stroke. She's been like that since she heard about . . ."

"Heard about?" Mary looked down on Betty, and she repeated, "Heard about? You mean since she burned Lally to death, and Jimmy nearly. That's what you mean." She looked toward the bed again, then took a step forward. There was no pity in her for the paralyzed form. "You took paraffin, didn't you, Ma, a tin of paraffin and set light to the wood outside, and tried to burn them alive? Nobody was going to get Moat Cottage, least of all Jimmy and Lally. You'd always had your eye on the place, hadn't you? And it was the last straw that they should be happy there. Well, I'm going to tell you something. Your son's been happier this year than ever he's been in his life. He had one year that few men ever enjoy." She turned her face toward Betty now. "And that's for your ears an' all." Looking back at her mother, she ended, "Your catch phrase was 'Everybody gets their deserts.' Well now, it's come true, hasn't it?"

The eyelids flickered, the face strained, the saliva ran out of the corner of the twisted mouth, guttural sounds filled the room, and Mary stood watching, pitiless in this moment. And then she said slowly, "I hope you live for years, Ma, years and years, until you're a very old woman." And on this she turned and walked out.

She was opening the door to go into the hall when Betty came scrambling after her and, looking up into her face, whimpered, "She didn't know, she didn't know they were in there. I told her they weren't going in until Monday; she wouldn't have done it, else."

"You knew then, you knew what she was going to do? Well, you're as bad as her. Whether she knew they were in there or not, she was going to burn their home down, and, whatever she or you might say, she would be wishing in her heart they were in there. And she got her wish. Well now, I said I hoped she lived for many a year. I hope you do, too; you'll be good companions for each other." She stared down into Betty's taut, trembling face, then she opened the door and went into the hallway, and as she went through the main door Betty's whimpering voice followed her, saying, "I'm not having it—she isn't my responsibility. I'm not having it all me life. She'll have to go to a rest home; I'm not having it."

12

When Mary brought the baby from the hospital the whole routine of the house was disorganized. Everything had to be adjusted to a delicate child who had an ear infection, who had to be fed every four hours and who cried most of the night; even when it wasn't crying she was aware of it, for she had the cot by her bedside.

Then Annie had to be moved out of her room and her bed put in with Cousin Annie's, not without protest from both of them. Although young Annie was fond of her Uncle Jimmy, and Cousin Annie was in sympathy with him in his trouble, neither of them wanted to be made uncomfortable because of him.

Why, they both asked, couldn't he go in with Granda?

Because he wasn't going in with Granda.

Mary gave them no further explanation. Jimmy, she knew, would take a long time to pull himself together. There would be nights when he would want to walk the floor and cry, so he would need to be alone.

It was ten days later when she brought him home. He sat like a child, looking so lost, so alone, that her heart was crying for him even while she said to him, "What's done's done; you can't make a better of it. I've been through a similar experience and you can't make a better of it. You've got to face it."

"Face what, Mary?" he said to her quietly.

"Life," she answered.

"What life?"

"Jimmy"—she sighed heavily—"you've got a child to see to."

"A child? Oh, yes." It was as if he had just remembered the child, and looking at her pathetically he said, "But you'll see to him, won't you, Mary?"

"No, Jimmy. No." She made her voice harsh. "He's your responsibility; you've got to face up to it."

She did not add, "I've got enough on my plate, with me da, Cousin Annie, and a daughter, and two businesses to see to, besides taking on you and the child permanently."

He looked up at her, and as if the child had never been mentioned he said, "Mary, I can't get it out of my mind what I've done. If I hadn't been drunk, at least tight. And if only I'd taken heed of her. She told me."

"Be quiet, Jimmy; it wasn't your fault."

"Oh! Mary, Mary." He shook his head from side to side and as he lowered it she looked down on the partly bare scarred scalp, and she wondered if the hair would ever grow again. From the front he looked bald; it made him look old.

She sat down in front of him and stared at him. Her mind in a turmoil, she asked herself should she tell him the truth, who really was to blame for the fire. But she was afraid of the effect of the truth on him at this moment; in his present state it wouldn't take much to unbalance him altogether. Perhaps it was better to let him bear the guilt for a little longer, until she got him on his feet. The doctor had told her he was in a very low state; he would need care, gentle handling and care.

Poor Jimmy!

The following morning she was down in the shop early. She had been up before six with the child and hadn't gone back to bed. She did not open the shop until eight o'clock these days and she was pulling the blinds when the postman pushed the mail through the letter box. She did not go immediately and pick it up; it would undoubtedly be bills and circulars. She never received personal mail; she had no one to receive it from. She picked up the half a dozen brown envelopes, and the white one, which was addressed to Mrs. Mary Tollett. She turned the envelope over, then looked at her name again before opening it. She hadn't thought to look at the postmark. The letter began: "Dear Mary," and went on, "I've never called you Mary before, but that's how I've always thought of you. I just want to say how sorry I was to hear of the tragedy to your brother and his wife—my mother wrote and told me. We are sailing for America tomorrow and I go with mixed feelings. I just wanted to say good-bye again in remembrance of the old days when we were young. Yours ever, Hughie Amesden."

She went into the back shop and sat down on an upturned box. In remembrance of the old days. What old days? In the old days when they were young, really young, he had never spoken to her except that once to say hello. What memory had he of the old days? Twice he had spoken to her in the shop, and once in the cemetery, and now he had gone to America. Why had he written this letter? To say he was sorry about Jimmy and Lally? He had called Lally Jimmy's wife; that was kind of him; but why had he written? She had thought that he was already in America. It was doubtful if they would ever meet again.

In memory of the old days when we were young.

She recalled the white light that had enveloped her and the feeling that it had given her. But he knew nothing about that; and even so, that light had faded and died when she met Ben. She went to crush the letter in her hand, then stopped herself. He was only being polite, kind to someone in the same boat as himself. He had lost his only child; she had lost Ben and David, and her grandparents, and they had all gone on the same night. He was seeing her as someone alone, a widow, and, therefore, showing his sympathy.

Alone! She looked upwards to the ceiling into the house up above. There were five of them up there now. Annie was twelve. In another five or six years she could marry and be gone, but for the rest—her da, Cousin Annie and Jimmy, and the child—she had them with her for life.

Suddenly she covered her face with her hands and tried to

stop the tears flowing, but they squeezed through her fingers and ran down her wrists, and no matter how she chided herself for being selfish and thinking only of herself, she couldn't stop crying. When at last she did, she looked at the letter on her knee and saw that her tears had made the ink run until the writing was blurred, one letter into the other.

It was almost three months later when she told Jimmy who was responsible for Lally's death.

Physically his body was recovering, and mentally, too, his mind seemed to be groping its way back to normality, for he had said to her yesterday, "I must start thinking about getting back to work. I'll have to use my hands sometime." And to this she had replied, "There's plenty of time for that. Go on helping Da downstairs; that'll give you plenty of exercise."

He had moods, black moods, when he was borne down with self-recrimination. It had been three weeks since the last one. When in these moods, he would sit staring before him and no one would get a word out of him; and he mightn't eat a bite for forty-eight hours. And when he came out of them he would always look at her and say, "Can I have a drink, Mary, just a short one?" and she would give him a drop of whisky.

It was around four o'clock in the afternoon when she returned with the child. She had taken him down to the infirmary for the weekly treatment on his ear. She was tired with the journey and also through lack of sleep. Her nights had been broken for months past. The house seemed full to overflowing; there was no privacy. And only yesterday Cousin Annie had told her out of the blue that she had sold her house in Wallsend, which meant that she was stuck with Cousin Annie for good. Well, she had always known this; but it was the fact that the little woman had gone about the business of selling her house in secret. Yet in a way she understood the reason for her doing this, for she was likely afraid that, had she consulted her, she might have been told it was about time she returned across the water. It was a *fait accompli*. Ben had often used that term. She hadn't

known what it meant until he explained it to her. But she knew
well enough now, for everybody seemed to have come into her
life in this way.

When she got upstairs it was to find Jimmy sitting staring
into the fire. He didn't even turn his head when she entered
the room.

"Oh, no," she said it aloud. Then going immediately out and
putting the baby in the cot, she pulled off her things, marched
back into the room, sat opposite him, gripped his hands and
said, "Now, look you here, Jimmy." She had to jerk him round
to bring his gaze to bear on her. "Snap out of it. Do you hear
me? I've got something to tell you. Listen to me." She shook his
arms, anything but gently, and he blinked as he said, "Aye. Oh,
yes, Mary."

"Listen to me, Jimmy. About . . . about the fire."

He stared at her. "About the fire?"

"You didn't cause that fire; you didn't set that place on fire.
Remember the insurance men who kept coming back and forward here? I didn't let them talk to you—you weren't fit. The
cottage was set on fire, Jimmy, deliberately set on fire."

He closed his eyes tight, screwed them up until they were
lost in their sockets, then stretched them wide. "Set on fire?"

"Yes." She was gripping his hands tightly now, staring into
his face. "With a tin of paraffin sprinkled all over the bomb-site
wood that you left outside. Remember? There was a pile of it
each side of the door."

"Paraffin? On the wood?"

"Paraffin on the wood, deliberately put there. You didn't set
that place on fire. It had nothing to do with the chimney. You
could have roasted an ox on that fire and the chimney would
have stood it. Don't forget you'd had it cleaned, you'd taken
all the soot down. The fire didn't start inside, Jimmy." She
bounced his hand up and down on his knee as she repeated,
"The fire didn't start inside, it was deliberately done from the
outside."

"Who? But who?" His face was stretched, his eyes wide. She

stared at him for a long while, and she gulped two mouthfuls of spittle before she could say, "Me ma."

She watched the expression changing on his face from amazement to horror, to disbelief, and back to horror again, before he said, "No! No! She wouldn't, not that. Bad as she is, not that."

"She did. She always wanted that cottage, remember? Remember years back when she wanted me da to take it, but the rent was too high? And when she knew you were going into it she couldn't bear it, she . . ."

She almost fell backwards when he flung her hands away. Then he was on his feet and running toward the door.

"Jimmy! Jimmy!" She caught him and hung on to his shoulders, crying, "Listen! listen! It's no good going to her."

He was looking down at her face. "You say she set light to the house, she burned Lally to death, and it's no good!"

Using all her strength she pushed him against the wall. "She didn't know you were in. Apparently she had got wind that you were moving in on Monday; she didn't know you had gone in on Saturday. She just meant to burn the place down."

"But . . . but she burned Lally." He put out his hand to thrust her away again, and she flung herself between him and the door and cried at him, rapidly now, "It's no use you going to her, I tell you, she's had a stroke, she's paralyzed, she's been paid out. I went . . . I went to the house—I was for murdering her myself—and then I saw her. She couldn't move hand nor foot, her face all twisted, the only thing left alive in her were her eyes. You'll do no good going. Leave her be. I told her I hope she lives for years, and I do. I hope she's pickled in the poison of her mind. Oh aye, I hope she'll live for a long time."

She watched him go limp. He seemed to lose inches. Then he was staggering back to the seat at the fire. And now he began to laugh, and this really frightened her, for this was like no laugh that she had ever heard. She pleaded with him, "Jimmy! Jimmy! Stop it!" But he went on laughing. She was gentle with him at first, saying, "Come on, lad, come on. I felt you should know. I had to tell you; you were flaying yourself. It's better you should know the truth. I waited. Give over! Give over! Stop it!"

When the laughter rose it became so loud that it filled the house. She took him by the shoulders again and shook him, and gradually it subsided. But he filled its place now with sobbing, and she didn't know which was worse. He cried loudly, not like a man crying silently, half-ashamed, but like a young lad or a young girl who had been faced with some unbearable catastrophe; and in between his sobs he kept emitting two words, "Me ma! Me ma!" Sometimes the name would reach a high crescendo, sometimes it would be just a muttering, but mostly it was a loud wailing cry, loud enough to be heard down in the shop and bring Alec and Cousin Annie upstairs, and to make the women customers look at each other and say, "He's calling for his ma. Aye well, it just shows, blood's thicker than water; it's your own you want when you're in trouble."

Jimmy stayed in bed until the following dinnertime, and then, unbeknown to Mary, he went out. Almost demented, she waited all afternoon for the police coming to tell her the latest news, but no one came. She waited all evening, and it was about half-past nine, when she was on the point of going to the police herself, that two men brought him home. One was a man who lived up the street, the other was a stranger. They themselves had also been drinking, but they didn't appear to be the worse for it. As one of them said, "It didn't take much to make Jimmy plastered." They left him on the landing floor and bade her good night, and as she looked down on him she knew that this was the beginning of the long end.

BOOK 3

The New
Species

JARROW 1973

1

"Do you mean to say that you've never, NEVER had . . . ?"

"Oh, be quiet, Maggie, you make things sound so—aw!"

"Aw! yourself. But honest, tell me. Why, I thought you and Cliff . . ."

"Well, you thought wrong then."

Maggie Pearce jumped up from the rug where she had been sitting in front of the electric fire, and, putting her hands behind her back, began to walk between the two single divan beds that stood opposite each other each against a wall of the long, narrow room. Her body half-stooped, her chin thrust out, she was mimicking a figure well known to both of them, that of Old Dodgett, Professor of Applied Mathematics. Now her tongue licking first one side of her mouth and then the other, she said, "Gentlemen, it seems that today: *virginibus puerisque canto,* for we have with us a specimen, one Patricia Ridley, with, of course, the prefix of 'miss,' who has for sale a maidenhead, and if we consider the students of this university as our universal set E, then she is the only element, I repeat, the only element of the subset virgins, V of the female set F."

"Stop it! You're bloody awful, Maggie. That's what you are, bloody awful."

"Ah! She's come alive. Do you know something?" With arms stretched wide, Maggie went toward the tall girl. "It's the first time I've heard you swear. Come into the fold, down to our level, join the band, you're one of us."

Pat slapped at the hands that were going round her shoulders, saying, "Thanks for the invitation, but I don't want to join the band. What are you, anyway, but a lot of mediocre-brained animals? It's . . . it's true what Tim Hanley said yesterday: half of your so-called band shouldn't be in the university, because you're making it into a cross between a whore shop and an abortion clinic."

"Aw, God Almighty!" Maggie's voice had a petulant note to it now. "You're talking like Mother Mary Magdalen. And you know something? I think it's all hooey; you're putting on an act, because you can't tell me you went rock climbing"—she stressed the "rock climbing"—"with a fellow like Cliff Spencer from Friday night until Monday morning and remained in . . . tact. Anyway, Cliff's version is different. He told Reg . . ."

"He's a liar. I tell you he's a liar. Whatever he told Reg, nothing happened. We stayed at the hostel, you know we did."

"Oh, my God! Don't be so infantile." Maggie put her hand to her head. "Honestly, you make me laugh, Pat; it's like talking to a six-year-old . . . not a seven-year-old, because they know it all. You should have got your mother to let you look in when they were giving them lectures on the telly. . . . Oh, for God's sake! Pat, you're not going to weep, are you?"

"No, I'm not going to weep." Pat marched down the room and flung herself on to the edge of her bed, and from there she cried back at her roommate, "But I'm going to tell you this: I'm getting out."

There followed a tense silence during which Maggie's jaw

slowly dropped, and then she said, "Look here, Pat, don't be a goat. I was only ribbing you."

"You've ribbed once too often, Maggie. You think I'm a fool, don't you? Oh, yes, you do. 'The git from Jarrow' you once called me."

"Oh!" Maggie shrugged her shoulders up around her ears. "That was years ago, when you first came. We were all new and stupid then."

"It isn't years ago, it's just over eighteen months." She sighed and stared at the wall opposite, then said slowly, "But at times it does seem like years. . . . Well, anyway I'm going to pack it in." Her chin gave a defiant jerk and she stared at Maggie, and Maggie, her voice high, cried, "What do you mean, pack it in? Are you talking about the room or the course?"

"Both."

"Oh, no!" Maggie was sitting beside her now. "You can't, Pat. All right, get a new place for yourself, but don't fluff the course. You're the only bright spark of the math lot; they say you'll get a first. And to tell you the truth, that's what niggles me." Her voice dropped and she said gently, "I'm jealous, jealous of what you've got in your noodle." She tapped twice on Pat's temple.

"It's no use, Maggie." Pat's voice was quiet too now. "I've been thinking about it for some time. The course isn't what I thought; I mean it isn't what I want to do."

"Well, what do you want to do?"

"I don't know. I'm all at sea. I only know one thing, I don't want to carry on."

"Just because I've ribbed you?"

"No, no, Maggie." She turned and looked at the red-headed girl, whom sometimes she liked and sometimes she loathed, and she said, "It's been fun on the whole, I mean living with you. You've taught me a lot besides"—she lowered her head and raised her eyebrows—"the three easy ways to lose one's virginity."

"There's only one, dear."

She was forced to laugh. Then Maggie said seriously, "Are you sure it isn't what I've done . . . or said?"

"Yes, I'm sure."

"But to give up math! Why, they're crying out for them; you could get anywhere. Look at that ad we saw yesterday for an actuary. And they're feeding slogans into computers now solely for mathematicians: 'Come, come, I want you only.' "

"Oh, Maggie, stop it. I don't want to laugh."

"Have you another subject in mind?"

"No."

"What will your people say? Have you thought of that?"

"Yes, they'll likely go round the bend, particularly my mother. I can hear her saying, 'After all we've done!' You know, the usual thing."

They nodded at each other.

"It isn't because you're getting such a small grant?"

"Good Lord! No. The money doesn't come into it."

"Well, anyway, I would think it over well before you tell them; let them have this weekend clear. And you might see things differently by Monday, too."

"I wasn't going home this weekend."

"But you said . . ."

"It's all right, Maggie, it's all right. Reg can come and take up residence as long as"—she now thumped her own bed with her fist—"and I repeat, as long as he doesn't sleep in here after you've had your weekly bust up. It'll be no use straightening it up because I'll know, mind."

"Cross my heart and swear on the pill, he'll not put a toenail near your virgin sheets."

"Oh"—Pat screwed up her face—"don't keep on about that. It's so stupid—sex, sex—you get sick."

"Well"—Maggie rose from the bed—"everybody to their taste, as the woman said."

"Yes, yes, I know—who kissed the cow." They both repeated the last line together, then laughed; and Maggie went on, "It all depends on how you look at it. Me, I enjoy it, I mean not being one, you know what I mean?"

"I know what you mean, Maggie. But if you'll take a word of warning from one so inexperienced as me, I'd say you'd better look out. If Ma Smith comes back early one night and finds Reg here, she'll report you."

"Not her. When Ma Smith comes home before twelve o'clock on a Friday or Saturday night I'll know she's hooked somebody and is going to be married to Mr. Fourth, God help him."

"Aren't you afraid she'd look in?"

"No, she's very considerate." Maggie laughed. "She tiptoes past the door. Anyway, we put a chair under the handle and by the time she moves that Reg'll be either under the bed or over the wall." She put her head back now and laughed heartily. "We did a rehearsal one night: into his clothes, out of the window, and over the back wall, three minutes dead flat."

"Well, all I can say is you're lucky it gives off into a cul de sac."

"Yes, aren't I? By the way. If you're not going home, where are you going, Jarrow?"

"Yes, to Gran Tollett's."

"Oh"—Maggie nodded—"that's something I meant to tell you. I saw her yesterday, in Northumberland Street."

"You did! Did you speak to her?"

"No; she was with a tall bloke."

"Fair, Swedish-looking?"

"That's him."

"That's my cousin Ben."

"Oh, so that's Ben. He's a looker. And your grannie, it's hard to believe she's your grannie. She knows how to dress, I'll say."

"What was she wearing?"

"Oh, a sort of mole-colored coat trimmed with fox, very fetching, and a fur hat. She's been a looker, she still is. Is the blonde married?"

"Ben? No; except to Gran. He's always trotting around after her. I think she gets a bit fed up at times."

"By the way, why aren't you going home?"

"Oh, they're going to Scarborough, to my father's people."

"Does your grannie know you're coming?"

"No." Pat laughed lightly. "I don't have to tell her. I can go anytime."

"Nice to have a grannie like that. Are you seeing Philip before you go?"

"Yes, I promised to call round at his place."

Maggie turned her face over her shoulder—there was a grin on it now—and said, "Ah-ha! mind yourself." Then putting her hand quickly over her mouth, she muttered, "Sorry, sorry—subject taboo."

Twenty minutes later they were both ready, Maggie to receive her current boyfriend, and Pat dressed for outdoors in a dark midicoat that made her appear inches taller than her five feet seven, and as she stood drawing on a pair of gauntlet gloves Maggie looked at her and said slowly, "Think it well over, I mean about packing it in. It's a serious step; you might regret it. You could go further and fare worse. It's a decent university. Oh, we grumble and growl, but that's the prerogative of youth, so they say. I could have gone to any one of three, as I've told you, and my headmistress even suggested Oxford or Cambridge, but because our Brian had liked it here so much, and the place and the people . . ."

"MAGGIE, what you trying to sell? It's my place, my home; you don't have to sell either the North or the university to me!"

"Oh, my God! I'm always putting my foot in it. All right, all right. Now don't, for God's sake, come the stout Geordie putting the foreigner in his place. I'm sorry. All I meant to say was you've been given the privilege of taking advantage of something good right on your doorstep, so don't kick it off without thinking hard."

They stared at each other and smiled, thin smiles. Then as Pat went toward the door, Maggie, her manner changing in its mercurial way, cried, "Give my love to the Swede. Ask him if he's got any saucy books I haven't read. He looked the type who'd line the mattress with them."

Pat went out and banged the door, but she was shaking her head and smiling to herself when she stepped into the street. Yet as she walked through the biting cold toward the bus stop she wondered whether Maggie really did have anything to do with her present attitude of mind about leaving the university. Then she rejected it. No, it wasn't Maggie, not more than any of the others. Perhaps it was herself who was at fault. Perhaps the trouble was she had got into the wrong set. She had met them through Maggie, and she had met Maggie because they were roommates. Perhaps her place was with the highbrows. But then she didn't consider herself intellectual enough to mix with them; and the fuds, the new evangelists who were trying to swing the pendulum from sex to saints, didn't appeal to her either.

Why, she asked herself, was there this great unrest in her? But didn't all universities breed unrest? They were the incubators of unrest. The name they gave to it was maturing, creating the complete personality. Perhaps she had put her finger on it. Perhaps she didn't want to mature and be equipped to grapple with life. When she faced up to herself she knew that she was bored by the prospect of what lay before her, a life of teaching, of ramming home mathematics, or of feeding programs into a computer, or of sitting in an office all day, as she would do if she became an actuary—that's if the opportunity presented itself, for there was all this talk of jobs going until you went looking for them. Some of the third-year students were experiencing this already.

When she studied herself she thought that she really must be backward in some way, for she was continually comparing her present life with her very young life in high school. She had enjoyed that life. But it wasn't only school that had made her happy then; it was the fact, she thought, that she had lived in Jarrow and within ten minutes' walk of her grannie. Everything had been close-knit; you always knew where to find people; her grannie's door was always open—perhaps it was because she kept the shop.

Getting her place in the university had changed not only her own life but that of her own particular family, for from that time her mother couldn't get away from Jarrow quickly enough, and her goal was Gosforth, in Newcastle. It appeared that her mother had never liked Jarrow, even though for years she had lived yon side of the station stairs in York Avenue, and her in-laws had lived near Laburnum Grove. And you couldn't get much higher than that in Jarrow. She knew her mother well enough to suspect that she wanted to forget she had been brought up over a shop and in the poorest quarter of the town and was just using the fact that her daughter was going to the university as a loophole. "We'll be on the university doorstep, so to speak," she had said, "so you'll be able to pop home at the weekends."

Pop home! And every other weekend, sometimes every weekend, they were away to Scarborough, where her grandmother and grandfather Ridley lived now.

Her mother, she considered, thought more of her dad's folks than she did of her own. Then, of course, they had much more money. . . . Now she was being bitchy. And as for more money, there was a question about that. They showed off more, but she bet that, if her grannie laid her pennies side by side with theirs, she knew whose would stretch the farther.

Her mother got very peeved with her grannie. She had no need to continue to live above that shop, she said, particularly as she had closed it three years ago. It was a pity, she said, that Cornice Street hadn't come under the demolition order right away; but its time wasn't far off.

They all wondered what her grannie would do. Three times in the last ten years she had been on the point of marrying again, and although her mother had put the blame for her grannie's failure to go through with the matches down to Ben, she knew that she was glad that her grannie hadn't married, for if she had taken a husband, it would likely have made a difference in her will.

Oh! she was being bitchy tonight.

When she got off the bus she pulled her hood further round her face. The cold was piercing. She wished she hadn't promised to call at Philip's place. She always felt slightly embarrassed there. She supposed it was because she rarely saw him alone; there were nearly always the other two students in his room, talking shop, or shredding some university rule to pieces. She didn't mind John Summners, but she just couldn't stand Angus Mills.

She entered the hallway and knocked on the first door to the right of her, and when Philip Smyth's voice called, "Come!" she opened the door, and there, astraddle a chair, which was his favorite pose, was Angus Mills. He had been talking. That was evident. He turned his head and looked at her but gave her no greeting. Nor did Philip get up off the couch where he was sitting, but hailed her with, "Hie there! Lord, you look frozen. Come on to the fire."

"It's bitter out, getting worse." She took off her hood and coat as she spoke, but before she had thrown them over a chair Angus Mills began talking again. It was just as if he'd never left off, or as if she had never come into the room.

"Regarding the exodus of the priests, it is not only the question of their marrying, which is really a red herring when you come down to basic facts, because those who don't have it on the side practice some form of eroticism. But on this much more fundamental issue of the confession. . . . Yet, this too is definitely linked to the question of their legally taking a wife. Now, whereas a certain percentage of the male Catholic laity might be for condoning this, the females will be dead against it." He paused here and stared at Pat as she took a seat beside Philip on the couch, while her eyes narrowed as she looked at him. His pauses always held large, silent question marks: why? And as if he were answering it, he said, "No Catholic woman would ever want a priest to marry, because the priest, let me tell you, is the other man in her life, he—he is her secret lover. He is the one she can spew out her thoughts to, dark, fearful thoughts; lustful, desirous thoughts; and she is not confessing them to God—or, as she kids herself, to the priest, she is talking to the other man—her other man, knowing he will understand, soothe and console her. And it's all legal with the blessing of God on it. You can't get divorced for chatting to the priest. What's more, he saves her a visit to the psychiatrist. But give him a wife, ah! and what then? He has taken another woman."

"SHUT UP!" Pat scrambled off the couch, spluttering now. "You're nothing. You're nothing but a dirty-minded swine. You're . . ."

"Pat! Pat!" Philip was pulling at her.

"Leave me alone!" She tore herself away from his grasp, and, bending toward the still seated figure of Angus Mills, she cried, "What do you know about the Catholic religion? You read bits here and there, pick up snatches from television discussions and whirl them round in your biased dirty little mind."

"Here! Here!" Philip had hold of her arms now and was shaking her, but when she gave a sudden twist to her body he found that he was no longer holding her arms but staggering from her, and he looked at her for a moment in amazement. She was so slim and fragile-looking, like a long piece of alabaster, yet her temper had given her a strength that had almost knocked him on his back.

Angus Mills had risen from his chair. He was stretching his short, thick neck up out of his collar as he stared at her, and then he smiled what could only be described as a pitying smile, which he accompanied with the single syllable "Huh!" The sound was derisive, and with it he turned and walked out, and he didn't bang the door as might be expected but closed it quietly, which seemed to put her further in the wrong.

She walked to the fire. She was feeling ridiculous, but nevertheless there was sufficient temper left in her to make her say, "I can't stand that fellow. What does he know about Catholics, anyway?"

Philip stood looking at her. His arms were folded and he said stiffly, "More than you, I should say. You've told me that your father is a Catholic and your mother a Protestant and neither of them practice. You said only last week that you were fortunate in being able to look in from the outside. That's what you said, wasn't it?"

She didn't answer but stared back at him.

"Well, what you don't know is that Angus is well and truly enclosed on his side of the fence; he's a practicing Catholic, a very practicing Catholic."

"Him?"

"Him."

"He can't be or he wouldn't say things like that."

"Oh, my God! Don't talk such rot. This is 1973, remember; you don't sweep the muck under the carpet any longer."

Philip threw himself on the couch, spread his arms wide along the back of it and stared up at her. He took in her thin legs, her small pointed bust, the clear pallor of her face, her dark brown eyes, and her hair, which was looped in a loose bun on the nape of her neck, and he knew what he had known for some time, that he wanted her and he was going to have her. There was in him a deep urge to break the alabaster of both her mind and her body. She was so damned narrow in her thinking, so plebeian, provincial. Yes, it was odd; possessing that startlingly keen math facility, she still remained provincial, low Tyne, back street he would call it. . . . And she was a virgin. He had no doubt about that, from what Cliff had said. Altogether she was a rare commodity.

Assuming an exaggerated drawl now, he said, "You know, Pat, you intrigue me, you worry me, and you fill me with, well, a sort of pity for you."

When she frowned and pulled her chin in he said, "Yes, pity, because you are missing so much. You won't let yourself go. . . . But at the same time I'm afraid of you, I'm afraid of your mind." He always found this worked. "I've always stood in awe of female mathematicians. Women shouldn't do math. Oh, I know all about it, equality, equality, the Liberation Movement." He patted the couch to the side of him now. "Come and sit down, come on, down to my level. But you'll have to unbend some way to get there." He laughed.

Slowly and like a child now, a chastised, deflated child, she came and sat by his side, and he put his arms around her and hugged her close, saying, "What is it? What are you frightened of? Look at me, Pat. I'm going to ask you something and I want a straight answer, just yes or no. But promise me"—he tapped her lips with his fingers—"promise me you'll tell me the truth."

"I always speak the truth."

"Oh, my God!" He put his head down now and held his brow in his hand. "That's another thing, you're such a mass of contradictions." He pulled himself back from her and surveyed her through half-closed eyes. "They say you'll be coming out top this year, yet you're so damned naïve, it's as if you'd been brought up in a MONUNSTERY."

"A what?"

"A monunstery"—he gave a high laugh—"a cross between a convent and a monastery, because the male in you is trying to dominate the female, and the female is petrified."

"Don't talk such rot. . . . And don't try to be another Angus Mills."

"Angus speaks the truth and I'm speaking it, too, and you know it, and with regard to you and truth, that's why you don't get on with people, isn't it? Oh, I know it's unfair, because you'd imagine that a truthful person should be loved, whereas in fact a truthful person is more likely to engender hate. . . . Don't you realize that people don't want to know the truth, that they cannot face it? They cannot face it in themselves, so it's not likely they're going to take it from another. Have you ever thought of that beautiful, beautiful word—diplomacy?" He waited while he looked at her, and when she made no comment he said, "It is a beautiful word. All right, it coats lies, but it does more good than harm, for it provides the lovely hot running butter to pour over the cobblestones of truth. . . . I like that bit." He laughed. "The cobblestones of truth. But tact and diplomacy, that's what you should take up, Pat, tact and diplomacy."

"Thank you." Her mouth was tight.

"You're welcome. Now, where was I? Oh yes, I asked you to speak the truth, but for the last time. Make it the last time."

He became silent now as he stared into her eyes, then slowly and softly he asked, "Have you ever been with a man?"

The alabaster skin was flushed to a deep pink.

"Now! Now! Now!" He was leaning back from her, wagging the fingers of both hands. "Come on, say it, yes or no. Say it. I know the answer—you've just given it to me—but I want to hear you say it." He bent swiftly forward and pulled her into his arms, and they overbalanced onto the couch, and as he held her stiff body to him he kept repeating as he laughed into her face, "Say it. Go on, be a devil and say it."

He didn't know how he came to roll onto the floor; she seemed to twist herself and then there he was on the floor. He got to his feet and looked at her where she was standing now pulling on her coat, and he went to her and said, "Ah look, Pat, I was only kiddin'. And I'm glad, I am. Of course I am. But I still say that it's a position that should be rectified, and soon, for your own sake. You'd feel better." He was looking into her eyes, and his voice was a whisper as he ended, "I promise you, you'll feel better."

As he stared at her he thought for a moment that she was going to cry, and he said with an eager softness, "Oh, Pat, I'm sorry. But I'm fond of you. I could go for you head over heels. I've been trying to stop myself. I might as well tell you I have, for I didn't want to go in off the deep end. But I'm afraid I'm toppling. And . . . and I want you to be happy. You like me, don't you? Or should I say, do you like me?"

Did she like him? Yes, yes, she supposed she was attracted to him—in a peculiar sort of way.

"Well?"

"I came here tonight, didn't I, half-an-hour bus journey and frozen stiff?"

"Then stay." His voice was soft, coaxing. "We can have it to ourselves." He looked round the room, then went quickly to the far corner and pulled open a drawer and took out a piece of board on which was written in large type: "IN SESSION." "When we want to work we pin it to the door. We call it rule 6." He pulled a face at her. "We could . . . work in peace."

Quite suddenly she felt sick, and she had the instinct to run, while at the same time she was saying to herself, "Well, you could get it over with here and now. No more conflict."

She walked slowly toward the door. "I'm . . . I'm going to Jarrow; I promised them I'd be there by eight."

He had her by the arms again, pulled her round. "You did nothing of the sort. And you're not going."

"I did. I am."

He was two steps away from her now. His look was puzzled; she had a way of snapping her arms down. She looked fragile, yet she was strong enough to push him, almost throw him off. "All right, all right. Good night," he said loudly and pulled open the door.

She went out into the little hall, then into the street. She kept her head down as she walked. Never before had she felt so young, silly and old-fashioned . . . or so alone.

2

Mary supported the glass in Alec's hand, and when he had drained the last of the hot whisky she wiped his mouth and said, "There now, get yourself off to sleep."

"Aye, lass, aye. By! that was grand, warmin', lovely. Eeh!

there's nothin' heats your belly more on a winter's night than a drop of the hard."

As she straightened the sheet under his chin he caught hold of her hand and murmured, "Aw! lass. Lass." And she said briskly, "There now! There now! Get yourself off to sleep." She stroked the thin strand of hair across the top of his scalp and added, "Now, mind, don't forget. Ring that bell if you want anything in the night, do you hear?"

"Aye, lass, I will. Good night and God bless you."

"Good night, Da."

She switched on a bedside lamp, then moved toward the door to turn out the main light, but before she reached it the door opened and a blond head was thrust round it, well above hers.

"Good night, Granda."

"Good night, lad. Where you off to tonight?"

"Oh . . . the high spots—bunny girls and strippers. Scampi and chips."

"Are you takin' the Rolls, lad?"

"No, the Bentley, Granda."

"Get out of it!" Mary pushed at the tall figure, then glanced back toward the bed. Alec was chuckling and she said, "Get yourself to sleep. You're as bad as him."

As she passed Ben on the landing where he was getting into his coat, she said, "I don't know about strippers and bunny girls, but you won't get to the club before it closes if you don't get yourself away."

"Well, that won't trouble me; I'm of two minds whether to go or not. Look, why not get Eva to come over and give an eye to Granda, an' come with me? There's bound to be something on. If not, there's always bingo. What d'you say?"

What did she say! Could she say that the clubs with their pile carpets, their last word in furnishings, their concert halls, their organs, irritated her more than they afforded her entertainment or relief from her mundane life?

Why was it she couldn't be ordinary and let herself go, have a drink and a laugh, carry on a bit, in fact? No, whatever club she went to. And she'd been to a few from Shields to Sunderland and Newcastle, from the social clubs, as they now called the glorified workingmen's clubs, to the nightclubs, where it always amazed her to see ordinary women gambling, women who, twenty years ago, would have had one main concern, whether they'd have enough money for the rent man on Monday. But in all of them she experienced a particular irritation, and she wondered whether it was because she felt an outsider, in that she hadn't her own man, for young Ben, no matter how he tried, could never fill that category. Or was it that she couldn't disassociate the women she saw at the tables from the years of dealing with bad payers? Bad payers always left a nasty taste in her mouth, like the ones who insisted on custard creams and boiled ham, when it should have been bread and potatoes; and she knew you couldn't do a night out at a club for less than three pounds, and that was putting it low. And some of them went two and three times a week.

But when she thought about it coolly in retrospect, she supposed that the social clubs did open up a new way of life for the women, and God knew that after what they had gone through in her time they needed a break. But still, they weren't her cup of tea. Could it be sour grapes because they had, in her case, come too late for her really to enjoy them? Could be, at that. Yet look at the old dears who went there, some of them dolled up like lasses. . . . Aw, why was she yarping on?

"What you standing dreaming about?"

"Who's dreaming? Me? Get yourself away out of it." She pushed at him, then exclaimed, "You haven't got a scarf on! Go and get a scarf."

"I don't want a scarf. I never feel the cold—you know I don't."

"Go and get a scarf on!"

"Aw, you!" He pushed at her, but gently, and he went into his bedroom and she into the sitting room.

The sitting room was furnished differently from what it had been twenty-eight years before, more expensively, but nevertheless it still retained the comfort of the earlier days. A chesterfield couch, its back supported with individual down cushions matching those of the seat, stood at right angles to the fireplace, which now held a low all-night-burning grate. The carpet was thick and plum-colored; a small modern piano stood to the right of the window. There were two sets of coffee tables, together with two occasional tables, dotted here and there; and the occasional tables at least had a period attached to them.

Mary herself, like the room, had changed. She was now fifty-six. She could have passed for forty-six and no one would have doubted her age. The only lines on her face were under her eyes, and these were a mere tracery. Her hair, which had begun to go gray about five years ago, she now camouflaged with a light brown tint. Anyone who hadn't seen her for twenty years would have found that the greatest change lay in her dress.

The expensive outfit she had bought for Annie's wedding in 1952 seemed to have given her a taste for dress. Before, she had never bothered much about dress; she'd never had time. But within one year the house had seemed to become empty, at least of half its occupants.

Early in 1952 Cousin Annie had died, and Jimmy shortly after. And later in the year young Annie, at nineteen, had been married. From then on there had been only Ben and her da to look after, and neither of them was much trouble. She remembered she had gone daft for a time buying everything she set her eyes on. She supposed, in looking back, it was the release from the irritation of Cousin Annie and the lifting of the weight from her shoulders of the responsibility of Jimmy.

She had been thinking a lot about Jimmy this last week. It was the clearing out of the store cupboard and coming across his books again and all his scribblings. She had made an assault on the store cupboard because she didn't want to have to tackle all the clearing up at the last minute. She wasn't going to take a lot of rubbish with her wherever she went.

It was odd, but the nearer the time came for her to leave this place, the more reluctant she became to move; and yet for years she had looked upon it almost as a prison, wondering when she'd be free, when she'd be able to be her own mistress and go where she willed; but now, with demolition almost on them, she was acting like a sentimental girl, hugging souvenirs to her.

She had just put her feet up on the couch when Ben came in. She watched him striding down the room toward her, and, as always when she looked at him from a distance, she was struck anew by his likeness to Lally. Naturally he would take after his mother, but her looks, represented in him, were quite uncanny. He was her all over again, except that he didn't appear flamboyant; he was too lean for that. Inside, too, he was like her, for his heart was kind. But there was also a good bit of Jimmy in him. He had Jimmy's mannerisms, his humor. Yet in one way he wasn't at all like his father, for he had no use for poetry. Nor did he dream; he was practical, was Ben, and he had known what he wanted to do since he was twelve years old. "I want to build cars, Mam," he had said. He had always called her "Mam," never "Aunt." Well, he hadn't built cars but he had serviced and sold them; and in his own business an' all, she had seen to that.

Young Ben was more like her son than Annie was her daughter. Annie was her own Ben's child, and therefore she should have loved her dearly. But Annie hadn't taken after Ben; strangely she had taken after her grandmother—not too much, but just enough to make her mean and contrary and selfish where her own needs were concerned.

But young Ben she had loved with a passion that a mother has for an only son. Perhaps it was because in his early years he had needed her so much. How often had she traveled with him down to the Shields Institution until he was five? She had lost count of the times she had walked up Talbot Road to those iron gates, the workhouse gates, as they were known. And her journeys had been in vain, because he was now stone deaf in one ear.

Because she loved him so much, she knew that she must try to throw him off, and the best way, she had considered, of doing this was to get herself married, but when it came to it she couldn't go through with it. Three times she had made a fool of herself, and the men. And he was as bad as she in letting people down. Look at the girls he'd had; they were round him like flies. They lasted a month or two. One had even lasted a year, but when he began to hear wedding bells he turned tail and bolted. She knew that people round about blamed her because he wasn't married. A big, hulking fellow like him, and twenty-eight years old, carting her around, they said. Wasn't natural, they said. He should be married with a family, they said. . . . Oh, she knew what they said.

She said to him now, "What you dithering for? Get yourself away, I've told you."

He looked down at her. "I don't like leaving you on your own. You look lost."

She drew in a deep breath, then pointed to a side table. "I've got a good book, a box of chocolates . . . drink through there if I want it"—she stabbed her finger toward the dining-room wall— "the telly, and if you don't mind, I'd like an hour to meself."

"You're an ungrateful old . . ." He put his hands on each side of the couch above her shoulders and bent his face down to hers. Then, wagging his head, he said, "I don't know whether to say 'bitch' or 'witch.'"

"I'll thank you to say neither."

He pushed his lips out and kissed her lightly, then grinned at her as he straightened himself, saying, "You're an old bag."

She grinned back at him but with her mouth compressed, then said, "I'll bag you one of these days."

He was walking toward the door when he turned round. "Oh, by the way, I forgot to tell you. You know what young Taylor said today when you came in to fill up?"

"No, what did young Taylor say today?"

"He said you looked smashing and you smelt nice. What have you got to say to that from a seventeen-year-old?"

"I would say he needed his ears boxed."

He went out laughing, and she laid back her head in the crook of the couch and repeated, "She looks smashing and smells nice."

Frank used to say that to her. "By! lass, you look smashing. What's that you've got on? You smell nice." Sometimes when she wasn't wearing scent he would say, "You smell nice." She regretted at times that she hadn't married Frank. It wasn't that she was in love with him. She'd never be in love with anybody again, at least she doubted it very much, and time was flying. But Frank had been nice and patient until that particular Wednesday in March two years ago.

She'd had to meet him that night to give him her answer. And it was going to be yes. Then, when she was almost ready, she had gone into the bedroom to get a handkerchief. The top drawer of the dressing table was inclined to stick and consequently she always tugged at it. This night she had tugged a little too hard and the whole drawer had come out, and besides the contents spilling all over the floor the drawer itself had fallen on her foot, and she had hopped around the room in agony for a moment. It was as she gathered the odds and ends from the floor that she picked up two envelopes which were as signposts to different periods of her life. One held the faded Valentine card: "From a silent admirer." She had opened it and gazed at the rose. It evoked no sentimental memory in her and she wondered, as she had done before, why she kept the thing. The other envelope held the last two poems Jimmy had written. She had taken these for herself; all the rest of his later writings were in Ben's possession, as was proper. And as she looked at them and read them again, she realized for the first time that Jimmy's hadn't been the wasted life that she had imagined. He'd had a year of wonderful happiness. Very likely some would say it was wrong what he did in leaving his wife and going off with Lally, but she would never say that. And some would say you always had to pay for doing things like that; yes, they would, and they did say that around these parts. Well, if they were right he had paid. God! how he had paid. He had tried to pull himself together time and time again, only to slip back. He'd had no stave to hold on to; she herself had just been a substitute mother and a nurse.

She, too, had paid for his one year of happiness, and had become weary of the struggle trying to prevent him from drinking himself to death. In the end she failed. But did he himself really fail? Because toward the end he had seemed to find something. He had said to her, "Do you think I'll see Lally again, Mary, I mean when I die?" She had not been able to answer him. How could she? She didn't know. But after he had gone she found two poems, among others, in his drawer, and they were significant of the change in him. One was entitled "I believe" and went:

Where do I go from here?
Don't tell me
Nothingness,
Into which no thought of mine
Will flow:
Dead, dead, deaded flesh
Meshed into mushed wood
And soil,
Rotten, spoiled,
Pressed down,
Food for geologists
In future mist-filled time.

Or still into nothingness
Burned,
While slow
Music drawn curtains
Bring flowing tears
Of the mourners
And fears
Of their turn.

Ashes spread around a rose
Cannot think
As they sink
Into the sod.
There must be something more,
There must;
If only for comfort now
I'll believe in God.

254   PURE AS THE LILY

The other was more significant still; it was his version of the
Lord's Prayer and entitled "As I Would Have It":

> Our Father
> Who is as a power
> Through all the universe,
> I would like to revere you,
> And be happy in doing so.
> We will take it at the start
> That goodness alone
> Comes from you and no evil;
> We want from you the power
> To earn our living
> In a way that will bring us contentment,
> And the power to resist harming human or animal,
> And the power to forgive ourselves our misdeeds,
> And the power to resist anything
> That our deep heart tells us is wrong,
> And the power to direct our mind
> To the realization that we are part of a great mystery
> That will one day be made clear to us,
> And hope that this will help us to come
> Nearer to you and say,
> In all humility,
> Thy will be done.

What struck her about this latter was that he had not translated
"As we forgive them that trespass against us"—no thought of
God could erase from his mind the open-eyed deed of evil perpe-
trated by his mother. Perhaps he had not lived long enough to
reach the point when the past becomes hazy and peace in eternity becomes a bargaining point.

Anyway, that night, after she had replaced the drawer, she'd
had to bathe her foot because it was paining, and as she did so
she began to cry. She didn't really know why, only that the pain
in her foot didn't warrant her tears.

At nine o'clock, when Frank phoned and she said that she
was very sorry but she wasn't coming and that it was no use, his
hurt pride had sizzled over the wires.

Frank had been a widower for four years; he was a healthy

sixty, he was about to retire, and the plan was that when they married they'd set off on a world tour.

The thought of the world tour had excited her, as had his quite grand home in the best part of Westhoe in Shields; yet the following morning she did not tell herself that she was a fool. And later, when she broke the news to Ben and he said, "Aw, thank the Lord. Oh, I am relieved. He was much too old for you. And for the life of me I couldn't understand what you saw in him—he was almost potbellied," she had laughed and said, "You're right."

Also she knew that she would never have forgiven herself if her da had died while she was away jaunting.

At odd times since, however, she had wondered if she had done the right thing, for in spite of Ben and her da, she was lonely. But once her da went—and God forbid that he should go soon, she didn't want that, but let her face it, once he went and Ben married (and Ben must marry)—the way would be clear; she would know what she was going to do with herself. For years and years she had longed to be free and to travel. Women traveled on their own all the time, and she would travel.

Got ticket, will travel.

She laughed to herself and reached out and picked up the book and the chocolates. She would indulge, stuff herself. What did it matter, another inch? She was past caring.

She had just settled back when she heard the staircase door open, and she thought, I bet that's him come back. Would you believe it? She looked toward the room door as it opened; then she swung her legs on to the floor and got up, crying, "Pat! Oh, how lovely to see you, dear. I thought you'd be going home. Come in, come in, you look frozen."

"They've gone to Scarborough. You don't mind, Gran?"

"Don't be ridiculous!" She slapped her granddaughter's hands. "Have you ever bothered to wonder before if I minded? What's the matter with you?" Then she exclaimed, "Oh, you're like ice. Come to the fire. You've just missed Ben."

"He's gone out! . . . On his own? He'll get lost."

"You cheeky monkey." She pushed her down on to the couch. "Sit there. Get yourself warm. Take your shoes off. I'll make you a drink."

"Thanks, Gran. . . . Where's Great-grandad?"

"He's in bed; he's had a cold all week. I had the doctor to him. He's got to go careful."

"Oh! I'll go in and see him."

"No, no, he'll be asleep now. Just leave him; you'll see him in the morning. What would you like? Coffee, cocoa, tea?"

"Tea, please."

"Same here."

Pat leaned back into the curve of the couch, her shoulders relaxed. The tension went out of her stomach muscles, and her feet fell sidewards away from each other, and she sighed. This was it. This was what she needed, just to stay here forever and ever. This was real, understandably real.

When Mary entered the room with a tray Pat asked, "Have you heard anything more about when you've got to go?"

"No, it could be next week, next month or a year."

"Have you found any place yet?"

"No, I haven't looked."

"Wouldn't you like any of the places they're offering? There are some nice flats, central heating, elevator, the lot."

"No, thank you. Wherever I go I want me own front door. And it's funny"—she laughed—"I've never had me own front door, only a back one."

"Do you fancy any place in particular, like Shields? There are some nice parts in Shields."

"Do you know"—Mary stopped in the act of pouring the tea— "I haven't given it much thought. It's very odd—I can't explain it—but I know I should be looking around, because this"—she wagged her head as she looked up—"could be around my ears in no time. But I just don't seem to want to bother. It's just as if, well—" She finished pouring out the cup of tea.

"Well what, Gran?"

"Oh, I don't know, I don't know, lass. But I've got no urge in me to look around. . . . The fact is I must be getting old."

"Don't be silly; you—old! But you'll have to find some place. You and Ben could go into a hotel, but there's Great-grandad."

"Yes, yes, I know all that, lass. You're right, I'll have to think about it or we'll land in one of those blocks of flats. Anyway, wherever I go it'll have to be somewhere near, so's Ben can get back and forth to the garage."

"He can get back and forth to the garage from any place in his car, and the rate he goes it wouldn't matter if it were John o' Groats."

"Oh, I think we'll find some place nearer than that." She laughed now, and as she sat down and sipped her tea she added, "But there's one thing I'm going to tell you: As soon as he marries I'm going to take a long, long holi—"

"Has he got somebody?" Pat's voice was sharp.

"No, not really. There's one at present called Irene, but she's been running a month, so time's nearly up, I should say."

"What's she like?"

"Small, dark, what you would call 'petite.' "

"I can't stand small women—they're always bitchy."

"I've known some tall ones who are, too."

"Oh, Gran!" She laughed, then leaned against Mary, and Mary said, "Hie up! Look what you're doing. The tea, over my good frock!"

"Oh, I'm sorry. It's lovely. What material is it?"

"They tell me angora, dear; and they also told me it was—almost—a model. But what they didn't tell me, but what I guessed, was that they were stinging me."

"You can afford to be stung."

"Listen to her!"

"You look lovely in it, anyway. I never look like you in clothes."

"I should hope not."

"You know what I mean. I'm . . . well, I'm like what Great-granda calls a 'yard of pipe water.' "

"Don't be silly, you're fashionable."

"Not any more, Gran. Where've you been? You can't get in the buses for the busts. Talk about strap hanging; some of them need jibs to support them."

They were leaning together again laughing, while Pat spluttered, "But honestly, Gran, you should see Maggie's falsies; they're like the old-fashioned pictures of the wartime barrage balloons, you know. I told Maggie that."

"What did she say?"

"Not what you would expect. She said she'd always wished she'd been old enough to be in the war, because her mother always talked of the great times she'd had, and her father, too. Apparently they both had the time of their lives. They enjoyed every minute of it, so much so that I don't think they've enjoyed their peacetime life together."

"By what you've told me I should think this Maggie has the art of enjoying herself well enough at any time."

"Oh, she has. She's got her current comforter in for the weekend. . . ."

"OH! Patricia."

Mary's attitude changed completely. There was no laughter on her face now. She hitched herself a little way along the couch and there was silence for a few moments, until she said, "I'm not stuffy, you know that, Pat. And I wouldn't care if they stuck to the one fellow. But by the sound of them, they're like a lot of half-breed bitches in heat."

"Oh, Gran!"

"Never mind, 'oh, Gran.' And another thing, I wish you weren't rooming with that girl."

"I won't be for very much longer."

"Oh?" Mary turned an inquiring glance on her. "You've got another place?"

"No, no, Gran. Like you, I haven't any place in mind. I think we're both in the same boat, and both at sea."

"What do you mean?"

"O . . . h! I wish I could tell you, Gran. If I could tell any-one, I could tell you. I'm all mixed up."

"Some fellow?"

"Yes and no. But it isn't actually; well, it doesn't really concern him. Gran—" She put down her cup, then took Mary's cup from her hands, saying, "I won't risk your spilling that again. But . . . well, Gran, I think I'm going to give it up."

"Give it up! You mean the university?"

"Yes."

"But, child!"

"That's it, Gran, I'm not a child. I'm nearly twenty."

"Well, you're still a child. Twenty or no twenty, you're acting like a child, if you're thinking of giving up your career. And such a career! I could have understood it if you had said this within a few months of your going there, and everything new, but you're in your second year and doing fine. Your father says you're doing splendidly."

"Oh, don't get up, Gran, sit still." She caught Mary's arm. "Yes, as you say, I suppose I'm doing splendidly. But, Gran, I'm doing splendidly at something I don't want to do splendidly at, if you understand what I mean. I just don't want to go on with mathematics. I'm not a dedicated person, and you've got to be dedicated."

"Aw, Pat." Mary now leaned back against the couch and stared at her as if to get her into focus, and then she said slowly, "There'll be hell to pay over this. You know that, don't you? Your mother will go mad. You might bring your dad round to your way of thinking, but not your mother. It was the greatest day of her life when you got to the university." Mary suddenly stopped talking, for her own words were recalling an echo from away down the years. It was her mother's voice, saying, "Our Jimmy's got through to the secondary school. What do you think of that now? And this is only the beginning. He'll go places, our Jimmy will, I'll see to that." When Annie received this news, she would react as her ma would have reacted toward Jimmy had he said he wasn't going to the Teachers' Training College.

But perhaps she was being a bit too hard on Annie; she wasn't really like her ma. But nevertheless, there'd be hell to pay.

"What's brought this about, lass?" She moved back up the couch, and Pat leaned against her shoulder again and said, "I don't really know, Gran; there's so many things. I . . . I don't seem to fit in. Perhaps I don't know when I'm well off, for they come from all parts of the country and consider they're fortunate to get a place there. It isn't the university, it's me, and"—she smiled faintly—"and I . . . I suppose my environment, my years around here." She spread one arm wide now. "This house, the shop, even the district set my pattern, because I was happy here; it was another world. You, Gran, and Great-granda and my Uncle Jimmy. I loved my Uncle Jimmy. Although I very rarely saw him sober, I still loved him. I can still hear him spouting his poetry. And you know something? He wouldn't have it was poetry; he just said it was verse. But compared with the stuff they publish today—why, if he were alive he'd be at university and he'd be hailed. He would, he would, Gran."

Mary was shaking her head as she said, "I'm not denying it. I'm just thinking it's odd how blood runs in the family. Jimmy and you going to college, and you're from my side, and I've as much brains as a flea."

"Oh, Gran!"

"It's true. And there's Ben, Jimmy's son. All he wants to do is work with his hands."

"Me Uncle Jimmy went off with a woman, didn't he—Ben's mother—and they weren't married?"

"Who told you that? I've never mentioned that to you."

"No, Mam did."

Mary just stopped herself from saying, "She would."

"Does Ben know?"

"Yes, yes, he knows. He was just turned six when his dad died. But by then he knew that his mother was the most wonderful person in the world, and it made no difference when he found out later that she and his dad hadn't been married, because he knew that his da had adored her, and that's the only word for it. I've never seen anything like it, and I know I never will again, the love that was atween Jimmy and Lally."

"But Mam said they called her 'doo-lally-tap,' Gran, and that means . . ."

"I know what it means, lass." Mary shook her head now and her voice was sharp. "And your mother had no right to say that. It was a nickname that her husband gave her, like you'd say to anyone, 'Aw, you're doo-lally-tap,' or 'up the pole,' you know, and it just stuck to her. Lally was no more doo-lally-tap than you are. She was gentle and simple, wise simple. Some people don't understand simplicity and kindliness and gentleness; they take it for softness, daftness; they think you've got a marble missing if you don't hit back at them. People are cruel, women are cruel. Oh aye, Pat, remember that"—she wagged her finger—"women are cruel. Seventy-five percent of women in my estimation are bitches—tall and short, an' that's being kind. But for the rest"— she gave a wry smile—"for the other few, they're lovely, and Lally was one of the lovely ones. Jimmy used to say she was fey, and that fey people dangled between eternities past and death. I've never really been able to work that one out."

"And Ben takes after her."

"Yes"—Mary bounced her head—"Ben takes after her. And don't say it like that. And get that smile off your face."

"I'm not saying anything."

"No, but with all you've got up top, me girl, you're still jealous of him and have been since you could crawl."

"Oh, really! Gran. Me jealous of Ben?"

"Yes, you jealous of Ben."

"Oh, Gran. Pour me another cup of tea. I want to swallow that."

As she watched Mary pour out the tea she thought, Nothing much escapes her, but something has this time. Yes, she had been jealous of Ben; but not in the way her grannie thought, or anyone else thought. She could remember the first feelings of jealousy she had concerning him; it was when she had just turned four and he was eleven or twelve. She had stood and screamed at him, demanding to know why he wouldn't play with her, and he had answered, "Because I want to be with me mam in the shop." And at that he had pushed her on to her bottom, and she had continued to scream, not through being hurt but in temper. And so it had been all down the years. She hadn't been jealous of his having her grandmother's affection but because he rejected her own. She had fought with him up till she was ten, and her grannie used to say, "You're a naughty girl, Patricia. Why don't you like Ben? What's he done to you?"

It was funny how people never understood your motives. Well, you couldn't blame them when you couldn't understand them yourself. She hadn't understood hers until she was sixteen, when there was talk of his going to be married.

"Ben is the star in your sky that will never fall, Gran, isn't he?"

"There you go again."

"Well, I mean he is, isn't he?"

"I brought him up from he was a few weeks old. He's like my own child—can't you understand that?"

"Yes, Gran." She closed her eyes and lay back and bit on her lip, and the next moment she was in Mary's arms, and Mary was murmuring over her, "What is it, lass, what is it? What is upsetting you? Come on, tell me. You know you can—you can tell me anything. You can't shock me. Come on, dry your eyes." She took a handkerchief and dried the pale face. "What is it? Something at home?"

Pat shook her head and swallowed.

"Well, is it a man?"

She turned her head away and looked toward the fire; then quietly she said, "What would you say, Gran, if I told you I was going away for the weekend, next weekend with . . . with a fellow?"

As Mary's arms slowly slid away from her, she still continued to look in the fire and went on, "I . . . I've never been with any-one, Gran, you know what I mean? And . . . and I think it's time. I , , ."

"STOP IT! Stop talking like an idiot. Why don't you say you haven't been on pot or L.S.D. and you think it's time you did? . . . You sit there and say you're going with this man because you think it's time—TIME! What do you mean by time? Are you in love with him?"

Pat turned sharply, crying, "I thought you said nothing could shock you."

"I'm not shocked, girl, I'm bloody well angry. You think it's time to do this. You're not doing it because you're worked up by love, or passion, or anything else. You just think it's time. You're not twenty yet and you say you haven't been with anyone, but you think it's time. . . . My God! I tell you one thing, I think it's time you did leave that university if this is the way it's making you think. . . . Now I could understand your going with a man because your feelings had driven you to him, but to coolly say . . ."

"What's this? What's this?"

Neither of them had heard the outer door opening, and now they were both looking at Ben and he at them. He moved slowly into the room, pulling his scarf off and unbuttoning his coat. Then, looking from one to the other, he asked in a tone of high surprise, "You two having a spat? I heard you at the bottom of the stairs."

"No, we're not having a spat." Mary let out a long, shuddering breath, then said, "What's brought you back?"

"Oh, just a minute." He grabbed up his scarf and put it on again, saying, "I'll go out and sit on the step until you let me in."

"You haven't been gone an hour." Her voice was quiet.

"No, I haven't been gone an hour, and if I'd known that Pat was here, I wouldn't have come back." He looked at Pat again. "You staying?"

"Yes."

"Well, what a pity you didn't phone. I could have made a night of it—as I said to Mam, high jinks, plush and slush, the lot."

"Oh, be quiet!" Mary had yelled, and he turned quickly and stared at her. Then, his own voice quiet, he said, "All right," and went out.

A minute later Mary followed him into his room, saying, "I'm sorry, I'm sorry, Ben. I'm all worked up."

"That's all right, dear." He was smiling at her. "I know that; I tell you I heard you at the bottom of the stairs. Even with one ear I could hear you. What's she done?"

"Oh, nothing, nothing, and don't try to get it out of me. It's nothing that I can tell you."

"Oh! Then it's bad." He bent down to the mirror and ran a comb through his thick fair hair as he said, "I didn't think she'd have any problems, not with that brain of hers that can sort everything out—Ridley's computer."

Mary came and stood close to him, saying, "She's going to throw that brain overboard; she's going to give up the university. And that's only part of her problem."

"What! No!"

"Yes. And just imagine what effect that'll have on your Auntie Annie."

"Oh, boy! What's made her take this line?"

"I don't really know; she's all mixed up."

"Aren't we all?"

"Now don't you be facetious."

"Oh! Oh!" He dipped his head and looked closely at her from under his brows. "Using big words, eh?"

"Yes, and I know what they mean. And when you come in there, be nice to her; don't tease her. You either tease her or ignore her. She's not a child any more and she's not even a young girl; she's a woman."

"You're telling me!" He put his hand on his hip and wobbled his buttocks, and she had to smile.

Slowly she rubbed his cheek with her fingers as she said, "Be nice to her, Ben, she's in trouble."

"What do you mean, trouble?" His face was straight. "She's not going to . . . ?"

"Oh, no, for God's sake! Lord, that's all it's been all night— men, sex, and now babies. No, she's not going to have a baby."

"Men, sex, and now babies," he repeated musingly; then said brightly, "Oh, well, no babies; that's one less worry for us, Mrs. Tollett. Our good name is saved."

"Oh, you fool. . . . But remember"—she turned as she made for the door—"be kind."

"All right, Mam." He nodded at her. "What you order, I'll serve, tea and sympathy."

During the next half-hour the conversation in the sitting room was stiltingly general. Mary sat in one corner of the couch, Pat in the other, and on the opposite side of the fireplace Ben sprawled in the easy chair, his legs stretching out halfway across the hearth rug. It was as he finished describing the tactics of Bill Thompson, his one-time mechanic, whom he had pro- moted to sales manager, doing his business of selling a car, that Mary happened to lift her glance from him and look at Pat and saw that her granddaughter was off guard. It was as if she were looking at her when she was sixteen, when she used to come and flop herself down and pour out the exciting doings of the day. Her whole face was relaxed. She was smiling at Ben's imitation of Bill Thompson, and as she watched her a strange thought pierced her mind. It came up as if through layers of years, and when it probed the surface it startled her. She looked across at Ben, then back to her granddaughter, then to Ben again, and she thought, None so blind as those who refuse to see. Whereupon she got to her feet, stretched her neck and said, "Here's somebody off to bed."

"So soon? It's not ten yet."

Ben was on his feet.

"When you get on about Bill Thompson and his antics one o'clock is early. If you two can do without sleep, I can't." She went now to Pat and, bending down, kissed her, saying, "Good night, dear. I'll switch on the fire and the electric blanket; it should be cosy by the time you get in."

"Thanks, Gran." Patricia reached up her arms and returned

the kiss, and Mary, patting her cheek, smiled and nodded at her. Then, looking at Ben, she said, "Good night, you."

"And good night, you."

As Pat watched them kiss and push at each other she felt pass through her a hurt that was painful enough to be physical. Their playful actions were almost childish, but they were the outward sign of something so deep in each of them that the loneliness which she had felt earlier in the evening was intensified.

"Well now!" Ben had not resumed his seat in the chair but was now sitting in the corner of the couch that Mary had vacated, and looking along at Pat he repeated, "Well now!"

"'Well now.' What does that mean?"

"Nothing, nothing; just, how are things going with you?"

"Oh, like they're going with everyone else, I suppose, up and down. The seesaw won't stay put in the middle."

"You'd get bored if it did."

When she made no answer to this but turned her head away and began to examine her nails, he said, "What's this I hear of your packing it in?"

Her head jerked round. "By! Gran wasn't long in passing the news on."

"Well, she just happened to mention it."

"You weren't out of the room five minutes, three minutes."

"Gran's a fast talker."

"I'll say."

"Well, are you going to leave?"

"I haven't made up my mind yet." She let out a long breath.

"It'll be a waste of good gray matter, of course, unless you've something better in mind."

"You consider I've got . . . good gray matter?"

"It frightens me."

This was the second time tonight a man had said her brain frightened him. Yet from what she saw in the university the majority of males weren't put off by brains; they married them and so ensured a good double income. Doctors, teachers, scientists: their basis for matrimony wasn't so much biological, as far as she could see, as financial. She had tried of late not to allow her sympathies to embrace the students who lived together and had the audacity to propose that the country support their desire not only for butter on both sides of the bread, but jam also, for their attitude at least seemed less calculated. . . . And they had nerve. She wished she had nerve, just a little bit.

She slanted her glance at Ben. "You don't say!"

"I do—and I mean it." He straightened his back against the couch. "It's always frightened me."

She turned her head fully toward him and said slowly, "Just because I do math?"

"Yes." He nodded, then looked downwards. "I was hopeless at math, even arithmetic."

"Yet you can build a car, even the engine."

"Oh, that, yes."

"Well, that's math; that engine wouldn't have come into being without math."

"I'm aware of that, but it's in being when I tackle it. All I do is put it together." He leaned forward, his elbows on his knees, his hands joined and hanging slackly between them, then he turned his head and looked at her. "What's brought it about?"

"Oh, I don't know. So many things." She was staring back at him defensively as she asked, "Did Gran tell you the lot?"

He paused while he stared back at her and considered; then he said cautiously, "She told me enough."

"And you're still speaking to me?"

"Why shouldn't I?"

"Oh, I'd have thought you'd get on your hind legs, you being so pious."

"What do you mean?" His voice rose sharply. "Pious! Me, pious? What makes you say that?"

"'Cos you are." Her own voice was quiet, clear and irritating.

"Now, don't you start." He wagged his finger at her. "We're never together two minutes before you start. Why can't we talk amicably?"

"Because you always get riled."

"Me get riled?"

"There you go, almost reaching top C, so is it surprising that I thought you would throw a fit?"

He stared at her through narrowed eyes. He was curious; he wanted to know what she considered would make him throw a fit. He parried, "Throw a fit in nineteen seventy-three?"

"Well, Gran did."

"Well, Gran, I mean Mam's Mam; she's . . . well, she's of another generation, two removed from you. Though you wouldn't think it. Nevertheless, it's true."

"You do surprise me!" She pulled herself to the edge of the couch, and now they were facing each other squarely. "I come to this abode of sanctity and say I'm going off for the weekend with a fellow, making my first trip as it were, and you take it as calmly as if you run a school for pros. . . ." As her voice trailed off she thought, I'm talking like Maggie, and the smile slid from her face as she watched his head come down like that of a bull about to charge. She saw his big square teeth grinding one set against the other. She watched the color flood over his fair complexion and up into his hair. She thought for a moment that he was going to strike her, and she leaned backwards from him as she muttered, "You . . . you said you knew; you tricked me into . . ." She jerked to her feet, and he with her, and when he gripped her by the shoulders she almost cringed under the pressure of his fingers. But she made no attempt to throw him off. She watched his tongue come out. It seemed to have to force its way through his teeth; and then he was wetting his lips as if to let the words slide through. "You . . . you came here to-night and you told Mam that, you told her that you were going off for the weekend with a fellow?"

"Well, whom else would I tell? I've always told her everything."

"You . . . you slut, you!"

"Take your hands off me and don't you call me a slut. Anyway, I'm going to do something definite about it, not like you, dithering about from one to the other and frightened of it."

When the flat of his hand came with a resounding slap across her face she was blinded for a moment, and she couldn't save herself as she went flying half across the couch and half onto the floor. When her vision cleared she stared up at him. He looked furious, wild. As the tears spurted from her eyes he turned and stalked from the room, and the banging of the door shook the house.

When the rat-tat came on Mary's door she called hastily, "Just a minute. Just a minute." Then, jumping into bed, she said, "All right."

As he barged across the room she was startled by the look on his face, "What is it? What's happened?"

"You'd . . . you'd better go in to her."

"What's happened?" She was getting out of bed again and grabbing at her dressing gown.

"I've just knocked her down."

"You've just knocked her down!"

"Just that."

She watched him leave the room as he had come into it, and she stood repeating to herself, "He's . . . he's just knocked her down?" Her mouth fell into a gape and when she closed it she said softly aloud, "Well! Well! Now would you believe that!"

3

"All right, all right, Dad, I promise to think it over."

"Do that, dear. She's dreadfully upset, and . . . and I'm afraid I am a bit, too."

"You took it very well."

"Perhaps, but that doesn't mean to say that I don't think you're being very foolish. But there, I suppose that's a sign of the times." Tom Ridley smiled wanly. "A few years ago I could have said you're under age, Miss, you will do as I say or else; but now, well, according to the law of the land you're a responsible woman. But please"—his voice dropped—"do think carefully. I've never seen her so upset. And don't take too much notice of what she said; she doesn't mean half of it. Look, are you sure I can't run you in to town?"

"No, Dad, no. Anyway"—she smiled—"her need is greater than mine." She pointed back toward the house, then said, "I'll get a bus from the corner; it's due in a few minutes."

"If Maggie's feeling so low, you should have brought her with you; a weekend in bed here and a bit of pampering would have likely got her round."

"Oh, no, she wouldn't have that. And . . . and she's not really sick, but . . . but I thought she should have somebody with her, you know, in the night."

"Yes, dear, I understand."

Patricia couldn't face the look in her father's eye. Tact and diplomacy; not lies, just tact and diplomacy.

"Bye-bye, Dad. And thanks for being so nice. I'll do as you say and have a good think."

"Bye-bye, dear. Mind how you go, it's frosty. Bye-bye."

As she hurried to the bus stop she thought, Who knows? After tonight I might change my mind. The end might justify the means. It was supposed to change your outlook, make you into a different person. It stretched the mind, Maggie said. . . . And Maggie said a lot more.

It was nearly ten o'clock when she got off the bus on the outskirts of Low Fell. This side of the river was new to her. Philip had said if he wasn't at the bus stop, she could easily find her way to Bailey Close, the first turning on the left, second right, and she'd be there, and he'd be on the lookout for her.

He wasn't at the bus stop, and he wasn't out looking for her.

She knocked on the door of number 5. It was opened by a young man, and on the sight of him she wanted to turn and run, not because he looked like a rough working fellow but because of the knowing look in his eyes.

"Is . . . is Mr. Philip Smyth in? He's . . . he's staying with his cousin, Arth—"

"Oh, aye. Aye, first floor, and the door straight opposite. You can't miss it."

She thanked him and went up the stairs. The place was well lit, there was carpet on the stairs and landing, and everything looked clean, surprisingly so.

She knocked on the door opposite the stairhead. When the voice said, "Yes?" she opened the door to see Philip, his upper part flat on a narrow couch with his legs hanging over the end of it. He swung them down and was on his feet in a second, coming toward her, saying, "Why! You're early."

"Early!" She looked at him disdainfully.

"You are. The ten-two, you said; you were getting the ten-two."

"I said I was getting the nine-two and I'd be here about ten."

"Oh, my God!" He thumped his forehead with the palm of his hand, then said, "Ah, well, you're here, come on." He pulled her forward, took the overnight case from her hand, threw it on to the bed in the corner of the room, then helped her off with her coat.

"You want a drink? You look frozen. . . . Aw, come here and I'll warm you first." He pulled her to him and, hugging her tightly, kissed her, and in the process his lips seemed to envelop the lower part of her face.

"Now, how's that for a start?" He gave her the thumbs up sign, then dashed through a door, saying as he did so, "You need a thawer; hot whisky and sugar, that's what you want, hot whisky and brown sugar."

She stood with her back to the two-bar electric fire, looking around the room. It, too, was clean. There was no clutter here like there was in Philip's own place, or in her room, for that matter. But the clutter there was Maggie's doing, not hers. The furniture was sparse: the narrow couch, the divan bed—she kept her eyes from this—the chest of drawers, an easy chair, a small table.

Philip came back into the room with a glass in each hand, both steaming, and, quick to observe that she had been looking round the room, said, "Nice, isn't it? Spacious. My dear cousin knows what he wants and gets it. Still, he's got to pay through the teeth for it. An old boy and his son run the house, do the work, the lot, even provide meals. There, get that down you."

She sipped at the hot whisky, then coughed.

"Go on, gulp. There's plenty more where that came from."

"I'm not fond of whisky; it's . . . it's like medicine."

"Well, treat it as such. Down with it, like this"—he threw the glass of whisky back, closed his eyes tight, coughed, choked, then doubled up, after which he burst into a paroxysm of laughter, and she with him.

"Clever bugger, me!" He was wiping the tears from his eyes. "You would think I couldn't take it. It hit the back of my throat, woof!" He came and stood before her staring into her eyes; then he placed the tip of his forefinger on her nose and he wobbled it round and round before saying softly, "I'll go and make some coffee, eh? Irish coffee and then we'll settle down."

She watched him go through the door again into what was presumably a kitchen. He was amusing, attractive, nice; but she also knew he was a little sly and cunning. Yet she liked him. But she didn't love him. LOVE—what had love to do with it? Her grannie had said she could understand its being done through passion or inexperience, but not because she thought it was TIME. Well, her grannie didn't know everything, and it was time. You dirty slut! he had called her, then knocked her flat. Why had she let him, why hadn't she put him on his back? She could have. Oh, be quiet! The voice in her head was yelling. Don't keep asking the road that you know, because you know perfectly well that road's blocked; he's blind, dead, impervious; he doesn't know you exist. Gran's the only woman for him. It's a pity a man can't marry his grannie . . . or his mam . . . or his aunt, whatever she is to him. God! Be quiet! Be quiet!

She sat down on the narrow couch, leaned her head back and closed her eyes.

"That's more like it; now we're at home." Philip came in carrying a laden tray. "Irish coffee. Southern Ireland—none of your Northern Ireland stuff." He nudged her. "Remember Riley at the debate yesterday. God! He was a scream. The Irish, they're so bloody bigoted, you'd honestly think to hear them, the Southern ones, that Northern Ireland was floating around the Fijis. Talk about the Berlin Wall. By the way, Angus was asking after you."

"Angus asking after me! Angus Mills?"

"Yes, Angus Mills. Oh, he thinks very highly of you."

"After what I said to him last week?"

"Thinks all the more of you for that. You know something?" He leaned toward her and began tracing his lips around her chin as he muttered, "He's got a thing about you. He doesn't let on, oh, no, but I, Philip Andrew Smyth, I'm well versed in the subtleties of hidden passions. Have you noticed that he doesn't look at you when you come into a room?"

"No, I hadn't noticed." Her tone was chilly.

"Well, I have; and a lot of his smart talk is just to impress you. He thinks you've got a masculine brain. Aye, me darlin' Pat"—he now rubbed his mouth up over her ear—"and you have, but you've got a female setup an' all. And he's not blind to that either."

"Oh! Oh!" She shuddered. "Don't do that."

"Ah!" He laughed at her as he wagged his finger in her face. "I touched one of the wires, did I?"

"Don't be so coarse."

"Ah now, coarse. We'll talk about that an' all. That's another thing you've got to get rid of, this differentiation between coarseness and subtle sensitivity. Wait till I pour the coffee."

He poured the coffee, added a good measure of whisky and topped it up with cream, then, handing her a cup, said, "There you are. Let that oil the works. Now, now"—he took a drink from his cup—"coarseness. You're always saying that, you know.

This is coarse, and that's coarse. Well, it's all tied up with the other thing; it's a reflex of an unused mechanism, because, after all, we're just machines, you know, that's all, just machines. Like cars. Leave a car in a garage and don't use it, what happens? It gets cold; yes, dearie, it gets cold. And when you press the self-starter, umph!" He bounced on the couch. "That's all the response you get, umph!" He bounced again. "No joy. Machines have got to be used, dearie."

"Philip, please! Stop being silly, please, and . . . and don't call me 'dearie.' I'm . . . I'm . . . well, I'm nervous."

"Aw, no." His voice was soft now. "I'm sorry; don't worry." He pulled her into his arms and began to stroke her hair while his lips moved in small circles around her temple. "We'll take it slowly. We've got all the weekend. Just think, all the weekend. We needn't move out of the door. Through there"—he thumbed backwards—"there's plenty of eats, and a john, and a shower. Listen, I'll tell you something that'll make you laugh. Olive told this one; it's very funny. There was this girl, she was fourteen, she was in a boarding school and one night . . ."

"Philip! I don't want to hear any of Olive's stories."

"No?"

"No."

"It's funny, it is; it's more risqué than rotten."

"Maybe so, but I don't want to hear it."

"Coarse?"

"Yes, perhaps, coarse."

He made a point of sighing heavily, then said, "Lot of hard work for me ahead, I can see that. But I've never minded hard work. I'm not the one to strike over night shift." His mouth fell sharply on hers, and again she felt swallowed up.

It was nearly an hour later. She'd had a hot whisky and two Irish coffees, and she should have felt very warm inside and quite relaxed, but she wasn't. The drink had only succeeded in turning the trembling in her stomach into knots.

Philip was being very amusing, very funny. The more he

drank, the funnier he became. She had lost count of the number of whiskies he'd had. He wasn't drunk, not really, just funnily tight. She thought she was a little tight herself. Well, Maggie always said you should get tight, but not too tight, because then you'd miss the fun. FUN! . . . What was she doing here anyway? Well, you thought it was time. Oh, damn you! Yes, damn her grannie, and damn him! Oh, yes, damn big blond Ben, damn him! Damn and blast him! Ben Tollett, who wanted to marry his gran, or mother, or auntie.

"What did you say, love? What?" Philip leaned over her. "You say you wanna go to bed?"

"I never said any such thing."

"But I'm reading your thoughts. You didn't know I was a mind reader, did you? Oh ye-yes, I am; it's one of my many acc-accomplishments. Did you know that I was going to be a psychi . . . psychi . . . psychiatrist? Hmm! I was, too. Medicine, that's what I was gonna take up, and psy-psychiatry. There's money in that. Get them on the cou-couch, boy, there's money in that. And the fun and games. An' you get paid for it. Come on, love, come on. An' I agree with you—what you're thinkin'. It's time you were in bed, high time."

He went to pull her to her feet, but she protested, saying, "Look, wait a minute. We were talking about Reed and the festival."

"Up you get! Never mind the festival—turn round."

When she turned round he unzipped her dress and pulled it down over her shoulders, and when it dropped to the floor she stepped slowly out of it. He picked it up and held it like an exhibit, waving it back and forth, before throwing it over the couch, saying, "Article one." Standing now a little back from her, he surveyed her through narrowed, laughing eyes as he said, "Oh! Slips. We wear slips. I didn't know we wore slips." When his hands came on her shoulders and he went to pull the straps down she spluttered, "Let . . . let me get my dressing gown."

"Dressing gown? What do you want with a dressing gown?"

"Well, it's early yet. I'm not tired. . . . We could talk."

"Talk? We've talked for hours."

"Don't be silly. I've only been here just over an hour."

"Jus' over an hour. It se-seems like ten. Anyway, what's there to talk about? We've gone through the whole gamut."

She pushed the straps back onto her shoulders, saying, "Look, I want to tell you about Reed. He said they'll be starting in the New Year and would I help, and . . ."

"Oh, for Christ's sake!" He flapped his hand wide. "Bugger Reed. He goes round farting festivals." As he spoke he caught hold of the front of her slip and pulled at it, and she cried, "Stop it! Don't!"

"Don't what?" He was standing in front of her now, his hands hanging slackly, his body bent toward her, his mouth open.

"D-don't use that expression—I hate it."

"What? Fa—?"

"Stop it!"

It was odd about swearing. She could stand "bloody," "bugger," "damn," but when it came to vulgarities, they jarred on her as much as the obscenities did.

"Aw, for Christ's sake! Far—"

"Stop it! Stop it, will you! You've no need to use . . ."

"Look here." He had her by the shoulders now. "What you gettin' at? Look, honey, these are jus' delaying tactics. Don' . . . don't tell me that your sensitivity is shattered by the string . . . stringing together of a few letters which only depict a minor body function. Ah, come on." When his hand went inside her brassiere and cupped her breast it was as if she'd had an electric shock. And he also. One minute he had been standing straight, the next his head was lower than his legs on the way to his lying flat on his back on the floor.

She watched him shake his head, blink his eyes, shake his head again, then make to get up; and she gasped at him, "Don't move, I'm telling you, don't move, because . . . because if you do I'll . . . I'll only throw you again."

"You'll what! You'll what! You'll . . . !"

As she grabbed up her dress and stepped into it she saw him look from one spread-eagled arm to the other, then with a twist of his body he was on his knees.

"I'm warning you! Mind, I'm warning you!"

"Judo! It's judo." His expression was comical, laughable, but it evoked no laughter in either of them.

She did not zip up her dress, just clipped the hook at the top, then snatched up her coat and slipped into her shoes, and still with her eyes on him she clutched the case from the bed.

When he made a dive at her she put out a leg and one hand in such a way that he tripped, his hands involuntarily going forward in an effort to save himself.

She did not wait to see the result of his fall this time, but pulled open the door and ran down the stairs and so into the street. The cold struck her shivering body and made her stop for a moment, gasping to get her breath.

It wasn't until she reached the main road and wondered if she had missed the last bus that she realized that she hadn't picked up her handbag.

Oh, no! No. Oh, dear God!

She hadn't a penny on her. What was she going to do? Far better had she left her coat behind than her handbag.

She was a good two miles from the flat. But anyway, she couldn't go back to the flat and face Maggie; Reg would be there. She'd have to go down to her grannie's. Oh, no, she couldn't face her grannie and Ben, she just couldn't. Well, where could she go? She couldn't go home.

She stood under the lamppost shivering and doing her utmost not to cry. She'd have to go to Jarrow and she'd have to walk, and she'd better keep to the main roads.

Before she got beyond Gateshead two cars had stopped, their drivers offering her a lift. To her curt refusal one of them said, "It's your loss," and the other, after curb crawling with her the length of a street, had been deterred only by her threat to shout for the police.

And then not only did it begin to sleet, but the heel of her tights must have become wrinkled, for she developed a blister. Another half-mile, wet through, her heel causing minor agony, her whole being in the depths of humiliation, she knew she couldn't go on, and she was going to be reduced to doing what her mind had suggested to her before she left Low Fell: get on the phone to her grannie by a reversed-charge call.

She hobbled for another five minutes before she came to a telephone box, and she hesitated as she picked up the receiver. Her head drooped and she muttered aloud, "I can't, I can't, I just can't do it."

When she gave the number she thought, They'll all be in bed; they mightn't hear it. But just as if someone had been standing close to the phone, a voice answered almost immediately, "Yes?" and the operator said, "Will you pay for a call from a Miss Ridley?"

She closed her eyes tight when Ben's voice came to her, saying, "Ridley? Yes . . . yes. Go ahead. Hello!"

She couldn't answer.

"Hello there."

"It's . . . it's me, Pat."

"Yes, I thought it might be . . . Miss Ridley."

"Ben."

"Yes?"

"I . . . I'd like to speak to Gran."

"She's in bed."

"Couldn't you get her?"

"No. She's been upset about something today. She went to bed early; she took a sleeping tablet. What's the matter? Where are you?"

Again she couldn't speak.

"Where are you?"

"I'm . . . I'm somewhere on the outskirts of Gateshead."

"On the outskirts of where?"

"Gateshead, on the main road near the traffic circle."

"What on earth are you doing there? Have you missed the last bus?"

"No. I mean, yes. Ben." There was a silence, and then his voice came low, saying, "What is it? Are you all right?"

"I . . . I haven't any money and . . . and I'm wet through and . . . and would you come and get me?"

There was another short silence. "Where did you say you were?"

She looked about her, then gave him a rough description.

"Stay in the phone booth," he said. "Stay put; I'll be with you as quick as I can, fifteen minutes at the latest."

"Thanks. Thanks, Ben." She put down the phone and leaned against the partition and waited. At one stage, when she saw a police car come racing down the road, she turned and pretended she was phoning.

It could not have been more than fifteen minutes later when Ben drew his car up alongside the curb, but it had seemed like an eternity, an eternity in which she'd had time to review her life, especially that part which had taken up the past eighteen months.

Having pulled open the heavy phone-booth door, he stood looking at her for a second, and she at him; then he put out his hand and took her case from her, turned and walked across the pavement to the car.

When she was seated he pulled a rug from the back seat and put it on her knee; he didn't tuck it around her.

He had been driving a few minutes and still he hadn't spoken, and she said softly, "Thanks, thanks for coming."

When still he made no comment she put her head down, and now, her voice angry, she cried, "Oh! Say something, anything. Ask me what's happened, why I was stuck out there."

He said, "I'll ask you all the questions you want when we get inside. I . . . I don't want Mam to wake up, that's if she does, and come out and find me gone; she would tell by my hat and coat being gone from the hall."

She just prevented herself from screaming at him, "Damn Mam!"

There was no more said until they reached the house; then

as he opened the staircase door he said, "Ssh!" and she limped up the stairs and across the landing and into the sitting room, he following her on tiptoe.

When he had closed the door gently behind him, he went to where she stood unbuttoning her wet coat. As he took it from her he looked at the long gap left by the open zip of her dress, and, taking hold of the bottom clip, he hitched it up in one swift, sharp movement.

She turned on him, her face scarlet; then bringing her joined trembling hands up to her mouth she pressed them against her lips but was unable to stem the flow of tears spurting from her eyes. As her body slumped forward he put his arms around her and said, "There! There! Don't." He did not add, "You'll waken Mam," but said, "Don't upset yourself. Come on, you mustn't upset yourself like that."

He led her to the couch and they sat down together. He was still holding her, and her head lay against his shoulder, and when she said softly, "Oh, Ben!" he looked down on her hair and became still. She felt the stillness and she muttered, "Don't be mad at me. Please, please, don't be mad at me."

"I'm not mad at you, Pat, I'm only—" He moved his head slightly and bit hard on his lip, and when he didn't go on she muttered, "I didn't go through with it. . . . I'm a fool."

"Oh."

She put her hand to her face now. "Oh, I don't mean I'm a fool for not going through with it. I mean I'm a fool for ever thinking I could. But still, at the same time, I . . . I feel an utter idiot, old-fashioned, behind the times. . . ."

"I'm glad."

She looked up at him, and they stared at each other, their glances deepening.

"I'm . . . I'm unhappy, Ben."

He took her hands and held them against his chest as he said softly, "You shouldn't be. You've got everything: the chance of a fine career ahead of you; you've got a brain above the av—"

"Oh, Ben, brains! Brains! Shut up about brains. A woman

doesn't just want brains; in fact, I think they're a disadvantage, I do, I do." She was shaking her head while sniffing loudly. "All this piffle about equality, running round the university forming societies for this, that and the other, all with the view toward equality. And the ones who get it, or think they've got it, you should see them. The more they get what they want, the more apart they become from those they want to be equal with. They herd together, and they talk—they're like overfed computers. You know, lately it's made me afraid of my mind." She laughed gently, derisively. "I suppose it's an awful admission, but there's something in me that doesn't want to be equal, and that's the truth. . . . I just want . . . oh, Ben!"

Their gaze deepened still further, until it reached a depth in which they were both swimming. "Pat." He was holding her face between his hands now, and again he said, "Pat!" Then she was being crushed tight against him while they rocked backwards and forwards. After a moment he held her from him and murmured haltingly, "All . . . all these years. I never knew. I . . . I thought it was all on my side. Why . . . why, Pat." Again she was held tightly to him, but now with his lips hard on hers.

When at last they drew apart she brought her hands up to her cheeks, one on each side, and standing like this she asked softly, "Will you marry me, Ben . . . soon?"

As she watched his blue eyes mist over, then saw him bow his head, she knew a moment's panicking fear and muttered in consternation, as he rubbed a hand across his eyes, "I'm sorry, I shouldn't have said it. It doesn't matter. I . . . ."

"Be quiet!" He was gripping her fiercely to him. "It's just that I never dreamed there was a chance . . . never, never thought you could. . . . I've loved you all me life, but I could see meself going round courting Mam to the end of me days."

"Oh, Ben! Oh, Ben! It's funny." Her voice was high, cracking. "Both thinking alike—you courting Gran, Mam. I've wanted to scream at you. . . . Oh Ben!"

They rocked together again, not knowing whether the other

was laughing or crying. Then, their faces close, she asked softly, "Do you think Gran'll be pleased?" and he answered, "Tickled to death. That's after she gets over the shock. And it's bound to be a bit of a shock after the way we've gone on at each other over the years." Again they clung together; then he said soberly, "Anyway, it'll help to take her mind off this other business."

"What other business?"

"Her mother, my grannie. The one I've never seen. They sent for her yesterday to go and see her."

4

Mary awoke around five o'clock on Saturday morning, feeling, as she put it to herself, like nothing on earth. She always did after taking a sleeping tablet.

The battle she'd had with her conscience over the past two days was something she thought she'd never have to face. It had begun with the policeman coming to the door. It was years since she had seen a policeman at the door; the last one had come about Jimmy: "I don't want to take him in, Mrs. Tollett," he had said kindly; "he's lying in a shop door in Ormond Street. If you'll go and get him, I'll pass by on the other side."

Now this policeman had asked, "Does Mr. Alec Walton live here?"

When she answered, "Yes," he had said, "Well, I'm sorry to inform you that his wife is dying. She's in the Old People's ward, the annex to the home, you know."

She hadn't spoken for a full minute, and then she said, "My father's ill in bed."

"You're the daughter then?"

"Yes."

"Well, perhaps you'd like to go along."

After a short silence he said, "Well, good night." And she, too, said, "Good night."

Her mother dying. She had thought, when she thought of her at all, that she might be dead already. The last time she had looked at her was as she lay in that bed paralyzed, speechless, when she had wished her long life. Well, apparently she had got her wish. But she shouldn't feel sorry about it, should she? And she wasn't going to. No, she wasn't going to. As for telling her da, that was the last thing she was going to do.

This had taken place on Thursday, and when she went in to him to say good night he had held her hand and said, "I've got a sort of funny feeling on me, lass."

"Funny feeling, Da?" she said.

"Aye, disappointed like, as if we were goin' off on a trip an' something had stopped us. You remember when I used to take you to Shields sands, we used to walk all the way to Tyne Dock and take the tram from there. And you used to wade, an' I used to buy you a stick of candy rock from that shop just afore you get to the Marine Park. You remember? The shop with all the spades and pails hanging outside. Eeh! Those were happy days, lass."

She had stroked his hand. Happy days, when they hadn't enough money to take the tram down to Tyne Dock! If they had taken the tram, there would have been no candy rock.

"Candy rock," he said. "Do you remember the fellow that used to come round the doors shoutin', 'Candy rock for stockin' legs!' You remember him? And the time you took a good pair of me stockin's out and when you came back and showed the rock to your ma she nearly went mad when she knew what you'd done?" His voice trailed away.

She had looked down at him. It was the first time she could remember his mentioning her ma's name during the last twenty-eight years. Her ma had died completely for them both when Lally died. She felt a shiver go through her as the thought came to her that perhaps, on her deathbed, where she was now, she was again forcing her will on him, as she had done all those years ago.

Yesterday he had said to her, "I still have this funny feelin' on me, lass."

"What is it like?" she had asked, and he had replied, "I can't explain it, except I'm depressed, like."

Then about eight o'clock last night he was sitting up in bed when she went in to him, and he said, "Aw, lass, I feel better. You know I'm going to get up tomorrow. Of a sudden I feel on top of the world, just like a bairn being let out of school, you know." He had laughed at her, and she had laughed back at him, saying, "A bairn being let out of school at your age! You're in your second childhood."

"I shouldn't wonder, lass, I shouldn't wonder. But I tell you what." He had leaned toward her, his eyes bright and happy. "You wouldn't have to press me very much to get me to take a double dose of me medicine tonight."

"Go on with you." She had slapped his hand, and when he saw the whisky she brought in to him was a double, he said softly, "Aw, lass, you're the best in the world." And when raising the glass to her, he sang in a cracked voice, "I love a lassie, a bonny, bonny lassie, she's as pure as the lily in the dell," it was all she could do to keep looking at him and stop the tears spurting from her eyes.

Years ago when he had sung these words, she had taken them as a recrimination for the mistake she made with Ben, but not any more, for she knew that to him she was still as pure as the lily in the dell, and he had forgotten she ever made a mistake.

And last night she had talked to Ben about her mother. "Ben," she said, "I've got something on me mind. The police've been and asked for your granda—me ma's dying and he expected one of us to go."

He had looked at her and said, "Well, what you going to do about it?" He knew all about his grandmother and what she had done to his mother.

"I don't know," she had answered him. "Yet if the situation

had been put to me, well, as a sort of—what do they call it?—hypothetical question, I wouldn't have hesitated for an instant. I would have said, No! No! If she was dying twenty times over, they wouldn't drag me to her bed. Yet now, here I am of two minds what I should do."

It was then Ben had said quietly, "If you're of two minds, then you know what you should do? You don't want anything on your conscience, Mam. Look"—he had ended—"do you want me to drive you there?"

"NO! NO!" she had protested firmly. "I'll have to think more about it. But I'm so tired; I didn't sleep last night at all."

"Take a pill," he said, "and in the morning things should be clearer. You'll know what to do then."

She had turned to him when she reached the door and said, "She might be gone in the morning."

"Yes, she might; but you'll have to face up to that an' all. Go on to bed."

Staring across the room at him, she remarked, "You look off color yourself," to which he had answered, "I'm all right."

She was thinking that Ben had been off color all week; it was that business last weekend. She wondered what that young monkey had done? She was worried stiff about her an' all.

It was at this moment there came a tap on the door.

When Ben came in with a cup of tea in his hand, she stared at him, saying, "You're up before your clothes are on, aren't you? It's just after five."

"Yes, it's just after five."

She continued to stare at him. His face was bright, his eyes were shining, and when he sat down on the side of the bed and handed her the cup she peered at him. "You're in fine fettle this morning."

"Never better, Mam."

"You must have had some pleasant dreams?"

"Marvelous."

"Good for you."

"Pat's here, Mam."

She gulped on the hot tea, put the cup back on the saucer and said, "Pat! When did she come? I never . . ."

"No, you never heard her. The pill had knocked you out."

"What time did she get in?"

"Well, let's see. What time did we get in?"

"We?"

"Yes, it's a long story." He leaned toward her and whispered, "But I'll tell you as briefly as I can."

And so he told her as briefly as he could, but in his own way. And toward the end of it she exclaimed, "Judo! Our Pat and judo! Knocking a man out! I don't believe you."

"Well, I'll leave it with you; she'll demonstrate later. And by the way, Mrs. Tollett, I'm going to be married, and right away." His hands went forward just in time to stop her cup toppling over.

"Mar—ried! Right . . ."

"Mar—ried, right . . ."

"Married! Who to?"

"Well, who do you think? Pat."

Mary leaned back against the pillows and let out a long breath; then said, "Oh!"

"Surprised? Shocked?"

"Surprised, shocked, me? No, no, not if you're going to marry Pat, I'm not."

His eyebrows went up, his face stretched. "You're not?"

"No, she's been bats about you all her life. Well, since she was about five."

"Oh, Mam!" He leaned forward and put his hands on her shoulders, and she said, "Hie up! This tea will be over me afore you're finished this morning."

"I've been bats about her for years an' all."

"Have you, lad?"

"Yes; I suppose you knew that, too?"

"Well, honestly no, no, I didn't. And honestly again, I didn't really know how things stood with her until last Friday night when . . . when I saw her looking at you—I must have been blind afore. And then, of course, when you hit her . . . well I knew for certain your side of it an' all."

He took the cup from her hand, put it on the sideboard and hugged her.

"We're going to be married next week."

"NEXT WEEK! Aw now, here, here."

"Never mind, here, here, Mam, I'm getting a special license."

"A special license!"

"A special license, that's what I said. Have you got a deaf ear, too?"

"And . . . and the university, her career?"

"Her career is ended, that career anyway. She doesn't want it, Mam. What she wants . . . well, she wants the same as me, a home and a family. That's all we both want, a home and a family. And, of course, you. You'll come along with us."

"NOT ON YOUR LIFE!" She pushed him roughly. "Now let's get this straight, lad. You can do everything you want, both of you, but don't try to settle my life."

"Well, where do you think you're going to go? You know, Granda's on his last legs, and you don't think we're going to let you live alone. You've looked after one and another for years and years; you've been at the beck and call of everybody."

"Look, Ben, please." She pointed stiffly at him. "As you say, for years I've been at the beck and call of everybody, an' that's true. For years 'n' years 'n' years I've felt encumbered. That's the word, 'encumbered.' Now, when you're settled, and when me da goes, I'll be free. And that's the word, that IS the word, 'free.' Don't you understand?"

He drew his head farther back and looked at her through narrowed gaze; then he said quietly, "You felt like this for long?"

"As I said, years and years."

"And I've been one of the encumbrances?"

"No, no, not you, Ben, you least of all. I could have done what I wanted to do with you alone; you know, get about, go abroad. No, lad"—she leaned toward him now and took his hand—"never you. You've been not my nephew, you've been like my own child; and you know that, don't you?"

He hitched himself up the bed and took her in his arms, and after a moment he said thickly, "But I'll be worried about you; I couldn't help being worried about you if you were on your . . ."

Again she pushed him away, but gently now, saying, "I'm not that old, fifty-six. I'm going to get about, see life. And I'll come and stay with you. I might even take a house near you, just so's you can park the bairns on me."

"Aw, Mam!"

She looked at him steadily now, and her voice held a deep and serious note as she said, "I'm happy for you, Ben. It's like a weight off me shoulders knowing you're going to be settled. How would you like to take a bit of good advice?"

"Always from you, Mam."

"Well, get it over and done with before you tell our Annie or Tom, because, well, I know my own daughter and she'll find some way of putting a spoke in the wheel. She had big things planned for Pat, and a mechanic didn't come into them, even the owner of a garage as he is now." She patted his cheek. "Annie's always had her eye on the scholastic world. Mrs. Patricia Blank, wife of Professor Blank, that's what she had in mind. Although she never said it, that's what she intended for her. Oh, I know my Annie. But anyway, see what Pat says."

"I think she'll agree, Mam. Oh, I know she will."

"Good. Good. Now leave me be. I've got some thinking of me own to do, you understand?"

"I understand."

It was ten o'clock the same morning when Mary entered the small lobby leading to the geriatric ward. The young nurse at the desk looked up and said, "Yes, can I help you?" and Mary had to wet her lips twice before she could bring out the words "I've . . . I've come to see Mrs. Walton, Mrs. Alice Walton."

The girl looked at her, then down at the ledger on her desk before saying, "Will you take a seat, please?"

Mary didn't take a seat but she watched the young nurse come from behind the desk and go toward the door at the beginning of the corridor; as she was about to knock, the door opened. She watched her step inside and heard her voice low and distinct say, "It's Mrs. Walton's daughter—she's come." Then another voice, equally low but clear, answering, "Oh! Has she?"

The woman who came out into the corridor and looked at Mary was evidently the sister in charge, and when their eyes met there arose between them an instant and mutual dislike. The sister was seeing "a well-dressed woman, one of those who get on and leave their folks to rot in loneliness," and Mary was reading her thoughts as clearly as if they had been written on a blackboard behind her.

"Good morning." The voice was icy.

"Good morning. I've . . . I've come to see Mrs. Walton."

"Oh." The sister now looked toward the desk and to the young nurse and said, "Wasn't it Thursday the information was sent out?"

"Yes, Sister."

The woman was looking straight into Mary's face now. "Thursday it was," she said.

"Yes, I know, but . . . but I haven't been able to get here before now."

"Well, that's a pity, because Mrs. Walton died at seven o'clock last night. Yes, she died last night. She's been here six years, you know, and has never had a visitor."

Their eyes were holding hard, and Mary's lips became tight as the sister went on, "She had been living in one room for years fending for herself, and partly paralyzed at that. Poor old soul. Then six years here without one visitor to see her. So you've come too late."

Mary hadn't felt rage rising in her for many a year, but now it was almost choking her. This woman was taking the place of

God, condemning her. She heard her saying now, "Do you wish to make the final arrangements?"

"No, I don't!" Her voice startled both the sister and the nurse. "I'll leave you to carry on with your self-righteousness."

"Self-righteousness! What do you mean? If you mean humanitarian . . ."

"Humanitarian be damned! What do you know about it?" Mary was almost spitting the words at her now. "Did you find Mrs. Alice Walton a sweet character to deal with? Did you?"

As the sister wagged her head slightly and pursed her lips, Mary cried at her, "No, you didn't! Well, neither did I. My mother, God forgive her, was the means of destroying a number of lives. Through her my husband was horribly disfigured. She disfigured him for life, but what was more"—she now bent from the waist toward the sister—"she burned her daughter-in-law to death, and drove her son almost insane and at last to his grave through drink. Go on. You carry on with your humanitarian principles; they make you feel nice, comfortable, and so very good, don't they? You should have had the dear old soul to live with in her fighting days—that would have tested your humanitarianism." For one moment longer she glared at the sister, then she turned and stalked from the lobby, leaving both the sister and the nurse gaping after her.

As she drove back home her rage gradually subsided, washed away on a flood of tears that almost proved disastrous to her driving.

When she arrived Ben and Pat met her at the top of the stairs, and when their arms came out to her she thrust them off, saying, "Leave me be for a while. Leave me be," and pushed blindly past them into her room. And there, throwing herself onto the bed, she sobbed as she hadn't done since Jimmy died.

"Eeh! lass, I can't understand it. I feel so grand, I feel I've had a new lease of life. Now you'll let me get up tomorrow, won't you? I could have got up today 'cos I've never felt better in me life. It's just as if I'd gone back forty years, aye, forty years."

Mary was not fanciful, but it was strange, she thought, that her da had had this feeling from around seven o'clock last night, just about the time they said her mother had gone. And he was looking sprightly; she had not seen him looking like this, not for years. Nor had his manner been so lively. Could it be that her mother, who was an evil woman—she would never think of her as otherwise—had weighed on him all these years? They said there was power in thought; but then it would have touched herself, wouldn't it, because her ma had hated her more than she had her da, she was sure of that. But she had been strong inside; she would have warded off any evil her mother had sent in her direction; her da had lain under it. It might all be fancy, but there he was before her eyes looking younger and talking with a lightness that did her heart good. It could be that he would get on his feet again and enjoy these last years of his life. She hoped so. Oh, she hoped so. In spite of wanting her own release, she hoped so with all her heart.

There was the sound of a thud from the direction of either the dining room or the sitting room and Alec looked at her and laughed and said, "What's that? Somebody emptying a load of coal upstairs?"

She laughed at him and, tapping his hand, said, "Somethin's fallen; I'll go and see."

Nothing had fallen in the dining room, but when she opened the sitting room door she saw what had fallen. There on the floor were Ben and Pat all twisted up together.

"Well, I never!" she said. "Did you make that thud?"

"Ma-Mam"—Ben was laughing as he spluttered—"she threw me, she's thrown me!"

"Don't be silly. Get yourselves up."

"I . . . I can't, Mam."

"Pat! Leave go of him."

When they were both on their feet and laughing like two children, she looked at them and said, "You didn't really throw him, Pat?"

"Course I did, Gran—watch."

"Oh, my God!" She sprang back as she saw her nephew, her big, strong, blond nephew, going head over heels, or legs over head was more like it, onto his back.

"There, Gran." Pat dusted her hands. "That's a demonstration of a hip throw. Now I'll show you a rear loin."

"No, you don't." Ben was pushing her away. "No!" Then coming at her, he cried, "This is the only way I'll be able to stop her, Mam." And he pinned her to him with his arms. When, the next moment, his feet again left the ground he yelled in protest, and again they were both on the floor laughing, with Mary standing looking down at them with a straight face and saying, "It isn't seemly, Pat."

"I agree with you, Gran."

From his prone position Ben spluttered, "Don't you worry Mam. I'm going to do something about it and right away. There's one thing I've learned: every move she makes can be countered, and I'll learn to counter them or die in the attempt."

"And you're likely to. Get yourselves up, the pair of you, and listen. . . . Oh"—she stopped and slapped at Pat—"I can't believe it. Just look at you, as straight as a drain pipe and able to topple him."

"The term is 'throw him,' Gran."

"Throw or topple, whatever, it's not right, it's unseemly, 'tisn't . . ."

"Womanly, Gran?" Patricia put her arms round Mary's shoulders. "That's the word you want, isn't it, 'womanly.' Well, that's how I feel about it, too. But, oh, it gives you a nice feeling on a dark night going up an alley."

When they stopped laughing she said to them, "Listen for a moment. Your granddad's had a new lease on life. I just can't understand it after what the doctor said. Anyway, I'll get him up tomorrow."

The following morning when she went in to her da with his early cup of tea the cup slowly tilted in her hand. Alec was lying on his back. There was a smile on his face, and under his hand on the counterpane was a small framed snapshot of herself taken on the Shields sands when she was about six years old. He had started on his last long trip.

5

An official had come to her and asked if she wished to make any arrangements about her mother's funeral and she had answered no. "None whatever?" he had said, and she had answered again, in his own words, "None whatever."

She felt now it had been a mistake going to the hospital. She knew that her conscience had no need to be troubled; the religious ones would say it was hardness of heart; if God could forgive, why not her? But she wasn't God. People were stupid who expected you to act like God. Yet she knew that there were men and women who had been tortured by the Japanese, and who had survived and yet held no grudge against their torturers. She knew there were Jews who had suffered under the Germans as no human being or animal should be made to suffer, and who afterwards held no bitterness in their hearts. But, on the other hand, she knew of those who had gone insane through the memories of what they and their people had suffered. And there were still people who could not sleep at night because of their memories. But the horrors these people had suffered had taken place during wartime. The evil in men erupted during wartime, and there was a license allowed for a certain amount of cruelty at such times. But her mother's cruelty had not been occasioned by war; hers had been bred of personal revenge. No, she was going to be no hypocrite. She was not going to manufacture forgiveness to lay as a salve on her conscience because of fear.

They buried Alec on the Thursday. Apart from Ben and Patricia, there were only Annie and Tom and a few neighbors present. As the pallbearers carried the coffin toward the grave, she followed with Ben's hand on her arm, and as she walked she was aware that, parallel with them on a side path, four men were carrying another coffin, and she knew without doubt that that coffin bore her mother. She had to fight the feeling of oppression that flooded over her. And when she stood by the side of the open grave and watched her da being lowered into it, if she prayed, she prayed that there would be no coming together in the great hereafter; her da had died smiling and she wanted him to go on smiling.

"It's scandalous," Annie said, "utterly, utterly scandalous, and for more reasons than one, getting married two days after Granda is buried. And then the sneakiness of it, and her career. This is the repayment I've got for the years of thought I've bestowed on her; and there's only one person to blame for it."

"And that's me," Mary said.

"Yes, yes, it's you, Mam. You've encouraged her."

"It's no use me saying I hadn't anything to do with it, is it?"

"No, because I wouldn't believe you."

"Ben. Of all people, Ben!" Annie literally stormed up and down the room while her husband sat with his head bowed and his hands between his knees, with Mary opposite him watching her daughter.

After a few minutes Mary said, "If she traveled the world over, she'd never do better than Ben."

"Never do better than Ben!" Annie had stopped in her prancing. "A mechanic!"

"A garage owner; he has his own garage, and this is only the beginning."

"He couldn't even pass the first level exams."

"No, he couldn't. But nevertheless he's got a head on his shoulders, a business head, and before many years are over he'll

have garages in every town both sides of this river; he'll be
another Adams and Gibbon, or better."

"Adams and Gibbon! That's got to be proved. As I see it now,
it's just high-faluting thinking."

"Well, if it is and he only has the one place, he'll still be well
off, because, I might as well tell you now, so's it won't come as
a shock to you later, he'll have all I've got when I go—all of it!"

"OH, MAM!"

"Yes, 'oh, Mam.' Tom there"—she nodded to her son-in-law,
who was looking at her now from under his brows—"he's able to
provide you with all you need, and more, and when Ben gets
my money he'll be able to provide Pat with all she'll ever need.
But as I sec it, he'll be doing that off his own bat afore long."

"You've always cared more about him than any one of us,
Pat or me or . . . oh!"

Mary looked at her daughter, and she thought, She looks just
like me ma in 1933, and she said, "He's been as a son to me,
Annie."

"And I've never been as a daughter?"

"You were married when you were hardly nineteen, and before that you were spoiled by your father, by your granda and
your Uncle Jimmy."

"But never you?"

"Well, somebody had to keep you in order." And she could
have added, "Try to erase your grandmother's traits that were
very evident in you from a child."

"Where've they gone, do you know, Mam?" It was Tom speaking now, and she answered, "Yes, I know, Tom, but I'm not
going to say. They'll be back at the end of the week."

"Where're they going to live?" It was a demand from Annie.

"Above the garage; they've got it all planned."

"Above the garage!" Annie tossed her head scornfully to one
side and gazed up at the ceiling, and Mary put in quickly, "Yes,
above the garage; not forgetting, Annie, that you were brought
up above a shop, and it didn't do you any harm."

"She's different."

"Yes, she's different," said Mary sharply now, "because she doesn't want to get away from her early surroundings. As strange as that may seem to you, she wants to live in Jarrow, because she was happy here. She was born here, she feels part of the place. Newcastle was like a foreign country. An' the university—oh, it's all right for some, but she didn't fit in."

"Not fit in? With her brains!" Annie's head was swinging from shoulder to shoulder. "Not fit in! She could have fitted in anywhere—Cambridge, anywhere. And now to live above a gar—"

"Stop it, Annie. Stop it. She can still use her brains."

"On what, I ask you, a bairn a year?"

"Well, she could do worse."

"That's a matter of opinion."

"All right, it's a matter of opinion. You have yours, and I have mine."

In the silence that followed Tom's quiet voice put in, "What are you going to do, Mam, now that you're on your own?"

"Live, I hope, Tom," she answered.

"Where?" Annie's voice now pronged her like a skewer being rammed into meat.

"I don't know yet." Mary's answer was sharp and loud.

"Then I think it's about time you did, if you say they've now told you you've got to be out of here in a month."

"Well, I've got a month then," said Mary. "I'll find some place. If not, I'll put the furniture into storage, the bits I want to keep, and then I'll have a look round. That is, after I've had a holiday, a long one, perhaps touring—round the world. Why not? I've promised myself this for years."

"Touring! On your own?" Annie's voice was scornful.

"Yes, I'm past school age. But what am I talking about anyway, school age! The youngsters hitchhike across Europe, so I suppose a boat or a plane will take me."

"Oh! Come on." Annie's voice brought Tom up slowly from his chair. Looking at Mary, he smiled gently as he said, "Well, if you're stuck, Mam, you know where to come."

"Thanks, Tom."

Annie came and stood in front of her now, her mouth a thin line, and wagging her head while she blinked the tears from her eyes she said, "I'll never forgive you, Mam."

"I know that, love, I know that, but at bottom, Annie, what you want, and what I want, what we all want, is Pat's happiness, and if she's going to be happy with Ben, and she is happy with him, then we should all be happy. . . . And what you don't know, lass, is she's been in love with him for years, chasing him for years."

"Oh, Mam! My Pat chasing Ben? Talk about imagination!"

"Yes, talk about it. Anyway, as I said, as long as she's happy, why should we tear each other's eyes out?"

"It's the way it's been done, underhand."

"Well, if they had tried to do it straight, you'd have put your spoke in and spoiled things. I'm sorry, I'm sorry"—she raised her hand—"but you know yourself you would; if you're honest with yourself, you know you would."

"I'm going."

Mary leaned forward and kissed the stiff cheek and smiled as she said, "Try not to hate me too much. And about me will, I'll leave you enough to buy a stick of rock candy. But don't think you're going to get it just yet." She poked her daughter in the shoulder, and Annie flounced round and went out of the room.

When Tom came toward her and kissed her gently, he whispered, "She'll get over it."

"I know, Tom."

"Tell Pat I'm glad she's happy."

Mary put her arms around her son-in-law's neck and they hugged each other, and she said, in not too low a voice so that it would carry to her daughter, "I know one thing, Tom. My daughter was damned lucky to get you, and if she's wise, she'll mind her p's and q's and hang on to you. With this self-service divorce business now and women snatching at blokes right, left and center, she should look out." She pulled a face at him and stabbed her finger toward the open door, and he doubled his fist and wagged it at her, and they both suppressed their laughter.

When they had gone Mary slowly sat down on the couch and gazed at the fire. There was a strange, soft hush over the house, and she attributed it for the moment to the snow that was falling and had been doing so all day. There was no sound of footsteps coming from the road or the street. Yet as she listened to the silence she knew it wasn't caused by the muting of the snow, but by the absence of people in the house.

For the first time in forty years she was alone in this house, and for the first time in forty years there was no one to call her name, bring her attention to them. She had achieved the state for which she had longed, the state of freedom. All the time in the future was her own.

She leaned forward and, resting her forearms on her knees, looked at the floor. She had at last got what she had wanted, but now she had got it, what was she going to do with it? She hadn't thought it would be like this; she had thought it would be exhilarating. She had seen herself dashing down into the shop, grabbing up a couple of cases and packing. She had seen herself telephoning a travel bureau and asking when the next ship was going to Norway, or how did she go about taking a plane to New York. She had gone over it all in her mind scores and scores of times.

She moved her head and looked around her. She was doing none of the things she thought she would do. She was just sitting here feeling like a lost old woman—sixty-six, seventy-six, not fifty-six. What was she going to do with herself in the future? Whether it was to be short or long, how was she going to fill it? Even tonight, what was she going to do with herself? She looked at the television. She could switch it on. She looked at the bookshelves. She could read a book. There was her knitting; there was a pullover for Ben half-finished. She could pick up the morning paper and look over the stock market; she hadn't looked at it for two or three days. But all she wanted to do was to sit there and cry.

Well, she wasn't going to!

She would start packing, because, whether she liked it or not, she must be out of here within a month, and there was all that stuff down in the shop to be got rid of. And whichever house she took she'd start from scratch. She wasn't going to carry bundles of memories with her, even wrapped up in furniture; she had enough in her head to last her the rest of her life. Yes, she'd start sorting out in earnest; she'd work it off. It was a good slogan, that, work it off.

She worked it off all the week. She burned business papers going back to when Ben's father first took the shop. She gave away boxes and framework and sweets bottles and all the paraphernalia that had gone to make up the shop, to the children and handymen around, and most of the contents of the rooms she allotted to the various neighbors to collect when she was ready to go. And in this way, miserably, she passed the first days of her freedom. Now it was Friday and she was longing for tomorrow when Ben and Pat would return.

It was about five o'clock when she decided to call it a day. She had a bath, dressed, made herself a cup of tea and was just settling down in the sitting room when there was a hammering on the back door and she heard a childish voice shouting, "Mrs. Tollett! Mrs. Tollett! Are you in, Mrs. Tollett?"

She went down the stairs and opened the door. It was dark in the yard, but standing on the step, shown up by the light from the stairs, was a small boy well known to her, Mrs. McArthur's grandson, Freddie.

"What is it, Freddie?" she said.

"This man, Mrs. Tollett, he's been lookin' for you. He asked us if you was still livin' hereabouts 'cos the shop's all boarded up, an' I said, Aye, an' you'd be in round the corner. An' you are."

Mary peered over the boy's head into the darkness. Then she lifted her hand and switched on the yard light, and there she saw the man standing midway down the snow-covered yard. He was a tall man, broad, wearing a heavy coat with a sort of astrakhan collar; he had a trilby hat on, which he now took off. He walked toward her, and when he was close he looked down on her and said in a thick, slow drawl that spoke of an American, "Mary Walton? I mean Mrs. Tollett?"

"Yes, yes."

She stared up into his face, then slowly raised both hands to her mouth and whispered, "Hu-Hughie Amesden!" She still continued to stare at him, then on a high note she cried, "Well! Come on up. What are you standing in the cold for? Oh, thanks, Freddie, thank you. See you in the morning."

"Aye, Mrs. Tollett. All right, Mrs. Tollett."

She stood aside, her arm outstretched, her hand pointing up the stairs, saying, "Go on up. Go on up. Please, go on up." She closed the bottom door, then ran up the stairs, and in the hallway they stood and looked at each other.

Hughie Amesden! She would hardly have known him. She could have passed him in the street. He seemed to be twice the breadth he had been when they last met. But the greatest change was his face. His skin was tanned to a reddy brownness. She remembered it had been very fair, beautiful skin, a beautiful face. He was still not a bad-looking man, but different, rugged-looking. There were lines all around his eyes and two deep lines running from his nose to the corners of his mouth. But he was Hughie Amesden.

"You haven't changed a bit." He was gazing at her.

"Oh, that's silly. All these years! What is it, twenty-five? Twenty-eight? But come along in. What are we standing here for?" She led the way into the sitting room. "I was just going to have a cup of tea; wait till I get another cup." She almost ran out of the room. When she returned he was still standing, and she said, "Take your coat off, do, and sit down."

"Thanks."

She took his coat and laid it over a chair; she noted that his clothes were very good—she had an eye for clothes, quality clothes. She picked up the teapot and as she poured the tea she said, "Fancy! The last person on earth I expected to see."

"It's been a long time."

"Are you on holiday?"

"Sort of."

"Have you been in England long?"

"No, I only arrived yesterday. To tell you the truth, I haven't long got off the train from London."

"From London?" She stopped, the teapot poised in her hand. "Why, you must be famished. I'll get you something."

"No, no, I had a good meal, in fact two, on the train. Quite good, quite good." He kept his eyes on her all the time he was speaking.

"Well, drink that cup of tea."

He sipped at the tea, then said, "Tea—this is English if nothing else. I drink mostly coffee now."

"Oh, I'll make you a coffee if you would . . ."

"No, no, no!" He shook his head. "I love a cup of tea."

She sat down on the chair opposite to where he was sitting on the couch, and, biting on her lip, she said, "I really can't believe it."

"Nor me."

"And you know, it's odd your calling at this time, for I'm . . . I'm packing up. Another week or so and I'd be gone."

"You're leaving here?" He raised his eyebrows slightly.

"Yes; they're demolishing the whole place."

"Really! Oh, well, I noticed the change as I came in the cab from the station; even in the dark and the snow, the whole landscape is changed."

"Yes, it isn't the same old Jarrow any more. It's better in lots of ways though, I suppose. Nicer for more people, although some still grumble and long to have the old times back—you wouldn't believe it."

"And so you are leaving?"

"Yes"—she nodded—"beginning of the New Year."

"Well"—he jerked his head a little to the side—"I'm just in

time. Lucky to find you. I . . . I didn't really expect to find you
here."

"No?"

"No, I thought you'd be bound to be gone . . . well"—he
pursed his lips—"married again."

"Oh, no." She shook her head. "I never married again. Anyway"—she laughed—"I hadn't time. You see, there was my father,
and my husband's cousin who was bombed out and came to
live here; then my own daughter, Annie, and my brother and
his child—his wife died"—she always referred to Lally as Jimmy's
wife—"and with one thing and another I've had my hands full
over the years, until . . . until this last week. My father died
just over a fortnight ago."

"Oh, I'm sorry; but he must have been a good age."

"Seventy-six. And then my nephew, Ben—he's my brother
Jimmy's only son, I brought him up—well, he got married to
my granddaughter a week ago."

"Your nephew married your granddaughter?"

"Yes; it's quite complicated, but that's how it is. My brother's
son married my daughter's daughter, if you can work it out."

He smiled, closed his eyes for a moment, then shook his head
and said, "Just."

"And there I was, I mean here I am, my own boss after all
these years." She paused for a moment and stared at him across
the space between them, then asked, "Your wife, is she over
here an' all?"

"No, she died a month ago, Mary."

"Oh, I'm sorry."

"I should say I am, too, but I can't; for her sake I'm glad
she went. You see, she's been in a sanatorium for the last six
years, and she didn't know me or anyone else. She . . . she never
got over losing our girl; she thought going to America would
erase the memory of it all, but it didn't."

"I'm very sorry."

He nodded his head slowly, and now she asked, "How do you
like America?"

"Oh, very well, very well indeed. I must say I wouldn't have done as well businesswise in England. You see, René's brother-in-law was in the car business, and he took me in with him and we went from good to better. Now we're quite a going concern, spread quite a bit."

"Isn't that strange? My Ben—I mean my nephew Ben—he's in the car business an' all. He's got his own garage."

"Oh, that's good."

They smiled at each other; then after a moment he put his head on one side and said, "I can't get over it. I can't get over it, Mary."

"Can't get over what?"

"About your not changing. You're just as I imagined you over the years. And this"—he put his hands down and patted each side of the couch—"I've often imagined me sitting like this talking to you."

She became still. She swallowed, while she stared at him. Not a line from him in twenty-odd years, nothing since she received that letter he had sent her telling her he was going to America. If he had been thinking of her, why hadn't he written? She said now with a slight trace of coquetry, "Oh, go on with you! If you'd imagined that, why didn't you send me a Christmas card to let me know you were alive?"

He didn't answer for a full minute; then he said slowly, "It wasn't because I didn't want to, Mary. It was because, because I was afraid to. Right from the time I left these shores I was afraid to."

She became still again.

Now she blinked, gulped, moved on her chair and, leaning toward the table, picked up the plate and said, "Would you like another scone?"

"No, I don't want any scones, Mary." His voice had a deep, rough sound to it now. "I . . . I want to talk to you, say something to you. An' I've come a long way to say it. I came just on the off chance, but I had to come. I didn't intend to go at it like a bull at a gap, but here I am not in your house ten minutes"—he stopped and looked around—"Do you know something? This is the first time I've ever been in this room, but the nights that I've stood outside yonder in front of Peel's doorway and looked up at that curtained window"—he pointed over his shoulder—"after you had married Ben Tollett. Well, they were countless."

Her mouth was slightly agape. She said softly, "You did that?"

"Yes." His lips twisted into a smile. "You must have known?"

"No. No." She shook her head emphatically. "No, I didn't dream. You see you never let on; in all those years you never spoke to me. Only once did you open your mouth, and then you said one word—hello. That's all you said."

"Well"—he laughed a deep, soft laugh as he shrugged one shoulder—"I wasn't a talkative fellow, and I was terribly shy. I used to let Paul—you remember Paul Connelly—I used to let him do the talking. Did you ever receive a card from a silent admirer?"

She joined her hands together and brought them to her breast as she said, "Then it was you who sent it?" And he nodded. "Yes, I sent that card. I paid threepence for it, and I didn't rub the price off the back, because it was a lot to pay for a card in those days."

She bowed her head and bit on her lip as he said softly, "And then, well, when you married Ben, I was sort of flabbergasted."

"But, Hughie"—this was the first time she had called him by his name—"you could have spoken to me."

"Yes, I could, but I suppose there was a real reason why I didn't, fear." He turned his head to the side. "You see, my dad was carrying on with a woman at the bottom of our street and I seemed to bear the brunt of it; my mother would talk to me for hours on end, and she nearly always ended by warning me to keep off the lasses. 'If I catch you going round with any of them,' she used to say, 'I'll . . .' Oh, well"—he spread his hands —"you know the jargon." He laughed again. "There was every lad in the place courting, in back lanes, over by the allotment, and the slag heap. I used to trip over them, but I didn't want to court anyone but you, Mary." He got to his feet. "That's why I came over. I had to come even if it was only to find you married, or dead."

He put out his hands and, taking hers, drew her up toward him. "I knew it might be one chance in a thousand but I had to take it. She'll be married, I thought; she's bound to be married, looking like she did. I had no means of finding out because we have no connection in Jarrow now. Why haven't you married, Mary?"

She was trembling from head to foot; she looked away from him as she said, "I had too many responsibilities, like I said." When she turned her head toward him again, she added, "Yet I nearly did, twice, three times, but something came up."

She could not keep looking at him—she had to bow her head—and it was bowed when he said, "You've been the only love of my life, Mary. It sounds improbable, I know, and very old-fashioned, but there it is. And now it seems as if a miracle has happened, to come and find you still where I left you. But about to fly. Can . . . can I ask you to fly in my direction, Mary?"

She lifted her head and looked into his eyes. They were the same eyes that she had dreamed about years ago; they hadn't altered; they were the same eyes that she had once walked toward, and they had dissolved into a white light. That white light, she knew now, had been love in its first unfolding, love as pure as the lily in the dell; love before it was touched by hand or marred by life; love as pure spirit. It had been a spiritual experience, that walking into the light. She had realized in past years that she had been fortunate in coming into the awareness of love like that before Ben had touched her.

She had loved Ben, but it had been a different love, an earthy love, a love linked to self-sacrifice from the day she had brought him back from the hospital and had accepted the death of romance and taken life as it was, and been thankful that she was loved by a man like him.

But now it seemed that the white light that she had walked through over forty years ago had been the beginning of the rainbow, and it had arched the years, and here she was at the other end. She wasn't seeing Hughie through a white light now; he was a man; he looked what they would term a "well-set-up man of the world," but underneath he was still Hughie Amesden, the silent admirer.

He was saying, "I'm not going to talk about love—it's too early yet. In fact, I can count the minutes we've been together. But I know how I feel, how I've always felt about you, Mary, and if you'll have me, I'll do everything in my power, God willing, to make you happy. To me it will be like picking up from where I left off standing across the street. Well, how about it, Mary?"

Her heart was racing. She blinked, she gulped, she was about to say, "Oh! Hughie," when her head jerked to the side as there came to her the faint sound of a key being turned in the staircase door.

The next minute there were pounding feet on the stairs. They came rushing across the landing, and the sitting-room door was burst open, and there were Ben and Pat, snow-covered, radiant, laughing. They came to a dead stop.

She hadn't moved from Hughie and they gaped at her, and she gaped at them, but just for a moment. Then she was going toward them gabbling. "Oh! Oh! Love." She took hold of both their hands. "I'm . . . I'm glad you've come. Oh, you look so happy."

"We . . . we thought you'd be alone." They said it together; then they looked at the tall man standing before the fire.

"No, I'm not alone. This"—she drew them toward Hughie—"this is Hughie. We knew each other years ago when we were young. He's . . . he's come all the way from America and"—she shook her head. And now the tears spurted from her eyes as she said brokenly, "I . . . I don't know how to tell you, I don't, I don't really, but . . . but I'm going back to America with him. We're go-going to be married . . . and . . ."

She did not finish. She was swung round from them and into the man's arms, and they stared open-mouthed as he kissed her hard and long, and when he had finished and she turned toward them again, Ben, who had looked bewildered but was now grinning, said, "Well! What d'you know. Talk about never rains but it pours. Anyway, we can show you how to go on, Mam; it only takes seven days for a special license."

"Oh, my dears! Oh, hinnies!"

They all began to laugh loudly now, almost hysterically. Then of a sudden they were linked together. She drew them, arm through arm, the divided generations, and she was gabbling, "I knew, I knew something was going to happen. That's why I didn't bother about getting a place. I told you, didn't I, Ben? I told you I'd wait. Oh, Hughie!" She leaned her head against the tweed-clad shoulder and as she did so Ben said, "I wish me granda was here. You know what he would have said?" At this he began to whirl them round in a ring as if they were children in the street playing long ago, and he sang as he went:

"I love a lassie,
A bonny, bonny lassie,
She's as pure as the lily in the dell,
She's as sweet as the heather,
The bonny, bonny heather,
Mary, me Scotch bluebell."